DRAGON'S WISP

A CASTOR'S GROVE YOUNG ADULT
PARANORMAL ROMANCE

A.J. RENWICK

ISBN (electronic): 978-1-960936-69-1

ISBN (print): 978-1-960936-70-7

1

YASMIN

Yasmin Gul's eyes flicked across the length of the cafeteria as she hunted for her next story. Whatever scandal she discovered needed to be big and irrefutably true. She couldn't suffer another humiliation.

At present, Yasmin was Folkestone High's walking joke. She'd spent the first week of her senior year hiding in the library. But even Mrs. Pence had made a snide comment after she'd caught Yasmin eating her sandwich behind a stack of books yesterday. The students weren't the only ones who'd read her blog post.

Why did that have to be the one that went viral?

Something pale moved at the corner of Yasmin's vision. She gasped and froze before recognizing it as a boy's hand. It grabbed her notebook and yanked it from her fingers.

"Look at that, Kal! I've got super speed." The comment did not deserve the loud guffaw that followed.

Yasmin forced a smile to stop herself from screaming as she spun toward the three idiots who'd taken her book.

Correction. Two idiots.

Zachary Wilson and Kalvin White were a pair of stooges

without their leader. Despite a dramatic difference in height and skin color, both boys shared the same lean physiques and obnoxious smiles. At present, Zach, the shorter of the two, waved Yasmin's notebook.

Brilliant.

"Keep it," Yasmin bluffed, shrugging as she turned to Zach. "I've barely used it."

She feigned a turn before spinning back and swiping. Her fingers brushed the pages, but she was too slow. Zach tossed it to Kalvin.

Yasmin's hand tightened around her pen, anxious one of the boys would grab that next.

It's just a notebook. Don't cry about it.

She couldn't give them something else to tease her about.

But it was a really pretty notebook. Yellow sunflowers popped on a dark, glittering green cover, and gold spirals bound the college-ruled pages. It wasn't for any of her classes. Even with barely any notes, she should've known better than to bring it to school.

Zach and Kalvin laughed. A third voice joined them.

Idiot number three: Mason Wick.

A group of sophomore girls followed the trio's unofficial leader with their eyes. He wore faded jeans, a gray shirt and the signature crooked smile that hid most of his teeth. *Sexy* and *shy* were the most common descriptors. Nonsensical. But Yasmin's classmates had invented a strange mythos around Mason, painting him as sweet and soft-hearted beneath a layer of easy-going charm.

Yasmin knew better.

The other girls were distracted by Mason's muscles and near-perfect features. The boys loved him because he was quick on the soccer field. No one cared that he talked only in jokes and meaningless platitudes. Yasmin would bet not even Zach and Kalvin could answer personal questions about Mason.

His smile was neither sexy nor shy. It was sly and secretive. Like he was hiding something dark.

"Come on, Kal. Give the book back." Mason ran a hand through his hair, sweeping the light brown strands from his forehead. His blue eyes caught the light from the ceiling, making them twinkle.

Do not notice his eyes.

Yasmin refused to count herself among the many girls who snuck glances at Mason, even momentarily. It was shock—not attraction—that made her stare.

Was Mason coming to her rescue?

If so, he undermined his attempt to play hero as he continued, "Gul's not the one with super speed. You can't expect her to get it."

Mason winked at her, as though he were being charming and not a colossal jerk.

Yasmin's jaw clenched, a muscle twitching on her cheek. *Is he too stupid to think of new material?*

Hair frizzed from Yasmin's braid. Her palms boasted near permanent ink stains, and she'd almost started crying because of a notebook. Clearly, Mason was too unobservant to notice any of that. He had to go for the most obvious joke and bludgeon it to death.

Mason took the notebook from Kalvin. Instead of offering it to Yasmin, however, the jerk flipped it open.

Oh no.

"Stop," Yasmin said, reaching forward. "That's priv—"

Mason stepped aside with annoyingly impressive grace, leaving Yasmin stumbling forward. He read the words aloud. "An investigation into unnatural phenomena in Castor's Grove."

It could've been worse. At least Yasmin hadn't had a chance to start pouring her heart into her notes. All Mason had read was a title. Nothing to be embarrassed about.

Until Zachary and Kalvin started snickering, and Yasmin suddenly wanted to sink into the floor.

Over the summer, she'd encountered a runner, a year older than her, who moved faster than humanly possible. Yasmin had seen it with her own eyes.

Breaking the news should have made her career as an investigative journalist. And for a blissful twenty-four hours, she'd thought it had. Traffic to Yasmin's blog reached an all-time high. Strangers from other schools shared her post on social media. It was as close to viral as any of her articles had come.

Until her success crashed and burned in a sea of laughing emojis and reports of bullying. Her blog was removed for *violating terms and conditions*, and Yasmin received a message prior to the start of term that she'd lost her position as the school newspaper's editor-in-chief. Folkestone High condoned neither bullying nor "inventing tall tales."

But I didn't make it up.

When Yasmin uncovered the truth and became a local celebrity, everyone who mocked her was going to fall to their knees groveling for forgiveness. Mason and his stooges should be the first in line. Especially given how Zach and Kalvin were laughing now.

"I think you might be wasting your time, Gul," Mason said. The jerk had the audacity to smirk as he passed the notebook, like he was doing her a favor by returning something she owned.

Yasmin snatched her notebook before Mason lifted it into the air. She clutched it to her chest, arms trembling as her anger snapped. "And I think that no one with a brain would listen to you."

Heads turned from nearby tables. Yasmin's voice had been louder than she'd intended.

Oops.

She forced her smile back into place, swallowing the anger and pretending not to notice the whispers rising around her.

Mason shrugged, unfazed by people staring. "Good luck then, Gul." He taunted her with a final crooked smile before moving back to his table. His stooges followed.

Yasmin stood alone in front the cafeteria doors, fighting the urge to hide behind her notebook. People kept glancing at her. She wanted to write the news, not star in high school gossip. There had to be a friendly face somewhere in the crowd. Yasmin had never been popular, but she had friends —didn't she?

Her eyes skipped over the popular table, where Mason and his goons would join lipstick-ed Gigi Davis, and the volleyball girls ruled by Lydia Prince. Most of the writers for the Folkes News shared a spot near the back.

Jeremiah Quick sat on the edge of the table, spider-long limbs sprawled over the bench. The pompous snot had been a pain in Yasmin's butt since they started high school. His writing was technically sound but hackney-ed and cliché. Him ending up as the newspaper's editor instead of her was something straight from an absurdist comedy.

He caught her staring and raised his hand.

An olive branch? Perhaps, as a journalist himself, he recognized that Yasmin was suffering for her work. Maybe, she'd misjudged him.

Jeremiah raised his middle finger.

Charming.

Yasmin spun on her heels and marched out the double doors. Sitting in the cafeteria was overrated anyway.

―――――

Yasmin's quest for privacy led her to the old gymnasium. It wasn't a glamorous lunch location. But it beat a bathroom stall.

She pushed open the doors on the old, graffiti-covered building and stepped into the half-demolished interior. A team had begun knocking things down before the school's administration crunched the numbers and realized that ignoring the gymnasium was cheaper than destroying it.

Sunlight streamed through a hole in the roof, high-lighting the dust floating in the air. Only one half of the bleachers remained. Wreckers had turned the others into rubble.

The scent of death filled Yasmin's nostrils as she moved further in. She kicked aside a deflated ball, lying among a pile of old floor mats and a fallen basketball hoop. The flat-tened lower half of a dead rat appeared. Yasmin covered her mouth with her notebook, gagging as she hurried past it.

The gym had to be breaking dozens of health code violations.

Yasmin ducked beneath the remaining bleachers. She swept aside cobwebs with her bag, settled on the floor, and unwrapped her sandwich. Foil-wrapped lunch in one hand and pen in the other, Yasmin opened her notebook. The title for her next story taunted her atop an otherwise blank page.

What unnatural phenomena had she heard mentioned in Castor's Grove? Where could she start her investigation?

Yasmin wracked her brain. By the time the lunch bell rang, however, the page remained just as blank.

Maybe she was as delusional as her classmates thought. Her intuition had sent her down an embarrassing rabbit hole. It would be safer if she—

A loud sneeze echoed through the gym.

Yasmin's back snapped straight. It was lucky she was short, or her head would have clonked against the underside of the bleachers.

Who else would come in here?

Yasmin twisted onto her knees and peeped through the slats.

Mason Wick covered his mouth, eyes squinting as he stepped away from the dead rat. His sneakers kicked at the dust causing it to rise around his feet in a white swirl.

Is he skipping class? Alone?

Mason stopped beneath the hole in the roof. He glanced over his shoulder, nose wrinkling as he scanned the gym. Sunlight streamed onto his face, highlighting his carved cheekbones and chiseled jaw.

Not that Yasmin noticed.

Something golden and yellow stretched from Mason's back. A trick of the light?

Yasmin's open book trembled as she hugged it to her chest. She blinked, trying to clear her eyes.

It wasn't light. It was scales—the most beautiful yellow she'd ever seen, soaked in warmth and gilded in gold as though someone had captured sunshine and turned it solid.

A gasp caught in Yasmin's throat.

Mason Wick has wings.

Her pen scribbled the words even as her mind struggled to believe them.

He couldn't. It was impossible. This had to be a trick.

Mason flapped the large, scaled wings—which he couldn't have possessed—and rose into the air—which was impossible. A second later, he disappeared through the hole in the roof—except he couldn't have because...

Yasmin's stomach turned as the contents of her lunch rushed in the wrong direction through her esophagus. Spots danced before her vision. She collapsed forward, head slamming against the bleachers.

Darkness pooled around the memory of Mason's sunlit wings.

2

MASON

Technically, Mason was breaking the law.

Flying across unsanctioned patches of sky was illegal. It broke the cardinal rule of being a Castor: Secrecy above all else. Remaining hidden was all that protected the magical citizens of Castor's Grove from being annihilated by humans.

Supposedly.

Color Mason skeptical.

Don't murder people. Now that was an important rule everyone ought to abide by. But secrecy? In his experience, that took care of itself. It took a particularly abrasive busybody, like Yasmin Gul, to notice anything amiss. And even her investigation was unlikely to yield anything.

He'd read her blog post. Yasmin had encountered a changeling with super speed and jumped to theories about extreme performance-enhancing drugs. Now she'd set out to find *unnatural phenomena*. Whatever she thought that meant.

Mason snorted.

Yasmin should've taken his advice and dropped it. Someone would have to mess up monumentally for her to discover the truth. Even then, her knowledge wouldn't last against amnesiac powder. A single serving of the enchanted dust was issued quarterly to every Castor. It was the King and his government's way of acknowledging that mistakes were inevitable while ensuring their citizens didn't grow too lax.

Mason wiggled his toes, feeling the satin pouch of powder tucked in his shoe. Truthfully, he'd love to encounter a human who required the enchanted substance. Most wiped their memories for him. Humans had an uncanny talent for lying to themselves. Especially when it came to magic.

Mason was a trick of the light, a shape in the clouds, a solar flare. At this distance, he couldn't blame them for not leaping to anything else.

The cars below looked like toys, arranged in rows and columns across the city's grid-like streets with blocks of mismatched buildings in between. Mason couldn't have identified his own father from this height.

Hopefully he wouldn't have to.

Mason licked his lips—forked tongue more reptilian than human in appearance.

Why do the Serpents want me at Pretty Pines Park?

Lunch had been almost finished when the message pinged on Mason's phone. He'd assumed it was one of his family, asking him to grab something from the store on his way home. How could he have guessed it would be anything sinister?

The Serpents were a criminal organization, known for being ruthless and mercenary with their dealings. They made their money through drugs, robberies, and illegal trades, procuring exotic meats for the carnivorously inclined and supplying prohibited ingredients for witches' spells.

Most upstanding Castors could go their whole lives without worrying about the Serpents. But the organization was a writhing shadow, looming over Mason.

His father, Lawrence Wick, had been a member.

A wisp of smoke curled from Mason's nostril. He sucked it in, a deep breath, squashing the frustration that threatened to rise.

It wasn't Dad's fault. I don't blame him for any of it.

After his wife abandoned him with a hungry four-year-old, Lawrence had been desperate for cash. He'd taken a loan from the Serpents to open a butcher's shop. It wasn't an unsuccessful endeavor. Customers liked the store. But when the Serpents returned for their dues two years later, they deemed the meager profits insufficient. Lawrence was forced to hike up prices to meet their demand. Instead, it drove off customers and sank the business.

In order to repay his loan and its rapidly increasing interest, Mason's father had joined the very organization that was bankrupting him. Three years later, Lawrence had been arrested for selling magical contraband.

Mason hadn't handled it well.

But both he and his father had served their time. Now, they were model citizens. Mason attended Folkestone High, and Lawrence worked as a gardener. They lived in different sections of the city—the courts never having seen it fit to return Mason to his father's custody—but they were still family.

And there was one rule Lawrence had made clear to his

son, more significant than secrecy, maybe more important than not murdering.

If the Serpents give you an order, follow it.

Those who didn't tended to turn up dead.

The Serpents' message instructed Mason to be at Pretty Pines Park by 2:00 p.m. He'd skipped his last two periods, giving himself over an hour to arrive. The flight took half of that, but Mason wouldn't have been able to concentrate on Steinbeck if he'd stayed another forty minutes at school.

And the extra time proved useful. The wind was on a mission to sweep everything east. It took Mason six blocks to notice and correct his course.

He still had more than fifteen minutes to wait when Pretty Pines appeared below. The park was a green square in a sea of taupe-colored buildings. Its namesake trees were surprisingly lacking. Maples provided the majority of shade for picnic benches and walking paths. The playground was left to bake in the sun.

Colorful specks moved over the climbing frame. Mason was all for scoffing at secrecy, but children could be perceptive when it came to magic. And flying into the middle of a park with his wings and tail out might be more than even the adults could reason away.

Instead, Mason landed atop a six-story parking lot, hid his wings, and took the stairs to the street.

Mason kept his head low, letting his hair hide his face as he passed the group of parents at the edge of the playground. His nostrils widened, taking in their scents. All humans.

The message had instructed Mason to wait by the park's exercise equipment. He sat at one of the outdoor machines and wrapped his hands around the silver bars. Elbows bent, he pulled the weights together before letting the equipment pull them away. The exercise targeted the chest muscles or maybe it was the biceps. Mason couldn't tell. Despite being on the thinner side, he could crush most humans in an arm-wrestling match.

Three-hundred-and-three. Three-hundred-and-four.

Mason fought the urge to lick his lips as they grew increasingly dry.

Five-hundred-seven. Five-hundred-eight.

Two o'clock came and went. No Serpent appeared.

Mason stopped pretending to exercise. He swiped his phone screen, willing another message to appear. He'd deleted the first—as it had instructed. Mason didn't have a way of responding.

I doubt it would have been possible anyway. The number was blocked.

But curiosity gnawed at Mason. His tongue tapped each second against the roof of his mouth. Had something happened or—?

"Mason!" A girl's voice shouted from the opposite corner of the park.

His head snapped up.

Kira waved from beneath one of the maples, rattling the silver bangles that adorned her wrist. Wagging his tail beside her, stood a creature that appeared to be a Pembroke Welsh Corgi—Comet.

Why are they here?

Mason lurched off the machine.

Despite Kira's darker complexion and Comet's four legs, both were Mason's siblings. Surely, messaging him as a Serpent wasn't their idea of a prank.

"See? I told you it was him." Kira directed her excitement to Comet before rushing across the grass, lilac shorts billowing into a skirt around her thighs. She wrapped her hands around Mason's arm. "Did you come to walk me home too? Comet got bored and decided to surprise me. But he's the slowest companion."

Kira pointed her sneaker toward their four-legged brother. In his true form, Comet preferred to fly. However, the enchanted orange collar that disguised him as a dog also forced him to rely on his weakened legs. His run was half-waddle.

"Is Jeremiah with you? Or did you ditch him because I'm cooler?" Kira grinned, flashing a pair of sharp white canines.

Mason blinked, his mind working slower than he liked. Kira had said nothing about a text. There was no hint of amusement or guilt in Comet's eyes. His siblings weren't playing a prank. They were there because—

This is the route Kira takes home.

She attended Westfield County Middle School, four blocks shy of Pretty Pines Park.

Panic fluttered in Mason's stomach. He swallowed it down.

"Of course, I came to walk you home!" Mason said, forcing a laugh as he wrapped his arm over Kira's shoulders and guided her back to the street. Comet trotted at their heels. "Jeremiah was too lame to skip class, but I thought this would be a fun surprise. Should we get ice cream?"

"Uh... yes!" Kira bounced on her toes in excitement. "We'll pass a Gelato Grove if we head south on One-Thirty-Seven."

Comet loosed an enthusiastic bark.

"Perfect." Mason marched them in the correct direction, nodding and gasping at the appropriate moments as Kira chattered about her day. But he couldn't concentrate on the thirteen-year-old's stories.

The Serpents had ordered him to wait at the exact spot Kira walked past each day. Was it a coincidence?

Or a message?

We're watching you, Mason Wick. And we know how to find your family.

3
YASMIN

"Why do you smell like puke?" Yasmin's younger brother, Hassan, turned and wrinkled his nose in disgust as she climbed into the backseat.

Because I passed out in my own vomit after watching Mason Wick grow wings and fly.

By the time Yasmin had regained consciousness, sixth period had been almost finished. Instead of trying to catch the last twenty minutes of AP Lit, she'd wandered to the nearest bathroom and scrubbed the mustard-scented sick from her face with cheap hand soap. A bruise blossomed at the edge of her hairline where she'd collided with the bleachers.

Had she hit her head so hard that she'd hallucinated Mason's wings?

It was a tempting theory. If super speed was far-fetched, her classmate having beautiful golden-yellow wings was a thousand times worse. Yasmin barely believed herself.

But the words were scribbled in her notebook. They slashed a diagonal across the college-ruled lines, a sign they'd been written by someone whose eyes were elsewhere. Writing was a natural reflex for Yasmin, but not even she could have managed it while unconscious.

She'd seen Mason's wings *before* she hit her head.

And if I tell anyone, they'll think I'm insane.

Yasmin shoved her knee against the back of her brother's seat, ignoring his question and turning to their father instead. "Baba, why is Hassan in the front?"

Amir Gul—father of three, widower, and unenthused electrician—scratched the black stubble on his chin. His lips pursed as though searching for an answer.

"I called shotgun," Hassan said, twisting so that he could push Yasmin's legs away.

"He called shotgun," Amir parroted his son's words.

"That's not a thing." Yasmin lifted her legs, trying to kick her brother's hands away. "The eldest sits in front."

"Exactly, and Nima's at college." Amir snapped his fingers as though he'd always meant for this to be the answer. "Now stop kicking your brother. Or I'll leave you both to catch the bus."

Hassan watched with an arrogant smirk as Yasmin moved to sit behind her father. She buckled the seatbelt and crossed her arms. "It's not fair. I'm sick."

Amir snorted as he started the car. Without so much as a glance into the backseat, he turned to Hassan. "How were soccer tryouts?"

I literally smell like puke and that's what you care about?

Yasmin was tempted to shove her knee into the back of her father's seat too.

But why bother? He was always like this.

Amir had never been good at hiding which of his children he loved and which he didn't.

Yasmin's older sister, Nima, was his favorite. She was the pretty one. Popular and perfect with a forced charm that everyone else swore was effortless. Yasmin knew how long it took her sister to get ready on a morning. A more traditional father might have taken issue with Nima's make-up and clothing—or lack thereof—and the way she enjoyed having boys follow her through the hallways. She'd gone through five boyfriends in high school. That averaged to more than one a year. Yasmin didn't know if their father was clueless or just didn't care. Despite claiming to be Persian, Amir was a third-generation American. He spent his Sundays watching NFL games on their flat-screen TV.

Hassan was right there with him. The two had more in common than could be considered healthy—identical loud sneezes, an aversion to asparagus, the same undiscerning love of sports. Yasmin could never predict what would be on when she heard the two yelling at the television: soccer, football, baseball, cricket. Once, they'd managed to get angry at a golfer. Hassan's position as second favorite was only because he ate all of Amir's snacks.

And then there was Yasmin.

"I had a big day today," she said, interrupting Hassan's never-ending monologue about his tryout. "I got an A in my AP Psych quiz."

"Why are they giving you tests? It's only the second week," Amir complained, and then they were back to Hassan's tryouts.

Yasmin closed her eyes and clutched her backpack to her chest. Her family wouldn't be able to ignore her when she was a famous journalist, when she revealed to the world that—that what?

She couldn't just announce that people had wings. Yasmin needed to understand how. Was Mason a government experiment with lab-grown wings bonded to the sinews of muscles in his back?

No, that wasn't right. Mason's wings were too pretty to have been engineered.

Yasmin had never seen such a beautiful yellow. The color was etched in her memory, as brilliant as the sun.

Amir stopped outside their building, letting his children out before he continued to his next job. The Guls apartment was on the fifth floor. There was no doorman in the lobby or fancy electronic keycards, only a classic lock on the knob, which no one ever bothered to use.

Yasmin and her brother rode the elevator to their apartment in silence.

Their key lived beneath the pot of a plastic plant hanging from the wall. Yasmin reached it before her brother and unlocked the door.

Hassan pushed past her to get to the living room. "Dibs on the TV! You need to shower anyway."

"And you need to take off your shoes!" His sneakers had tracked dirt over the cream carpet. "I'm not cleaning up after you."

Yasmin closed the door, letting a curtain of straight, black hair sweep toward her nose. She inhaled. The scent made her wince. Maybe there was still some puke. She crossed the hallway in her socks, heading to the bathroom.

Mason's wings occupied Yasmin's thoughts as she washed her hair.

They were covered in scales. Not feathers. Not skin. What creature has scales on their wings?

Taxonomy had never been one of Yasmin's passions. She wrapped herself in a towel when she finished showering, hurried to her room, and pulled her laptop and note-book from her bag. There was no desk. None could fit. The small room was cramped with shelves. With Nima at college, all of them should have belonged to Yasmin, but her older sister had refused to relinquish any of her space. She'd left half her clothes, her collection of trashy romance novels, and the extra make-up she couldn't fit in her suit-case. There was enough to supply a small shop.

Yasmin's half of the room was as organized as the space allowed. A narrow wardrobe held her clothing, and her shelves were lined with books. There was true crime, literary journalism, and field reporter memoirs. A less impressive collection of fiction displayed some of the clas-sics. The largest section, however, belonged to the note-books. Writing helped Yasmin process her thoughts.

And she had a lot of thoughts. Especially now.

Yasmin settled on the double bed. Conditioner that she'd failed to rinse from her hair dripped onto the sunflower patterned sheets as she opened her notebook. At least with Nima gone, she didn't need to worry about anyone peeping over her shoulder while she wrote. Yasmin didn't hold back in her description of Mason's wings. She wanted to capture the sense of magic she felt in the memory.

What is Mason Wick?

Not a butterfly. Not a moth. Not a bumblebee.

After learning that insects had scaled wings, Yasmin scrolled through photographs of bugs on her laptop. None of the images matched with Mason.

Not a mosquito. Not a cricket. Not a dragon—

Yasmin's hand froze over the trackpad. She hadn't considered mythical creatures.

But why not? They were as real as a person with wings. Maybe Mason was a fire-breathing, gold-hoarding dragon.

Except he looked human. How could he—?

I'm going about this entirely the wrong way.

Studying pictures of winged creatures wouldn't tell her what Mason was. If Yasmin wanted to know, she needed to go to the source.

4
MASON

Mason stared at the blank page as he tapped his pen against the desk.

After ice cream, he'd returned home with his siblings. Uncle Lee, their official fairy godfather, had been waiting in the kitchen, eager to assign tasks to anyone with time to spare. The old Victorian property collected dust with enviable enthusiasm, and its five bathrooms didn't clean themselves.

Both Mason and Kira had waved their school bags, faked apologies, and vanished to their rooms. Only poor Comet had no excuse. He'd removed his collar, returned to his true form, and clamped his teeth around the handle of a broom.

Watching Comet hover three feet in the air—orange wings flapping to keep himself aloft as he struggled to sweep—had amazed Mason to no end when he'd first moved in. He'd never met a great dragon before, far less a dwarfed one that did housework.

Did the Serpents know Comet would pass the park today too?

Panic seized Mason's chest. Great dragons were considered sacred, but Comet's deformities lessened his status. Born stunted, with twisted legs and a truncated neck, his wings spanned barely three feet. But it wasn't Comet's size that had caused his mother to abandon him. His deformities meant he produced no flames—a death sentence for a great dragon. His original name, *Cometsroar*, had been struck from draconic record and he'd been tossed into a bin, still half in his egg.

Luck and Uncle Lee had saved him, and despite the odds, Comet thrived. Proof fire wasn't the blessing dragons claimed it to be.

Not that Mason needed more evidence.

He inhaled, closed his eyes, and tried to focus. He wasn't worrying about the Serpents. He was writing his college essay. Supposedly.

Mason opened one eye. The empty page glared back.

As part of their admissions process, Castor's Grove University required a personal essay be submitted with all transcripts. For those with magic, the response needed to be handwritten. That wasn't the aspect bothering Mason, however. It was the prompt: *Write about a time your emotions got the best of you. How did you handle it? What did you learn?*

Mason knew the answer he was expected to write. His first foster home, right after his father's arrest, he'd—

Nope. Flames sparked in Mason's stomach. He flung his pen onto the desk and stood. He needed a distraction.

Kira's room was on the opposite wing of the house. Comet could be anywhere. If Mason tried to find either, Lee might spot him and assign him dinner-prep duty. Peeling potatoes left the mind much too free.

He had a closer sibling: Jeremiah Quick. The fifth

member of their government-mandated family unit slept across the hall.

Mason left his room to knock on his brother's door.

"Can I not have ten minutes before I'm expected to chop vegetables?" The door swung open, and Jeremiah appeared. He wore the same cream polo and slacks he'd worn to school. Only now a pair of large, pointed elf ears twitched on the sides of his head. He lifted a pale eyebrow. "Oh, it's you. I might have preferred Lee."

"Careful what you wish for," Mason advised as he stepped into the room.

It was twice the size of his with half as many things. Jeremiah had adapted to his disguise as a human and embraced the digital age. His shelves functioned as charging stations for various electronics. The only books he owned were for school. Even those looked sparse.

"You're back late," Mason pointed to the unpacked gray satchel at the foot of Jeremiah's four poster bed. "Were you out on a date? Was he cute?"

Mason grinned, taking an unoffered seat at the edge of the mattress.

Jeremiah sighed as he closed his door. *Annoyed* was the elf's default response, but Mason knew better than to be offended. His brother enjoyed his company. Jeremiah just also enjoyed complaining.

"I had a meeting with Miss Montgomery," the elf explained, taking his bag and beginning to unpack his books.

"Weird date. Didn't think she was your type."

That was funny. Their English teacher was pushing fifty with dyed pink hair and a love for all things tie-dye. Mason liked to think Jeremiah was laughing on the inside as he rolled his eyes.

"We were discussing the newspaper." Jeremiah froze, staring at a copy of *King Lear* he'd just pulled from his bag. "Speaking of disgraced former editors, did you get a message from Yasmin Gul?"

Mason snorted. He assumed Jeremiah was joking.

"She asked me for your number," the elf explained. "Said you two were working on a project for AP psychology."

Mason groaned. "Yasmin *is* a psych project."

It wasn't an insult. Just a fact. Despite being in high school, Yasmin had deluded herself into thinking she was an investigative reporter and built a personality to match. She was dogged, abrasive, and a complete kiss-ass when it came to teachers. Her new interest in *unnatural phenomena* might prove amusing, but Mason intended to watch from a healthy distance.

"You didn't give her my number, right?" he asked.

"Course not. But it looked like she was forwarding the question to every contact on her phone. I figured someone would. You really haven't heard from her?"

"I don't know. My phone's in my bag. I haven't checked it since I got home." That was a lie. Mason had stared at it for the first hour, waiting for the Serpents to message again. He'd had to put his phone out of sight before it drove him mad.

"How is that even possible? I check mine..." Jeremiah trailed off, head tilting to the side as his ears began to twitch. Elves had the most acute hearing of any species in Castor's Grove. "I think your father is downstairs."

———

Mason raced down the winding Victorian staircase toward the archaic parlor.

Kira had once described their home's entrance room as *a cheap tearoom on Valentine's Day* while Lee called his decorating style *ironically cheesy.* Either way, the space featured heart-shaped everything from the pink cushions on the lilac chairs, to the fuzzy red rugs, to the white coffee tables.

In his army green shorts and grass-stained shirt, Lawrence didn't belong in the parlor.

He leaned against the wall, arms crossed, and shoulders hunched. His features were the older version of Mason's own—same thin lips, straight nose, light eyes. But prison and manual labor had weathered Lawrence's skin, giving him a permanent tan and deep wrinkles.

Uncle Lee stood a few feet away, arms wrapped around his shoulders, clinging to a pastel shawl. His mouth twisted in an uncomfortable frown as he listened to Lawrence.

Mason caught the end of his father's story.

"... must be something valuable. Otherwise the Drages wouldn't be so anxious. Lucky I have an alibi." He pulled a pair of ticket stubs from his pocket, waving them as though the fairy had requested proof. "I don't envy any of my coworkers with a couple hours they can't account for."

"Why not?" Mason asked, slowing as he stepped from the carpeted stairs onto the white wood floor. He didn't want to appear like an overeager child racing to his dad. But he couldn't hide his curiosity. "Were the Drages robbed?"

Lawrence and Uncle Lee turned to Mason as though noticing him for the first time.

"Finished your homework?" Uncle Lee asked. Despite the fairy's small stature, his angular features gave him an air of aristocratic authority. "Kira and Comet are dicing onions for dinner. I'm sure they could use the help."

"Cruel of you to abandon them then," Mason said, grinning so that all his teeth were visible.

Uncle Lee's frown deepened at the joke. The fairy wasn't in the mood to banter. He seldom was when Mason's father appeared.

"Did you come to see me, Dad?" Mason asked, turning to Lawrence and keeping his voice as steady as he could manage. But a flutter of optimism made his pitch rise and his words rush the next second. "Want to stay for dinner?"

Real smooth. Why don't I just draw him a picture and ask him to hang it on his fridge?

Mason was certain that his father *loved* him, but Lawrence didn't *like* children. It had been difficult for him to raise one alone.

"Oh, I—uh..." Lawrence stuttered as he straightened, pushing himself off the wall. His boot had left mud on the skirting board. "Can't tonight, I'm afraid. The Drages want to speak with me. Another time, kid. Come by me, and we'll have a real dinner. With meat."

"Sure, Dad." Mason scratched the base of his throat, fighting to keep his smile in place. His father didn't suggest a day. He never did.

But he's here now. That has to count for something.

"What brings you by?" Mason asked, hating the nervous quiver in his voice, the strange edge of formality.

"Just was in the area, and—"

"Mason!" Jeremiah shouted over the white banister at the top of the staircase. He waved. Something dark flashed in his hand before he descended, his speed transforming him into a cream-colored blur.

Jeremiah barreled into Mason, knocking them both against a portrait of Eros on the wall. The heart-shaped gold frame clattered to the floor.

"Jere, what the hell." Mason pushed the elf off of him. "Are you—?"

Mason's voice caught as the front door creaked shut. A single moment of confusion and his father snuck off without a word.

Didn't he come to tell me something?

"I thought that fostering teenagers would mean less commotion," Uncle Lee said, pink fairy wings unfolding with a buzz. "I trust there's a reason you've whirled into the parlor to scatter my belongings?"

"Yes," Jeremiah said, though he didn't sound as confident. "There's a girl trying to get in touch with Mason." He raised his hand, revealing the item he was holding.

My phone.

"It's Yasmin," Jeremiah said, lowering his voice and raising his eyebrows as he shoved the device into Mason's hands.

"That's what this is about?" Uncle Lee slapped his palm to his forehead, but there was a hint of amusement beneath the exasperation. "She better be someone special."

She really isn't.

Mason didn't understand what Jeremiah was so worked up about, but the elf's eyes kept flicking to the phone. Uncle Lee must have noticed as well.

"I take it I can't hear whatever you're about to say next." The fairy shook his head. "But do be quick, otherwise you two can clean up alone tonight. Then, you can discuss this Yasmin as much as you like." He flew off toward the kitchen.

The moment Lee was out of earshot, Jeremiah grabbed the phone once more, typing in the passcode to unlock it.

"You made a massive mistake," he hissed, shoving the phone into Mason's face. Thirty-two messages and eight missed calls, all from the same number. Had Yasmin gone—?

Burning hell.

Mason's eyes widened as he scanned the messages. A lot were repetitive ramblings, but he got the gist.

Yasmin had seen his wings. And she was threatening to tell the entire school.

5
MASON

"Would you relax?" Mason clung to a support bar, bracing himself as the streetcar screeched around a corner.

Jeremiah, who'd been busy hyperventilating and inventing worst case scenarios, stumbled backward into an unamused businesswoman. The six-foot tall elf shrank beneath her glare as he regained his balance.

Mason had hoped that a night's rest would soothe Jeremiah's nerves. Instead, the elf's dreams had conjured an impossible scenario where Yasmin revealed the existence of magic and Castors were hunted to extinction.

"All I'm saying," Jeremiah said, slinking back into his position and steadying himself on the bar, "is what if the amnesiac powder doesn't work?"

"It will." Mason wiggled his toes against the bag in his sneaker. "The powder erases memories of magic from a human's mind."

"But what if you don't have enough for all her memories? I mean, how long has Yasmin known? What if she's been onto us for ages? What if she's—"

"Trust me. I have enough."

After Mason hadn't responded to any of her thirty-two messages or eight missed calls, Yasmin had left him a ten-minute long voice note—about half of which was an unnecessarily formal preamble given that her ultimate goal was blackmail. She wanted to interview him. It would be anonymous if he agreed. Otherwise, she would reveal his secret.

Yasmin's messages had said as much, making the voice note superfluous. Mason was worried he'd wasted ten minutes of his life.

But in her speech, Yasmin did let slip when she'd seen his wings.

How did I not smell her in the gym yesterday?

Dragon's noses were designed to pick out human scents, and Yasmin's smell was easy to recognize.

The damned rat must have thrown him off. It had reeked of death and internal fluids.

Jeremiah's lips twitched as his brain searched for some other horrible suggestion. "What if she's already told someone?"

Mason snorted. "Who cares? No one would believe her."

The streetcar slammed to a stop. Mason grabbed the back of Jeremiah's shirt before the elf lurched into another unsuspecting passenger. But he wouldn't have been the only one to lose his balance. People tumbled and tripped, knocking into one another like bowling pins.

"Attention, passengers," a voice came through a speaker in the roof. "Due to a sudden technical difficulty, you are all being asked to disembark. This car will be down for the next hour for maintenance."

There was a chorus of groans mixed with more than a few curses. Those fortunate enough to be seated rose, and the mass of people shoved their way down the aisle and toward the street.

"Fantastic," Jeremiah said as they pushed their way out. "Just what we needed. Now, we're going to be late."

"You could run," Mason suggested, kicking a pebble as they continued on the sidewalk.

Jeremiah scowled. "I don't think now is the time to be lax about secrecy."

The nearest bus stop was at the Ivy Street intersection. They stopped beneath as more people from the broken streetcar arrived.

A red luxury vehicle pulled up beside them. The front window rolled down, and a young man in his mid-twenties with dark blond hair and an expensive watch leaned out of the window. He lowered his shades, and his eyes landed on Mason.

Is that Eli Drage?

The last person Mason expected to see on his way to school was the son of his father's wealthy employer.

Eli flashed him a sharp-toothed grin. "You're Lawrence's son, right? Mason?"

Why does he know my name?

Mason managed to nod.

"Need a lift?" Eli offered, pointing toward the back of his car.

Mason's eyebrows rose. The appearance of the wealthy dragon just when they needed a ride was too fortuitous not to be suspicious.

"Yes, thank you!" Jeremiah answered, rushing toward the car.

Did he use up all of his anxiety worrying about Yasmin?

Mason wasn't used to being the cautious one but being around the Drages made him uncomfortable. It wasn't that the wealthy family of dragons were cruel. Far from it. They'd given Lawrence a chance when few others would. That was already generous. Mason didn't deserve any more of their kindness.

But Jeremiah was halfway in the car, and Eli was watching.

Mason smiled, nodding in gratitude as he took a seat beside the elf.

"Where to?" Eli asked, pulling out into the road.

"Our school. Folkestone High," Jeremiah answered, his voice growing smaller as he said the name. Castors didn't attend human schools if they could help it. The Drages were wealthy and influential. Eli would have attended a magical academy elsewhere in the city. He'd probably never heard of Folkestone High.

But Eli entered the school's name into his GPS system without comment. His arm flexed as he leaned back and started driving again. Dragons naturally had more muscle than humans, but Eli had the physique of a fighter, lithe but tough as though, despite growing up in luxury, he knew how to throw a punch.

"You have a really nice car," Mason said, hiding his discomfort behind the compliment as he studied the clean, dark leather interior. The Drages' symbol and house words were embroidered in blue thread on the seat covers: a dragon's heart consumed in fire with the motto above. *For loyalty, we burn.*

"I'm lucky that my family have a lot of nice things. Though many resent us for it," Eli said, stopping at an orange light. His eyes met Mason's in the rearview mirror. "Did you know something was stolen from us yesterday?"

"That is a travesty," Jeremiah responded a beat too fast. "Some people let jealousy get the best of their morals."

He's not talking to you, moron.

Mason fought the urge to elbow the elf's ribs.

"My father mentioned something," Mason said, careful to keep his tone relaxed. "But he wasn't at work yesterday. What did the thief take?"

"No, he was at a movie theatre." Eli ignored the question, draping his arm over the center console with a casual lean. The muscles flexed. His eyes remained on Mason. "What about you? Any idea as to your whereabouts yesterday between twelve and three?"

Mason fought the urge to lick his lips. "I'm a suspect?"

"Of course not." The light turned green, and Eli sped off. "Should you be?"

"We were at school during those times," Jeremiah said. "Our last class doesn't finish until two fifty-five."

Mason nodded. He didn't mention that he hadn't been at school yesterday afternoon. He'd been waiting for a criminal who never showed. Kira and Comet could confirm his whereabouts only after 2:15pm. And they were his family, not the most reliable witnesses.

The timing was unfortunate. But Mason hadn't committed any crime. He didn't need to worry.

Unless the Serpents are framing me.

"Of course," Eli said. He turned left. Three blocks later they were outside Folkstone High. He stopped in the middle of the street, unconcerned by the drivers honking and shaking their fists behind him. "I'm sure your school's attendance records will show you're innocent."

Mason's stomach leapt into his throat. He didn't dare open his mouth, afraid what might come out.

If I'm not a suspect, why would you check my attendance records?

Mason hurried from the car, Jeremiah close behind. They watched as Eli sped off.

"That was weird," Jeremiah noted, arranging his hair before turning to enter the school's compound. "Are the Drages planning to question every Castor about their whereabouts yesterday?"

"I doubt it." Mason's voice hissed, strained from heat. He pressed his hand to his chest.

Inhale. *Stay positive.*

Exhale. *Just focus on the facts.*

A theft had occurred. The Serpents had robbed Mason of an alibi. Now, he was being questioned.

Optimistic theory? The three weren't connected.

Less optimistically? Mason was going to need a damn good excuse as to why he'd been absent from class during the exact hours when a crime occurred.

6

YASMIN

He's not going to show.

Yasmin had told Mason to meet her in the library at 8:00 am for the interview. She dismissed a text from Nima and checked the time: 8:20. The only other person there was Gigi Davis, who'd spent more time posing with the books than reading them.

"Want to walk to AP psych together?" Gigi offered, making a crying face as she took one last picture beside a textbook.

Yasmin's brow furrowed. Despite attending school together for the past three years, they'd never been friends. Gigi loved shoes and makeup, and she'd once done a presentation on why her dream job was *influencer*.

"You're okay being seen with me?"

Gigi chewed the end of a blonde ringlet. She'd painted her lips a cherry red, which was against the dress code. "I was friends with your sister. Nima was always super nice."

Brilliant. A pity invitation. Yasmin wanted to throw up in her mouth.

"How is she?" Gigi asked.

"Perfect. As always." Yasmin forced a smile and marched into the shelves. The Folkestone High library was smaller than she would have liked. Its ten rows housed little in the realm of nonfiction beyond textbooks, and seating areas were crammed into the corners of the room.

Yasmin clutched her notebook to her chest instead of returning it to her bag. It contained the list of questions she'd planned on asking Mason.

What if he denies having wings?

For all her threats, Yasmin was toothless. She was the girl who'd cried super speed. If she proclaimed Mason to be a creature from a fantasy book, she'd be accused of bullying. Or insanity.

What I need is undisputable evidence.

Until she found a way to obtain it, research remained her best option.

Yasmin weaved through the rows of books, enjoying the scent of the pages. Her fingers trailed across the spines until she reached an encyclopedia of mythological creatures.

"I doubt I'm in there."

The sound of Mason's voice made Yasmin jump. She pulled her hand away from the encyclopedia, feeling like a child caught stealing baklava.

Mason stood at the opposite end of the row, watching her with his crooked smirk.

"Sorry I'm late. Had to wait for Gigi to leave. You could've refused her invite a bit more courteously. She's nice."

More like Mason thought she was pretty. Most of the boys did. But most of the idiots probably thought that was Gigi's natural lip color as well.

But Yasmin hadn't asked to meet to give Mason a crash-course in make-up. She smoothed the collar of her blue button down, and tightened her grip on her sunflower notebook, holding it like a shield before her.

"I'm pleased you decided to join me, Mr. Wick." Yasmin lifted her chin in an attempt to seem taller. "I wanted to discuss—"

"My wings. Yes. I was too illiterate to understand the thirty-two texts, but your voice note cleared it up."

Yasmin's eyes widened. She hadn't expected him to come out and admit it. Where was her phone? She needed to record this.

Mason drew closer, and his smile grew wider.

His teeth!

They were straight and white and predatory. The large, pointed cusps of his canines sparkled, perfect for ripping into meat.

Yasmin's fingers tightened around her notebook as though its pages might save her from an attack. Her shoulders bumped against the bookshelf. She'd stepped backward without realizing.

"Not sure why you're not curious about the tail or the ridges on my back," Mason continued, stopping before her.

Was he teasing her? Or had Yasmin been so mesmerized by his wings that she'd missed those details?

Mason rested a hand on the shelf, blocking her escape to the left. He was average height for a boy, but he towered over Yasmin. No amount of holding her chin high could make her feel otherwise.

"Do you know what I am?" Mason asked. His eyes picked up the blue of the walls, cool and beautiful. There was a hint of something else in them—amusement?

He's toying with me.

What if Mason was the type of creature that hunted humans? That would explain the high cheekbones, the perfect nose, the dazzling eyes. Yasmin had always judged the other girls for giggling over him, but what if she'd been lying to herself? She'd been so enchanted by his wings the memory had followed into her dreams.

Mason lured his prey with his looks, then attacked.

He's going to eat me. This is just the equivalent of him playing with his food.

Yasmin's voice stuck in her throat. She shook her head.

"Do you want to?" Mason asked. He pushed his hair away from his face, and his tongue flickered over his lips. It was thin and forked, like a snake.

Heat flushed through Yasmin. The strange tongue should've made him less attractive, and yet—

"You're a dragon." The guess slipped from Yasmin in a whisper. She could think of no other winged mythological reptiles.

But it was a ridiculous guess.

Dragons were four-legged creatures with long necks who breathed fire. Mason was missing at least two of the criteria. She expected him to laugh in her face.

Mason's jaw slackened into an open-mouthed grin, revealing more sharp teeth toward the back. "You are clever."

Yasmin's insides quivered. It might have been better if Mason had laughed.

"I won't let you eat me," she said.

The smile slid from Mason's face. "What?"

"Dragons eat humans." Yasmin wasn't an expert on mythological creatures—though she swore that she'd become one if she survived this—but she was confident that was true. Why else were there tales of knights hunting them?

"That is incredibly offensive." Mason crossed his arms,

stepping back to lean against the opposite bookshelf. "Dragons don't eat humans." Under his breath, he muttered, "Not since it became illegal three hundred years ago."

His addendum did not inspire confidence. But it was new information. The bell rang. First period was about to begin. It was the perfect excuse to escape.

"Dragons have laws?" Yasmin asked. Her feet glued themselves to the floor; her eyes refused to move from the boy before her. He looked human again now that his mouth was closed.

"Of course," Mason said. "All Castors do. That's the name for the magical population that live in the city. You humans are Grovers. The rest of us are Castors."

Yasmin's fingers jumped toward the pen in her shirt pocket. Mason was answering questions before she could voice them.

But why is he being so forthcoming?

She'd hoped to strong arm Mason into an interview. He was acting like he wanted to tell her the truth.

Yasmin clicked the cam of her pen three times before pointing it at her winged classmate. "You're messing with me."

"No." Mason shook his head. "I want to make a deal."

Yasmin's eyebrows rose. She lowered her pen.

"Instead of wiping your memory,"—

Excuse me? When had they discussed that possibility?

—"I'll teach you about the magical world. I'm sure you're curious. And in exchange, you're going to tell people that we were together yesterday afternoon. Studying. In here." He pointed to the library floor.

Yasmin pursed her lips. She wanted it to look like she was deliberating over the proposal. In actuality, she was hiding a smile. Mason Wick, the school's beloved, needed an alibi. It wasn't a big enough story to make national news, but it soothed Yasmin's soul to have her skepticism of his good-natured persona reinforced.

"What did you do?" she asked.

"Nothing. I'm innocent." Mason crossed his finger over his heart. "But something was stolen—"

"Okay, I'm in." Yasmin held out her hand. Whether Mason was innocent or guilty was irrelevant. Robbery wasn't murder. If it got her proof that magical creatures existed, Yasmin could make a small ethical sacrifice and cover for a thief.

Mason's crooked smile returned as he reached for Yasmin's hand. He paused. "You understand that you can't tell anyone else about magic? What I teach will be only for you."

"Deal." Yasmin shook Mason's hand. Behind her notebook, she crossed her fingers.

7
MASON

"That's your plan?" Jeremiah's fist curled in his hair as he leaned over the desk. "Are you absolutely mental?"

Mason raised a finger, trying to get the elf to lower his voice. In order to survive in the loud environment of Folkestone High, Jeremiah wore plugs to dull his enhanced hearing. Sometimes, they worked too well.

Mr. Clark shot them a look from the front of the classroom. The AP Calculus teacher allowed students to work in pairs, but he also enjoyed dolling out detentions for *disrupting others' learning.*

"It's illegal to tell a human about the magical world," Jeremiah whispered, scooting his chair closer. "They won't send you back to juvie for this. It'll be straight to Iron Vault."

An extended stay in the Castor prison—isolated in the woods, with dark walls that leeched magic—was precisely what Mason was trying to avoid.

"I told you what happened yesterday," Mason said,

copying the derivative example from the board. Focusing on the math helped keep his emotions steady. "How do I explain my absence if Eli checks the attendance records?"

"The same way you did to me this morning." Jeremiah twisted the green glass earring that made his ears appear human. "Though it might help if you had the original text as evidence."

"It wouldn't matter if I did." Mason studied the equation, trying to make sense of the numbers. "We can't tell anyone else the truth. The Serpents didn't set me on Kira's route by accident."

"You think they would—?" Jeremiah's lips tightened, unable to finish his question.

But Mason understood.

Would the Serpents hurt an innocent thirteen-year-old girl?

"Yes." Mason swallowed the heat that rose in his throat. He copied a new question as Mr. Clark added it to the board.

Inhale. *Focus on the positives.*

Exhale. *Kira will be safe.*

"That's why I'm using Yasmin," Mason said, shrugging, and forcing a smile. As far as alibis went, his hyper-intrusive classmate would not have been his first choice.

Or second, or third, or hundred-and-fifth.

But Yasmin seeing his wings and fainting meant that she'd been absent for the same classes as Mason. That would be important if Eli checked the attendance records.

"No, you're not," Jeremiah said, shaking his head. "I was on the newspaper with her for three years. Trust me, thirty minutes and you're going to shower her with amnesiac powder. And I will be right there to say I told you so."

———

"Why is Jeremiah here?" Yasmin's eyes narrowed as she stepped into the old gymnasium.

Mason sighed, glancing at the elf beside him. "No idea."

"Because I like being proven right," Jeremiah said, not looking up as he pulled his lunch from a paper bag and sprawled his long legs across the bleachers. "This isn't just any human you're trusting. It's Yasmin Gul. Moral scruples aren't exactly her thing."

Mason winced. He wasn't fond of Yasmin either, but she didn't need to hear them insulting her.

Unfortunately, Jeremiah's worry about the Drages and the Serpents had replaced his earlier concerns about the amnesiac powder. The elf's faith in the enchanted dust was at an all-time high. So was his certainty that Mason would *do the right thing* and use it. Jeremiah assumed Yasmin would forget any insults.

"That's a bold statement from the boy who stole my paper," Yasmin said, placing a hand on her hip as she marched forward. "Though I can't say I'm surprised to learn you're not human. What are you? A slug in human skin?"

"See?" Jeremiah wiped a peach on the edge of his shirt and pointed a thumb toward Yasmin. "She's already revealing that she thinks being *human* is inherently good. Not trustworthy."

"It's better that she doesn't have a moral compass," Mason responded before Yasmin could issue a retort of her own. He stepped down the bleachers, holding his arms up in peace as he turned between his friend and his new co-conspirator. "I'm asking her to cover my tail. Literally."

He laughed, trying to diffuse the tension. Neither of the others joined in.

"You two keep talking about me like *I'm* the criminal." Yasmin's eyes flicked over Mason. They were large and brown, like a doe.

If a deer delighted in others' misfortune.

"I'm not a criminal," Mason corrected her.

"Though you did do a stint at Ember Rise Reformatory," Jeremiah said.

Heat burst in Mason's stomach as he glared at his friend. *Why is he telling her that?*

Jeremiah pointed at the toe of Mason's sneaker where the amnesiac powder remained.

"What's Ember Rise Reformatory?" Yasmin asked, using her shoe to brush the dust from a cleaner patch of floor. She took a seat, crossed her legs beneath her, and opened her notebook.

Jeremiah bit into his peach. "It's a juvenile detention center for magical kids. Mason spent two—no, almost three years there." Juice trickled down his chin.

Frustration bubbled within Mason. He clamped his jaw. Jeremiah was trying to goad him into using the amnesiac powder. But the Reformatory had taught Mason how to keep his cool.

Inhale.

The sweet floral scent of roses filled his nostrils—Yasmin.

If it was a perfume that she wore or something else, Mason didn't know. But the unique smell had surrounded Yasmin for as long as they'd attended Folkestone High, mixing with the soft-fleshy scent that marked her as human.

It was a testament to the stench of the dead rat that Mason had missed her in the gymnasium yesterday.

Unlike its high-strung owner, Yasmin's scent was soothing.

Mason let it wash over him, and the heat dampened in his stomach.

Positive thoughts.

He looked down at Yasmin and spotted her notebook. "Why are you writing about Ember Rise Reformatory?"

"Not that you seem to know, but it's rude to read other people's notes," Yasmin said, pulling the book to her chest. She glared up at him. "Isn't that our deal? I get lessons on magic and all the different creatures that apparently live in our city. It's not much given I'm perjuring myself for you."

Yasmin's mouth spread in a massive fake grin, so wide it threatened to crack her cheeks. She used the same smile when she wanted to impress teachers. How it worked, Mason couldn't understand. The grin was better suited to a haunted plastic doll. It disguised the fact that Yasmin, with her big brown eyes and long lashes, was pretty.

Probably for the best. Otherwise, people might mistake her for someone normal.

"Just the look that'll charm the Drages," Jeremiah said, clapping in slow sarcastic beats from his position on the bleachers. "Come on, Mason. You have to see that besides this whole thing being completely illegal, Yasmin lacks the likeability to be a good alibi."

The fake smile faltered on Yasmin's face. Her eyes flicked to her notes, blinking a few too many times. She didn't retort.

That upset her more than she wants to let on.

Mason rubbed the back of his neck, looking down at the human girl. Jeremiah was being too cruel. For all her flaws, Yasmin wasn't a *terrible* person.

Nor was she an ineffective one.

Part of why Yasmin frustrated her peers was because, despite her abrasive nature, she knew how to get her way. When sweet-talking teachers failed, strong-arming them did not.

"Yasmin is plenty charming," Mason said though *convincing* might have been a more apt term. He grabbed her hand and pulled Yasmin to her feet. She was too caught off guard by the gesture to object. "I have complete faith in her."

Mason wrapped an arm over her shoulders, spinning her so that they faced Jeremiah together. Perhaps presenting a united front would stifle the elf's objections.

Yasmin didn't get the message. She stiffened, turning into a plank of wood. Instead of glaring at Jeremiah, her eyes widened as they turned to Mason.

She's not seriously about to berate me for being nice, is she?

Before Yasmin could voice any bizarre objections she had at being complimented, Jeremiah clicked his tongue, drawing their attention.

"Yasmin could be the most charming human in the world," he said. "But it wouldn't matter. She'd still be a human. It's one thing for the Drages to check attendance records. But you really think one of the wealthiest families of dragons is going to be willing to take her word on anything?"

Jeremiah stood, one pale eyebrow arched as a smile crept on his face. He knew he'd made a winning argument, and his gaze fell once more to Mason's sneaker.

Burn it! He does have a point.

Mason had been so focused on securing an alibi, he hadn't considered that aspect. Dragons didn't eat humans —anymore—but there was a level of animosity that remained among the elite of Castor's Grove. Would the

Drages listen to a creature their ancestors had considered prey?

Inhale. An idea formed in Mason's mind as he breathed in the rose perfume, almost over-powering the human scent beneath.

"Well then," Mason said. "Maybe Yasmin isn't human."

8

YASMIN

It was embarrassing to admit, but for a few seconds, Yasmin thought Mason meant that she was magical too. The idea made her heartbeat so loud it echoed in her ears. She preferred to focus on facts, but it would be a lie to say she'd never indulged in such fantasies as a child.

But Yasmin didn't have magic. She was very human. What Mason was proposing was a disguise.

It wasn't the worst idea.

Going undercover as a magical creature could make my story more compelling.

Last night, Yasmin had been envisioning a newspaper article, but this was enough information for an entire book. What would she call it?

My Time Among the Dragons...Magic: An Exposé...The Enchanting Discovery of Yasmin Gul.

"I think the Drages will notice when they can't find any Guls listed in the Archive of Legends," Jeremiah said, descending from his seat on the bleachers to argue with Mason. The two faced one another a few feet away from Yasmin.

"That doesn't matter." Mason waved his hands. "The archives only track magical families that have been living in Castor's Grove for generations. My mother's a dragon. She's not in there."

He just admitted his mother's a dragon.

Had Yasmin learned nothing in the library? She needed to record Mason. Without sufficient evidence no one would believe her, and she could kiss her future book—and all its imaginary titles—goodbye.

"Yeah, but Yasmin's family are from here," Jeremiah said. "If they look into the Guls, they'll see that they're human."

"Okay, except that her—" Mason broke off. His eyes narrowed at Yasmin. "What are you doing?"

Yasmin stopped rummaging through her backpack as her fingers clasped around her phone. "Getting ready to take notes," she said, pulling the device free and waving it before her. "Easier to type."

Mason shook his head. "You hate typing. All your notes are handwritten. Even some of your assignments."

How does he know that?

Maybe Yasmin's note taking in class stood out, but she hadn't thought any of her classmates paid attention to the essays she handed in.

Were they a secret source of mockery? It would be on brand for Mason and his friends to make stupid jokes about how long it took Yasmin to write her essays.

Then he has the gall to call me charming.

It was all part of Mason's nice guy act. He hadn't meant the compliment, even if a small part of Yasmin wished he had.

Whatever. She'd leave *charm* to people like her sister and Mason. Yasmin didn't need it. She was clever.

"I thought it would be better to keep my notes more secure in this instance," Yasmin lied, keeping her expression neutral. "My phone has a passcode. Anyone could pick up my books, and you said I had to keep this secret."

"Precisely why no one should tell you in the first place," Jeremiah muttered, shooting her a glare from the corner of his eye. He probably intended it to be withering, but Yasmin had seen worse.

Mason chuckled. "Trust me, even if someone does pick up your notebook, they won't believe anything you've written."

That's what I'm afraid of.

Yasmin smiled and rested her phone on the floor. It would seem strange if she insisted on typing now, and Mason might notice if she tried to take an audio recording. But perhaps, she could convince him to show her his wings again. Then, she could snap a picture—a perfect piece of evidence.

The memory of Mason's wings, glowing gold and yellow in the sunshine made Yasmin's breath catch.

They were so beautiful.

"If we're going to pretend you're a Castor, you need to know the basics." Mason turned from Jeremiah and knelt on the ground before Yasmin. "Castor's Grove was founded in the year sixteen twenty-eight by Prince Martin Roserun, one of the sons of the Fairy King of—"

"Wait, slow down." Yasmin blinked, feeling her body grow hot. How had she lost focus thinking about Mason's wings? Better than noticing his muscles or his eyes like most of the other girls, but still very unprofessional. She scrambled to free her pen from the spirals of her notebook. With a click, she hurried to write what Mason had said, then paused. "Did you say a *prince* founded the city?"

"Yes, in sixteen twenty-eight," Mason repeated, perhaps missing the reason for Yasmin's confusion. "Initially, the settlement was called Fairy's Home. The prince and his people were searching for a new land where they'd be safe from the persecution of magic that plagued Europe at that time..."

Yasmin hadn't expected to learn an alternate history about the founding of the city. All the books she'd read claimed Castor's Grove had been built at the turn of the eighteenth century by a group of scholars out of New York. She struggled to write everything down. The reality of magic proved more challenging to process than Yasmin had expected. On more than one occasion, she found her pen freezing and her jaw growing slack.

"And you all still have a king." Yasmin shook her head as she stared at the page.

"Castors have an unusual fondness for hierarchal nobility. The witches have their matriarchs. The elves have princes." Mason shrugged. "I wouldn't worry too much about that aspect. The nobility keeps to themselves. You're not going to meet any of them."

Yasmin nodded, but her mind felt numb. Learning of the existence of a monarchy in modern America baffled and embarrassed her in equal measure. Everyone in Castor's Grove accepted the existence of the city's downtown palace as an architectural eccentricity, the design of a family with more money than sense. Tourists flocked to it for photographs. But Yasmin prided herself on her observational skills, her natural investigative talent. How had she never questioned any of this before?

According to Mason, Castor's Grove existed as a magical utopia. Enchanted locations and creatures of every variety hid in plain sight: fairies, dragons, pixies, elves, were-wolves, nymphs, harpies. The list went on.

"The city's motto is Castors in Heart." Mason placed his hand to his chest, and flicked his eyes to Yasmin's note-book, reminding her to keep writing. "It's the only city where different magical species identify under a single, united banner instead of keeping to our respective groups."

"You make it sound like a paradise," Jeremiah scoffed from where he'd sprawled near the bottom of the bleachers. It wasn't his first interjection. "We're not that united. The fairies hoard most of the wealth, and our fabricated little aristocracy lords over everyone—all obsessed with blood-lines and sigils. They barely look out for their own kind. Most vampires wouldn't piss on an elf if we were on fire."

Tensions among magical population. Yasmin made a note. In a smaller font, near the corner, she added: *Jeremiah = elf?*

"I thought elves were the little people who made shoes," Yasmin blurted. "Like the story."

Jeremiah rolled his eyes. "You're thinking of brownies."

His tone made it seem like the comment was stupid. But how was Yasmin supposed to know the difference between elves and brownies?

"Actually, scholars think it was a wingless species of pixie that inspired that story," Mason said, though after catching Jeremiah's eye, he hastened to add, "But definitely not elves."

Yasmin pursed her lips, hiding her thrill at Jeremiah being corrected. Who knew Mason Wick could be a know-it-all when he wanted?

But his clarification had done little to define *elves* to Yasmin. What distinguished them from humans? Mason had wings, a tail, a forked tongue, and sharp teeth. Objec-tively, he was attractive. Jeremiah was just pale and lanky.

"Could we disguise me as an elf?" Yasmin suggested.

Jeremiah's nose wrinkled in disgust. "Certainly not. A troll, maybe."

Yasmin didn't need an extensive knowledge of Castors to know that was an insult.

Mason laughed, trading a look with his friend. "Hey, don't insult the trolls like that. A lot are decent."

So I'm less attractive than a troll according to Mason.

Yasmin's jaw clenched. At least Mason wasn't pretending to be nice and giving her compliments he didn't mean any more.

What was he doing at a juvenile detention center?

Mason had more secrets than his wings and tail. Yasmin intended to expose him as much as any Castor in her tell-all book, title TBD. How many of her classmates would continue gushing over Mason when they learned the truth?

Yasmin just needed to uncover all of it.

"So not an elf, or a troll, or a dragon," Yasmin said, plastering a smile on her face to hide her annoyance. She tightened her grip on her pen to keep her concentration from slipping. "What could you disguise me as?"

Their answer, she hoped, would give hints as to how to identify magical species. Yasmin could fill a chapter on that alone.

"No one ruled out dragon," Mason said, turning back toward her. He grinned, revealing his massive teeth. They added a hint of danger to his features, at odds with the dimple that appeared on his right cheek.

Yasmin's heart skipped. The pen slipped from her fingers. There was something entrancing about the juxtaposition of Mason's features.

No. Stop. You do not find him attractive. He just has some sort of human-alluring magic. Focus.

"How would we disguise me as a dragon?" Yasmin asked.

Mason kept grinning. "Make massive papier-mâché wings and stick them onto you."

The breath escaped Yasmin in an exasperated huff. She lowered her gaze to the floor and grabbed her fallen pen. Mason was an idiot. They weren't in class. Who was he trying to impress with his dumb jokes?

Evidently himself since he was the only one laughing.

"I think the inability to breathe fire would be more noticeable," Jeremiah said, rolling his eyes from his perch on the bleachers.

The smile slid from Mason's face.

Yasmin scribbled the note. "You can breathe fire?"

"Oh yeah," Jeremiah started to answer for him. "If Mason were to get angry—"

"Not all dragons breathe fire," Mason interrupted. He raised his hands, and there was something severe about the gesture, an insistence that Jeremiah stop talking.

Something the elf said had struck a nerve.

Mason inhaled, and his voice calmed when he spoke again. "So should we continue with your lesson? I thought you wanted to learn about Castors."

"And I thought you wanted me to be your alibi." Yasmin forced a smile, charming or not, and stared at him over her notebook, trying to act innocent as she pried. "How am I going to play a convincing Castor if I don't know about dragons?"

A muscle twitched in Mason's jaw. His crooked, close-lipped smile returned, and he nodded. "Why don't we focus on something you could pretend to be instead?"

Is he avoiding the topic?

If so, he'd done it effectively.

"Like what?" Yasmin asked.

Mason's vicious canines appeared again as his grin broadened. "You, Yasmin Gul are going to be a witch."

9
MASON

Mason regretted mentioning witches about ten seconds after the word left his lips. Now that there was a specific topic for her focus, Yasmin had a thousand-and-one new questions.

What do witches look like? Can they really cast spells? What types? How do they work? Can they heal people or cure diseases?

Home brought little reprieve from her hounding.

Mason's phone vibrated in his pocket. He stabbed a piece of lettuce on his plate, pretending not to notice.

"That's the fifth time in the past hour," Jeremiah muttered, tips of his ears rising as he glared across the dining table.

"Interesting." Uncle Lee dabbed a cloth napkin over his lips before leaning back in the tall mahogany seat. His eyebrows quirked in amusement. "Yasmin by chance?"

"No," Mason lied.

But at the same time, Jeremiah ratted him out. "Yes."

Mason considered throwing the lettuce at his brother. Their fairy godfather was getting the complete wrong impression.

"We have an AP psych project together," Mason borrowed the lie Yasmin had used when trying to get his number. "She's a little... intense."

"What's the project about?" Kira asked, wrinkling her nose as she considered a cherry tomato on the end of her fork. Almost a year living with Uncle Lee, and she still hadn't grown accustomed to the fairy's vegetarian meals.

"Building a psychological profile on a fictional character."

Comet sat up on the table. He retained the sparkling sense of magic that clung to all great dragons, but in his case, it was undercut by almost cartoonish cuteness. His massive round eyes—a similar fiery orange to his scales—blinked at Mason as he tilted his head. Comet flicked his tail up and snorted. No smoke accompanied the gesture.

A selfish part of Mason was grateful for that.

"We haven't chosen a character yet," Mason said, answering Comet's wordless question. "That's why she keeps messaging. Can I be excused? I need to start researching."

Without waiting for a response, Mason stood, crossed the dining room, and pushed open the burnished oak door to enter the kitchen.

Uncle Lee's manor lacked the modern niceties of newer construction. A wood-burning stove burrowed into the base of a stone chimney, and an old fridge hummed in the corner. Water ran through the taps, sourced from a well near the back of the property. The only dishwasher in the room was Mason.

He rinsed his plate and cutlery, glancing over his shoulder before checking his phone. Yasmin's messages consisted of a fresh set of thirteen new questions. Annoyingly complex ones about woodswitch culture and elvish society, which she'd latched onto as tangentially relevant given their shared use of the forests.

More aggravating, she was probably right.

Mason scanned the list, head spinning. *I don't even know the answer to half of these.*

Not that he intended to admit that to Yasmin.

Comet flew through the door, angling his body to allow his wings to pass. His mouth clamped around his plate. He settled near the edge of the sink, eyes flashing to the phone screen.

Great dragons couldn't speak. But they could read.

Mason hid the screen as he typed: *Stop messaging. We'll talk at lunch.*

Comet washed the plate with his tail, wide mouth twitching into a Cheshire cat styled grin.

Evidently, Lee wasn't the only one misinterpreting things.

Mason opened his mouth to argue, but paused. Bizarre as it was to have his family teasing him about Yasmin Gul of all people, it beat them learning the truth. They couldn't know the Serpents were involved.

Lee would fall into a state of panic. Comet would attempt to fortify the manor. Kira might suggest taking down the Serpents themselves.

And they know how to find her. What if—

A jet of water spouted onto Mason's face, shaking him back to the present

Comet moved his tail, and the stream fell harmlessly back toward the sink. His ears twitched, eyes narrowing as much as they could before widening in a suggestion.

How the hell had Mason's expression led the great dragon to that conclusion?

"I'm not standing here worrying if a girl likes me. I'm

just—" Mason couldn't explain that he was panicked for their safety. "—distracted. I have work to do."

Mason shook his wet hair onto Comet's orange scales in vengeance before ducking from the room.

A short passage led from the kitchen to the parlor. Instead of climbing the marble stairs to retrieve his school bag, Mason continued to the opposite hall, following the dark corridor to the end.

If he wanted to disguise Yasmin—or answer her incessant questions—Mason needed to research.

The door at the end of the corridor led to the manor's library. Rows of colorful books lined the shelves, stretching from the floor to the vaulted ceiling. A plush plaid carpet gave the room a mossy glow and large lamps stood as beacons in the corners. In the center, a yellow Queen Anne chair waited for a reader to settle in.

Uncle Lee's collection of titles was impressive. The fairy enjoyed the human classics, but the shelves also boasted historical texts and personal records, copied with magic from before the printing press became common place. Within such books, the writing appeared handwritten on the yellowing pages.

Mason walked to the section on witches. Everything related to the covens within the city.

The soft jingle of metal bangles hitting one another made Mason pause.

"Whatchya doing?' Kira stretched the question out as she jumped into the library. The thirteen-year-old was all long limbs, loose braids, and massive grin.

"Looking for information on woodswitches," Mason said.

"For your project?" Kira guessed. "Check the elf biographies. They interact a lot."

Another point for Yasmin. Dammit.

"Want help looking?"

"Depends. Are you avoiding scrubbing pots?"

Kira grinned, spun, and began searching the shelves. She'd already grabbed two books for Mason to consider by the time he reached her. "Comet thinks you have a crush on a human."

"Comet's as mental as Lee."

"Good. Dragons aren't supposed to date humans." Kira passed him the books. "Even hanging out with them so much is—"

"Humans are fine, Ki," Mason said, cutting her off before she said something thoughtless. Few dragons opted to spend time with humans, or even certain other species of Castor. Old prejudices seemed to thrive in their fires. Lawrence had expressed similar distaste when learning his son was attending a Grover high school. But Mason liked most of his classmates. "We're lucky we get to know them better."

"Lucky. Right." Kira hugged her arms across her chest. Her eyes grew heavy and dropped to her feet.

Flames, I'm a moron. Why would I call her lucky?

Kira's parents were dead. She'd been taken in briefly by an uncle who'd then relinquished to the system. Her first home had been with a pair of elves. Mason didn't know why she'd been removed from their custody, but it couldn't have been anything good. She flinched when Jeremiah approached too fast.

"Do you ever think about the nymphs you lived with before?" Kira whispered.

A chill crept over Mason. He shook his head and considered the books she'd given him. His eyes flitted over the handwritten spines: *Wandering Elf: a tale of the city's first murderer. The Harrow King and other Stories.*

Good texts if Mason was really do a psychological profile on a fictional character.

"What you did was incredible," Kira said.

Mason kept his eyes on the titles. What was the story of the Harrow King again?

"Not the—what happened, but your fire."

An elf king born with the powers of witches sought to master the abilities of every magical species. But when he went to the dragons, they laughed and burned his hands. Or something. Mason didn't remember, only the final line: For only a dragon can control—

"I've heard it was unbelievable how much you summoned. You must be one of the most powerful dragons living."

Mason blinked. Yellow flames danced over the back of his eyelids. The memory of ropes bit into his wrists. An iron bar stuck between his teeth.

Screams. Heat. Fury.

Kira brushed his shoulder. "I've been wanting to talk to you about—"

"No." The word came harsher and more abrupt than Mason intended.

Kira pulled her hand back. Her green wings and tail broke free, short spikes leaving marks in the carpet. A defensive reflex.

Shit.

Mason inhaled. *Think positive.*

Exhale. Was it power if you weren't in control?

"Why am I the only one cleaning the kitchen?" Jeremiah's voice made Mason jump. Unlike Kira, the elf had no bangles to warn of his arrival.

He stood in the doorway, arms crossed, and lips twisted in an unimpressed scowl.

"Because we're working on Mason's project," Kira said, throwing him an uncertain glance. "He's doing a profile on a woodswitch."

Jeremiah barely glanced at Kira. "Have you considered not choosing a woodswitch?"

The elf's tone dripped with double meaning, which Mason chose to ignore.

"Because a vampire would be better?" Mason suggested. "They are the battiest of the Castors. I'd stake my life on it."

Kira exploded into a fit of giggles.

Jeremiah took a second longer to get it. Then, he rolled his eyes. "You should be banned from making jokes."

"You should fire him," Kira suggested, still giggling.

Mason hated the reference. But it was a good pun. He forced a grin.

"What is that?" Jeremiah's eyes landed on a dark green scale by Kira's feet. In an instant, he was beside her, bending to grab it. He raised it and waved it in her face. "Can you not pick these up?"

Kira crossed her arms in defiance. "They disintegrate."

"And leave dust. Last time Lee found one of Mason's scales, he made us deep clean the entire dining room. You want to clean all these shelves? Take it and throw it away." Jeremiah pointed to the doorway.

Kira rolled her shoulders, hiding her wings and tail once more. She took the scale, hand flinching at Jeremiah's touch. She muttered under her breath as she stomped out.

"You should be gentler with her," Mason noted. "She's our sister, and you scare her."

"Kira's too bullheaded to be scared," Jeremiah

muttered. "And I wouldn't call a kid we've known nine months our sister.'

"We're brothers."

"That's different." Jeremiah waved his hands as though frustrated by the entire conversation. "You're trying to avoid a rational conversation about what you're doing."

Of course, he was. They'd had several on the way home.

"Teenagers aren't sent to Ironvault for telling one classmate the truth, Jere," Mason offered the reassurance for the hundredth time. "Besides, I won't get caught."

"Really? Because you think a criminal syndicate is framing you. They might have a plan."

Mason's stomach turned. Membership in the Serpents didn't stop at the individual who bought in. The gang offered a packaged deal. Lawrence had joined. That meant the Serpents owned Mason. He'd assumed they'd decided to ignore him due to his prior incident. But just because he couldn't be trusted as an official member didn't mean he couldn't be a patsy.

"Do you want to be my alibi?" Mason suggested. It wouldn't work. Jeremiah had been in class, and he was his brother to boot. No one would believe him.

Jeremiah voiced neither point as his reason for objecting. "You don't need an alibi if you're really innocent."

And there it was, obvious in the sudden increase in the elf's pitch: doubt.

Mason shook his head, swallowed, and moved past his Jeremiah. He couldn't keep arguing. His point had already been proven.

If Mason's own brother doubted him, he definitely needed Yasmin's help.

10

MASON

Despite Jeremiah's objections, Mason spent lunch on Thursday training Yasmin in the old gym. He wouldn't call the experience pleasant.

The more familiar Yasmin became with the concept of magic, the less her focus drifted. Their forty-five minutes had featured several not-so-subtle attempts to pry into Mason's personal life. Her mind had latched onto Jeremiah's mention of Ember Rise.

But, for all her many flaws, Yasmin was an excellent student. She parroted facts, asked insightful questions, and agonized over the details of her notes. If they dealt with a lax enough official, she might pass as a woodswitch by tomorrow.

"Wick, what are you doing?" Coach Robinson shouted from across the soccer field, shaking Mason back to the present. "You have to chase the ball. You're playing midfield." He waved his hands toward the opposite goal.

Mason's team were making a play.

Dust!

Mason slapped his cheek and burst into a sprint. Friday

morning soccer practice was not the time to be distracted with concerns about Yasmin.

You're putting far too much effort into this for someone who's innocent.

Mason's chest tightened. It was Jeremiah's voice, quiet but sharp, like a dagger pressed into his spine. They'd been assigned kitchen duty the previous night, and the tension between them had prickled with every passed plate.

It's been three days. The Drages could have found the real culprit. Why are you still worrying?

Because Mason hadn't hallucinated that text, and it hadn't been a joke. Whatever was going on, the Serpents were involved. Mason would be a fool not to worry.

A boy in a lime green overshirt balanced the soccer ball with the tip of his shoe. He scanned the field for an opening. His eyes locked onto Mason. He grinned and kicked.

The ball spun toward midfield. Mason ran forward and stopped it with the side of his cleat. The moment the ball was in his possession, two orange shirts rushed.

Mason ran the ball closer to the goal, searching for an open teammate as he avoided another orange shirt's attempt to steal.

A few feet from the goal, Zach had slipped away from whoever was guarding him.

Perfect.

Mason aimed and—

A flash of eggplant purple caught his eye. Across the field, a blond-haired man walked through the rows of cars in the parking lot. From the distance, the stranger's features were obscured, but the uniform's color was distinct—the Castor's Police.

Mason's stomach flickered. What was an officer doing at Folkestone High?

Kalvin—dressed in a mesh orange overshirt—swiped the ball from Mason's toe. The game turned, and the other players raced across the field again.

Mason remained frozen. The policeman turned. Their eyes locked.

He's here to arrest me.

Mason's heart pounded. His stomach bubbled, a cauldron starting to boil. Every instinct told him to summon his wings and flee. Yasmin couldn't be his alibi, not yet. She wasn't ready. She was missing crucial elements of her disguise. Mason had been planning to collect them this afternoon.

I'm too late.

A whoop of excitement rose from the opposite goal post. Coach blew his whistle.

The policeman disappeared into the school's administration office.

"You're killing me today, Wick!" Coach's hand snapped like a vice onto Mason's shoulder. "If you're playing like this next practice, I'm benching you for the game against Dashmoor. You're supposed to be our best player! Where the hell is your mind?"

Coach pointed to the opposite corner of the field where the other boys were pulling off the overshirts.

Mason shuffled toward them, glancing over his shoulder at the administration office. The Castor's Police department must have obtained a warrant to check Folkestone's attendance records.

What are the chances they're incompetent enough to only look at if I was present on Tuesday morning and not consider the individual class logs?

Not high, but Mason clung to the shred of possibility.

"Did you not see that I was open?" Zach flicked a sweat-covered green shirt against Mason's side as he reached his teammates. "We could've won."

"Uh. Doubtful," Kalvin said, wiping a bead of sweat from the edge of his curls. "We were clearly the superior team."

Mason forced a laugh as he removed his overshirt. "It's true, Kal. You were unstoppable today."

"He was not." Zach objected. "You were distracted. Have been all week."

The team moved toward the showers. Mason dragged his feet. If he was going to be arrested, he'd prefer it happen while his friends were elsewhere.

Unfortunately, Zach and Kalvin stopped beside him.

"Looking for someone, Mase?" Kalvin asked, there was a hint of amusement in his voice.

Yeah, a big strapping man in uniform. Mason's chest was too tight to make the joke.

"Maybe a girl with a long black braid and big brown eyes?" Zach suggested, batting his lashes before bursting into a laugh.

Mason flicked his gaze away from the admission building's entrance. "Are you talking about Yasmin?"

"You both disappeared Tuesday afternoon, and you've spent the past two lunches alone with her," Kalvin said, raising his eyebrows. "One of the sophomores told us that she saw you two going into the old gym yesterday."

Burning shit.

Mason hadn't realized they'd been spotted.

Maybe it's a good thing.

At least if the policeman asked around, it would support Mason's alibi. It might not even matter that Yasmin was human!

Except that it would prove her mind could be easily

manipulated. A good lawyer would argue that Mason had bewitched her after the fact in order to concoct an alibi—ironically, not far from the truth. The Drages wouldn't have a good lawyer, they'd have the best.

"You can tell us," Zach said, nudging Mason's ribs. "Are you hooking up with Gul?"

"What?" Mason had never heard such a preposterous suggestion in his life. It was one thing for his family to jump to conclusions. His friends knew Yasmin. "Have you both gone insane?"

"We wouldn't judge you," Kalvin said, holding up his hands. "She's a pain, but she's not unattractive. And you know what they say about girls who act like prudes."

"I don't." Mason's eyes narrowed at his friends. Judging from the grins on both their faces, Kalvin and Zach had invented a significantly more titillating version of what was happening. Yasmin would not want a rumor like that spreading. "You have the complete wrong idea."

"Really. You and Gul are sneaking into the old gym to study?" Kalvin snorted.

"As a matter of fact, we are. She's…" Mason's voice trailed off as the policeman emerged. There was a thin beige file in his hand.

"Secretly in love with you?" Zach suggested, resting his head onto the side of Mason's shoulder with an exaggerated dreamy sigh. "She was desperate to get your number a few days ago. Did she write you a love note begging you to tutor her? So nice of you to say yes."

"Would you stop making things up?" Mason shoved his friend away before Zach attempted another joke.

Over in the parking lot, the policeman pulled out his phone. He pressed it to his ear as he climbed into his car. He was going to drive off. Maybe the Castor's Police operated with the exact level of incompetence Mason needed.

He relaxed as he turned toward his friends. "Yasmin's tutoring me in English, that's all."

"Why didn't you ask Jere?" Kalvin asked, still sounding skeptical.

"He said he's too busy," Mason lied, waving his hand and fighting to keep a smile from his face.

Maybe Jeremiah was right. Mason had panicked over nothing.

Except the police car hadn't driven off.

The door swung open. The officer climbed out once more, no longer on his phone but still clinging to the beige file. Without glancing at the field, he walked into Folkestone High.

He doesn't know I'm me. The officer must've been hoping to find Mason Wick inside. He had no idea that it was the same boy he'd seen fumbling on a soccer field.

I still have time to run.

But he'd need to take his alibi with him.

11

YASMIN

"Thank God you're predictable."

Yasmin jumped at the sound of Mason's voice.

She slammed her notebook shut as he stepped out from behind a row of books. Yasmin had been brainstorming chapter ideas for her magic-exposé. She wanted to blend informative and narrative, mixing details about each species with her personal memoir. Witches would be chapter one. Elves, chapter two. She was torn for chapter three. It made sense to pry Mason for information about dragons—and she was desperate to uncover what he was hiding. But from a story-telling perspective, she liked the idea of saving them for last.

If Mason saw what she'd written, that would be the end of Yasmin's internal debate. He'd wipe her memory with his magic powder, burn her sunflower notebook with the fire he wouldn't discuss, and force her to say farewell to her future best-seller.

"What are you doing in here?" Yasmin asked, clutching her notebook to her chest. The bell had rung five minutes ago. Mason should've been on his way to physics, but he hadn't changed since soccer. A light sheen of sweat made his white t-shirt cling, outlining the muscles on his abdomen. Yasmin's face heated. She wasn't trying to stare, but his abs were at eye-level.

"Getting you, obviously," Mason said. He grabbed her bag from the table and slung it over his shoulder alongside his own. "We have to go. There's a policeman."

Yasmin didn't stand. "How did you know I was here?"

"Because this is the only place you go when you have a spare period. Now would you stop being difficult? If he picks up my scent, I'm screwed." Mason grabbed Yasmin's hand and pulled her up, dragging her behind him as they weaved through the bookshelves.

He was *very* strong.

Yasmin stumbled after him, afraid her arm might be yanked off if she didn't keep up. Mason's answer had only confused her more. How did he know that she had a spare period now? And where was he taking her? And why were they running from the police?

"You are the most suspicious innocent person I've ever met," she said as they reached the front of the library.

Mason pressed his finger against her lips. They were close enough that the gesture felt embarrassingly intimate. His skin felt so warm.

"You can have that conversation with Jere," Mason said. "I'm being framed. And I don't plan to underestimate my opponents."

Yasmin's eyebrows rose. Even without magic, Mason's story might be shaping up to make a decent true crime podcast.

He slipped his head through the door, flaring his nostrils as he inhaled. "Sorry, could you step back?" Mason released Yasmin's hand, staring at his feet as he explained. "Your scent is throwing me off."

Her *what*?

Yasmin didn't smell. Was Mason mocking her again?

"Coast's clear. Hopefully, Mr. Wilson's already told the officer to check the soccer field for me. Come on." Mason took Yasmin's hand again and pulled her into the corridor.

From there, skipping school proved unexpectedly simple. One of the janitors snapped at them to stop running through the hallways, but he made no effort to pursue them. No one else even glanced in their direction.

Yasmin and Mason slipped through the school's back exit and found themselves facing the familiar outline of the crumbling gym.

"Now what?" Yasmin asked as they crept along the edge of the school.

"Dust!" Mason's nostrils flared as he turned the corner. He spun and grabbed Yasmin's waist. Given the strength he'd displayed earlier, his touch was surprisingly gentle.

A flush crept up Yasmin's neck as she looked at his hand. This was not a detail she'd include in her book.

"Let's hope my scent masks yours."

"What are you—" Yasmin's objection was cut off as Mason scooped her into his arms. One of his hands brushed her ass. Her eyes widened.

He'd tossed her over his shoulder with their school bags. Yasmin wasn't heavy, but still.

How much can he lift?

Unencumbered by the additional weight, Mason ran across the field toward the old gym. They were almost through the door when Yasmin caught sight of the reason for his sudden panic.

A golden-haired man, purple uniform bright against the

green field, rushed toward them. Coach Robinson jogged behind their pursuer, shouting at Mason to stop.

"I think your cop may have spotted us," Yasmin said.

"Stunning observational skills," Mason grunted. "You should be a reporter." The door swung behind them as they entered the gym.

The stench of decomposing rat soured the air, its potency enhanced by time and heat. Yasmin's eyes watered. She buried her nose in Mason's shirt, afraid overexposure to the smell might make her ill. Even sweat would have to be —oh.

He smells good.

Like a warm mix of smoke and salt. How was that possible when he'd been on the soccer field minutes ago?

Mason raced across the floor, making a direct line to where the roof had fallen. He shifted his grip, hands moving to Yasmin's waist and swinging her forward so that she was in his arms.

Are we going to—? Yasmin was afraid to hope as they stepped into the pool of sunlight. She wrapped her arms around Mason's neck, staring over his shoulder.

The gymnasium door opened. The policeman stepped in.

Brilliant golden wings unfurled from Mason's back. He flapped and his body rose into the air, carrying Yasmin with him.

The officer shouted at them from beneath.

Yasmin didn't register the words. She clung to Mason. Eyes full of the sunlight dancing on his wings.

She was flying.

12

MASON

"You do have a tail." Yasmin's words escaped in a breathless whisper; her arms locked in a vice-grip around Mason's neck. They were a hundred feet in the air, but instead of marveling at the clouds or the view of the city, her eyes were glued to his back. "And spikes."

Yasmin's fingers inched over Mason's neck, tracing the protrusions of bone that rose like golden hills along his spine. Her hand crept lower until she brushed the base of his wings. Her touch tickled.

Mason's tail curled, cheeks growing hot. He wasn't used to someone touching his scales, especially not when he was flying, and Yasmin was whispering about him like he was a specimen under a microscope.

"They're so..." She didn't finish her thought.

Mason frowned. What? Weird? Strange? Off-putting? Not that he cared what Yasmin thought of his wings, but she didn't have to be so open with her judgement.

"What are we—I mean—where are we going?" Yasmin asked, hand retreating to his neck once more.

"Downtown." Mason's afternoon trip had been moved

forward thanks to the officer. "There's something I need to collect. You can wait at a café while I grab it."

"Absolutely not. I'm coming with you."

Mason turned his head. Yasmin's face was closer than he'd realized, all big brown eyes and parted lips. Perhaps he couldn't blame Kalvin and Zach for leaping to assumptions.

Except that she's also the most demanding human in existence.

"You understand I could let go right now, and you'd plummet to your death."

"Yeah, but you wouldn't." Despite her tone, Yasmin's grip tightened.

So she is a little afraid.

Good.

Mason trusted his grip, but he preferred her clinging tight all the same.

"I don't know, Gul. I'm a hardened criminal who needed an alibi." Mason grinned, revealing his teeth. "You're putting a lot of faith in me."

Yasmin's lips pressed together, eyes widening as though she'd just realized what a leap of faith she'd taken. She looked down at the streets below, squeaked, and buried her face in Mason's shoulder.

He tried and failed not to laugh.

———

Mason's heels dropped against the smooth roof as he landed on a skyscraper in the heart of downtown Castor's Grove. He'd used the building as a landing-pad before. The glint of sunlight on the glass walls masked his wings, and the seldom used roof-top bar meant an elevator into the city.

Yasmin untangled her arms from Mason's neck and wriggled free. His chest felt suddenly exposed. He'd grown accustomed to the feel of her—small and warm—pressed against his body.

On her own feet again, Yasmin crossed her arms, lifted her chin, and spun toward him. "I'm coming with you wherever you're going. Otherwise, I won't be your alibi."

Mason's jaw clenched. He should've known Yasmin's silence hadn't been acquiescence.

"You are the most stubborn—" Mason cut himself off. Took a deep breath. Ridiculous as it was for Yasmin to bully a fire-breathing beast whose ancestors might have eaten hers, he couldn't get annoyed. "You know what, sure."

"Oh." Yasmin's lips pursed before relaxing into a smile —small and guilty, but also genuine. It made her eyes light up like a kid who'd just discovered where their parents stashed the cookies.

It's much cuter than her fake grin.

Mason's brow furrowed. Had he just thought of Yasmin Gul as *cute*? Attractive, fine, if you could look past the personality. But *cute* suggested a sweetness that Yasmin lacked. She'd just strong-armed her way into accompanying him.

"What's the worst that could happen?" Mason shrugged as he folded his wings. "A vampire discovers you and turns you into a blood smoothie? No scales off my back."

None of that was true. In a worst-case scenario, Yasmin's memory would be wiped, and she'd return to her normal life. The one at risk was Mason.

But no one at the Purveyor would snitch.

Probably.

———

"This is where we're going?" Yasmin moved her hand from the strap of her bag to her hip. She frowned at the shabby exterior of *Dilly Dally*. A pane of murky glass, set in the crumbling brick wall showed the cluttered gift shop within. Children's toys balanced on notebooks; coffee mugs and commemorative glasses intermingled on the shelves. The rotating displays didn't distinguish between keychains or earrings.

Mason chose to be amused instead of annoyed at Yasmin's abrupt shift in mood. When they'd first started walking through the old alleyways near the edge of down-town, she'd been thrilled. Most of the surrounding build-ings were residential. Perhaps she'd thought they were about to visit a witch.

"You could wait out here," he suggested.

"Absolutely not." Yasmin tossed her braid over her shoulder. "This will be my first test. I'm supposed to be a witch, aren't I?"

"True. And Douglas won't be able to smell you."

"I don't smell."

"You do."

The sign on the gift shop door read: *Out for lunch. Back whenever.*

Yasmin opened her mouth to argue. Mason cut her off before she could.

"It's not an insult." Mason pulled open the door, ignoring the sign that read: *Out for lunch. Back whenever.* "Some Castors have more acute senses, that's all. The man who runs this shop is a fairy, so he doesn't."

Yasmin's face fell as she stepped into the cramped, disorganized shop. She lifted a hat from atop a stuffed crocodile and hung it on a peg. "Do dragons have this superior sense of smell?"

"Rivals werewolves in some cases." Mason strolled through the mess of things until he found a sign with a toilet and an arrow pointing right.

Yasmin rearranged the items as she followed. "Hmm. So, an enhanced sense of smell, super strength, fire-breathing, magical allure."

Mason stopped walking. His lips twitched. "What was that last one?"

"Allure," Yasmin repeated, examining an *I heart Castor's Grove* mug in the center of a group of unfolded t-shirts. She lifted it and scanned the racks as she explained, "That's how you hunt, right? You draw people in with your—"

Her eyes moved to Mason, and she cut herself off. His grin must've given it away. But he couldn't help it.

"Keep going." Mason's grin continued to spread. Not that he cared what Yasmin thought of his appearance, but it didn't hurt to have an ego boost. He leaned closer, struggling to keep his voice soft and seductive instead of bursting into a laugh. "Are my looks luring you in?"

"No, I didn't say—" Yasmin's eyes widened. She twisted the mug as though ceramic warded dragons. "I mean, all the—I was talking about your wings! Obviously, I found them mesmerizing. They're beautiful."

Mason's eyebrows rose. A compliment from Yasmin? That had to be a first.

Yasmin slammed her mouth shut, as though as shocked as Mason. Cheeks flushed, she turned and shoved the mug onto a shelf beside a pile of shirts. "When is the owner going to be back?"

"Up here? Who knows," Mason said. "Come on."

He grabbed her hand, fighting not to laugh at her

obvious confusion. A rack of coats hid the door to the men's bathroom. Mason pushed it away and pulled Yasmin into the stall behind him.

"Excuse me?" She twisted free, pulling away from him as the door closed behind them. "Just because I admitted I find your wings attractive doesn't mean I'm into you."

Mason's brow furrowed. "What do you think we're doing in here?"

"I don't know." Yasmin crossed her arms, but she didn't try to leave. "Two of us alone in a bathroom while we wait for a store owner to return. What am I supposed to think your intentions are?"

"Your imagination is as active as Kalvin and Zach's." Mason grinned. He knew that comparison would annoy Yasmin. The fact that she wouldn't understand what he meant made it all the better.

"This..." Mason went to the sink, counted three up and two to the left of a single blue tile, then pressed the wall.

Yasmin gasped as it moved.

"...is the entrance to The Portentous Purveyor."

13
YASMIN

The Portentous Purveyor was as cluttered as the gift store that disguised it, but there was an elegance to the chaos. Bottles of liquid glowed on long rows of shelves, their strange light glinting on curious metals. Flowers blossomed beneath glass jars, and colorful vines trailed across the hardwood floor. Weaponry and tapestries hung on the walls, décor plucked from a history book.

Now this is a magical store.

Yasmin descended the final step into the dim room, trying not to gape at the rainbow of colors that swirled through the shelves. Light didn't emanate that way from ordinary items. This was magic—reminiscent of the sunlit sheen of Mason's wings.

Not that Yasmin would be making that comparison aloud. She'd embarrassed herself enough upstairs.

Why did I suggest he uses his looks to lure in humans?

She clung to the desperate hope that her hunch was right, and he'd lied to embarrass her. The alternative meant that not only was she pathetic enough to get distracted by Mason, she'd all but admitted it to him.

Now, he'd lump Yasmin in with the rest of the girls giggling over him at Folkestone.

He'd be sorely mistaken.

Yasmin could—begrudgingly and preferably not out loud again—admit that Mason was objectively attractive. But she had zero romantic interest. A suspected thief who'd done a stint in magical juvie? Not a chance. Mason's amiable persona hid more than just wings.

Yasmin intended to learn what.

"I'm going to speak with Douglas to see if my order has come through," Mason whispered. "Try to blend in."

He moved deeper into the store, inching along the wall until he vanished behind the last row of shelves.

Yasmin found herself unsupervised. In a magical shop.

Her fingers tingled. She clutched the strap of her bag, pulling it tighter to her chest as she stared at the display before her. To convince people that the events in her future best-selling exposé were true, Yasmin needed evidence. Now, she was surrounded by it.

What do I investigate first?

Her head felt light and giddy. Everything caught her eye. She skipped forward to examine the nearest shelf of glowing bottles, full of potions and powders. Yasmin struggled to decipher their handwritten labels. The illegibility of the slanted scrawl could rival any doctor's note.

Flowers winked their petals as she passed. The leaves on the floor's creeping vines illuminated whenever her toe tapped too near, surrounding her black flats with auras of red and pink and blue. Humans could achieve a similar effect with electronics, motion sensors, and a few colorful LEDs, but there was an otherworldly essence to the vine.

A flickering orange light on the third row of shelves caught her eye. A flame, suspended in a thin glass vial, spiraled in a DNA-like helix.

How can it survive with no oxygen?

Yasmin knew the answer even as she reached for the glass. Magic made the impossible true.

The glass felt cool beneath her fingers. Any heat the flame held remained sealed within. A piece of tape on the shelf bore three words: *Dragon flame—NFS-C.* Beneath was a date.

This is what Mason's been hiding?

Compared to his wings, the fire in Yasmin's hand bordered on mundane. True its existence in the glass betrayed the laws of reality, but it was still just fire. Why was Mason so reticent to discuss it?

A shadow stretched against the wall. Yasmin slipped the flame into her bag, hiding it before Mason rounded the corner. Any mention of dragon fire made him tense. He wouldn't react well if she asked to purchase it.

But the flame was—if not indisputable proof of magic —a good place to start for collecting evidence.

Yasmin just needed to convince Mason to head up the steps before her so that she could buy it.

Except it wasn't Mason who rounded the corner.

A girl, almost as tall as the shelves, stepped into the row. An elastic tie struggled to contain wild dark curls. She stared at Yasmin, and her hand curled around a leather belt at her hip.

She looks like an Amazon.

Yasmin's breath caught. Her legs trembled. But under-cover journalists didn't have the luxury of panicking.

Blend in.

Yasmin turned back toward the shelf and feigned fascination with the first bottle her eyes landed on—a small, glass eyedropper, filled with a rich blue. She squinted, trying to read the tiny label looped around its neck.

Three tense seconds later, the Amazon eased, turning her narrowed gaze toward the shop's wares.

Yasmin lowered her chin to hide her smile.

See? I blend in. No one would guess I haven't visited this shop a dozen—Ya Allah!

Yasmin froze, eyes stuck on the Amazon. How had she missed the ears? They were massive, tapering to the top of the Amazon's frizz.

She's an elf.

At least, her appearance matched Mason's rough description of the species. Yasmin had rewritten and reorganized her notes on them last night, brainstorming her second chapter before she'd finished the first. Jeremiah had been her only reference. She'd assumed all were pale and gangly.

The Amazon's coppery skin rippled with muscles. Her curls bordered on black. But the ears gave her away, larger and more pointed than Yasmin had pictured. They quivered, twitching and drooping in the manner of a dog's tail.

I have to get a picture.

Yasmin's mind felt unsteady, like everything was taking place underwater. But she pushed through the liquid, slipped her hand into her bag, and searched near the bottom. Journalists took photos all the time when they were investigating. She just had to be covert—no flash, pretend to type for a minute, make the angling of the phone appear natural. Yasmin had practiced plenty of times on her family.

Her fingers closed around the device. She pulled it out

and tapped the screen. No light appeared. She pressed the power button. Nothing.

The Amazon cleared the few feet between them in the space of a heartbeat.

Yasmin's stomach jumped into her throat.

She has super speed.

"What are you doing?" The Amazon's hand latched around Yasmin's wrist. Her voice quivered with an unusual mixture of anxiety and power as she growled the question. "Who are you?"

Yasmin's insides trembled. The Amazon towered almost a foot above her. She could pick Yasmin and fling her across the store like a stuffed bear.

But that would be ridiculous.

I didn't even do anything suspicious yet.

"I'm Yasmin." She straightened her back and lifted her chin, stretching to her full height, a whopping five feet and two inches if she measured generously. "I'm a woodswitch. Who are you?"

The Amazon ignored the question. "Why did you take out your phone?"

"To message my friend. I wanted an opinion on this." With her free hand, Yasmin plucked the eye-dropper potion from the shelf and waved it. Mind still swimming, it took all her effort to remain standing and feign the appropriate frustration. "Why do you care?"

"Because every Castor knows better than to use their phone in a magic shop."

Wait. Why? Yasmin struggled to recall Mason's lessons.

"And—" The elf hadn't finished. Her eyes narrowed on the eyedropper. "—even a woodswitch should be competent enough to change an item's color without a potion."

"Uh..." Yasmin struggled to formulate a response. This was Mason's fault. He'd failed to prepare her for today.

Of course, I insisted on coming and then risked trying to take a picture of an elf.

Whatever. She and Mason could share the blame later. Now, Yasmin needed to talk her way free.

"Is that what the dropper does?" She attempted a disappointed frown as she glanced at the vial. "I couldn't read the label. That's why I wanted to call my friend. Guess you've saved me—"

In an instant, the Amazon's hand lashed out, wrapping around Yasmin's other wrist. She shouted, "Finn, we have a problem! There's a knight in the shop."

14

MASON

"We agreed on two hundred, Douglas." Mason tapped his fingers against the wooden counter, focusing on his breaths. Bargaining was a necessary evil when dealing with illicit goods, certainly no reason to lose his cool. But wisps of smoke still curled from Mason's nostrils.

Behind the counter, a small older gentleman with gray whiskers and bright green eyes watched the tendrils rise into the air. If the smoke worried Douglas, he didn't show it.

The old fairy held out his hands in an apologetic shrug. "A witch-scented perfume is an uncommon request. Procuring it proved more challenging than I anticipated."

Mason doubted either of those things were true. After thirty years in the business, Douglas knew how to haggle with suppliers and predict prices. He also knew how to read customers.

I must reek of desperation.

But then, didn't everyone who ventured into The Portentous Purveyor? The shop operated without a permit, which meant Douglas' sales went unchecked by officials. Only a certain type of clientele sought out an illegal, over-priced racket for untraceable purchases.

"I've only brought two hundred," Mason said, pulling the cash from his pocket and laying it on the counter.

"I recall your father trying the same tactic."

"And I recall you having a heart and lowering the price when you realized he had a poor, hungry child to feed." Mason stuck out his lower lip, making his best attempt to look pathetic. "I'm still poor and hungry."

Douglas snorted, and his dragonfly-shaped wings fluttered. Flecks of gold flashed against the bright green as he flew toward the ceiling. At his touch, a compartment opened in the wooden panels. "We're discussing a repayment plan. You aren't as cute as you once were."

Mason nodded fast before the fairy changed his mind.

Douglas returned to the floor, holding a glass bottle with a gold bulb attached. He rested it on the counter with a theatrical flourish. "You're lucky I sent my boy for it today."

"Your boy?" Mason reached for the perfume. "Have you taken in a street urchin?"

"Something of the sort."

"Finn, we have a problem!" A woman's voice rose from the middle of the shelves. "There's a knight in the shop!"

Burn it, Yasmin!

Hadn't he told her to blend in?

"Not a common request at all," Douglas muttered, voice turning cold. His bright eyes narrowed to thin slits, and he snatched the perfume from Mason's hand. "Are you trying to disguise a human?"

Before Mason could explain, a wooden door at the back of the room flew open. An elf—well above six-feet with

broad shoulders, a chiseled jaw, and rich auburn curls—
emerged. He paused, just long enough to pose in a manner
better suited to a comic book hero, then dashed forward.

Shit!

Douglas' business model ensured the fairy looked the
other way in most instances. But nothing about this elf's
appearance suggested that he belonged in a seedy shop. He
was a wild card. Mason needed to figure out how the elf fit
into things before anyone got the brilliant idea of covering
Yasmin in amnesiac powder.

Then, Mason could worry about saving his own ass
from prison.

15
YASMIN

"I just wanted to message my friend, I swear!" Yasmin leaned back with her full weight, trying to pull her wrists free.

The Amazon shifted, and the edge of her shirt rose, revealing a muscled stomach. Something bronze protruded from the waist of her shorts—the hilt of a small blade, pommel fashioned into a burning star.

"Technology doesn't function when exposed to unfamiliar magic," the Amazon explained. She lifted Yasmin into the air, bringing their faces closer. "Whoever taught you about woodswitches should have mentioned that."

Mason had. An image of the note in her book flashed before Yasmin. She'd forgotten. She'd messed up.

A laugh slipped from Yasmin. Disgust flashed across the Amazon's face.

"Xena!" A boy's voice, far too cheerful, spoke, "You found a human?"

A red-haired, borderline giant stepped into the row. His ears marked him as another elf.

Yasmin kept giggling as she kicked her legs, searching

desperately for the floor. Instinct told her to run. The pulsing in her brain told her she'd struggle just to stand.

"Stop, she's not a knight. She's with me!" Mason appeared behind the elves. A moment later, so did a gray-haired man with dragonfly wings.

Magic vines. Glowing potions. Elf ears. Fairy wings.

Yasmin's laughter grew higher, more desperate. Her eyes landed on Mason's own. Their blue looked stormy in the dim light.

The Amazon—Xena?—turned to Mason as well. "You admit to breaking secrecy?" She sounded surprised. "No, I'm sorry. This is too far, Finn. We have to report this."

"That is not the arrangement," an old voice—the fairy? —said. "If you work here—"

"I don't," Xena snapped. "And neither should Finn. Your entire operation ought to be shut down."

"Whoa! Let's not overreact because of a human," the boy elf—Finn probably—stepped between them. "Just wipe her memory and poof. Problem solved."

Yasmin's chest tightened. If they tampered with her mind, she'd forget everything. Her chance to uncover the truth about magic would be gone before it began.

A good investigative reporter would talk their way out of this situation.

But Yasmin's voice had fled. Her mind felt addled, full of too many things and nothing all at once. Maybe she wasn't as talented as she thought.

Goodbye, best-selling novel. Goodbye, fame. Goodbye, magic.

This strange world Yasmin had managed to slip into would be lost to her. Forever.

And it was entirely her fault.

Mason stepped forward, moving with a predatory grace

he seldom displayed. Golden scales flashed against his back. Their glow made the rest of the magic dim. An aura of power clung to him, making the air around him tremble and the elves shrink. Yasmin's eyes latched onto him like a drowning man with a rope.

"No one is wiping her memory."

"Listen, I get it," Finn said, with an uncomfortable laugh. "But we can't stand by while you break secrecy laws to conspire with a human. We have a civic duty—"

"As do I," Mason interrupted, drawing closer. Without turning his gaze from the elves, he rested a protective hand on Yasmin's shoulder, pulling her lower.

Her toes brushed the ground, then her heels.

Heat radiated from his fingers, making Yasmin's skin buzz. He leaned closer and bared his teeth in a sharp smile that transformed his face from cute and boyish to handsome and dangerous. His tongue flicked over his lips.

Maybe it wouldn't have been so bad to make out with him in the bathroom.

Wait! No, no, no. Yasmin had not just thought that. What was going on with her brain? At least one plus side of having her memory wiped would be forgetting how bizarrely intriguing she found Mason's tongue.

Except that, given Mason's smile, Yasmin wouldn't be losing her memory. He was going to save her.

How? A blast of fire? Tearing into the elves with his teeth? Yasmin wanted to escape, but—

"Don't hurt them," she said. "This is my fault. They're not doing anything wrong."

"They're working in an illegal shop," Mason responded without taking his eyes from the giant red-headed elf. "And I have a civic duty to inform the city of any shady dealings done by our nobility. Wouldn't you agree, Prince Finnian?"

16

MASON

Mason thanked every deity he could name for the fact that Yasmin had started quizzing him on elves. He was no expert on noble lineages, but several texts he'd skimmed mentioned *Prince Finnian Starling*—a reused moniker among the nobility of the Reul Aingeil, the Star Elf clan of Castor's Grove. It couldn't be a coincidence that their sigil, the fiery star, marked Xena's pommel.

At the word *Prince*, four heads snapped toward Mason —well, three. Yasmin had already been staring.

"Elves that break the law are banished from their clans, isn't that right?" Mason kept his tone congenial, as though it were an innocent question and not a thinly veiled threat. "I'd think working at an unregistered shop with unsavory clientele would qualify."

"My parents wouldn't cast me aside for a bit of harmless fun," Finnian said, waving off the accusation. But panic flashed behind the prince's smile. His eyes flicked to his companion.

Gotchya.

"What about your bodyguard?" Mason pointed to Xena.

"She's not my bodyguard," Finnian objected, but his eyes grew nervous again.

"Enough!" Douglas flew between them, glaring at the prince and Mason in turn. "This is bad business. Bad business either way. There's no rats in this shop. And no knights. You swear she's not one of them?"

"Cross my heart." Mason drew an *x* across his chest.

Douglas' wings twitched as he eyed Yasmin. It was obvious he wanted to ask more, but ignorance and discretion made for a happy partnership.

"Perfume's price has tripled. You'll need more than a scent for her to pass. Finn, do something useful and *help* our customer." The fairy stalked back to his counter, muttering beneath his breath about secrecy and discretion.

Mason relaxed, until he'd processed the full implication of Douglas's displeasure.

Did he say triple?

Mason didn't have that much cash. He'd have to beg Kira. The thirteen-year-old would make him pay her back in chores, but she was his only choice. Jeremiah would refuse. Comet wasted his allowance on hoardable trinkets.

Finnian nodded at Xena. With a sigh, the warrior released her grip.

Yasmin's arm dropped. She stumbled backward and into Mason, body turning to press against his.

Is she hugging me?

No. That would have required Yasmin to lift her arms. Instead, her cheek sunk against his chest. She stared up at him, and a sheen of amazement glistened in her eyes.

Shit. Overexposure to magic. At least she hadn't passed out.

"Are you two dating?" Finnian snapped his fingers. "You must be disguising her to take home to meet your parents!"

It was a good guess and an innocent explanation. The smart thing to do would be to play along.

"Definitely not." Yasmin pushed herself away from Mason and shot him a glare as though it was his fault she was struggling to stand straight. "We're not together."

Yasmin pulled her braid over her shoulder, finger twisting the bottom as she stared up at Finnian.

Oh, I get it.

Mason rolled his eyes. The elf checked all the boxes for a human girl: tall, handsome, a prince.

So much for my dragon powers of allure.

Not that Mason was jealous or anything. He didn't care if Yasmin found the prince attractive. It was just annoyingly predictable.

"Definitely not together," Mason agreed. No point using the perfect cover story Finnian had offered them. Yasmin had already blown it so she could flirt with a prince. Did she really think she had a chance? "I prefer to date girls with a shred of dignity and self-awareness."

Yasmin stopped twirling her braid. She turned her forced grin toward Mason. "Odd comment from someone who's faking their entire life."

Ouch. Mason wasn't faking anything. Pretending to be human was a necessary lie all Castors told.

"Mason and I are allies of convenience," Yasmin continued, blinking some of the sheen from her eyes as she addressed Finnian again. "Were you going to show us some wares?"

Despite Xena glowering a foot away, the prince's eyes twinkled at the prospect, no hints of his previous misgivings. "I've never disguised a human as a witch. Clothing seems like a good place to start. There's a couple of outfits you could try."

Mason's jaw twitched. Why was Finnian's first suggestion to have Yasmin model clothes for him?

He wasn't the only one who found it suspicious.

"How about *I* help her find clothes," Xena offered, stepping forward to take Yasmin's wrist once more. At least she didn't lift her into the air this time.

"Oh no." Yasmin's eyes widened. She flicked her gaze to Finnian. "I think I'd prefer—"

"Don't be silly." Xena's lips twitched into a smile, more intimidating than reassuring as she pulled Yasmin away.

Given that, less than a minute ago, the elf warrior had wanted to wipe Yasmin's mind, perhaps she wasn't their best option for customer assistance. But Mason didn't see how Finnian would be any better. The prince watched the girls retreat a few seconds too long. Then, he remembered Mason.

"How about potions?" Finnian suggested. "Can't be a witch if you can't do magic?"

The prince palmed a small bottle of blue liquid and began snaking his way through the rows, examining items as they passed.

Mason followed. He knew better than to pry when it came to nobility, but evidently Yasmin's nosiness was contagious. "How'd you end up working for Douglas?"

Finnian paused, a jar of sleeping powder pinched between his fingers. "I may have broken a valuable orb while examining a sword. Didn't want to ask my parents for the money to replace it, so Douglas and I made a deal."

"I thought Star elf nobility weren't allowed to use weapons."

"Drums! What are you? An elfish scholar?" Finnian

reached the counter and dropped the bottles he'd gathered on the glass. "I've conversed with at least fifty customers the past couple months. No one's identified me."

Or they were smart enough to keep their mouths shut. Threatening the nobility wasn't a risk Mason would've taken under normal circumstances.

No sense reminding Finnian about their power imbalance. But the prince watched Mason like he expected an answer.

"My brother's an elf. Adopted brother, obviously." Mentioning Jeremiah seemed safer that admitting he'd been pouring over elfish lore to teach an overly inquisitive human.

"A dragon with a wandering elf for a brother. Interesting." Finnian hopped over the counter and reached for something on a shelf below. "You see this?"

The prince slapped a copy of *Witch Whisper* on the glass. The magazine was a Castor gossip rag. Jeremiah and Kira were both fans, but Mason never bothered. The writers enjoyed salacious details more than accuracy.

Occasionally, however, a kernel of truth slipped through.

The prince pointed to the headline: ***Hidden Heist at Drage Manor? What these Decadent Dragons May Have Lost.***

Mason's heart stopped. He turned the magazine and scanned the article. Most was wild speculation. Different writers theorized on the nature of the stolen item: a priceless artifact, a sentimental keepsake, a compromising oil painting of Pyrrhus Drage's late wife.

Finnian talked as Mason read, "The robbery definitely happened. But I hear they're avoiding talking to the police.

Too embarrassed to admit their security was breached. You know how proud dragons can be."

And yet Mason was humble enough not to argue despite the prince being wrong.

The officer at Folkestone High proved the Drages had gone to the police. The investigation must've been a secret. Even from the nobility.

"Think your brother has any contacts in the world of thieves that might know anything?"

Mason stopped reading. "Excuse me?"

"The wandering elf. Most are thieves, or at least descended from them."

Mason's jaw tightened. He knew nothing about Jeremiah's family. His brother never spoke of his life before being taken in by Uncle Lee. But that didn't matter.

"My brother's the most strait-laced person I know. He doesn't have criminal contacts."

"Pity. Everyone's dying to know what was stolen. The way the Drages are acting, my money's on the painting." Finnian laughed.

Mason didn't. The question hit too close to home. "Let me see the potions."

The prince brandished his hand across a collection of bottles he'd plucked from the shelves, explaining each of their properties with a grin.

Mason did his best to focus, but his eyes continued to flick from the potions to the *Witch Whisper* article.

What item had the Drages lost? And, more importantly, why were they being so careful to keep any information about it a secret?

17
YASMIN

Yasmin hurried to get the long burgundy gown over her head. She didn't like standing in a storeroom with only her underwear for cover, even if the boxes hid her from view.

Maybe it is better Xena came.

Finnian seemed chattier, and he hadn't left bruises on Yasmin's wrists. But it would've been uncomfortable modeling outfits for a boy she'd just met.

Yasmin shimmied the dress lower. The hem trailed across the floor, waistline cinching on her hips and leaving her chest far too exposed.

Is this what Mason expects me to wear?

Yasmin couldn't see anything *dignified* about this outfit. And what had Mason meant that she lacked self-awareness? Had he noticed her staring at him?

Oh, please no!

Yasmin slapped her hands over her face. There had been a moment—maybe two—where she'd thought about kissing Mason. She'd love to pretend otherwise. Unfortunately, despite accusations to the contrary, she was *very* self-aware.

If Mason didn't have powers of allure, then what did that mean?

Nothing. It meant nothing.

The idea had simply been in Yasmin's head from when he pulled her into the bathroom. Then, he'd come to her rescue, and her mind had been addled, and a natural adrenaline response must've kicked in.

Now, in the dark storage room, Yasmin had regained control of her thoughts. Her interest in Mason was purely professional. The dragon was all red flags.

Secretive. Went to juvie. Committed a burglary.

Maybe not that last one. Over the past few days, Mason had remained adamant of his innocence. What if his bizarre story about a text message happened to be true?

"You must be finished." Xena stepped behind the boxes. Her eyes flicked over Yasmin, taking in the dress. "This could work."

"Are you joking?" Yasmin gestured to her chest, but it was impossible to tell with the massive sleeves flapping over her hands. "I'm drowning, and my arms look like wings."

Xena caught the fabric of the sleeve. Her fingers undid a row of silver buttons, making the already loose material open wider, into a bell.

"That's how witches style their clothes. They have compartments where they hide spells." The Amazon pointed to a zipped pouch stitched into the interior of the sleeve.

"Why?" Yasmin shimmied the fabric up her arm to reach the pouch. This couldn't be the most practical option. "Do bags repel magic or something?"

"No, they just look suspicious." Xena's eyes narrowed at Yasmin's school bag, resting beneath her folded jeans and shirt.

I am so doomed if she looks in there.

Yasmin's notes made it obvious she was writing an exposé on Castors. She would never have brought them on an investigation with her, but visiting The Portentous Purveyor hadn't been on her Friday timetable.

"If you want to read my thoughts on *As You Like It*, go ahead," Yasmin bluffed. "It's mostly a rant on why siblings are the worst."

Xena tapped the side of her hip where her dagger remained belted. Her lips pursed as she considered the offer. She almost looked tempted. That had not been Yasmin's intention.

"Do witches hide magic by their shoes too?" Yasmin lifted the skirt of the dress, trying to shift the Amazon's attention.

"No. You're just short." Xena grabbed the collar of the dress and pulled the material higher. "Know a good seamstress?"

Yasmin shook her head.

"Maybe you can pin it."

Fantastic. "Anything smaller for me to try?"

Xena sighed and disappeared behind the boxes. A few seconds later, she tossed over two more dresses. The first, a shade of sickly green, was twice as large again. Yasmin would get lost in the fabric just attempting to put it on. She rested it over her bag in dismissal, before considering her next option.

Ribbons and lace adorned a deep fuchsia dress. The color coupled with the swirling details around the skirt screamed for attention. Yasmin wouldn't have chosen it in a million years. But it was the smallest option.

She slipped the dress over her head, huffing as she struggled to find the opening through the sea of ribbons.

Silence came from the other side of the boxes.

Had Xena slipped out without Yasmin noticing? Could elves cloak the sound of their movements? Or was the Amazon special?

"Mason called you the prince's bodyguard," Yasmin said, searching for a casual conversation topic as her head broke free. She pulled her hair after, losing the tie at the end of her braid. "Is it common among elves for women to act as protectors?"

Silence. Only Yasmin's own breath—three nervous inhales. Then, finally, Xena answered, "Depends on the clan."

A woman of few words.

No issue. Yasmin had interrogated her share of unwilling interviewees. Badgering wore anyone down. "Are the clans very different? Which one are you and Finn from?"

The question had barely left Yasmin when the Amazon appeared. The tip of Xena's dagger pressed against Yasmin's throat. "*Prince* Finnian. He's not your friend."

Yasmin gasped as the cold steel left from her skin. She grabbed her neck. No cut. No pinprick of blood. A warning.

Include in Chapter Two: Elves don't play when it comes to titles.

"Finn's always been overly curious about humans," Xena said, voice calm as though she hadn't just threatened to slice Yasmin. "But the only ones I've ever seen interact with magic are knights. Why are you pretending to be a witch?"

"Uh... we..." It was difficult to invent a lie while staring at a dagger. Yasmin should've said she and Mason were dating like Finnian guessed. But after fawning over his wings, Yasmin didn't dare give Mason more ammunition to mock her. "He needs me to provide an alibi, and he doesn't think the police will believe a human."

"They wouldn't." Xena tossed her blade up and caught the handle. She didn't sheath it. "What crime is the dragon suspected of?"

"I don't know. A theft of some kind. Seems serious."

"But you think he was with you when the robbery occurred?" Xena's voice softened. If she didn't still have her weapon at the ready, Yasmin would almost think the Amazon's tone compassionate. "Sometimes memories are false. We have potions. Humans are the most susceptible to—"

"Mason didn't drug me."

"How can you be sure?"

"Because if Mason could choose someone to be his alibi, it wouldn't be me." Yasmin didn't know why her tone sounded so bitter.

"I'm not so sure." Xena rested a hand on Yasmin's shoulder, spinning her around.

What is she doing?

After the knife on her throat, Yasmin wasn't keen on the idea of turning her back to the Amazon. But she was in no position to resist.

"You're handling magic better than most humans." Xena's fingers pulled the ribbon on the bodice of the dress, tightening a faux corset around Yasmin's waist.

"Really? How do most humans handle it?" Yasmin's voice lifted. A smile blossomed over her face. Maybe she'd write nice things about Xena in her book after all.

Another tug cut off Yasmin's breath.

"Most can't comprehend that magic exists." Xena slackened her grip as she tied the first bow. "The few who notice usually faint or throw up and forget the entire thing."

"How embarrassing." Yasmin forced a laugh. She'd done two of those. But she hadn't forgotten.

Mason's wings haunted her dreams like an enchanting ghost. Proof that humans could accept magic when confronted with sufficient evidence. Yasmin couldn't be the first.

"What about the knights you keep mentioning?"

"They're the humans who don't forget." Xena cut off Yasmin's air a second time as she moved to the next ribbon. "They become hellbent on the eradication of magic."

"That's ridiculous." Children dreamed of magic. Even Yasmin, who prided herself on being practical, had indulged in a fantasy or two. Learning of its existence should feed that desperate, communal wish, make humanity believe in miracles anew. "I know the truth, and I don't want to destroy magic."

If anything, Yasmin wished she could possess it.

Imagine being able to change the appearance of an object with your will, or fly, or breathe fire.

"You're in the minority." Xena finished the last bow. "History does not lie. Humans don't react well to forces beyond their comprehension. The dragon should never have risked telling you of our existence."

Yasmin's chest felt tight. It wasn't the ribbons. She turned from the cluttered storeroom to face the Amazon. "You think humans can't handle learning the truth?"

"No." Xena's lips parted into a silent sigh, and she cast her gaze to the wall of boxes, eyes heavy. "I think we can't survive the strength of your fear when you do."

18

MASON

By the time Yasmin stepped from the storage room, Mason was eager to leave. His pockets were empty, and his signature scrawled on several *IOUs*. Douglas offered no option to work off the debt.

Guess that repayment plan is only available for princes.

Mason was as far from nobility as you could get. At least he'd been spared of providing the fairy with the collateral he usually requested from dragon clientele.

"Does this work?" Yasmin asked, hiding behind a veil of dark wavy hair as she stepped out.

Mason barely glanced at her. He shifted the bag on his shoulder and grabbed her hand. "Perfect. Let's go."

"Wait. I have to pay still." Yasmin's eyes flicked to Finnian, smiling at her from behind the counter, then back to Mason. "You go ahead."

Mason rolled his eyes. They didn't have time for Yasmin to flirt with a prince. "I already covered the cost of your dress."

In fact, Douglas had included the price of several outfits in an IOU he'd made Mason sign.

"Come again soon," Finnian shouted to them as they climbed the steps. His voice echoed through the slanted passage. "I work Mondays and Fridays. I'd love to hear how your disguise works!"

Yasmin looked over her shoulder as Mason pulled her up the steps. "I really think I should say goodbye."

"Why?" Mason pushed the wall at the top of the staircase. It opened, revealing the white tiled bathroom once more. "You want to kiss the prince farewell?"

"Excuse me?" Yasmin wrenched her hand from his grip as they stepped through the wall. Now that she'd been called out, she made no attempt to return.

"You can't swoon over every noble Castor you meet," Mason explained. He touched the correct tile and watched the wall bolt back into position. "The Drages aren't princes, but Eli is wealthy and just as disarming. He might seek you out, and you can't go making doe eyes at him if he does."

"I wasn't making doe eyes at anyone. Finnian isn't even my type."

Mason snorted. "What. Too tall?"

"A bit. Yes."

Sure, cause girls hate that. Yasmin was just embarrassed to admit that she'd been taken in by an elf prince. Why else would she want to *say goodbye?*

Mason opened his mouth, ready to call her out. Then, he noticed the dress.

Large pink sleeves and a lace-covered skirt created bell shapes around her limbs, but the fabric hugged her upper body. No straps covered her shoulders. Dark brown waves fell across the smooth, exposed skin. She brushed a lock over her shoulder drawing his attention to her chest.

Damn.

"You look really good." The comment tumbled from

Mason before he caught himself. Shit. That wasn't what he meant to say. He added quickly, "Like you could definitely be a witch."

A smile spread across Yasmin's face, eyes fluttering between him and the floor, as though she'd grown bashful. The color of the dress accentuated the flush of her cheeks, the deep pink of her lips. She untucked a wave of hair and twirled it in her fingers. The light illuminated the dark brown hues.

She's beautiful.

No wonder Finnian had offered to help her try on clothes. Maybe Mason shouldn't have been so quick to tease Yasmin for thinking he wanted to kiss her earlier.

What am I thinking? This is still Yasmin Gul. She's a pain in the ass who pries into people's personal lives to turn their trauma into news stories.

Being alone with her in the bathroom was clearly doing strange things to Mason's mind.

"We don't have all day for you to admire yourself," he said, turning before she realized he was the one staring. "There's more to being a witch than the right outfit. Skipping school doesn't mean you get out of learning. And believe me, you still have a lot to learn."

———

Mason scanned the street as they walked, searching for a suitable place to slip into and hide. Leaving the bathroom at The Portentous Purveyor might have been a mistake. Humans overhearing a discussion about magic wouldn't matter, but Castors were a different story. If the wrong person eavesdropped, Mason could find himself in trouble.

They needed a semi-private location to sort through the

magical items he'd purchased. Until then, walking in silence seemed safest.

So why was Yasmin's lack of questions bothering him?

She stared at the sidewalk, twisting her hair into a curl and clinging to her bag. Not even a collection of offices that had been designed to resemble giant, blocky cacti made her glance up.

Burn it. Her silence is worse than the risk of being overheard.

Mason stepped from the sidewalk onto a stretch of grass beneath the shadow of a green building. Whoever the architect was, they'd half-assed it. A desert would've had sand, not bright green AstroTurf.

He spun to Yasmin, forcing her to stop as well. "We were in a magical shop. With elves and a fairy. Why aren't you bombarding me with questions?"

Yasmin froze, finger locked in her hair. Her eyes flicked to Mason, then back in the direction of The Portentous Purveyor.

If she's being quiet because she's thinking about Finnian, I swear—

"You didn't tell me about the knights."

Mason blinked. That was not what he'd been expecting. "It's been three days. I haven't told you about a lot of things."

Yasmin crossed her arms beneath her now more exposed chest.

Don't glance down. Don't glance down.

Mason fixed his gaze on her forehead.

"Seems like an important detail not to mention," Yasmin continued, voice more anxious than annoyed. "Why wouldn't you tell me that most humans who learn about magic turn evil and attempt to hunt Castors to extinction?"

Mason shied away from the darker elements of Castor's

Grove History, but even he knew that was a gross oversimplification of the issue.

"I doubt *most* humans do," he said. "The knights came into existence centuries ago when our laws were a lot more lax. Annihilating magic sounds reasonable when you think your friends are at risk of having their blood drained by a vampire."

"Or being eaten by a dragon?"

Behind his lips, Mason's tongue flicked over his teeth. Eating another sentient species had never crossed his mind, but he knew his kin hadn't always made such a distinction.

"Sorry I asked," he muttered, moving from the Astro-Turf back to the Luck Street sidewalk.

Yasmin kept pace with him. "Why did you? I thought you'd be happy I was quiet. I know my questions annoy you."

"Not all the time," Mason admitted, scanning the street once more. Part of him had enjoyed the challenge of finding answers for her this week. It was just when she pushed too far, tried to force the conversation in dangerous directions. "My real issue is your motivation."

Yasmin's brow furrowed. "What do you mean?"

Wasn't it self-explanatory?

Mason stopped at the corner, gathering with a waiting crowd of pedestrians, all watching the traffic light. "Everyone knows you want to be a journalist. Why?"

"Because my mother thought I'd be good at it."

The answer, soft but honest, caught Mason by surprise. His attention flicked from the crosswalk light to the girl beside him, twisting her hair once more. Yasmin never mentioned her mother.

"The last eight months of her life, she was stuck in bed," Yasmin said, staring at the back of a redhead's ponytail. "I read the paper to her every morning, and we watched the news together every night. I always had so many questions, and she'd say, *you should be the journalist, then you could find out.*" Her eyes dropped to the hem of the long pink dress. "I got quite into conspiracy theories for a few years after she died. Wondered if there was a secret cure for cancer that I might uncover."

The walking man lit up on the opposite side of the street. The rest of the crowd moved. Mason and Yasmin remained still.

"I'm sorry, Yasmin. I don't think witches have a potion to cure leukemia."

"I know—I didn't—" Yasmin blinked as she turned her gaze toward him. "How do you know my mother died of leukemia?"

Was it a secret?

"Science fair. Grade Nine," Mason reminded her, hurrying across the street as the seconds started to count down. "You did your project on it, and your sister started crying when she saw your stall. It stuck with me."

"Oh. That's...I didn't think anyone noticed." Yasmin jogged behind. "My father was furious. He said I shouldn't dredge up the past, and that I ought to have known it would upset Nima. She's his favorite. Then my brother, so..." She stopped as they reached the sidewalk again, tossing her hair from her face to stare up at Mason. "How's that for self-awareness?"

Despite the soft, vulnerable glisten in her eyes, her chin jutted forward in a challenge.

What is she—Oh right. I said she lacked dignity and self-awareness, didn't I?

Shit. Maybe that had been harsh. Yasmin was more sensitive than she pretended. But Mason had only made that comment because he'd been annoyed about how quickly she tripped over her tongue to tell a prince she was single.

There was no way to admit that without sounding petty.

"Your mom was right," Mason said. He resumed walking, focusing on a bright pink colonial-style building a few feet ahead. "You'll make an amazing journalist someday. I'm glad I trusted you to be my alibi."

"Mason, wait!" Yasmin grabbed his sleeve, fingers twisting around the fabric. "You shouldn't—I did something bad."

19
YASMIN

Yasmin's hand trembled around her smoothie as she slid into the seat opposite Mason. They were at the Upside-Down Watermelon—a smoothie and burger place four blocks from The Portentous Purveyor. The restaurant's interior resembled the inside of a piñata. Bright streamers spiraled from the ceiling, Latin music bounced from the speakers, and smiling fruits waved from the wallpaper.

The restaurant was an unscheduled stop. But Yasmin needed to come clean.

Not about her novel. If she told Mason about her plan to write a tell-all revealing magic to the human world, he'd wipe her mind. And maybe he'd be right.

Yasmin squeezed her eyes shut. She didn't want to worry about the implications of exposing the Castors. She wanted to be a revered reporter.

Why did Mason have to say he trusts me?

Yasmin tightened her grip on the smoothie, trying to stifle the guilt churning in her stomach. Her tell-all wasn't the only crime she needed to atone for.

"I'll go back and pay for it," she promised, wincing at the thin glass vial resting on the table. The stolen dragon flame spun within.

The muscles in Mason's face tensed.

"I wanted to earlier, but you wouldn't let me," Yasmin reminded him. "But trust me, I recognize the irony. I'm supposed to be your alibi for a theft, not implicating you in one. I'll go back and pay for it."

"Don't," Mason whispered. He pried his gaze from the fire, but his posture remained uneasy. One leg swept toward the booth's exit like he might bolt at a moment's notice. "Every dragon's fire has a unique magical frequency. Douglas takes flames as collateral. Some desperate fool probably offered it in exchange for something he couldn't afford, and the prince put it out by mistake. If the fire gets used in a crime, it'll be traced back to the owner."

Yasmin's fingers curled around the vial. She studied the swirling helix of flames. "So it's like a fingerprint."

Mason nodded. "You should get rid of it."

Yasmin's brow furrowed. *She* should get rid of it? He was the dragon. But Mason was always strange when it came to dragon fire. This was the most he'd touched on the subject.

No, it's not just dragon fire.

Yasmin recalled their chemistry class in grade ten. Mason never touched the Bunsen burner. At the time, Yasmin had assumed it was because Zach, his lab partner, was a borderline pyromaniac who leapt at the chance to turn on the flame. But what if Mason had avoided the task on purpose?

"How do I get rid of it?" Yasmin asked.

"Let it loose on something insignificant. It'll burn itself out without doing much harm. How's the smoothie?"

He was trying to change the topic. Yasmin didn't intend to let him. "Won't the fire spread?"

"Only if you stole an amplification spell too." Mason chuckled. "Or you get someone to control it."

"Can you control fire?"

Pain flashed across Mason's face, so quick Yasmin might've imagined it.

"Elemental bending is more common among fairies and nymphs. Let me taste this." Mason stole her smoothie, sipped, and wrinkled his nose. "You should've gone with the peanut butter one."

Yasmin swiped it back from him. She considered the plastic container, then the orange helix in the tube. So far, it was the best evidence of magic she'd collected.

He didn't answer my question.

Could Mason control fire?

Yasmin pushed the top off the tube. The flame leaped free, straight toward her smoothie.

"Stop, what are you—?" Mason leaped to his feet. There was no doubting the fear in his eyes.

"You told me—ow!" Yasmin had been watching for Mason's reaction, not paying attention to the flames. Sparks flew from the orange blaze of smoothie, leaping onto her palm.

Mason grabbed Yasmin, pulled her up, and wrapped his arms around her shielding her from the fire. His body felt like a furnace. His breath grew fast and hot in her ear. Yasmin's heart pounded. So did his. So loud, she could hear it.

The dragon fire sizzled out, leaving a muddle of melted plastic and smoothie. It hadn't singed the table, and other than a few welts from the sparks, Yasmin was fine. No one else in the restaurant even seemed to have noticed.

Unleashing the dragon fire had been as damage-free as Mason claimed it would be.

So why had his heart not slowed?

Yasmin looked up and found the answer clear as day in Mason's eyes. "You're afraid of fire."

Mason reacted like she'd slapped him in the face. He dropped his arms, and scoffed, and turned away. "Don't be ridiculous. I'm a dragon."

That's what makes it so odd.

Mason swore he wasn't a thief, but had no qualms about her stealing the flame. He acted nice, yet he'd been to juvie. It was obvious he had secrets, and Yasmin had a hundred questions for him.

But, for possibly the first time in her life, she held her tongue. She'd settled on *Dragons: The secrets of Mason Wick* as the tentative title for the final chapter in her tell-all. Bombarding him with questions was sure to reveal something useful. It always did.

But Mason had questioned her motivations. Maybe he had a point. Was she so curious about him because she wanted to expose him to their classmates or because she thought it would make a compelling story? Or was her growing fascination something different entirely?

Suddenly, Mason wasn't the only one who wanted to change the subject.

Yasmin grabbed several napkins from a dispenser on the table and began wiping the melted remains. "I can't be the only one who got something from the shop. What did you buy?"

20

YASMIN

The bright blue door to the single stall bathroom at the Upside-Down Watermelon swung open. A tall brunette with tortoise shell glasses stepped out, flicking droplets of water from her hands as she returned to her table.

"Should I go in with you?" Mason leaned over Yasmin's shoulder, whispering the question in her ear. "Or are you worried I use my powers of allure to trick you into making out with me?"

His breath—warm and smokey—sent goose bumps down Yasmin's neck. The heat crept up to her cheeks. "I didn't think—"

Okay, maybe she had. But did Mason have to tease her? She felt stupid enough as it was.

"Just give me the bottle," she said, not meeting Mason's eyes. His crooked smirk was already too self-satisfied. He didn't need to know how effective his comments were at embarrassing her.

Mason slipped his hand beneath the long pink sleeve to

pass her the perfume. His fingers brushed her skin, and a shiver ran up her arm.

Yasmin hurried into the bathroom and swung the door closed, relieved for the barrier. Years spent ignoring how attractive her classmate was had vanished in a flash of his wings. Yasmin needed to get a grip. She held literal magic in her palm.

An automatic light illuminated more smiling fruit on the bathroom walls.

Yasmin studied the bottle in the mirror. Crosshatched grooves gave the glass a thorny exterior at odds with the soft gold squeeze bulb. Dark pink liquid sloshed within.

Magic perfume.

Her hands tingled as she sprayed her wrists. Cool droplets settled on the skin. Yasmin waved her arm, letting it dry, then pressed her nose to where the scent should be.

Nothing.

Maybe I'm just too human to smell it.

Yasmin tried not to let that upset her as she spritzed more of the perfume onto her neck.

I don't want magic. I want to write about it. I'll go down in history, and everyone will be amazed, and...

Yasmin sighed. The idea wasn't comforting her the way she'd hoped.

She pulled back the long sleeve on her left arm and found the pocket in the interior. Yasmin unzipped, hid the perfume within, and stepped back into the restaurant.

Mason waved her half-finished smoothie from the entrance. He'd attracted the attention of a group of middle school girls, who kept giggling and turning around in their seats to peep at him.

And he says he doesn't have powers of allure?

Yasmin hurried past the bar, ignoring the glances her dress earned from the people in line. "So, how do I—?"

Before she could finish the question, Mason's hand went to the small of her back. He pulled her toward him, pushed her hair back, and leaned in.

Yasmin's breath caught as Mason inhaled. His nose brushed her neck. His hair tickled the bottom of her jaw. His lips were less than an inch from her skin.

The middle school girls kept giggling. From their vantage, it must look like Mason had bent over to kiss her neck.

Heat locked Yasmin's her limbs. Her heart pounded.

Please don't let Mason hear that.

"Did it—uh—" Yasmin squeaked. She swallowed, trying to return her voice to its usual pitch. "Did it work?"

Mason released her and stepped back. "I think it must have."

A flash came from the corner.

Please tell me those girls weren't taking pictures.

Yasmin pushed the door open, eager to leave. "How can you not be sure? I thought you had the most incredible sense of smell."

"Not as good as a werewolf. Or some other dragons," Mason muttered, following her out onto the street. "It probably worked. You don't smell human. I just thought it would mask all of your scent, but you still smell like..."

"Like what?" Yasmin stopped at the corner of the street and spun to face him.

"Roses."

The word slammed into Yasmin like a memory. Unexpected tears gathered in the corners of her eyes. "My mother's room used to smell like roses."

In her final months, Fatimah Gul had covered her sheets

and pillows with her favorite perfume in an effort to mask the scent of sickness. There was a bottle left when she passed. Yasmin had wanted it, but her older sister got to it first.

And that was it. Amir would never compel his favorite child to share, and Nima had a talent for hiding things. No matter how hard Yasmin had hunted, she'd never found the bottle.

I still smelled the roses sometimes though.

Some nights, after particularly difficult days, her mother's scent followed Yasmin from her dreams into the real world. The scent would wrap itself in her blankets like a warm hug or slip into her father's car or her brother's freshly washed shirts.

Forget about Maamaani's perfume.

Crying because Mason mentioned a flower would give him another reason to mock her. Yasmin pressed a knuckle against the corner of each eye, soaking the tears into her skin before they fell. The gesture wasn't as subtle as she'd have liked.

"That explains it then," Mason said, and Yasmin braced for the inevitable joke. "The scent attached to your soul. Maybe there's a little bit of magic in you after all, Gul." He knocked her shoulder the way he might one of his friends, grinned, and turned east. "Let's pay a visit to the Crown Gardens."

Yasmin stared at him as he walked ahead. Her brain struggled to formulate a response. Not only had Mason been genuinely sweet, he'd suggested they go to the most popular date spot in all of downtown.

———

Obviously, it wasn't a date. Had Yasmin had even a fraction of a doubt, Mason's current behavior made it painfully obvious

"You really thought it was going to break." Mason leaned against a stone pillar on the perimeter of the park, clutching his side as he laughed.

Yasmin fought back a scowl as she bent to retrieve the fallen perfume from the sidewalk. Of course, she'd expected it to break. It was glass.

But it was also magic.

"I'd never suggest you practice with breakable glass that I paid—" He cut himself off with another laugh.

What. A. Jerk.

Yasmin considered throwing the bottle at Mason. She doubted it would hurt a dragon, and it would make her feel better. But she'd probably miss, and then he'd make fun of her again.

"I know. You've seen me in gym," Yasmin said, straining to keep her voice polite. "As you told those two."

She glanced at the retreating backs of a pair of well-dressed men. They'd heard her scream as they left the gardens and hurried over. Mason had informed them that she was an *uncoordinated woodswitch* and that they should *hear her in gym when a volleyball came toward her.* Yasmin's attempt to explain that she'd only screamed once, and that Lydia Price spiked like she had a vendetta had only made their laughter louder.

"I had to say something," Mason lowered his voice to a whisper. "They were nymphs."

Yasmin understood. Mason had explained that the Crown Gardens were popular with Grovers and Castors alike. She was officially in character.

And most woodswitches wouldn't scream when they dropped enchanted glass.

Another mistake. Her what—second? Third? She was losing count. At least she could blame this one on Mason. He'd insisted she practice retrieving the perfume like a witch. That meant using her left hand to unzip the interior pocket without being noticed. Or trying. Most of the walk Mason had snorted at her lack of subtlety. Yasmin had almost suggested he put on the dress and give it a try.

And just when she thought she'd succeeded, she'd fumbled, and the bottle dropped.

"Silly me," Yasmin said, making a point of putting the bottle in her right sleeve this time. She forced a smile as she stood. "Being worried about a perfume that matters to no one but me."

Mason's eyes flicked toward the gate as a couple holding hands strolled out. "You're right. I'm sorry." He didn't sound it. "No need for sarcasm, or your weird, fake grin."

"I have no idea what you mean." Yasmin adjusted her bag, tossed her hair, and marched toward the gate.

Cobblestone paths wound their way through a sea of curated greenery. Vines full of pomegranates and passion fruits twisted over low stone walls. Flowers burst in swirls across sloped mounds. Honeybees buzzed among the colorful petals, and birds cooed overhead.

Every aspect of the gardens threatened romance.

Not that Yasmin noticed. She wasn't paying attention to the pink rose bush sculpted into a heart, or the trickling of the brook, or the presence of her classmate.

Yasmin forced her grin bigger.

"Seriously, stop. Your face looks like it's about to crack."

"Rich of you to lecture me on fake smiles."

"I don't look like I'm plotting to kill Batman." Mason stepped in front of her, blocking her path over a wooden bridge. Sunlight caught the twinkling amusement in his eyes. He lifted his hand and poked Yasmin's cheek.

A familiar heat flushed through Yasmin. Her smile deflated into a pout, and she swatted Mason's hand away. If her face turned red, she needed him to think it was from anger.

"That's it, just embrace the annoyance." Mason had the audacity to smirk at her response. "You're much cuter this way."

"I—" Yasmin froze. Mason had just called her cute. A thought flashed into her mind—so quick, she could almost pretend it hadn't.

Maybe I wouldn't mind if this was a real date.

Yasmin's cheeks flushed. She slapped her forehead, trying to get her brain functioning. That had not been an acceptable thought. She did not want to go on a date with Mason!

But in a place like this, she needed to be careful. Otherwise, Yasmin might find herself daydreaming about him again.

21

MASON

large lawn sprawled in the center of the park. Colorful picnic blankets spread across the grass. Mason's nose suggested only half were human. But all were couples. They cuddled on blankets, laughed over shared plates, traded cards in games. Few glanced up as Mason led Yasmin over the grass, yet he felt hyper aware of the impression they made.

He'd suggested the Crown Gardens because Yasmin's scent put the idea in his head. Not in a romantic sense. He'd forgotten it was a popular date spot. But she smelled like roses, and the garden—burn it. Why was he feeling flustered? A secret date was the perfect explanation for why two teenagers would skip school and run from a cop. Love —or lust—could explain a lot of idiotic decisions.

"This looks good." Mason stared at an open stretch of lawn. He hadn't packed a blanket. His bag held schoolbooks and a change of clothes he'd rather not get dirty.

But he'd spent a lot of money on Yasmin's dress.

"Here." Mason pulled his t-shirt off and spread it on the grass. He gestured for her to sit.

Yasmin didn't move. She stared at him, shaking her head. "Ab-absolutely not. You can't just—Put that back on."

Mason's jaw tensed. Really? Was his bare chest that offensive to her? He knew he lacked the bulk of an action hero, but dragons bore naturally muscular physiques. Most girls—Oh.

He considered Yasmin again, doe eyes wide, lips parted. She clung to the lock of hair that refused to stay behind her ear. A red undertone crept across the exposed skin of her chest.

Mason grinned. "Does it distract you?"

"No. That's not—I meant your wings when—" Yasmin's voice shifted between squeaks as she struggled to find her usual pitch. "And where are your eyes?"

Yasmin crossed her arms in an x over her chest, trying to cover the exposed skin.

Oops. Mason pulled his eyes up to her face. His smile turned guilty. "It's a very flattering dress."

"Yeah, cause it's padded," she said, rolling her eyes. "And the ribbons cinch my waist. Honestly, guys are so easily duped." She slumped onto Mason's shirt, keeping her arms crossed. Her hand fluttered within the sleeve.

She's trying to get the perfume.

Mason hid a smile. He had to give it to Yasmin, she was determined.

"No wonder Nima always got so much attention. *Oh Amir, your oldest is so beautiful. She's going to marry a very wealthy man.*" Yasmin affected the lower, grumbling tone of an older gentleman with surprising success. "We'd all be beautiful if we covered our faces with makeup and stuffed our bras."

Mason's eyebrows rose. He'd struck a nerve. Did Yasmin always respond so poorly to compliments?

"You want to talk about why you're the one with magic, but you're jealous of your sister?" he asked, crossing his legs and joining her on the grass.

Yasmin's head snapped toward him, confusion furrowing her brow.

Please, don't tell me she's forgotten she's in character.

The elves in the park would be able to overhear their conversation. Mason wanted any eavesdropping Castors to be assets, not liabilities.

"I'm not *jealous* of Nima," Yasmin said. "It's just frustrating to work ten times harder and still have everyone prefer your sibling."

Wow. Yasmin Gul—the girl with observational skills so keen she'd discovered the existence of magic—was blind to her own emotions?

"You could start stuffing your bras too," Mason offered, holding back a smile. "I won't tell anyone."

Yasmin glared at him from the corner of her eye. Her hand continued to squirm within the sleeve. "The dress isn't *that* padded."

Mason grinned. "Noted."

"No, I wasn't—I just meant—I don't want—" Yasmin stuttered for an explanation, chest flushing with embarrassment once more before she snapped, "Don't you have an essay you want help with?"

"Yeah." Mason glanced at his backpack. Truthfully, the only thing he wanted to do less than work on his admissions essay was work on it *with* Yasmin. But he'd invented the cover story himself. And—given the policeman this morning —she'd need to provide a convincing alibi very soon.

Mason stifled a sigh, reached into his bag, and found the paper tucked into his folder. He handed it to Yasmin, sliding it beneath her sleeve. "Here, bask at it in all its glory."

Yasmin tossed the fabric aside to unfold the page. Her lips pursed. "It's blank."

"That's how every masterpiece starts."

Yasmin rolled her eyes, but she had no come back. Instead, her lips mouthed the prompt, handwritten in unfading ink at the top of the paper: *write about a time your emotions...*

Mason slid onto his back to avoid watching her. He knew what was coming. A hundred prying questions. And he'd have to answer. If he'd been skipping classes with a witch to get help on his essay, he should have something to show.

I should've just said we were hooking up. No one would make me prove that.

"It's a difficult topic," Yasmin said. She stretched her arm toward Mason offering him the paper beneath her sleeve. Her eyes focused on him with an intensity hot enough to burn.

Mason's fingers locked around the page. His jaw clenched.

Here come the questions.

Yasmin turned away, setting her gaze on the edge of the trees.

What the hell?

Mason had just presented her the perfect opportunity to pry into his business, and she'd gone silent. That couldn't be right.

Except, Yasmin had done the same thing earlier. Mason was afraid of fire, and she knew it. He'd overreacted to the dragon flame and his denial hadn't fooled her. Yasmin was —for better or worse—far too clever.

But she hadn't pushed.

Mason held the unwritten essay toward the sky. Sunlight streamed through the paper and the enchanted ink darkened in response, making the question impossible to avoid. "What would you write?"

He waited for Yasmin to call him out on the hypocrisy. He'd criticized her for prying. What was he doing?

Yasmin stared at him, mute for a few seconds until she lifted her chin to the sky. "After my mother's death, I sank into a bit of a depression. My father didn't believe in therapy, but my school's counselor started meeting with me in her office. She suggested I find a safe release for my emotions. That's when I started writing everything down."

"Like in a diary?"

"Like case notes," Yasmin corrected him a bit too fast. "Details and discoveries. But I include my thoughts. It can be therapeutic."

That sounded like a diary, but Mason didn't press the issue. Yasmin tended to take his jokes personally. And her current pose—arms hugging her knees, doe eyes staring at the clouds—added a soft vulnerability to her beauty, like a captured princess from a fairytale.

Not that Mason should think of Yasmin as a damsel in distress. She was the one saving his ass.

But she couldn't do that unless he gave her the tools to provide an alibi. Which meant, Mason couldn't keep avoiding his essay. It was time to face his past.

22

YASMIN

"My father got arrested for dealing illicit substances when I was ten." Mason stared at the clouds as he spoke, his voice soft and distant, like he was telling a story about a stranger. "A pair of nymphs volunteered to foster me. They had a lot of rules."

Yasmin's fingers closed around the zipper beneath her sleeve. She didn't open the pouch, didn't move, didn't breathe, afraid any subtle shift might spook Mason.

He stretched on the grass like the cover model of one of Nima's romance novels, chest golden in the sunlight. But a heaviness clung to his features: tensed his jaw, tightened his lips. Whatever memory stirred within him, whatever he intended to reveal was Mason's real secret—not his wings.

"One night, I got thirsty, so I snuck out of my room and poured a glass of coke." Mason stopped, eyes on the clouds. Yasmin worried he'd fallen silent for good.

"You weren't allowed coke," she guessed, trying to keep her tone light, like she hadn't spent nights obsessing over what Mason was hiding.

"I wasn't allowed to leave my room," he corrected her. "Unless I was supervised. Probably why they usually refused when I asked for a drink. Anyway, I tripped and spilled the coke on a rug. They caught me trying to scrub it clean."

Mason stopped again. Yasmin didn't interrupt this time. She counted his breaths. Five. Deep and steady, making his muscles rise. His next words came very fast.

"They used to tie me up and lock me in the closet when I misbehaved. Usually, just for a few hours. But this time, they forgot me. I watched the sun rise and set. The iron bar in my mouth started to burn. I tried screaming, but then I... lost control. I breathed more fire than I could handle, and—"

Yasmin's chest tightened. She'd invented a dozen reasons why Mason might've been involved with criminals and locked in a juvenile detention center as a child. She'd wanted a story that would shock her classmates. Could she take back that wish?

"The place crumbled to ashes, and my foster parents—" Mason's voice hitched. "—well, nymphs aren't fireproof. Manslaughter carries less charges for a minor, so I was sent to the Reformatory for the next three years. They taught me to keep my fire from escaping, so don't worry. You're in no danger."

He laughed. It was a hollow sound that made Yasmin's chest ache. All this time, looking for flaws and cracks in Mason's smiling mask. She'd never considered—

"That wasn't your fault. You know that, right? That's not— They were abusing you, and it was an accident." Yasmin's hand shot out from beneath her sleeve, abandoning the captured zipper. She wrapped her fingers around Mason's own and squeezed.

His gaze dropped from the clouds. His eyebrows rose.

I'm holding his hand.

Yasmin pulled back, turned away, tried not to notice Mason's eyes—two pools of shimmering blue, assessing her with a curious expression. Or the corner of his lips, pulled together in a manner that no longer made her think of hidden darkness, but of childhood pain. Or his chest, tanned muscles still exposed and threatening to send her mind spiraling toward fantasies of—

"Where was your mother?' Yasmin lowered her gaze to her sleeve. She refocused her efforts on finding the zipper, and desperately filled the silence. "Is she—?"

"In Europe, yes. Castor's Grove wasn't for her. Too much comradery, I think. She went back to Switzerland when I was four." Mason sat up and shook his head. Grass fell like rain from the thick waves of his hair.

Yasmin needed to find the zipper. She was an undercover reporter, on the edge of the biggest story in history. This was professional. Her motivation was professional. Her curiosity was professional.

"Your mom left you behind?"

"She wanted freedom. Not a kid." A sudden hitch in Mason's voice—stifled fast as he closed his mouth and forced a smile—threatened to crack Yasmin's heart. She'd often thought nothing could be worse than her mother's early death.

But Maamaani didn't choose to leave me.

"Mason, I'm—" The apology caught in Yasmin's throat.

"She and my dad were a bad fit. It happens. What about you? What's your type, Gul?"

The zipper slipped past Yasmin's fingers. She refused to turn to look at Mason. How had he changed the topic so suddenly? And why to that?

"Only curious since you claim it's not tall, big-eared princes."

"Seriously? Why do you care if—" Yasmin caught the zipper. She opened the pocket and slid her fingers around the perfume bottle. A smile snuck onto her face. She'd done it! Yasmin turned, ready to reveal the bottle clutched in her fist, and froze.

Sunlight basked Mason's skin, creating etched grooves in the lines of his abdomen. The muscles on his chest and shoulders shone. His hair turned the same gold as his wings.

Yasmin's body grew hot.

Mason grinned, teeth white and dangerous beneath the shadow of a perfect Grecian nose. A dimple blossomed on his cheek, and his eyes caught the brightness of the sky. He leaned closer, took Yasmin's wrist, and pushed the fabric aside to reveal her hand, clutching the perfume bottle. "That's a good start, but I hope you didn't have plans for the afternoon. Because I think between my essay and your sleight of hand, we both have some work to do."

23
MASON

The streetlights flashed on as Mason walked home. He'd spent longer with Yasmin than intended.

Or necessary.

The first hour, he'd watched her practice. The second hour, she'd helped him draft his admissions essay. The hours after?

I did promise to teach her about the founding of the city.

But they hadn't just discussed historic battles or ancient Castors. Their conversation had shifted toward school and classmates. Yasmin had shared her many observations. Some seemed absurd, others insightful and amusing. Who knew Yasmin could be funny?

Mason had ridden the subway back toward the south with her as well. He'd found a Castor-free carriage where he could pass her the other items he'd purchased from Douglas. They'd been stuck shoulder-to-shoulder in the cramped seats as commuters filed in. Her scent provided a floral oasis in a desert of sweat and dirt. His nose had latched onto her—calming, soothing.

And problematic.

How confident am I that the perfume is disguising her?

Mason thought he detected a whiff of witch beneath the roses, but what if the smell was a placebo?

He rolled his shoulders as he turned the corner toward his home. His nose was average by dragon standards, but he should've been able to tell. Why did he find Yasmin's natural scent so distracting? Was it attrac—?

Nope, nope, nope! Not going down that road. Maybe she's more fun than I expected but—

All thoughts of Yasmin vanished from Mason's mind as he spotted the indigo car parked on the grass before the crumbling Victorian manor.

The Castor's Police were at his house.

Mason's shoulders itched, wings ready to break free and escape into the clouds. But he couldn't keep running. He'd spent the day prepping Yasmin. He had an alibi.

Mason hurried across the grass and jumped the three stairs onto the large patio. His mind ran over his prepared excuse: *We thought you were trying to help the gym teacher stop us from skipping class, not that you wanted to talk to us about a crime!*

Not perfect, but if Yasmin stuck to the same story when they spoke to her, there'd be no proof it was a lie.

Mason took a deep breath, pushed open the door, and entered the parlor.

Before him was the scene of a valentine's breakup. Shredded wallpaper littered the floor. Toppled furniture lay among the stabbed remains of the heart-cushions. Goose feathers floated through the room and hid in the crevices of the ripped paintings.

"But why are they here?" Kira's voice whined from the kitchen to Mason's left. "I don't understand what's going on."

If anyone answered, it was too quiet for Mason to hear.

Stomps pounded on the floor above—heavy, purposeful. Mason tiptoed up the staircase toward the wing he shared with Jeremiah.

"You've got to give me a bit more detail, Drage." A deep, gravelly voice came from Mason's bedroom. "How am I supposed to know if it's his flame or yours? He's a dragon too, ain't he?"

Mason froze in the center of the passageway. The police were hunting his house for dragon fire? And they were speaking directly to—

"Dragons don't keep samples of their fire trapped," Eli responded. The wealthy dragon was in Mason's room, personally overseeing a police search.

"You obviously did. How else did it get stolen?"

"I said the item in question bears a resemblance to my flame. I know you're not a genius, but you understand what *resemblance* means, don't you, Brager?"

An orange helix flickered in Mason's mind. Could Yasmin have—?

The bedroom door opened, and Eli stepped into the passage, blond hair tied in a small tail at his neck. His pale eyes focused on Mason like a hawk spotting a rabbit. "Mr. Wick. Just the man I was hoping to find."

Eli's voice dripped sugar. He approached with the confidence of the wealthy, unaccustomed to resistance and unconcerned by the prospect.

Mason's tongue flicked over his lips; his shoulder blades twitched. Dragons postured by flaunting their scales and blowing flames. The passage was too narrow for wings. Fire wasn't an option. The best he could manage was a straight back and puffed out chest.

"Why are you ransacking my family's house?" Mason kept his tone as casual as he could manage.

"Take a guess." Eli's smile was all teeth. There was no hint of aggression in his voice, but blue sparks flickered into the air with his words.

Whatever he's missing must resemble a blue flame.

At least that eliminated the one Yasmin released. Mason felt silly for worrying. His initial thought when he'd seen the trapped fire had been just as wild. He'd thought—but it didn't matter. The fire was gone.

Blue embers danced into the air, sizzling out just before they reached the wooden floor. Not a threat, but a promise that one could be issued soon.

Mason flinched as one of the sparks popped by his hand. "My name wasn't on the attendance records. I realized my mistake a few minutes after you left."

"Oh?" Eli's brow quirked up. His smile broadened, and he rested his hand on Mason's shoulder, wrapping it around the strap of the school bag. "I do love a good explanation. Why weren't you at school?"

Mason's instinct was to fight Eli's attempt to take his backpack. But Yasmin had anything that might look suspicious, and Douglas didn't give receipts.

"Funny story," Mason said as he released his bag. "I was with..."

Footsteps clattered in the parlor below. Eli dumped the bag's contents unceremoniously onto the floor, unconcerned by the commotion. Uncle Lee's voice shouted at someone to stop.

Mason turned in time to see Kira racing up the winding staircase. The thirteen-year-old grabbed the banister for a second, catching her breath before placing both hands on her hips and glaring at Eli Drage.

Burning hell.

Kira had more bravery than sense. The glint in her eye suggested she was a heartbeat away from summoning her own fire. "Don't hurt him! Mason didn't steal anything from you. None of us did."

"Would you hush, child?" Lee was a frantic flurry of pink wings as he flew toward Kira. His hands zipped over his lips, a desperate plea to stay quiet.

"No, I'm telling the truth," Kira objected. "You said the robbery was this Tuesday, and—"

She's going to come forward as my alibi.

But it wouldn't work. The timeline raised too many questions. Going off course and arriving early to the scheduled meeting at Pretty Pines Park meant a two-hour window where Mason's movements couldn't be tracked. Attendance wasn't taken at lunch. Jeremiah's word—if he'd provide it—would matter little. If anything, it would seem like all of Mason's siblings conspiring to cover up for him.

And how would I explain what I was doing at Pretty Pines?

Mason couldn't risk mentioning the Serpents. Not when they could hurt Kira in retaliation.

"—and I was at school," Mason broke in before Kira could finish, spinning back toward Eli. "Just not in class. That's why I'm not on the attendance records."

For a moment, the only sound Mason heard was his heart thumping in his chest. Then, the bedroom door creaked. A man dressed in a dark purple uniform with the gold crest of a Castor's Police Lieutenant stepped out. Hair fell in dark waves around his sunken cheeks. His eyes glowed with an almost yellow hue above his thin nose.

Mason didn't recognize him.

"And no one to confirm your whereabouts," the lieutenant said, offering a sarcastic grimace of sympathy. "What a pity."

"I didn't say I was alone," Mason corrected. Fear fanned the fire in his stomach, and trails of smoke escaped him. He swallowed, trying to dampen the rising flame. He needed to appear calm. He had nothing to hide. "I was with a woodswitch. Working on my university essay. Here. See?"

Mason reached down and lifted one of his notebooks from the floor. He flipped to the page with the draft. His quick, messy cursive mixed with Yasmin's smaller, neater font.

The lieutenant snatched the book from Mason's hand, glanced at the page, and tossed it back to the ground. "I say we take him in for further questioning."

"Thank you, Lieutenant Brager, but I'm inclined to believe Mr. Wick. Providing his alibi check out." Eli's gaze shifted from something behind Mason. A curious smile curled his lips. "Tomorrow, four o'clock. My estate. Bring your friend, Mr. Wick. I'm always delighted to make the acquaintance of a witch."

24
MASON

Mason was not popular that night.

Uncle Lee downed five cups of *soothing chamomile* tea, which failed to live up to their name. Mason couldn't tell him the truth. Just a whisper of the Serpents would give his fairy godfather a heart attack. Mason offered reassurances instead.

This was a misunderstanding. No, he wasn't lying about the woodswitch. Yes, Lee had heard them mention her.

A flicker of curiosity illuminated the fairy's eyes when he learned that they were talking about the girl who'd been messaging Mason recently. But he didn't pry for more details—a sign that Eli's visit had unnerved him. Instead, Uncle Lee set Mason the task of clearing the parlor.

An eerie silence had settled over the room: no footsteps, no whispers, not even the wind. A carpet of ripped fabric and shredded wallpaper covered the hardwood floor. Disemboweled pillow fluff rested atop.

Mason released his wings and flapped. The movement created a gust that pushed the debris toward one corner. Mason would salvage what he could and transport the rest to the garbage. He turned to grab the broom and dustbin from the corner.

Jeremiah stood before it.

"Damn." Mason jumped back then slapped his forehead at his own response. Living with an elf meant accepting silent and sudden appearances.

"Do you know what I'm going to ask?"

"Whether I think Eli was desperate to find whatever was stolen or just offended by the tacky décor?" Mason joked, gesturing to the destruction around them. He chuckled at his joke.

Jeremiah didn't.

"Lieutenant Brager ripped everything. Not Eli," the elf corrected, tone clipped and cold. "And another policeman showed up at Folkestone today. Officer Sable. He had a lot of questions about you and the Drages. I got interrogated in your stead. Where the hell were you?"

"Shit, Jere. I'm sorry." His brother hated cops. Like most kids in the system, he'd developed an understandable distrust of authority. "I skipped school with Yasmin. We went down—"

"You were with Yasmin?" Jeremiah's nose wrinkled as though her name tasted sour. "Since this morning? You've lost your mind. Drums! Give me your phone."

Mason pulled it from his pocket and passed it without question. "Yasmin's doing better than you think."

Outside of being identified as a human by an elf. And suffering from magical overload in Douglas' shop. And still smelling like roses.

Shit.

The perfume had to be working. Mason needed it to. He couldn't risk worrying about worst-case scenarios.

Keep your thoughts positive and the emotions will follow.

Mason's Ember Rise motto.

Jeremiah snorted in obvious doubt. His fingers paused whatever they were doing on Mason's phone. Then, he leaned over, lowering his voice so it was barely audible. "What are you going to do if there's human-proof protections on the property?"

The hair rose on Mason's spine. Magical protections to dispel humans existed throughout Castor's Grove, but they were costly to maintain and upkept by a single coven of witches who knew the spell. While the government funded a number of safe zones,—the hospital, the castle, the zoo, certain forested land—the average civilian couldn't afford to protect their private homes or businesses.

But the Drages' wealth was far from average.

Jeremiah scoffed. "You didn't think about that aspect, did you?"

"All spells have a weakness," Mason said, parroting a common saying among most non-witch Castors. Whether it was true, or a reassurance passed down from a time when they were enemies and not allies, he couldn't say.

Jeremiah evidently believed the latter. "Forget it. I'm sorry I asked. You and Gul are partners now. I don't want to know about whatever other crimes you commit. Just—" He shoved the phone back toward Mason and sighed. "—try to survive when this all blows up in your face."

———

Where am I sleeping tonight?

Mason stared at the carnage that had once been his bed. His belongings had taken the worst of the werewolf's claws. Shreds of his former mattress blended into the splinters of his desk drawers.

The softest option for sleep were the clothes strewn from his overturned wardrobe. Mason shook out a few of his thickest sweaters and layered them atop the closet. Jeremiah's warning repeated in his mind.

Possible anti-human protections. A perfume that only maybe worked. What if Mason got Yasmin caught? Was it safe? Should he message her and—?

Kira's lightly charred scent entered Mason's room before she did.

"Why did you—Woah! Your room is way worse than mine." Then, with barely a pause, she relaunched her original question. "Why did you lie about being with a woodswitch? We both know you weren't."

Mason turned and pressed a finger to his lips. Voices traveled in the manor. Lee would drown himself in tea if he learned his charge had no real alibi.

"It's complicated," Mason whispered. He didn't want to panic his sister about the Serpents, but he was grateful for a distraction from his own growing nerves. So he explained the issue with the timeline as he stacked his clothes.

Kira leaned on the shell of desk that remained, arms crossed over her blue crop top. "You'd need to be a phenomenal flier. And an exceptional thief."

"For all Eli knows, I am. Besides, only you and Comet can vouch that I was in Pretty Pines Park at two fifteen. And you're my family. Not exactly unbiased."

"I could convince him," Kira muttered. She twisted one of her bangles, then frowned. "Who's the woodswitch you've got covering for you?"

"Just a girl at our school." Mason shrugged. His makeshift mattress threatened to collapse as the pile of clothes grew. "You didn't think Jere and I were the only Castors at Folkestone."

"No, but I've never heard you mention any others before." Kira moved from the desk and waded through the stuffing and splinters to draw closer. "You sure this woodswitch isn't the unbiased source?"

"Meaning?" Mason flung another shirt on the pile, knocking out a sock and a pair of striped boxers in exchange.

"Girls don't just agree to lie to for any boy who happens to be in their class, Mason." The thirteen-year-old lowered her tone, as though she were the adult explaining. "Sounds like she has a crush on you."

Mason laughed. That was absurd.

"I'm serious." Kira lifted his underwear, pinching them between her fingertips with more disgust than warranted. She pretended to gag as she tossed them toward him. "Ugh. I'd rather suffer the full force of werewolf stench than smell your lavender-scented underwear."

Mason rolled his eyes as he caught the underwear. At least she'd acknowledged they were clean. Wait... Mason inhaled. All he got was a faint hint of lavender and their own smokey scents. "You can still smell that officer?"

"Yeah, the room is too earthy. Like we're outdoors."

A lightbulb flicked in Mason's mind. "Do you want to meet Yasmin?"

"The woodswitch?" Kira's eyebrows rose. Her smile turned suspicious. "Why do you want me to meet her if she's just a friend?"

To ensure that she smells like a witch because if she doesn't, I might need to change strategy and plan a very hasty escape to find my estranged mother in Switzerland.

"Do you want to or not?" Mason asked.

"Yes, obviously!" Kira's grin widened. "Any *friend* of yours is a friend of mine."

"Great. I'll tell her to come by tomorrow before we go see Eli," Mason said, ignoring his sister's not-so-subtle implication. He sat on his makeshift mattress, using his elbows and knees to wrangle the escaping clothes.

"At least Uncle Lee won't have to worry about you sneaking her up to your bed."

Mason didn't see a pair of boxers, so he flung a sock at Kira instead. She dodged and ran out his door in a fit of laughter.

At least someone finds the situation amusing.

One unforeseen problem, and Mason could find himself in a host of trouble. Yasmin needed to be convincing. The perfume had to work.

And I have to get Yasmin onto the Drage's compound. Magical protections be damned.

25
YASMIN

Yasmin had never wished for a desk more. She sat on the carpet, squashed between bed and bookshelf, and boxed in by her notebook, pen, and an array of curious glass vials.

Magic.

Yasmin's fingers tingled as they flittered over the three glass vials. She'd already made notes on the perfume.

Pink. Scentless. Doesn't hide that I smell like roses.

A smile snuck across Yasmin's face as she glanced at that last sentence. She recalled Mason words to her earlier: *Maybe there's a little bit of magic in you after all, Gul.*

The light had softened the blue of his eyes, and he'd given her that annoyingly attractive smile—crooked beneath a perfect nose. Yasmin had taken pains to describe it in her notes. She liked to record every detail of a case. Including her thoughts.

Which was exactly why she needed to stop thinking about Mason. Real-life magic waited on Yasmin's floor. She did not have time to write about a boy. Even a very attractive one.

Yasmin leaned forward and grabbed the remaining vials.

The first, small and flat, contained a pale blue powder. Yasmin wrote the description on a fresh page in her notebook. According to Mason, if she blew a little of the powder into the air, anyone who inhaled would fall asleep.

Maybe I'll test it on Hassan.

The second was an ornate glass dropper with blue liquid within. Yasmin had recognized it before Mason explained—the color changing dye. A real witch wouldn't need it, which meant her sleight of hand needed to be perfect.

Yasmin tucked the eyedropper up her sleeve, practicing slipping it out and opening it within the shadow of the fabric. Only once she'd managed it three times in a row did she reward herself by testing the magic. She pressed a single drop onto a fresh page in her notebook.

The white darkened to a rich blue.

Yasmin's eyes widened. She hurried to record her findings, though she had to squint to make out the black ink now.

Better than any dye. The magic is precise. The paper is dry. Only a single page changed color. No hint of blue has leaked through elsewhere.

"Yasmin!" Her brother flung open her door without knocking. "Nima's on the phone. Dad says—" He broke off with a snort and pointed at Yasmin. "What are you wearing?"

"A dress. I didn't know you were blind," Yasmin spat back, resting a billowing sleeve on the floor to ensure the magic remained hidden behind her bookshelf.

"Yeah, but why is it so low. You haven't got anything to show." Hassan paused, eyebrows lifting as though he'd just had an epiphany. "Oh, damn. I'm a poet." He raised his arms and moved his knees in and out in some sort of victory dance. Evidently his wit was so lacking, he had to celebrate his ability to accidentally rhyme. He paused suddenly, eyebrows rising. "Wait. Is it like triple padded or something?"

Yasmin grabbed a pillow from her bed and flung it at her brother. Unfortunately, her aim was terrible. The pillow fell inches shy of his feet.

Hassan exploded into a fit of high-pitched hysteria before he remembered why he'd barged in. "Dad says you have to come talk to Nima. Though you should probably change first."

Yasmin folded the arm that wasn't blocking the magic over her chest and glared. "I can't. I'm busy."

"Doing what?" He leaned further through the door, angling to read her notebook.

Which contained personal observations and thoughts on magic. And on Mason. Yasmin slammed the cover shut.

Her brother stuck out his tongue, then turned and shouted into the hall, "Yasmin says she's too busy for her family!"

"I did not," Yasmin objected, though it was the phrasing that bothered her more than the sentiment. Nima's existence consisted of make-up, bands, and boys who fawned over her. Yasmin didn't want to hear about her sister's life, and the feeling was mutual. Nima's recent messages with vague requests to "talk" only meant she wanted a favor. Whatever it was couldn't be more important than studying magic. Even their father would understand that if he knew.

But Yasmin had no proof. She'd gotten rid of the dragon flame. And for what? She'd learned Mason was afraid of fire, but his essay would've given her that insight anyway. Her impulsive decision had proved to be a major mistake.

Unless I don't want proof.

Did humans who learned the truth really seek to destroy magic? Was that even possible to do?

No, Xena must've been exaggerating. Yasmin was over-reacting. She hadn't destroyed the flame on purpose. Of course, she still wanted to write a tell all—maybe she'd keep Mason's secrets out of it, but some human was bound to learn the truth and expose it eventually. Why couldn't it be Yasmin?

"Tell your sister I'm confiscating her phone if she doesn't come," Amir's voice called back.

"Ooh." Hassan whistled. "Baba says—"

"Yeah, I heard him." Yasmin didn't know why her father hadn't just yelled his message directly to her. Or why he was threatening her phone. Even he knew to go for her notebooks when he wanted to punish her.

"Better hurry up then because you definitely want your phone." Hassan sang the last bit as though hiding a secret.

Yasmin's eyes narrowed. She'd left her phone charging in the kitchen so that the unfamiliar magic didn't continue to leech its battery. "Did you do something to my phone?"

"No, but I saw a message come through. Mason Wick invited you over."

26

MASON

No welcome mat greeted visitors. No decorations sat on the small patio. Wooden shutters sealed the windows. At a glance, it would be easy to assume no one lived at Townhouse 23 in the Quintessential Living Complex.

Mason knocked on a blue door with paint peeling from its corners.

Feet shuffled within, followed by a groan, then the scraping of a metal bolt.

Lawrence Wick, gray bathrobe open to reveal a white tank and polka-dot boxers, raised a hand, shielding his eyes from the sun. "What've we said about showing up unannounced, kid?"

That it's the only option because you're never available if I ask ahead?

"I brought coffee," Mason volunteered, holding up two large to-go cups with a green mermaid stamped on their sides.

Lawrence sighed and turned, but he left the door open.

Mason followed him in.

The townhouse's front entrance led to a small kitchen with dated brown cupboards and white appliances that didn't match. A stove in the corner told the wrong time, and a package of sliced bread grew mold on the counter. The old white refrigerator hummed. Within would be the finest slices of meats, purchased from butchers across the city.

Lawrence grabbed a cup from his son and leaned back against the counter. "I'm afraid I don't have time for much, kid. I'm getting ready. I start work in an hour."

That last might have been true. But the Drages lived only a few blocks away, and nothing about Lawrence's appearance—bare feet, pajamas, gray morning whiskers—indicated he'd been in the midst of preparing to leave.

"I just need five minutes, Dad," Mason promised.

"Guess I'm here till I finish this." Lawrence lifted the coffee cup and took a sip. His nose wrinkled in distaste. "Too cold."

Mason tested the beverage in his own to-go cup. There was still some heat left.

Lawrence opened his lips in a small circle. A jet of orange flame shot from his mouth. It consumed his hand, the paper cup, and the liquid within.

Mason's throat tightened. He didn't dare blink, lest the image of the fire slip beneath his lids and turn yellow.

I can't let him see that I'm scared.

The panic was irrational. Unlike his son, Lawrence controlled his flames. The bright, flickering ball didn't so much as singe the paper. When the coffee reached his desired temperature, he blinked, and the fire vanished.

"That's impressive," Mason said, eyes dry. He inhaled, trying not to gasp and reveal he'd been holding his breath. "Perhaps you could teach me sometime?"

"You're a bit old for lessons now. Eighteen officially, right? An adult by most standards. You don't need me."

It was a human notion that at eighteen everything changed. Castor laws had always been more fluid, perhaps due to the varying ideals of adulthood found among different species.

But his father knew that.

"Unless you're here now for a five-minute lesson. Doubt we'll have time for a follow up." Lawrence laughed, higher than his voice, eyes flicking around the kitchen like a captured animal looking for an escape. Perhaps he thought Mason had shown up to waste his time with chatting.

"Dad, I'm a—" Mason stepped forward as he began to explain. The shift in position meant that the kitchen wall no longer blocked his view of the small living area beyond.

Lawrence had never been one for material possessions beyond his exotic meats. His aesthetic surpassed minimalistic. He purchased cheap, plain furniture that could be abandoned without fuss if he chose to pack up and leave in the middle of the night.

But a broken television, gutted couch, and shred floor matt took things to the extreme.

Mason stared at a hole, punched in the wall beyond. "The police searched your house too."

"The Drages," Lawrence corrected him. "Suspicious bunch. They're looking at all their employees, I guess. Even the ones with—what do you mean too?"

"Your kitchen seems fine."

"Werewolf probably didn't like the smell. They never search as well when they don't like the smell." Lawrence rested his coffee on the counter. "Now, tell me, what were the police doing at your house?"

"I'm a suspect in the robbery at the Drage's manor." Mason explained his situation as succinctly as he could.

Lawrence drummed his fingers against the counter as he listened, expression darkening. "I had no idea," he muttered. "None. I mean—what evidence do they have that points to you?"

"I don't know. But the Serpents must've planted something."

"Don't be absurd." Lawrence waved his hand. He paced the short length of the kitchen. "Someone else must have messaged. You're not important enough for the Serpents to frame for a crime, or recruit, or take any interest in at all. Not without serious cause."

Mason winced, hand tightening around his own cup. Coffee sloshed within. Fire turned in his stomach, rising to heat his chest. The forgotten child within him wanted to scream, *I am important.* Instead, he clamped his mouth tight and swallowed.

I'm sure he didn't mean it like that.

Lawrence was a good father. He'd stayed when Mason's mother hadn't, provided food and shelter, the necessities. Sensitivity went against his nature, but children grew stronger from harsh truths than coddling. Any emotional outburst from Mason would lose his father's respect.

"Someone must have wanted me in the park for some reason," Mason said, keeping his tone matter of fact.

"Certainly an unusual coincidence." Lawrence stopped pacing to rub his chin. "But I can't imagine—I mean, you can't control your fire. You would be useless to the Serpents. They wouldn't want you."

Why? Because you and Mom didn't?

Mason clamped his jaw to hold back the childish retort. He didn't see why his inability to control his fire mattered anyway. The Serpents were framing him for theft, not arson.

"Can you get an alibi?" Lawrence asked, pacing again. "Not one of the castaways you live with. Though maybe Lee could—"

"That's why I'm here," Mason interrupted, relieved that his father wanted to help save him. "One of my human classmates learned the truth about magic and offered—more or less—to help. She'll cover for me, but in order for her word to be taken seriously, we're disguising her as a woodswitch."

"We? Who's we? Not me." Lawrence cleared the distance between them in two steps and pressed a hand over his son's mouth. Mason was an inch taller, but he felt like a child beneath his father's glare. "I'm not helping you with this, understand? You shouldn't even have told me that. What if I went to the police?"

Mason clamped his jaw. He didn't like having his mouth covered any more than having his limbs bound. The sensation returned him to the dark closet. Ropes bit into his wrists. Iron blocked his mouth. He couldn't breathe.

Fire rolled inside Mason's stomach, rising to his chest, his throat. He clenched his jaw, holding back the flames until his skin grew hot. Smoke curled from him, his fire seeking an escape.

Lawrence moved his hand and resumed pacing.

Air flooded through Mason's nose. His panic subsided as his breath returned. The fire retreated with it, vanishing as fast as it had grown.

He licked his lips, dried and parched from the heat. "Would you go to the police?"

"Of course not. You're my son. And I've got my own qualms with law enforcement. But you don't know that."

Lawrence pounded the heel of his palm to his forehead as he walked. "And you think the Serpents are interested in you? You have no understanding how anything works. Kid, you can't trust people like that when you're doing something illegal."

An orange helix swirled in Mason's mind. A question rose with it. He knew better than to ask.

"I'm sorry." Mason stared at his coffee cup. "It's just that Eli wants to meet the woodswitch this afternoon."

"Of course, he does." Lawrence stopped pacing to slap the counter. "Bastards are always looking for witches. You better hope your human is up to the task or who knows what they might do to her." He stared at the coffee cup, a dark expression on his face.

"That's why I'm here. I wanted your help—or your advice rather—on how to sneak her in," Mason admitted. "Past whatever protections the Drages have against humans."

Lawrence chuckled. There was nothing cheerful about the sound. "You don't need my help, kid. Humans can come onto that property no problem."

"Really?" Mason sipped his coffee. The caffeine did little to help steady his thoughts. "Why wouldn't they pay for wards? Do they want humans to be able to come on?"

"Must do." Lawrence said, tapping the edge of his cup. Then, before Mason could ask, his father answered his next question as well. "Couldn't tell you why. Maybe they eat them."

27
YASMIN

This is where Mason lives?

The sprawling property hid behind a row of small, single-family homes. Tall hedges guarded most of the land from view, but beyond their leaves rose a steep gabled roof and two curved towers in white-washed brick.

Mason had mentioned his foster family yesterday. He'd failed to add that they lived on a miniature estate.

Yasmin's heart pounded. She didn't know why. The dangerous part would be later when she needed to convince an unknown dragon of both her identity and Mason's alibi. This first meeting was just to confirm the disguise worked.

But what if they don't like me?

Stupid thing to worry about. What did it matter? Yasmin should have been thinking of this as an opportunity to gather more information for her exposé.

The hedge before her shuffled. A pair of large orange eyes opened amongst the leaves.

Yasmin squeaked and stumbled back. Her instinct was

to hide behind a notebook, but she'd abandoned her usual defense. On her possession instead were the vials of magic and her phone. Whether by enchantment or careful design, the items remained stationary in her pockets. No rattling betrayed their presence, and when Yasmin reached for them, they'd be exactly where she'd placed them.

If I remember to reach for them.

A woodswitch wouldn't squeak and hide. She'd ready her magic. Yasmin couldn't panic every time something surprised her. Though it would have been nice if Mason had mentioned owning a plant with eyes!

"Comet, get away from there before someone spots you," a voice called beyond the hedge.

A low rumble came from within the hedge, and an orange scaled head emerged revealing the true owner of the eyes. Comet's gaze bored into Yasmin. His slitted nostrils flared.

He's smelling me.

Comet's mouth opened into wide smile, thin tongue unfurling over a row of sharp teeth. He loosed a sound eerily akin to a dog's bark, and his small ears twitched. Ignoring the warning he'd been given, the dragon pushed through the leaves.

Yasmin's jaw slackened despite her best efforts.

Mason had explained that there were two species of dragons. Bipedal dragons like himself—human in appearance with the ability to hide more of their reptilian qualities—and great dragons.

Comet was a creature from a fairytale. Four short legs dangled from a round torso, kept aloft by a pair of flapping wings. Bright orange scales covered his skin, and rounded white spines ran in two parallel rows across his back. Behind his ears shone a pair of small white horns.

Forget fire that existed without oxygen. If Yasmin got a picture of him...

Comet grumbled and swooped lower. His wing tapped the back of Yasmin's calves, herding her onto the property like she was a sheep.

Yasmin twisted her hand beneath her sleeve, trying not to stumble over the curved drive as she unzipped. Hopefully the magic hadn't fried her phone just yet.

Comet leaned his head back and whistled, more bird than dog in his sounds now.

At his alert, the manor's front door flew open, and a dark-skinned girl in a red dress skidded onto the long patio. She was taller than Yasmin with a body comprised of mainly limbs. Two curls, loose form her ponytail, bounced to either side of her long, narrow face. Her silver bracelets jingled as she rushed forward.

"You must be Kira," Yasmin guessed, stopping at the base of the patio steps. "Mason's told me so much about you."

"Interesting." Kira's lips pursed into a curious smile. "What did he say?"

That he's worried a group of criminals will hurt you if he explains the real reason he wasn't at school?

Yasmin obviously couldn't say that.

"You're his sister. And a dragon." Yasmin gave up on her plan to remove her phone. Kira studied her openly. Comet hovered in the air between them, mouth open in a relaxed smile that gave him the appearance of an amused spectator. Yasmin felt like an article being scrutinized for typos by a vindictive editor. "Is Mason inside?"

"He'll be down in a bit." Kira spread her arms, stretching between the wooden railings and blocking the entrance. Her broad grin revealed human-crunching teeth.

Yasmin's stomach turned. But this was ridiculous. Fire-breathing dragon or not, Kira was still a middle schooler. Yasmin could handle any questions a kid might have about her parentage. She'd stayed up all night studying her backstory. There was no reason to be nervous.

"Do you have a crush on Mason?"

Yasmin's chest grew hot. That was not what Kira was supposed to ask. Why would she even—Ugh. Middle schoolers came up with the most absurd ideas.

"You totally do."

Oh no. Yasmin had forgotten to answer.

"Of course not." She tried to step around Kira.

The middle schooler, still smirking, mirrored the move, blocking Yasmin's access to the patio. Comet made a noise suspiciously like a chuckle.

Where was Mason? When he'd invited her over, Yasmin had assumed he'd make the introductions. She would never have allowed Hassan to welcome one of her guests. When she saw Mason, she would—what? Complain because Kira thought Yasmin liked him? Mason would probably burst into laughter and ask if his sister was right.

"If you really want to know, I think your brother is incredibly annoying," Yasmin said. "He makes far too many jokes and tries to change the topic whenever things get uncomfortable. I'm helping him write his admissions essay, and it's like trying to draw blood from a vampire."

Kira's lips pursed. She appeared unconvinced. "Quite the favor for a boy you *don't* like."

"Oy!" A man in a lilac suit and deep indigo shawl fluttered on a pair of pink wings by the door: Uncle Lee, Mason's fairy godfather. "Kira, are you harassing Mason's friend? Invite her in."

The middle schooler stepped aside with a toothy grin, and Uncle Lee ushered Yasmin in.

Two dragons and a fairy.

The lightheadedness that had swept through her in The Portentous Purveyor threatened to consume Yasmin once more. She squeezed her palms into fists to remind herself not to gape at the glittering orange scales or fluttering pink wings. She'd traveled less than twenty minutes from her home yet found herself in a whole new world.

"Forgive the lack of furniture," Uncle Lee said, holding the door open to reveal a large, empty room with a winding staircase like what debutantes descended in movies. Remnants of heart-covered paper clung to patches of the walls. "We had a visitor yesterday, searching for a stolen dragon flame. I'm sure Mason's mentioned."

Yasmin almost tripped over her feet. She'd exchanged several messages with Mason since they'd parted ways yesterday evening. None had mentioned a stolen dragon flame.

Had Douglas missed the one she'd taken?

Uncle Lee ordered Kira to fetch cups of tea, sat Yasmin on the stairs, and began questioning her under the guise of small talk: *What classes do you take? How did you realize Mason was a dragon? Where in the woods is your family from?*

This was the line of interrogation Yasmin had anticipated. She eased into character, answers flowing naturally.

"Unfortunately, my mother passed before she could teach me much," Yasmin finished, addressing the tea stains at the bottom of her mug. "That's why I agreed to help Mason with his essay. He offered to help me learn."

Kira still looked suspicious, but Uncle Lee offered a sympathetic look. Comet, who lay on the step beside Yasmin, rested the edge of his wing on her knee. Another wave of amazement knocked into her at his touch. She couldn't afford to lose her mind in awe.

Yasmin stood. "Can I use your bathroom?"

Uncle Lee pointed her in the direction, and Yasmin followed the passageway until she reached a white door. She opened it, turned on the tap, and splashed water on her face before she remembered that she'd applied some of her sister's makeup.

She dabbed her face fast before the mascara could start to run, then froze. Was she imagining it or had something in the bathroom started to hum?

28

YASMIN

With every second Yasmin spent in the bathroom, the sound increased. It couldn't be the plumbing. But there was no sign of anything unusual—only the toilet, the sink, and a built-in ceramic tub.

Empty patches of gray interrupted the pink floor tiles. Recalling the secret entrance to The Portentous Purveyor, Yasmin crouched, tapping each with her thumb. Nothing.

Maybe overexposure to magic had turned her mad.

Yasmin reached for the door. The hum grew desperate and wild, a plea in her ear. "If you want me to find you, you have to tell me where you are."

The humming stopped, then resumed, softer and with an obvious direction. It was somewhere in the bathtub.

And it had understood Yasmin's question.

"I'm losing my mind." Yasmin double-checked the lock before climbing into the ceramic tub. She felt along the smooth walls, tracing every inch until she was on her knees. Her fingers brushed the metal edge of the drain. The humming grew into a frantic, desperate crescendo.

She couldn't be imaging this.

Yasmin leaned forward and pressed her eye to the drain. "Are you down there?"

A warble echoed up the pipe.

What would a fairy, an elf, and three dragons have hidden in their bathtub drain?

And should I be trying to free it?

Probably not. But the hum filled Yasmin with a feeling she struggled to explain—kinship, maybe? But how did you feel connected to a sound?

The drain protector was loose. Yasmin pulled the colander-like silver circle from the pipe and reached in. But her fingers could only fit so far.

She took the enchanted dye from her sleeve, removed the dropper, and traced the inside of the pipe until it bumped against something—a string. Yasmin caught the cord on the glass dropper and lifted. The steady excitement of the hum strengthened as its source drew closer to the surface.

The creature responsible for the sound was—

A dragon's flame?

Only, this one appeared to be a hundred shades of blue. And it hummed.

Yasmin's fingers trembled as they latched around the thin glass tube. Uncle Lee had said that people came looking for a stolen dragon flame. Yasmin had worried about the one she took from Douglas, but what if this was it?

Mason needs me to be an alibi for a robbery, but he never told what was stolen.

Yasmin leaned against the back of the tub, holding the glass toward the light. The spark within bobbed up and down, a glowing wisp of crackling blue. A buzz emanated from within as its movements grew erratic. The miniature fireball hit against the glass.

By the time Yasmin recognized what it was doing, it was too late. The trembling tube—rocking from the spark's momentum—slipped from her fingers. It shattered on the ceramic floor.

So much for enchanted glass.

The fireball broke free.

Its hum rose to a victory march. Then, the sound turned hungry. It latched onto the enchanted vial of blue dye. The glass melted, but the blue fire didn't vanish like the one Yasmin had released yesterday.

The blue fire grew until it was the size of a burning fist. No amplification spell required. Yasmin needed to escape before it spread to her dress. She tried to stand but slipped on the tub.

The magic dye had burned to nothing. The wisp of fire gave a satisfied burp, then turned its attention to Yasmin and rocketed toward her face.

29
MASON

A loud knock came on Mason's door a second before it swung open. Kira and Comet barged inside.

"Wrong order guys," Mason said, buttoning his soft gray shirt. A wrinkle creased the collar. Spending the previous night as part of a mattress hadn't been kind on the material. "I'm supposed to say come in first."

Kira wore a red dress and smug grin. "Your *friend* is downstairs."

Mason stopped tugging at his shirt. "Yasmin is here? What time is it?"

He'd wanted to introduce her to his family, see how Comet and Kira reacted to her scent. Had the perfume worked?

"You're fine. She's early." Kira stretched and studied the room. Her smile grew, like she knew a secret. "I see why you've been studying woodswitches."

Flames! If a thirteen-year-old can clock Yasmin as a human, what's my backup plan?

Grab a bag and get to an airport.

"You did tidy up in here," Kira said, giggling. She glanced at Comet as though they'd discussed it.

They probably had.

Kira had been by a friend when Mason got back from his father that morning, and Jeremiah had vanished too. However, Comet had helped Mason sweep the debris and return the closet to its usual state. Though the lack of a bed made the room appear empty, it was at least clean.

Comet's forehead moved as though wagging nonexistent eyebrows. Mason understood. The great dragon had been making similar gestures throughout the morning.

His siblings hadn't noticed that Yasmin was a human. They thought they'd discovered a secret romance.

"I'm not trying to impress anyone," Mason objected for what felt like the hundredth time. All his arguments fell on deaf ears. "I'm not even bringing her up here."

Though given Yasmin's penchant for snooping, she might wander up on her own if she had the chance. He'd rather not give the impression that he was a slob who slept on piles of his own clothing.

"Bet she'd come if you asked," Kira teased. "She totally likes you."

Comet snorted his agreement.

Mason shook his head. Of course they thought that. They couldn't conceive of another reason why Yasmin would lie for him.

Of course, Uncle Lee believed Mason's alibi to be true, and the fairy had similar suspicions.

Wait. Had Kira and Comet left Yasmin alone with Uncle Lee? What would the two of them talk about? Him?

Mason grabbed a yellow tie from his closet, pulled it through his collar, and hurried to make a knot. His siblings watched. "You guys should head back down," he suggested. "I want to get your opinion of her."

"Oh, that's easy," Kira said. She didn't move from his doorway. Neither did Comet. "She's smart, easy to fluster, kind of clumsy, and—I think you know—very pretty. But it's kind of a waste of your raw power to have kids with a witch."

Mason's hands slipped from his too-slack tie. Forget rushing downstairs. Yasmin hearing embarrassing adolescent stories from Uncle Lee might be safer than letting Kira loose.

"I meant get a sense of her as an alibi," Mason grumbled, fixing his tie. "Not as the future mother of my children."

Comet opened his mouth in a rumbling purr. He approved of Yasmin for both.

"Well obviously you think that," Kira complained, shooting Comet an annoyed glare. "You don't have fire. You don't get how important it is. We can't weaken our lineages. We'll end up destroying our own species and breeding only..."

Mason froze.

But Kira was childish, not cruel. She'd likely heard sentiments about dragon supremacy from her uncle and parroted them without thinking. Now, as she realized her mistake, she quickly switched topics. "I think Eli will love Yasmin. She's too pretty for a boy not to want to trust her, and he said he likes witches. Think she knows any spells with dragon fire?"

"Unlikely." Mason finished his tie and moved toward the door. Kira followed him out. Comet came a few seconds after, movements slow and large orange eyes turned to the floor.

Kira may have caught herself, but they all knew what she'd wanted to say: *We'll end up destroying our own species and breeding only deformities.*

Like dwarfed great dragons with stubby legs and no flames.

Mason's chest tightened. He wanted to tell Comet that he'd prefer a brother who helped him clean his room to one who could burn a house down any day. That fire was over-rated. That his mother hadn't wanted him either.

But the words caught in Mason's throat. He'd never been good with difficult conversations.

The sound of shattering glass cut through the tense silence. Mason froze at the top of the stairs.

Lee sat near the bottom, sipping his tea. The fairy was alone.

Where the hell was Yasmin?

30
YASMIN

Yasmin screamed and raised her hands in a futile effort to block the onslaught of flames barreling toward her.

She'd always assumed the cliché *curiosity killed the cat* had been invented by someone too dull or too corrupt to question the status quo. But maybe it was cherished wisdom after all.

Why didn't I ignore the humming? Why didn't I just leave the bathroom instead of snooping?

Now, Yasmin was going to burn to death.

Warmth spread through her hand as the fire engulfed it. She gritted her teeth, waiting for the pain.

It didn't come.

"Huh?"

Yasmin opened her eyes. Blue flames clung to her right hand, crackling and hissing. But her skin wasn't burning.

How is that possible?

The orange dragon flame had singed Yasmin's fingers. She had the raised pink welts to prove it. And she'd just seen this blue wisp obliterate a glass vial.

"You're different, aren't you?"

The wisp's hummed a frequency that reverberated in Yasmin's chest, matching the rhythm of her own heart, her own breath.

A loud rap came against the door, followed by Mason's panicked voice. "Yasmin? Are you okay? We heard something break. And then you screamed."

The fire shrank to its original size, little larger than a bee, and flitted to Yasmin's neck, hiding behind the veil of her hair. Its frequency shifted. She could feel its fear.

It didn't want anyone to know she'd found it. Or maybe it didn't want *Mason* to know.

"I'm fine. Just dropped my phone," Yasmin shouted the first excuse she could think. "You know I scream when I drop things."

She expected laughter. Instead, she got concern. "It sounded like something broke."

"The screen. I'm cleaning it."

"I'll get you a broom." His feet pounded away before she could refuse.

Mason was fast. He'd be back soon. Yasmin didn't have long to figure out what she'd just discovered.

A stolen flame? Was Mason the thief?

All the suspicions Yasmin had dismissed yesterday rushed back. How much could she trust Mason? Maybe he was a criminal mastermind toying with her emotions. Maybe he did have magical allure that he kept using. Maybe he'd invented a past that would tug at her heartstrings and make her trust him.

Mason knocked again before she could figure it out. "Can I come in? I'll help you sweep."

"No!" Yasmin leapt from the tub and hurried to the

door. The wisp hid beneath her hair as she grabbed the dustpan and broom from a concerned-looking Mason.

"You sure you're okay? You seem rattled."

"I'm fine. I just don't want you coming in the bathroom with me." Yasmin slammed the door before he could make any jokes.

Her chest grew hot. No, wait, that was the wisp of fire. It had come out from behind her hair and nestled in her cleavage now they were alone.

Brilliant.

Yasmin swept up the glass. The wisp hummed against her skin. Unlike the dragon fire she'd encountered before, this one felt alive. Emotions pulsed within—worry, distrust, and relief. For some reason, it seemed to have decided Yasmin was safe. Still, she assumed it would fly to freedom once clear of the property.

But when—after disposing of the evidence and offering the perfunctory farewells— Mason and Yasmin left, the wisp did not.

Instead, it slipped beneath her dress to nestle in her palm—a stowaway in Yasmin's sleeve.

31
MASON

The soft rattle of the subway buzzed in Mason's ear. Yasmin leaned against the wall in the seat beside him, hands folded in her lap. She'd spent the past twenty minutes staring at her sleeves, barely speaking as they moved toward downtown.

"Did something weird happen with my family before I came downstairs?" Mason asked. "You seem... off."

"Just nervous," Yasmin mumbled, not turning her head. She'd forgone her braid, and a curtain of dark waves hid her expression.

Why is she avoiding looking at me?

"You talk more when you're nervous, not less," Mason informed her. He reached over and brushed the hair from her face. The strands were soft and silky. He liked how they felt against his fingers.

The intimacy of the gesture didn't occur to him. Until he heard the hitch in Yasmin's breath. Her floral scent washed over him, almost intoxicating. He wanted to keep his fingers wrapped in her hair, to lean in, and—

Shit. I must be the one nervous about the Drages.

Mason pulled his hand back, crossing it to his chest and trying not inhale. Despite going to efforts to see Yasmin's face, he addressed the subway map on the opposite wall. "You're lost in thought about something. I want to know what."

Yasmin pursed her lips. A sheen of gloss accentuated their natural pink. Coupled with the smoky shadows around her eyes, the effect was almost sultry.

No wonder Kira kept commenting on her looks.

Mason's stomach flipped.

His family had said something weird when he wasn't there, hadn't they? His sister had made an inappropriate comment, or Uncle Lee had asked if they were in a relationship. Yasmin loved to overanalyze things. She might be ruminating over the challenges dragons faced when dating humans.

"What was Eli Drage looking for when he searched your house yesterday?"

"Oh." The back of Mason's head slumped against his seat. His shoulders fell as an unexpected sense of disappointment hit him. Had he wanted Yasmin to ask him about human-dragon relationships? "Something that looked like a blue flame, I think."

"Why didn't you tell me before?" Yasmin's voice was clipped.

"Because it didn't matter?" Mason had been trying not to think about it himself. He needed to clear his name, not worry over what the Serpents wanted with fake dragon fire.

"Why'd you come check on me in the bathroom?"

Mason's brow furrowed. These questions were getting weird. "You screamed. We were worried."

"Your family were concerned?" Something sparked in Yasmin's eyes. She leaned closer. "Who? Lee?"

Shit, she was close.

Mason's throat went dry. It took all his effort not to look down. But staring at her eyes proved equally dangerous. Her thick lashes were all damsel-in-distress, but the curiosity burning in her gaze was wild and unstoppable, like a force of nature.

And she thinks I have powers of allure?

Evidently, all Yasmin needed to do was put on a low-cut dress and a bit of makeup. No magic required.

"Sure." Mason cleared his throat. "Kira and Comet too. They thought you saw a mouse."

"Nothing else?"

They'd also teased Mason about how quickly he'd run to check on her. But Yasmin didn't need to know that.

"How much do you know about your family?" Yasmin asked. Her hand twitched beneath her sleeve. "I mean, you've been with them for—what? Four years? You're not blood relatives. How does that change things?"

"It doesn't." Annoyance gave a sharp edge to Mason's voice. The threat of a spark burned in his stomach. "They're my family."

"Yeah, but how do you know you can trust them?"

Mason's jaw clenched. She had not seriously asked that.

"Can your sister trust you?" He asked, locking his teeth into a grin as phony as the one Yasmin liked to use. "That's her makeup you're wearing, right? Did you call and get permission? Or has your jealousy gotten to the point where you're just stealing her look?"

Red flushed Yasmin's chest. Her arms trembled, but she kept them folded in her lap, head snapping away from him instead as she turned toward the subway window. "You're a jerk."

"I thought you'd be happy. Didn't you want a guy who could notice when you wore make up?"

"Didn't you ask what I was thinking about?" she bit back.

Mason's tongue clicked against the roof of his mouth. Yasmin had him there. He'd insisted she share her thoughts then gotten annoyed they weren't about what he wanted.

But couldn't she have just liked my family?

The subway arrived at their stop. Mason and Yasmin pushed through the sardined bodies onto the platform. A large clock hanging on the station wall reported the time as 15:05.

Fifty-five minutes to get to the Drages.

The walk should only take fifteen, but Mason might need longer to fix whatever was going on between him and Yasmin.

Why did I choose now to get into a fight? She's about to be my alibi.

They slunk up the subway steps in silence. Only once they were outside, walking in an uneven strip of shade—the result of mom-and-pop diners mixed with skyscraper offices and commercial apartments—did Mason attempt to break the silence.

"So—uh—you ready for this?"

"To lie for you, you mean?" Yasmin's tone made it clear they were still fighting.

Mason glanced around, nervous someone might've overheard, but they weren't close to the Drages yet. He inhaled—just to double check. The soft, soothing scent of roses rolled over him. It calmed him. He hated that. Yasmin shouldn't get to smell like that when she was being difficult.

They walked another few blocks, passing the coffee

shop Mason had visited earlier that morning and the group of town houses where his father lived.

This time, Yasmin broke the silence. "Would you want a fire that stops burning?"

Mason rolled his shoulders. "All fire stops burning eventually."

"No, I mean one that keeps existing, but stops burning. You'd like that, right? Because you're scared of fire."

Mason's jaw tensed. Now who was being a jerk?

"Or would you still be afraid?" Yasmin continued. Her interrogation didn't seem to require Mason. She responded to her own questions, walking down the street faster than should've been possible given her short stride. "It's likely. The fear is emotional, not logical. You're fireproof. So what would you do with a flame that didn't burn? You could use it for exposure therapy, I suppose. But would that be worth the trouble?"

Yasmin was so lost in thought, she walked straight past the massive stone wall of the Drage's estate. Mason had to grab her elbow and pull her back in the correct direction.

"I don't know what is going on in your mind, but can you please focus?"

Yasmin shook her head. "I didn't think I cared, but I do."

"Care about what?"

"That you're innocent."

Mason's heart stopped. He spun toward her, putting their faces as close as he dared. They were three feet away from the Drage's gate. "You're asking me this now?"

"I didn't ask. I said I'm trying to ascertain," Yasmin whispered.

Mason couldn't believe her. She'd agreed to be his alibi, but this whole time, she'd thought he could be a thief?

She's not the only one.

Jeremiah wasn't annoyed just because he thought disguising a human was a hair-brained scheme.

He thinks I might be guilty. Eli definitely will. And the cops.

The truth wouldn't help Mason. But who was he to ask Yasmin to lie?

He'd killed two people and gotten off light. Maybe suffering for a crime he didn't commit was the universe's way of evening the score.

Sparks fluttered in Mason's stomach. He squeezed his eyes shut, clamped his jaw, and took three deep, rose-scented breaths.

"Listen, Yasmin," he whispered, managing to keep his voice even. "I won't blame you for what you do. Most people wouldn't believe me. But you need to decide now. Either you want to help me, or you don't. Which is it?"

32
YASMIN

"That's a false—" The word *dichotomy* died on Yasmin's lips.

Mason's face was a mask of stoic calm, but his eyes betrayed him. They'd picked up the shimmering gray of his shirt, and the hurt rolled within like rain clouds in a storm. Beautiful, and powerful, and so sad it made Yasmin's heart break. Mason had trusted her, and she hadn't trusted him back.

Why did her mind always spin stories? Why couldn't she ever give people the benefit of the doubt?

But this was different.

Maybe Mason didn't steal the fire, but someone in his family did.

And he had no idea.

"I want to help you," Yasmin whispered. She meant it. "But in my palm—"

The last part of her sentence was lost to the wind as Mason's wings unfurled, solid sunshine in the center of a gray street.

Yasmin's breath caught. Words vanished from her

mind. Would she ever get used to seeing something so stunning?

"Good." Mason wrapped his arms around her waist and pulled her toward him. Her body pressed against his muscles. His head bent; his lips tickled her ear. "Because I desperately need you to."

His whisper quivered with a sadness he usually hid. The rawness of his voice, soft against her skin, made Yasmin forget the information she'd been about to provide. She released the blue wisp, hoping it might escape as she wrapped her arms around Mason's neck. Her fingers locked over the armored ridges of his spine as his wings swept the air into a frenzy around them.

Yasmin sank against his chest as they rose. Her heart pounded; her body grew hot. Too hot.

The wisp hadn't left. It zipped about beneath her dress, matching the pounding of her heart.

Does it want to stay with me? Or is it trying to return to its owner?

Yasmin didn't know, and she wasn't sure it mattered. How could she be Mason's alibi, if she got caught transporting the very thing he was accused of stealing?

———

A gray-scaled dragon with a silver spear guarded a circular gate carved high in the stone.

Mason gave their names. "We have an appointment with Eli Drage."

"Ah yes, the woodswitch." The guard's nostrils flared as he appraised Yasmin. "Got anything in your sleeve?"

Just your boss' stolen fire.

The wisp shrank into the curve of her elbow, heat

sinking into her skin as though it wanted to hide within her.

Yasmin held her chin up. Mason had taught her how to answer. "I'd be a fool to meet dragons if I didn't."

Boldly admitting that she was hiding magic in her sleeves felt like announcing that she'd smuggled a gun in her backpack. But the rules of weaponry were different among Castors. In many cases, their defenses were built into their species. A dragon couldn't put their fire aside any more than a werewolf could forgo their strength. Most witches refused to meet without protections of their own in place.

The guard grunted, slipped a key from his pocket, unlatched the iron gate, and admitted them to the compound.

———

The Drages' property made Mason's home look like a shack. Bright green lawn, brilliant flowers, and carved topiary bushes stretched the entirety of a block. In its center, a blue and white mansion, with sprawling terraces and high towers, rose toward the sky. Its spires were ten feet higher than the surrounding walls, yet the house had been invisible from the street.

Striking as the manor was, however, it was the many Castors who caught Yasmin's eye.

A pair of yellow-skinned men in suits and ties argued near the edge of a pathway. A woman with vines on her skin and butterflies in her braids poured water onto a bed of hydrangeas. A blond boy, about Hassan's age, raced across the grass, pointing toward a giant brown rabbit.

A thin elf in a tuxedo chased him. "Master Jack, I must implore you—"

"I'm not going to eat him, Nigel." The boy unfurled a pair of scaled, sapphire wings. "He's for my magic trick."

The rabbit disappeared into a row of hedges, followed by the boy, who was followed by the elf.

What kind of magic tricks would a dragon perform?

Yasmin might've pursued as well just to find out, but she didn't think their escort would approve.

Two bipedal dragons, dressed in silver uniforms, flanked either side of her and Mason. They'd introduced themselves in gruff barks as Jim and Jarl. The former was taller, with a larger nose and paler skin, while the latter bore a thin face and long limbs at odds with his muscular physique. Both dragons displayed similar moss-green wings, spiked tails, and disinterested scowls.

Despite the blatant magic on display, Yasmin's mind remained clear. Except when she glanced at Mason.

The sunlight danced on his scales, soaking into the rich yellow gold. Even folded, Mason's wings held a hypnotic, otherworldly beauty. Staring at them should've burned her retinas. Instead, they made Yasmin worry she'd lived in darkness her whole life and could only now see. She wanted to run her fingers over the scales, feel the warmth and power of sunshine made solid.

Heat fluttered against Yasmin's chest, stronger and more intense than her usual flush. She used her sleeve to hide the flicker of blue in her cleavage as the wisp pulsed in time to her heart. Was it reacting to her attraction?

That would be embarrassing. And bizarre.

Why would it react to my emotions?

The wisp hummed against her skin in response. Only,

the sound wasn't external. It resonated inside her chest and buzzed in her mind.

Mason nudged her. He flicked his eyes toward a burning topiary bush a few feet to their right. A man stood before it, staring at the plant through dancing orange flames. Blackened leaves curled, crumbling to ashes as the fire diminished.

Yasmin's eyes widened, unable to hide her shock. What remained of the greenery had been shaped into a dragon.

"That's my dad," Mason said.

The man turned, and Yasmin saw the resemblance: same light eyes, natural tan, good bone structure, even the scales of his wings glinted a similar yellow. But when Lawrence spotted them, there was no smile—crooked or full of teeth. He nodded and returned to his hedges.

"He has excellent control of his fire. And an artistic eye." Mason chuckled nervously as Jarl and Jim opened the manor's doors. "Neither of which I inherited."

"No, but you're beating me in AP Calculus," Yasmin whispered, drawing toward him on instinct and covering the wisp as she did. "That's more impressive."

———

"You two are early," Jarl informed them as they entered a massive chamber. Light flooded a blue satin chair, raised on a dais near the far wall. "You'll have to wait." He pointed his spear toward a series of benches arranged to face the seat, then positioned himself at the door with Jim.

Yasmin followed Mason down the carpeted aisle. The wisp stopped spinning. Its heat crept up her side, beneath her armpit, and down her sleeve, until it zipped out from beneath the fabric.

What are you doing? You can't be seen!

Yasmin didn't dare speak to the wisp aloud. Instead, she tried to catch it in her palm, but the wisp slipped through her fingers to balance on her skin. It tapped the back of her hand, and small blue sparks flew free. They drifted toward the door despite the lack of wind.

The wisp's hum changed, still nervous, but with a new hint of determination.

And somehow, Yasmin understood.

There's something in this mansion that it wants me to find.

33
MASON

The Drages' waiting chamber resembled a throne room. Stained glass great dragons flew along the walls, bewitched to reflect a nonexistent sun. Between rows of benches, a white carpet ran toward a three-foot high dais of carved white marble. Atop, a blue padded chair displayed a silver back, designed to mimic the leaping flames of a massive fire.

Mason shuffled onto a wooden bench. Whatever audience visited this chamber, the Drages cared little for their comfort. "You'd think given the display of wealth they could have sprung for cushions," he mumbled as he inched across, making room for Yasmin beside him.

She didn't sit. "How long do we have before Eli arrives, do you think?"

"About thirty minutes," Mason guessed. "Assuming he's ready to meet with us at four." Sometimes, the wealthy liked to keep their guests waiting, remind them who was in charge.

Mason scratched his throat. Despite the space, the room felt stifling. He rolled his shoulders, letting his wings flex.

Yasmin's eyes flicked toward his back. Something blue fluttered by her chest.

Or did Mason imagine that?

Her hand blocked whatever it was before he could see.

"I'll be back." Yasmin spun on her heels, steps brisk as she marched toward the door.

What the hell? Where was she going? Had she changed her mind about being Mason's alibi again?

She's going to get me arrested.

Mason didn't understand. Yasmin had been excited to pretend to be a woodswitch and confront Eli yesterday. What changed?

Chest tight, Mason jumped from the bench. His longer stride and faster speed allowed him to catch Yasmin as she reached the guards.

"You're not wandering through this property alone, witch," Jarl said, adjusting the grip on his spear. "If you need the bathroom, you'll have to wait for another two guards to come and escort you."

"That's utterly ridiculous." Yasmin waved her left hand in protest, her right hung still at her side. "Just let me walk by myself if you can't split up. Or would you rather my dress be soaked with urine when your boss comes."

Something blue flickered against the back of her neck, its glow just visible through her hair.

I'm not imagining it.

There was no doubting that the source of the light was magic. But what magic hovered near humans? Was it a spell his father didn't know about—placed by the Drages to identify intruders? An effect of the perfume? Some other magic Yasmin had taken from The Portentous Purveyor?

"How about all four of us take a trip to the bathroom?" Jim offered.

"Too late. Do you smell that?" Yasmin's right hand twitched in her sleeve.

Oh no, don't tell me she's—

Twinkling blue powder rose like pollen on the wind. Mason held his breath. The guards were less observant.

"I don't smell—" Jarl's voice cut off as he inhaled the powder. His eyes drooped, and he fell face first onto the floor. Jim collapsed a split second after.

"Burning shit, Yasmin," Mason grabbed her arm, pulling her away from the toppling guards. "Are you insane? You can't attack them. How is that going to look to Eli?"

"I don't know. I'm sorry," Yasmin pushed her hair back. "But they weren't going to let me leave, and I have to find something."

"Excuse me?" She was making no sense.

The light flew from behind Yasmin's neck into the open. And Mason's heart leaped into his chest. A chill, cold enough to quash any heat in stomach, shot through him.

A ball of fire hovered beside Yasmin. Shades of blue twisted in its flames—deep sapphire, soft periwinkle, bright cobalt.

Mason's tongue felt like sandpaper as it flicked across his lips. He pointed at the fireball. "What is that?"

"What do you think it is?" Yasmin snapped, but her tone was more anxious than angry.

Blue dragon fire.

No, worse. Something that *looked* like blue dragon fire. Otherwise, it would be latching onto something and burning.

The blue light flew to the door then back again. It tapped Yasmin's shoulder and shot sparks toward the exit.

"It wants me to follow." Yasmin shook free of Mason's grip.

"Does it?" Cold sweat dripped down Mason's temples. "The fireball is speaking to you?" He wanted the comment to be a joke. This was absurd.

Yasmin didn't laugh.

Oh shit.

This was not how Mason's meeting with Eli was supposed to go. His biggest concern was Yasmin being outed as a human. It hadn't occurred to him that she might bring the stolen item onto the property with her.

Maybe she didn't. Maybe that's not the stolen flame. Maybe this whole thing is a test that the Drages have to see how their guests respond.

The wealthy could be eccentric.

Mason clung to that tenuous hope as he followed Yasmin into the massive hallway.

"You don't have to come," she whispered.

"Oh no? Fantastic, I'll let you sneak around the mansion and get caught by yourself," Mason hissed, following her as she turned in the opposite direction to how they'd entered.

The fireball led them deeper into the building, hiding beneath Yasmin's sleeve whenever a servant passed. Mason flexed his wings at the few who glanced their way.

At least if we get caught it'll prove my innocence. I'm not good enough at sneaking around to rob a place like this.

Except that none of the servants sounded the alarm. Either Mason was better at blending in that he thought, or the Drages' workers were accustomed to strangers moving through the halls.

. . .

They arrived at a dark staircase that wound deep into the earth. The fireball buzzed and flitted ahead, bouncing with an agitated eagerness.

Burn it. Now I'm interpreting it.

Fire didn't have emotions. Nor did it communicate. It wasn't alive.

Yasmin was quicker to follow, which meant they descended into the darkness with her at the lead. Mason didn't like that. Whether she refused to be his alibi or not, he'd brought Yasmin into this. He had to keep her safe. The twisting staircase must have been the one narrow passage in the Drages' home. If something dangerous waited at the bottom, it would be difficult to jump in front and protect her.

When his father mentioned the Drages eating humans, Mason had laughed it off as Lawrence's dark sense of humor. What if the warning had been real? What if this wisp was leading Yasmin toward a giant cooking pot where servants stewed human meat?

Mason swallowed. "Yasmin, where exactly did this flame come from?"

"I think we're about to find out."

A massive steel door waited at the bottom of the steps. Clamped around its handle was a heavy padlock with no hole for a key.

Firelock.

The enchanted defense system was popular among wealthy dragons. Witches used a mixture of potions and enchantments to calibrate the metal so that it required a specific flame to open—not dissimilar to the fingerprint scanner humans utilized.

The fireball charged toward the lock, growing larger. It consumed the metal. And the lock melted.

Mason's eyes widened. That wasn't—Firelocks couldn't be burned away. That was the whole point. How had it—?

Before Mason could think of an explanation, Yasmin pushed open the door.

34
YASMIN

Another dark corridor twisted before them. The wisp hovered before Yasmin. Its soft blue light guided her through the cool, damp stones. Despite the lack of stairs, she sensed they were descending deeper into the earth. But the further they went, the warmer the air grew.

"Yasmin, what if Eli finds us snooping around his property?" Mason whispered, worry evident in his voice.

He had a point, but colors flickered on the walls ahead. The wisp's hum grew excited. This was what it wanted Yasmin to see.

She brushed Mason off. "We'll think of something."

A sharp turn brought them to the source of the light. The end of the corridor opened into a dome-like cave, burned from the surrounding earth and etched with strange runes. In its center, a massive gold chalice provided the hearth for a blaze of colors. Wisps of fire swirled together, casting the symbols on the walls in an array of hues—deep reds, bright whites, somber grays, soft lilacs, forest greens.

A thousand soft hums spread from the tiny flames, slow and sad like death itself.

Tears rose in Yasmin's eyes. Her body trembled as a silent sob caught in her throat.

The blue wisp reverberated with the same sad tune, beckoning Yasmin to follow as it approached the blaze.

What is this place? Why do I feel like this fire is calling to me? Like it wants to tell me something.

Yasmin lifted her hand toward the wisps.

"Stop!" Mason rushed forward. "Don't touch—"

But it was too late, Yasmin's fingers brushed the edges of the flames. Yellow sparks trailed up her hand, disappearing beneath her sleeve.

Mason pulled her away. "Are you crazy? You don't know what that could do." He took her right hand in his, brushing aside the sleeve to inspect her skin. His eyes—a hundred shades in the iridescent light—widened. "It didn't burn you."

"I don't think it's fire," Yasmin whispered. Her chest felt too heavy to raise her voice. The mournful hum filled her mind. By her shoulder, the blue wisp shivered. It kept its distance from the rest of the blaze as though afraid to approach and be consumed.

"It is. Or at least, it used to be." Mason's voice was as soft as her own, his eyes still on her hand. "The scent is like dragon fire, but wrong somehow. Fleshy, alive. Maybe even human." He dropped her hand and stepped away, head tilting back as he studied the room. Shadows and firelight danced across his face. "This is a potions den. For witches. The Drages must've had them alter the flame somehow. But why? What does it do?"

Excellent questions.

Mason would make a good investigative reporter himself.

"I think it's trying to tell us," Yasmin said, watching the colors twist. "Can you hear it?"

"No. What's it saying?"

"I don't know. But it's sad and scared. There's something it wants me to know."

"Tell it to talk fast then. We need to get back to that waiting room before Eli realizes we're missing."

Mason was right.

Yasmin closed her eyes, listening to the hum and letting the emotions within fill her chest: sadness, loss, the faintest tremble of hope. Then, panic overtook her. The blue wisp slipped down the back of her dress, trembling in the indent of her spine.

A warning.

Yasmin grabbed Mason's hand. "We need to go. I think someone—"

Before she could finish her sentence, a man's voice interrupted, "What fresh level of incompetence is this?"

35
MASON

"How could you all forget the firelock?" Eli's frustration echoed through the corridor. He must've been by the door they'd entered through.

Shit. This is not good.

At the sound of Eli's voice, the blue fireball ducked beneath Yasmin's sleeve. Mason's hand flinched away for a moment before he caught himself and grabbed her again, pulling her close.

"Eli's going to find us," he whispered, leaning so close to her ear that his lips brushed her skin. "We need to find another way out of here."

Yasmin shook her head. "There isn't one."

"How could you—?" Mason started to argue, but he could see the certainty on her face.

Flaming hell! She'd asked the fireballs somehow, hadn't she?

A pair of voices responded to Eli. Their answers came like muffled echoes through the corridor. Both seemed to be trying to pass the blame.

Mason couldn't afford to worry about which servant would be reprimanded unfairly. If he and Yasmin couldn't run, then they needed to hide. But the curved walls provided no corners to duck behind, and the human-scented fireballs illuminated the entirety of the space. They couldn't even find cower in some shadows and pray.

Eli's footsteps, and those of his companions, reverberated through the corridor. In less than a minute, he would discover Mason and Yasmin at the scene of the crime. What good would an alibi be then? Eli would probably assume they'd come back to steal more of his strange flames.

Unless I can give him another reason.

Why would two teenagers have snuck down a dark flight of steps and nosed their way into an obviously private, secluded area? Mason could think of only one reason. Yasmin wouldn't like it.

Mason took her wrists and spun her around, pressing her to the wall so that their eyes met. Her cheeks flushed at their closeness.

Yeah, she's really going to hate this.

But Mason couldn't think of anything else, so he whispered, "Kiss me."

36
YASMIN

Heat flushed through Yasmin. Shades of blue flashed like lightning in Mason's eyes. His face was mere inches away.

Was he playing a joke on her? Now of all times! Or was he serious?

"Unless you can think of a better reason for us to have snuck in here," Mason whispered.

Oh! Of course that was why he was suggesting it. He didn't *want* to kiss her. He was looking for another alibi.

"No way!" Yasmin whispered and shook her head. It was a terrible idea! No one would believe they'd snuck away just to make-out.

Or maybe they would.

Yasmin once caught her sister making out with a boy in one of the storage rooms in their building's garage.

But, surely, she could think of something better.

The footsteps grew louder. Mason hadn't moved away.

Yasmin's heart pounded. Heat rose to her chest. She was certain that she could have come up with a better excuse, except that she couldn't think with his lips so close.

"You do it then," Yasmin whispered.

Mason's eyebrow rose. He must've thought it was hilarious that just the thought of kissing him had her half-immobilized. But Yasmin had never initiated a kiss before.

Luckily, Mason didn't have time to tease her. His fingers brushed against her cheek, softer than she'd expected. He tucked a stray piece of hair behind Yasmin's ear, then tilted her chin up.

It's just a kiss. You're acting. It doesn't mean anything.

Yasmin closed her eyes as Mason's mouth pressed against hers, soft and gentle. She copied his movements, tasting his lips as they slipped between her own. She hadn't expected to enjoy the flavor of him—sweet, smoky.

Mason's thumb traced her cheek, fingers sliding between her hair. His other hand slipped around her waist, pressing her hips toward him.

The fire against Yasmin's chest grew hotter, her heart wilder.

Her hand roamed over his chest, feeling the muscles beneath his shirt. Her other arm wrapped around his neck, and her fingers brushed the skin on the inside of his folded wings.

Mason's body trembled against her. His hand tightened in her hair, pulling Yasmin closer. For a split second, their kiss deepened. Yasmin moaned against his lips.

"Ahem!" A sudden loud cough crashed Yasmin back to their present situation.

Mason broke their kiss and stepped away. Breathless and overheated, Yasmin stumbled back, body supported by the wall. The wisp hummed in delight against her chest.

Or perhaps, Yasmin's mind was the source of the emotion, and the fire was only imitating it.

No, no, no. I did not enjoy that!

It was a meaningless kiss. A performance. For an audience that Yasmin had somehow forgotten about.

Three dragons stood at the entrance to the dome-like room. It was easy to identify Eli Drage among them. Though he stood a head shorter than his two gray-winged guards, there was something lethal to his movements as he stepped toward them. He seemed as likely to strike as to laugh.

"You're in a relationship with your alibi?" Eli's expression remained unreadable, but his tone had settled on amusement.

Mason rolled his shoulders. His scales shot twinkles of gold across the walls so that he appeared to be standing in a storm of falling stars. It highlighted the sharp lines of his jaw and the curve of his lips. They'd been so soft and smoky, and he'd felt—

"We're not into labels," Mason said.

Seriously? Yasmin wasn't good enough to even be his *fake* girlfriend?

"Or common courtesy," Eli noted, lifting an eyebrow and surveying their location. "Do you make a habit of escaping guards and snooping around the homes of your hosts?"

Yasmin didn't think he would've appreciated if she'd answered that honestly.

"We're so sorry, Eli," Mason said hurriedly. "We shouldn't have left the meeting room. Or knocked out your guards. That was stupid, and reckless, and—"

Eli lifted his hand, cutting Mason off. "Whose idea was it?"

The wisp shrank against Yasmin's skin. It crept deeper into her dress, as though hoping to hide beneath her armpit.

"Mine," Yasmin answered before Mason could. She stretched to her full height, crossed her arms, and stepped forward. The bolder she acted, the less suspicious it would seem.

At least, Yasmin hoped so. Both Mason and the wisp were depending on her now.

"Oh?" Eli's lips curved, and his eyes trailed over Yasmin in a manner that made her skin crawl. She'd seen boys give her sister the same look before. It usually meant they were picturing—Wait! What did he think she was admitting to? He'd only caught them kissing.

Although would two teenagers have gone to so much trouble just to make out?

"No, we weren't—That's not why—" Yasmin wished the wisp would keep its heat to itself instead of sharing it. She was certain her face was turning crimson. She needed to take control of this situation.

I am not a flustered human standing before a creature that could eat me.

Yasmin was a woodswitch, who was bold enough to knock out guards and sneak into obviously off-limit rooms. It was time to start acting like it.

37
MASON

"Why do you even have a potions den for us to sneak into?" Yasmin asked, tossing her hair over her shoulder and stepping forward. "It's a waste of effort for a family of dragons."

Mason's heart leaped into his chest. Was Yasmin insane or had he not impressed upon her that Eli could reduce her to ashes with a cough?

"If the witches mixing your fire told you they needed this set up, you should hire better people," Yasmin continued, sneering at the walls. "My mother didn't need anything this fancy to work magic."

Burn her, she could act. Mason almost believed her.

Eli definitely did. His eyebrows rose, expression immediately curious. "You know about mixing flames?"

"I know some of the theory," Yasmin's voice faltered for a second before she waved her hand. "I'm sure I could figure it out."

In a flash, Eli grabbed Yasmin's left wrist.

Mason moved to defend her, but luckily caught himself before a rash decision proved their undoing. Eli hadn't lashed out with the aim of hurting. Instead, he studied Yasmin's hand.

"Seems like you couldn't." A smile flickered over Eli's face. "Did you try to touch the fire?"

"Mason said it smelled different, and I thought..." Yasmin trailed off, casting her eyes to the floor.

Was she feigning embarrassment or struggling to think of an excuse? Either way, her crumbling confidence seemed to please Eli more than Mason's immediate acquiescence.

"It does have a curious scent," Eli agreed. "A prank played by my witches, I suspect. But it's just mixed dragon fire."

Then why are you so concerned that someone stole a piece?

A dangerous question.

"Should we go back upstairs?" Mason suggested instead. "I'm sure you have questions about where I was on Monday."

"No," Eli said. He crooked a finger, and his guards inched closer. "I doubt I'd get the truth without a great deal of coercion."

Shit. This is bad.

If Eli hadn't bought their excuse for being in the potions den, what could Mason do? Any physical altercation would be three-against-one. Terrible odds, and Mason's tail already set him at a disadvantage. Unlike Eli's massive spikes or his guards' blunted studs, Mason had no weapon-built into his form. Historically, the Wicks had been servants and craftsmen, not warriors.

Whatever happens, I need to get Yasmin out.

She was only here because of Mason. Perhaps he could trade his freedom for hers.

Or he could hand over the fireball that was hidden somewhere beneath her dress. Returning the stolen item would look suspicious, but it might be enough to earn Eli's forgiveness.

As if he could read Mason's thoughts, Eli held out his palm. But it wasn't the fireball he wanted. One of the guards passed him a clear bag. Mason caught a glimpse of yellow-orange dust within.

"Show me your scales."

Mason didn't question Eli's order. He turned and spread his wings as much as the room allowed.

"Three missing, boss," one of the guards said.

Suddenly, it clicked what was in the bag: a crumbling, molten scale. That's how Eli had narrowed down his suspects. Had the Serpents planted it at the scene of the crime or—?

"Would you say that color's the same?" Eli asked.

Over his shoulder, Mason could see the wealthy dragon holding the bag up to his guards. They squinted.

"Hard to tell in this light," one admitted.

"Obviously, it's not the same," Yasmin said, voice soft and breathy despite the unadvised boldness answering displayed. Her eyes flicked from Mason's wings to the bag of dust. "Can't you see the way the light dances on his scales? They glow. What you're holding is dull."

Burn it to ashes! Was Yasmin seriously arguing colors with Eli Drage?

"Molted scales always lose some of their shine."

"Do they lose their warmth? That color is approaching a cool orange. Mason's wings are—" Yasmin cut herself off, crossing her arms beneath her chest and turning away as though embarrassed.

Or because the fireball had gone to her chest again.

Shit. They were so screwed.

"Women certainly pay attention to the hue of your

wings, Mason," Eli said, lips twitching. He slipped the disintegrating scale into the pocket of his pants. "I believe your woodswitch is right. The scale isn't yours."

Wait, he believed them? Relief flooded Mason as he folded his wings But the sensation was short lived.

Something about this felt too easy.

"My name is cleared?" Mason clarified as he turned to Eli. "Yasmin and I are free to go?"

"My men will escort you and your woodswitch to the exit so that you don't go on any more *excursions*," Eli said. "But yes, you're free. Though I think I think I'll keep an eye on you going forward. I'm always on the lookout for talented. And we might want to employ your services you after all."

Mason's brow furrowed. Eli had wanted to imprison him yesterday. Now, he wanted to hire him. For what?

"That's nice of you to say, but I haven't got any talent," Mason said.

"Not many dragons can turn a stone house to ash. And we have such similar taste in friends. Choosing the right people is its own talent." Eli's eyes roved over Yasmin with a hunger that made Mason's jaw tense.

Can he smell that she's human?

No, that couldn't be it. The perfume worked. And when Eli's smile turned back to Mason, the hunger remained, a cold glint in his eyes as he said, "You would come highly recommended, Mr. Wick."

38
MASON

Mason's heartbeat pounded in his ears as they walked toward downtown. Instead of relishing the freedom, his mind spun, trying to hold onto a hundred thoughts at once.

Human-scented fire. A yellow-scaled thief. The stolen flame attached to Yasmin.

She said it called to her. How is that possible?

Mason tried to understand, but he only heard half of Yasmin's story about finding the fireball in the bathtub drain.

Why would Eli want to hire him? And why only now check the color of Mason's scales? Had Lawrence—?

Mason pushed the thought away. The only *recommendation* Eli could have been referring to was one from himself to his own father. Pyrrhus Drage would be in charge of hiring for their estate. And Eli had said they'd need to wait and see when Mason had pressed for an explanation.

I'm being paranoid and overanalyzing.

Eli probably just assumed that Mason shared

Lawrence's control and would be a master at sculpting hedges.

At the thought of gardens, the scent of roses tickled Mason's nose. His thoughts spiraled in a new direction, remembering Yasmin's lips pressed against his. He'd have been doomed if she hadn't agreed to kiss him. No scale could have exonerated Mason if he'd been found at the scene of the crime without an excuse.

Yasmin's hair had been soft beneath his palm, and her dress was like silk. His fingers had slid over her waist, and then she'd brushed the sensitive skin on the inside of his wings and—

What is wrong with me?

Mason shook his head, trying to concentrate on the present. His kiss with Yasmin had been the least significant thing to happen in the past hour.

"The Drages must be planning to use it for something," Yasmin continued speaking, unaware that her audience had been only half-listening. She stared at the fireball hovering in the curve of her palms, hidden from the view of other pedestrians. "Do you know what they want with you?"

Now she's talking to it.

The fireball flickered, scattering sparks. Mason flinched as they landed on Yasmin's skin. But she remained unbothered.

How could a human command fire? It wasn't fair.

"You should have returned it," Mason said, glancing at the cars on their left

"It didn't want to go back."

"Bit odd that it traveled all the way then. Why bother descending to the potions den if it was so scared?"

"Because it wanted to show me the others." There was a

defensive edge to Yasmin's voice. She stopped, and spun toward him, blocking the middle of the sidewalk.

A pair of girls stepped onto the road to race ahead of them.

Mason pushed the hair from his forehead, sighed, and did the same to avoid Yasmin. He didn't intend to argue over the motivations of a semi-sentient flame.

But Yasmin hadn't finished with their conversation. "We need to find out who stole it in the first place," she said, hurrying after him. "The suspects are obvious. But the motive is more complex."

"You're talking like we're detectives."

"Investigative reporters," Yasmin corrected him. "Now, you know your family better than I do. Who do you think stole it?"

Mason stopped as abruptly as if he'd slammed into a wall. "Excuse me?"

"Uncle Lee seems the most likely." Excitement lit Yasmin's eyes, and her fingers flitted before her as though she were scribbling notes in the air. "Or maybe Jeremiah. I almost forgot he lived with you too. He's the most suspicious, though we shouldn't rule out Kira or—"

"Yes, you should!" Kira and Comet had been at the park with him. Jeremiah hadn't left school. Uncle Lee was the opposite of a criminal. "Rule them all out. And then forget about any investigations. My name is cleared thanks to you..."

Kissing me.

"...being my alibi." Mason rolled his shoulders and resumed their journey. The traffic was evidence that they were almost downtown. Instead of waiting for the crosswalk light, he weaved through the lanes of unmoving cars.

"Oh come on. You're too clever to just let this go. Don't

you want to know why you're being framed?" Yasmin followed a few feet behind. Cars honked at her as their light turned green. She lifted the dress to run and almost lost her shoe.

Mason stopped beside a young maple that had been planted in a green square in the center of the sidewalk. Was he being framed? He'd been certain before, but now something felt off. If the Serpents wanted Mason convicted to the point they hid the stolen goods in his home, couldn't they have done better than an off-color scale?

"Look at the evidence," Yasmin continued. "The thief had your number. They knew what to say to get you to show up. They had access to your house. Occam's razor. The simplest solution—"

"Is that my family wouldn't frame me. So drop it. I'll help you with a different story if you want."

Yasmin pursed her lips. The fireball peeped out from her sleeve, traipsing over the fabric to climb onto her hand. She lifted her arm, bringing it between them.

Was that yellow flashing in the center of the blue?

"No, this is the story," Yasmin said, and the excitement that had animated her earlier took on a serious edge. "I thought it was about exposing magic, but it's about something different."

"I'm sorry." Mason must've misheard. "You thought it was about what?"

Yasmin squeaked and slapped her hand over her mouth. "I changed my mind. I know about the knights, and how dangerous humans can be now. I swear."

Her eyes were big. Beautiful. Sincere.

Coupled with the calming scent of roses, Mason might have managed to swallow the flames, rising in a spiral up his throat. Forgive and forget, another Ember Rise motto.

But Yasmin didn't stop. Her voice grew higher, faster, trembling with an eagerness she couldn't hide. "And I don't need to tell that story anyway. We've stumbled onto a better one: the mystery of these wisps."

She held the fireball up again. Too close.

"We have to find out the truth. Whoever stole it must know something. We just need to interview your family and—"

Mason shook his head. First, Yasmin admitted to wanting to reveal magic, then she accused his family of being criminals. He wanted to defend them, to chastise her for never thinking about the consequences of her stories.

But his eyes were glued to the yellow core at the center of the wisp. Bright flames, like the sun crashing to earth, licked at Mason's mind. Fire turned in his stomach. If it escaped, he couldn't control it. He would burn the entire street.

Including the girl before him.

"This story matters," Yasmin continued. "I can feel it, and—Are you okay?" She reached toward Mason. The fireball rode on her wrist.

"Stop!" Mason leaped back and turned away, covering his mouth before sparks could escape. He couldn't lose control. He needed her gone. The fireball as well. "We're done, Yasmin. Go home."

"But don't you want to solve the mystery?"

"No. I don't. And you can't." Mason sucked in air, then spoke fast, trying to drown his fire with words. "You're not a real witch, Yasmin. And you're not a real journalist. You're just a pain-in-the-ass who pries into people's business, and—"

A sob came from behind him. Yasmin's footsteps

pounded on the pavement. The scent of roses grew fainter as she fled.

I'm an asshole.

Mason clenched his jaw, inhaled through his nose, and glanced over his shoulder. Dark waves hid most of Yasmin's back. One arm bunched the fabric of her dress higher, the other stuck out at ninety degrees in an effort to keep her balance. Even for a human, she was slow.

Mason didn't pursue.

Yasmin wanted a story. She wanted to catch the thief.

Mason didn't. Because he suspected Yasmin was right. Someone in his family had stolen from the Drages. And deep down, Mason knew who.

39
YASMIN

Heat pulsed against Yasmin's chest as her pen moved across the page. The wisp echoed her emotions back to her: excited, scared, annoyed.

Stupid Mason.

Yasmin had heard people mock and doubt her hundreds of times. No comment had hurt as much Mason's own. Forget forcing a smile. Yasmin hadn't even been able to stop her tears.

She'd fled before Mason could see them. But even as she'd sat shaking on the subway, she'd hoped he'd appear. It didn't matter that the stupid mascara she'd borrowed was running. She'd wanted Mason to follow her.

Why? So he would apologize, or keep yelling, or...

Kiss me again?

Yasmin reached that moment in her rewriting of the day, spared no detail in her notes. She wanted it all recorded.

Beneath the blue t-shirt she'd changed into, the wisp grew increasingly hot. The heat spread through Yasmin with every word she added to her page. It wasn't anger. It was longing.

Despite her very real desire not to, Yasmin had fallen for Mason Wick.

"I have a magic fire, and I'm sad because I had a fight with a boy." Yasmin buried her face in her notebook and collapsed backward onto her pillows. "This really is my lowest moment."

The wisp's hum reverberated through her. Somehow, it managed to feel both conciliatory and amused.

Yasmin peeped out from behind her notebook and found the blue light hovering in the air above her. She sat up.

"I am going to figure out what your story is. Even if Mason thinks—" Yasmin's tears returned without invitation. "Why did I tell him that I wanted to expose magic? Or keep insisting it was one of his family members who stole you? Of course he lashed out. I'm such an idiot."

Now, instead of gaining an annoyingly attractive and impressively observant investigative partner, Yasmin had alienated Mason.

Fine. So what? She'd always investigated on her own.

The wisp nuzzled against the crook of her neck. Its warmth turned soothing.

Yasmin's lips twitched into a slight smile. "Sorry, I did get a partner."

She raised a finger, and the wisp flew to perch on the tip of her nail. She raised another. The fire bounced onto it.

"Are you following my movements?"

Yasmin experimented, holding out her left hand. The flame zipped onto her palm. With another gesture, she summoned it back to her right. She pointed behind her neck, twitched her eyes up into the air, rolled her arm to signal a spiral. Each time the wisp followed the silent commands.

She'd just twitched her shoulders, summoning it between her shoulder blades. Amazing. If Mason could see—

Hassan burst into the room. "Baba wants your help."

"Do you understand the concept of knocking?"

"Do you understand the concept of locking your door?" Hassan fired back. His eyes landed on the sunflower notebook. "Didn't your last story cost you your blog. You should seriously give up."

Yasmin slammed the notebook shut. Mason's name was all over those pages. "What does Baba want, Hassan?"

"He can't figure out how to set up the new microwave."

"He's an electrician."

"Yeah, we plugged it in. But you're the one who pestered him into buying a new one. Come figure out the settings."

Hassan had fried the Guls' previous microwave by attempting to heat foil. Their father swore he could fix it, but three months had passed with little proof. Maybe Yasmin's reminders had been frequent, but she hadn't *pestered* anyone. They'd needed a new microwave.

It didn't make sense to argue.

Yasmin sighed, rested her notebook on the bed, and stomped to her feet.

"Nima messaged too," Hassan informed her as they walked down the passageway. "She says you're ignoring her, and you're going to regret it. She got a new boyfriend too."

Of course she did. Yasmin rolled her eyes at the threat. "Wow. Lucky number seven."

"Don't be jealous just cause you can't get one."

That stung a little too much at present.

Yasmin shoved her brother, causing him to stumble into the living area. His attempts to trip her in revenge failed as they walked toward their father.

Amir sat at a small round table, which just fit in the center of the claustrophobic kitchen. A refrigerator was crammed in one corner, while an after-thought of an oven jutted out to impede the doorway. Both appliances had once been white.

"I got saffron chicken and rice for dinner." Amir waved a plastic bag full of takeaway containers. "But we need to heat it. And since you have a brand-new microwave..." He pointed to the single silver appliance in the center of the counter. "You're welcome."

Am I supposed to thank him for making me heat up dinner?

Yasmin took the chicken and rice out of the containers, portioning the food onto microwaveable plates.

Hassan grabbed the other chair, squashing into the kitchen so there was no room for anyone to move. He and Amir struck up a conversation about a recent football match, studying the statistics on their phone.

Yasmin would have to squeeze past them to reach the microwave.

Do they even remember that I'm here?

She wanted to scream at her family. The anger burned against her stomach.

No, that was the wisp.

Checking that neither her brother nor father were watching, Yasmin lifted her hand. The wisp zipped upward, and out through her sleeve, following the gesture just like it had before.

A smile spread across Yasmin's face.

Forget using the microwave. She had something better.

40

MASON

Mason hefted a large shopping bag over his shoulder. Bolts of fabric poked through, stuck between heart-shaped cushions. Instead of sleeping in on Sunday—or celebrating his now cleared name—Mason had been sent to purchase supplies. The house needed fixing.

Beside him, Kira carried paint samples, a rug, and a heart-shaped picture frame she'd insisted Uncle Lee would love. Jeremiah struggled beneath two inflatable mattresses that would be their beds until the new ones arrived. Comet trotted at their feet in the form of a Corgi, holding a pink squeaky ball between his jaws. His previous one had been popped and deflated by Lieutenant Brager.

"I still think you could carry more," Kira noted, narrowing her eyes at Comet's wiggling rear end. "No one's going to see a dog dragging a shopping bag and assume you're a dragon in disguise."

Comet grunted in objection.

But Kira wasn't wrong.

Humans loved to latch onto the easiest explanation.

Unless they're wannabe reporters with too much curiosity.

Mason hadn't heard from Yasmin since she'd run off yesterday—not a single message. Insults had never dampened her eternal quest for information before. Why had she gone silent now?

And why did it bother him so much?

Yasmin had treated his family like suspects in a game of Clue. Was it Uncle Lee in the potions den with a spell book, or Jeremiah in the bathroom with a stolen flame?

She'd also kissed Mason when it counted. And defended him to Eli.

And she found the stolen flame.

"Have you guys ever heard of the Serpents committing a robbery?" Mason asked, kicking a pebble with his shoe.

Jeremiah sighed. "Why are we still talking about the Drages?"

Kira's eyebrows rose. "You think the Serpents robbed the Drages? No way! They're too important. Secret organizations don't go around stealing from powerful people with connections to the police."

"Criminal organization," Mason corrected her. But *criminal* and *secret* weren't mutually exclusive. A high-profile robbery wasn't the Serpents typical MO. Though, given the curious nature of the Drages' fire, perhaps they'd made an exception.

Mason stopped a few feet shy of the turn to their house. "What would you do with a fire that didn't burn?"

The others turned to look at him. Comet's corgi-head tilted to the side.

"Is that a riddle?" Kira guessed. "Ooh, would you set Yasmin's world on fire but make sure she never burns away from you?"

Mason swung the shopping bag at his sister. "That is an offensively bad joke."

Kira dodged easily and raced ahead laughing. Comet went with her, but Jeremiah slunk closer to Mason.

"Tell me you're wiping Gul's mind on Monday," he whispered.

Mason stumbled over an uneven slab in the sidewalk. He'd promised Yasmin she could learn about magic in exchange for the alibi. It hadn't crossed his mind to betray their agreement.

I could though. She was going to break it.

Yasmin had intended to expose the existence of magic to the human world. That violated her initial promise. Mason should want to wipe her memories. It would absolve him of any breach of secrecy.

But Yasmin would forget everything. Their trip to The Portentous Purveyor. Their day downtown after. Their kiss.

Mason rolled his shoulders. "She's nicer than you think, Jere."

"Tell me you're joking."

"I know she asks a lot of questions, but she's kind of brilliant."

Yasmin had molded herself into the persona of a witch in less than a week. An enchanted fire had attached to her, and instead of panicking, she'd wanted to help it.

And her theory about the thief—

Mason pushed away the thought. But it returned in full force the moment he rounded the hedges onto their property.

Uncle Lee held the door open, waving Kira and Comet in. There was someone else with them—Lawrence Wick. He disappeared into the manor.

Mason jogged forward, dropped the shopping bag by Uncle Lee's feet, and turned toward the hallway.

Please, let me be wrong.

"Where is he?"

"Guest bathroom," Uncle Lee said. "You can have two minutes but come find us in the garden. We have to weed..."

Mason didn't hear what chore the fairy had planned. He'd already taken off.

41
MASON

"Occupied," Lawrence's voice called over the sound of running water.

Mason rattled the knob, jaw clenched. The taste of smoke pressed against his tongue, and gray coils slipped between his teeth. He needed to get control, but fury and panic coursed through him in equal measure.

I went to him for help, and he said nothing.

Mason slammed his fist against the door. "Let me in before I burn it down."

For once, it wasn't an empty threat.

Lawrence muttered a string of curses. The tap went silent. He opened the door. Despite the bathroom's lack of towels, his hands were dry. Fear burned in his eyes. "Kid, I'm not in the—"

Mason didn't let his father finish. He pushed his way into the bathroom and slammed the door. Smoke hissed through his teeth. "Missing something?"

Realization flashed across Lawrence's face. He glanced at the drain. His jaw tensed, just like Mason's did when he was holding back anger. "What did you do?"

"What did *I* do?" Fire licked Mason's inside. He almost laughed at the absurdity of the question. "You stole from the Drages. You hid their fire here. Did you not think—Did you not care how that could've affected me?" Yellow and gold sparks flew from Mason's tongue. He couldn't stop them. "I almost took the fall for you!"

Fire barreled up Mason's throat. It escaped in a jet of golden light straight toward his father.

Lawrence winced as the flames hit, but dragons were fireproof. The rest of the room was not. The shower curtain exploded into a wall of flames. Golden sparks leaped free igniting the toilet paper and whatever garbage had been in the bin.

Shit, I didn't mean to—This is bad.

Smoke twisted through the rich yellows. Mason's eyes burned. It felt like staring directly into the sun. He slammed his mouth shut, blocking the escape of further flames.

"Damn kid." Lawrence dabbed his forehead. Dragons couldn't burn, but they could feel heat. "One decent thing your mother did was pass on that raw strength."

I have to put it out.

Mason searched his mind for some semblance of a connection. It was his fire. He should be able to mentally grab hold, gain control. But it was like grappling with a snake covered in slime. Each time Mason's mind brushed against them, and he issued a command, they slipped free, haunting him with memories. The dead screamed in Mason's ears. Pain shook his limbs. He trembled.

Everything is fine. Everything is fine.

The yellow flames grew larger, more out of control, licking the edges of the bathtub, the corner of the sink. Ceramic bubbled threatening to melt.

What if Lee and Jeremiah were back inside? Mason

couldn't let his new foster family go the way of the old. Desperate, he searched the smoke for the tap. Maybe if he took a sip, it might soothe—

"What are you doing? Didn't they teach you anything in that damned reformatory?" Lawrence shoved him away. "Water won't help. Only fire beats fire."

Lawrence exhaled a controlled wave of dark orange flames. They spread through the bathroom, consuming Mason's blaze. For a second, everything burned. Then, with the clench of his fist, Lawrence quashed it.

Ashes dusted the floor where the toilet paper roll had been. Melted ceramic solidified in a waterfall along the tub.

Mason didn't dare exhale. The heat remained within him, turning as he stared at his father. His anger had given way to pure, raw terror. There was so much he needed to ask, but he couldn't speak.

Lawrence clamped his hand over his son's mouth, and shoved Mason against the wall. "You know what your problem has always been, kid? You're too sensitive. Everything comes down to emotions. You're an adult now. Grow up and use your brain."

He rapped the side of Mason's head.

"Hiding it here wasn't personal. Just convenient. whatever conspiracy you've concocted, I'm not dumb enough to make my own son a patsy. I went to a lot of effort to get a doppelganger spell from Douglas so I had an airtight alibi. I didn't think the Drages would look at you in a million years."

Mason squirmed beneath his father's grip. He hated having his mouth covered.

"So maybe I'm not father of the year. But I stuck around. That's more than your bitch of a mother did. I had to raise you alone. You know how much that cost me? The universe owes me. You owe me. And that flame is my ticket out of this city. So where the hell is it?" Lawrence slammed the wall beside Mason's head. One of the tiles fell loose.

Mason pushed his father back and gasped. The sudden intake of air chilled his lungs. He tried to push that coolness into his stomach.

"The flame's gone. I released it."

Lawrence shook his head. "You're lying. You wouldn't do something so stupid." When Mason didn't rush to admit otherwise, the fear returned to Lawrence's eyes. His jaw shook. "No, you can't have—do you have any idea—I've got debts."

Of course, that's what his father was worried about.

"I got rid of the fire you left with Douglas," Mason said. A wave of self-loathing fanned the sparks in his stomach once more. He'd recognized his father's flame in that tube the moment he saw it. That's why he hadn't made Yasmin return it, why he'd encouraged her to get rid of it. But he'd refused to acknowledge it because, deep down, he'd known if his father was trading in dragon fire for magic he couldn't afford, Lawrence was up to his old tricks.

And his debts weren't only to Douglas.

"Why did you steal the flame?" Mason asked. "Did the Serpents order you to?"

His father was still in their debt. He wouldn't refuse.

Lawrence leaned back on his heels, his head tilted toward the ceiling, and he loosed a low, wheezing laugh until tears pooled in his eyes.

"You really are an idiot, know that?" He wiped one of the tears, shaking his head as he turned back to Mason. "I wasn't following Serpent orders. I was stealing from them."

Mason's brow furrowed. Did his father mean—

"The Drages didn't take me in out kindness. Working

for them has been part of repaying my debt. The Drages are the head of the Serpent, and that flame ain't dragon fire. It's a weapon. Worth an intoxicating amount to the wrong people. And you just released it into city. You better hope it burns itself out quick, or you're going to have a lot more deaths to answer for, kid."

The words slammed into Mason like a punch to the gut.

If his father was telling the truth, then that meant—No. Mason couldn't let anyone else burn.

42
YASMIN

Yasmin directed the wisp's movement across a frozen package of chicken sausages. Water dripped down the plastic. Boiling would've been faster.

But this wasn't about speed. Yasmin was learning.

Why won't you burn anything?

It had been the same yesterday when she tried to use the wisp instead of the microwave. Yasmin had warmed only a drumstick before her father accused her of wasting time.

Her father's tablet rang on the counter, the obnoxious trill of an incoming video call. Nima's image appeared on the screen, and Yasmin's concentration slipped.

The wisp zipped from the sausages to the tablet.

The ringing stopped. Then, Nima tried again.

Stifling a groan, Yasmin grabbed the tablet and answered.

Nima's face popped onto the screen—brown eyes made massive with eyeliner, lips painted a dark red. She looked like if someone had drawn Yasmin with sharper lines and a larger nose. Her hair hung in manufactured waves just above her bare shoulders. Her background showed a sea of purple pillows.

"Baba's out on a job," Yasmin said, adjusting her braid to hide the wisp, which had settled against her neck. It peeped out at the screen. "Call back later."

"No, wait!" Nima brought the screen closer to her face. A silver stud glistened in her nose. "How are you?"

"Busy. I'm working."

Nima scoffed. "You're in the kitchen. You haven't brought a book in there since Hassan smeared mustard on your math homework when you were twelve." She raised her screen, likely searching for her best angle. "Listen, I really was hoping we could talk. I need a favor—"

"Is that Nima?" Hassan bounded into the kitchen. Whatever sports game he'd been watching continued to blare from the television. "Let me talk to her."

Hassan pushed his way through the narrow space between counter and table, nearly knocking over one of the chairs in his rush to shove his face in front of the screen. He wrapped his arm around Yasmin's shoulder, pinning her in place. "Guess who has a crush on Mason Wick?"

Yasmin froze. The video showed the flush spreading from her chest up to her cheeks. How did he—?

"She's writing fanfic about him in her diary." Hassan pointed at Yasmin with a smug grin.

Her mouth opened, and Yasmin found herself gaping like a fish as both her siblings exploded into laughter. The wisp buzzed against her neck. Its heat pulsed with growing dread.

"You read my notebook?"

Yasmin couldn't believe it. She'd left the notebook in

her room for what—twenty minutes? Why had Hassan chosen now to get curious about her notes?

It wasn't just Mason. Everything Yasmin had learned about magic was in there. If Hassan read it, then he knew— Wait. Had he called it *fanfiction*?

"She made him a dragon. Did you know Yasmin was one of those weird fantasy chicks? There's like a hundred descriptions of his wings." Hassan stuck his finger into his mouth and mimed throwing up.

He'd had just read the truth about magic. But he wasn't searching for enchanted potions in her sleeves, or even looking for the wisp.

"You're such an idiot." Yasmin meant the statement more than she ever had before. She pushed her brother away and fled.

Hassan's howling laughter at her retreat mocked Yasmin until she slammed her door shut. He'd left her notebook open on the bed. And he'd drawn hearts around Mason's name.

I'm going to murder him.

"Are you really writing a story about Mason Wick?" Nina's voice trembled with suppressed amusement.

Yasmin jumped. She'd stormed off with the tablet and forgotten to hang up. Brilliant.

"No—I—Ugh." Yasmin raised the tablet to glare at her sister "If you tell any of your friends, I swear I—Would you stop giggling?"

Where was the button to end the call?

"I'm sorry, but this is the most human I've seen you act. Normally, you're like a perfect robot child."

Yasmin's thumb froze over the red circle. "You think I'm perfect?"

"Trust you to ignore the robot part." Nima sat up to

reveal posters of bands on the wall behind her bed. Her eyes narrowed. "I need a favor. I left something at home and—Is that mascara smudged under your eyes?"

"No." Yasmin's gaze darted to her image on the screen. She'd scrubbed her face yesterday, but still woken up looking like a raccoon.

"You stole my makeup." Nima looked more thrilled than annoyed. "You should've called. I could've given you tips."

The wisp buzzed against Yasmin's back. Its heat pulsed, hot then cold, anxious then annoyed. She knew this feeling. She hated it.

"I don't want your advice, Nima," Yasmin snapped. "I don't want to act like you. I don't want to be anything like you."

"Okay, chill. I didn't say you did."

But everyone thought it. Even Yasmin sometimes.

The wisp's hum softened to a comforting tune. It nestled against her neck.

I have my own little piece of magic, but I'm jealous because people like my sister more?

Maybe Hassan wasn't the only Gul who could be a brat.

"What did you forget?" Yasmin flipped the screen to show Nima the shelves. "I'll send it to you."

"It's not in the room." Nima's image trembled as though she were tapping her foot. "I told you'd regret it if you didn't help me. You've been dying to know where my hiding spot is since elementary school. I'm going to tell you."

———

A loose tile in the ceiling of the laundry room held a secret crawl space. Yasmin had to climb onto the dryer to reach it.

Her sister's birth control tablets sat in a metal container within.

"Of course, that's what she wanted," Yasmin muttered as she pulled it out. Her own judgement reverberated in the wisp's hum. It felt strange having her own emotions echoed back to her, and embarrassing.

Nima had been almost sweet during their conversation. She hadn't teased Yasmin, had barely even mentioned her new boyfriend. The closest she'd come to mentioning boys was saying that she didn't mind sharing her makeup or talking for real if Yasmin ever wanted. Plus, she'd finally revealed her hiding spot.

"Maybe she is actually nice."

For a change, the wisp didn't mimic Yasmin's feelings. It nestled against her neck with a reassuring warmth as if to say, *you're nice too.*

But she wasn't.

When she first learned that Mason had gone to juvie, she'd been eager to assume the worst. It hadn't occurred to her that he'd been the victim in the situation. And she'd acted the same way yesterday, jumping to accuse Mason's family of theft.

I barely know them.

Mason probably hated her now. He'd be back to mocking her on Monday. Or worse, he'd ignore her. It would be like none of this had happened.

The wisp spread its warmth through Yasmin like a hug, filling the room with its hum.

No, there would be no going back to how things were before. Yasmin had magic. She had a partner. The wisp had chosen her, by necessity or something more it made no difference. Yasmin would do whatever it took to be worthy of it.

The mechanical shrill of the doorbell made Yasmin jump. She hurried to put the tile back. The last thing she needed was for someone to discover the crawl space. She had plans to—

"Yasmin!" Hassan's shout echoed through the hallway. "You're never going to guess who's here."

43
MASON

"Are you here to talk about the game?" Hassan asked, grinning as he turned back to the doorway.

"I'm looking for your sister," Mason said. He'd thought that obvious. Why else would Hassan have shouted to Yasmin?

The smile slid from Hassan's face. "But you're not friends."

"Sure we are." Assuming Yasmin wasn't holding a permanent grudge. "Can I come in?"

Mason smiled, looped his thumbs in his pockets, and leaned forward, studying the television room beyond Hassan. A bag of chips spilled off the coffee table onto a carpet. Getting the crumbs off would be a pain in the ass for whoever did the vacuuming.

Hassan eyed him like he was a cobra. "Why are you suddenly interested in my sister?"

"Uh..." Mason's mind blanked for a second. He hadn't expected an interrogation from Yasmin's fourteen-year-old brother. He thought Hassan liked him.

Did Zach and Kal spread some stupid rumor?

"She's helping me with an English assignment."

Hassan's eyes narrowed. "If you try anything with her, I'll beat you up."

The threat would have been more effective if Mason wasn't taller, broader, and a dragon. A gentle nudge could send Hassan toppling backward onto his open bag of chips.

Do not laugh at Yasmin's brother.

"Understood." Mason nodded with grave sincerity, and Hassan stepped aside.

A rack of sneakers sat beside the door. Mason bent to untie his shoes and add them to the collection.

Hassan watched him. "Are you related to Jeremiah Quick?"

Mason frowned. That was a sudden shift. He gave the answer they always offered the humans at Folkestone. "No, we live in the same neighborhood, so we catch the same subway, but we're not related." He pulled his second set of laces loose. "Why?"

"Just something I read."

"Hassan!" Yasmin shouted at her brother as she raced from a narrow passageway into the main room.

The scent of roses flooded Mason's mind. Relief came with it. The fireball hadn't grown and consumed Yasmin during the night, or stolen her soul, or done whatever terrible thing it was capable of. It must have fled somewhere else because Yasmin was fine.

More than fine.

Yasmin wore black leggings and a white shirt that hugged her body, accentuating subtle curves. Her dark braid fell across her shoulder, and a few loose waves framed her face. A flush in her cheeks brought out the color in her lips. Fury flashed in her eyes, but they softened as they landed on Mason, turning wide and doe-like and unbearably beautiful.

Mason's heart skipped.

Above him, Hassan cleared his throat.

Oh, shit. Mason's eyes had trailed over Yasmin, and her brother had been watching.

"Ignore anything Hassan told you," Yasmin said. She grabbed Mason's arm and pulled him to his feet. Her eyes were on her brother, however, expression murderous. "We're going to my room. If you follow me, I will forget to pay the television subscription for the next several months."

"You can do homework in the kitchen," Hassan shouted, but Yasmin's threat must've worked because he didn't pursue.

She dragged Mason down the narrow passage toward the second door on their left. He wanted to make a joke.

Taking me to your bedroom, Gul? Maybe you're the one who's trying to take advantage of me.

But between making her cry last time they spoke and her brother's warning, Mason decided to hold his tongue.

Plus, maybe there was a tiny part of him that wouldn't be joking. He wouldn't mind if Yasmin was pulling him into her room because—

She has a weapon created by the Serpents, which Eli is panicking to find. That's why I'm here. That's the only reason I'm here.

And maybe also to apologize.

A bedroom packed with more things than floor space waited behind the door. Shelves and cupboards lined the walls, creating a tunnel toward a twin bed with a sunflower blanket. Yasmin's notebook lay open on top. Red ink stood out against the blank of her writing.

Had she drawn hearts around the page?

Yasmin ran forward with speed she'd never displayed in gym class and slammed the book shut. She clutched it to her chest. "What are you doing here, Mason? I thought you never wanted to see me again."

"I didn't say that," Mason objected. He rolled his shoulders, and his gaze shifted to the shelves.

Yasmin shared the room with her sister. That was obvious from the polaroid photos of Nima and friends displayed in frames on one of the shelves. The other half of the room, however, was pure Yasmin: a copy of *All the Kings Men* with colorful tabs sticking from the pages; a box of newspapers; notebooks that occupied nearly two shelves on their own. Fake sunflowers in a glass vase squeezed between the books.

Kind of ironic. Shouldn't she have roses?

"I guess I just assumed," Yasmin said, dropping onto her bed. Her voice was heavy, but it held more hurt than anger. "Given that I'm a *pain-in-the-ass* who's *not a real reporter*."

Ah crap, is that really what I said?

"Yasmin, I'm sorry, I—" Mason's voice cut off as something hummed a note that resounded with a soft reassurance.

The blue fireball rose from Yasmin's chest, settling against her neck. It had been hiding under her shirt.

"Careful!" Mason moved toward her. He needed to capture and contain the fireball before it activated and became the weapon his father swore it was.

Blue sparks flickered.

Mason's stomach tightened. But this wasn't the time to be afraid. He needed to save Yasmin.

He reached for the fireball.

It darted back down Yasmin's shirt, hiding exactly where it knew he wouldn't put his hand.

Dammit. Maybe the thing was sentient.

A soft blue glow pulsed between Yasmin's breasts. He could hear it. The hum continued, nervous and unsure. If it really was a deadly weapon, why did it seem so docile?

A new note rose in the humming. Embarrassment? No, why would a fireball feel embarrassed. Why would a fireball feel anything at all?

Maybe the weapon worked by confusing you with its sounds.

Yasmin raised her notebook higher on her chest, blocking the fireball. Red colored her cheeks. "Are you trying to steal the wisp back?"

There was that word again.

"It's a weapon," Mason corrected her.

The blue fireball hummed its objection from within Yasmin's shirt.

"It says it's not," she informed him.

"I heard it," Mason said, which was concerning in itself. Weapons weren't supposed to communicate. That suggested consciousness, which meant independent thought.

Why would the Serpents make a weapon that could rebel against them? It didn't make sense. Was his father lying? It wouldn't be the first time.

Mason pushed his hair from his forehead and sat on the corner of the bed. He'd come because he'd begun to worry that he'd made a mistake letting Yasmin keep the fireball. But he saw nothing to suggest it would hurt her. Or anyone.

Yasmin sat at the other end of her bed, still clinging to her notebook. Concern filled her eyes. "Who told you it was a weapon?"

"My father," Mason admitted. "He's the one who stole it."

44
YASMIN

"And he said the Drages want to sell it to the Knights?" Yasmin's brow furrowed as she considered the wisp. It had come out to hover in the center of her palm as Mason explained what had happened with his father.

"The Serpents," Mason corrected. "Though I guess that's the same thing. Eli's stepped up to run things for his dad. Guess he's more ruthless about what weapons they'll traffic in. And less discerning about recruits."

"You think he sent you that message to meet in Pretty Pines Park." Mason hadn't come out and said it, but it was an obvious conclusion.

"If he did, then he knows we lied about you being my alibi."

"But he'd know you had one," Yasmin said, which would explain Eli's willingness to believe them despite finding them at the scene of the crime. "Maybe he was watching you in the park but decided to lay low when he saw Kira and Comet."

"Out of concern for children and reverence for great

dragons?" Mason's tone was skeptical, but then he shrugged. "Maybe. But you have to be twisted to create a weapon for the Knights. Or to sell to them..." The usual warmth vanished from Mason's voice as anger bubbled to the surface. He clenched his jaw.

He's thinking about his dad.

Lawrence had wanted to sell the stolen wisp. He'd planned on approaching one of the Knights himself. Mason knew it. Yasmin could tell from the way he'd weaved around the topic, tensing his jaw and swallowing his words.

The wisp hummed in concern. Yasmin ran her finger over the fire, stroking it in agreement like it was a tiny, fiery cat.

I know. I'm worried about him too.

Mason's real secret wasn't some dark, sordid crime or even his identity as a dragon. He hurt, and he didn't want anyone to notice.

"I'm sorry," Yasmin whispered.

Mason's eyebrows rose. He looked away from the wisp to meet her gaze for the first time since it had come into the open. "For what?"

"Take your pick," Yasmin suggested. "Misjudging you, planning to reveal the existence of magic, accusing your family of stealing—"

"You were right about that," Mason cut her off, unfamiliar coldness creeping into his tone once more. His eyes flicked to the wisp, then back to her. He forced one of his crooked smiles. "I'm surprised you're not gloating."

He was trying to make jokes again.

"I'm not that petty," Yasmin said. "Anyway, I wasn't right. I accused your foster family." Mason's father hadn't crossed her mind—an obvious oversight given the scale. "I'm sorry."

Mason smirked. "Two apologies? In one day? Maybe that thing is affecting you after all."

The wisp chuckled. Not in the traditional sense, but the noise emanating from it carried the cadence of a short laugh. Its sparks bounced to match. A sense of its amusement swelled in Yasmin's chest. It felt warm and human.

If the wisp had been designed as a weapon, it didn't want to be one.

Yasmin's fist closed around its light. She held it safe in her palm and set her gaze on Mason.

Any delusions she'd had about him forgiving her were about to crumble to dust.

"I'm not returning the wisp," Yasmin said, holding up her chin, and feigning confidence. She had no real defense against Mason. The wisp didn't burn, and her notebook was more liability than shield. Still, she had to try. "It doesn't want to go back to Eli. Whatever he's planning, it didn't like it."

She waited for Mason to argue. Yasmin was a human. What right did she have to keep a magical wisp?

Mason leaned his head against her wall. "You think I'd take a potentially deadly weapon back to the gang that created it?"

"No, but—" Yasmin faltered. "What are you proposing?"

"I don't know." Mason ran his fingers through his hair. He had one foot propped on her mattress, arm casually draped over his knee. The pose made look like a clothing model in a magazine.

Except he's sitting on my bed.

The wisp pulsed with eagerness, mimicking Yasmin's heart. Heat flushed through her.

Don't give me away like that!

Mason could hear the wisp. She didn't need him knowing that in the middle of a very important discussion, she'd gotten distracted by his looks.

"I'm not going to take it from you," Mason whispered. "But we do need to investigate and find out what it is. Eli's looking for it. My father might be too. He knows it didn't vanish after being released. If it can be turned into a weapon, we need to keep it out of the wrong hands."

Yasmin nodded. She knew what Mason was saying was serious, but a delighted hum had filled her mind. "Did you say *we* needed to investigate?"

"Shit. Sorry, that was presumptuous," Mason said. "I didn't mean—Look, I'd love your help. You're brilliant at this sort of stuff. But you can't publish in a Castor paper, and a human one won't believe anything you write about magic. There's no story in this for you."

That wasn't true. Yasmin didn't need to publish to have a story. Especially not when it was this important.

"Maybe I can still help. If you tell me I'm brilliant again," Yasmin suggested, holding back a smile as she leaned against her pillows. The wisp's internal humming must've been affecting her rational thinking because her tone sounded almost flirtatious.

Mason grinned. "I think I'd prefer to just steal the notes you've undoubtedly already made on the *wisp* and be on my way."

"Absolutely not." Yasmin leaped from her bed before Mason could make a swipe for her notebook.

"You've been clinging to that thing more than normal. Do you have something in there you don't want me to see?"

He snapped his fingers and pointed at the sunflower cover. "You wrote about me and my family, didn't you?"

The wisp spread its heat through Yasmin. It seemed to enjoy doing that whenever she got embarrassed.

"Whatever you wrote must be awful if you're so determined not to let me see," Mason said, thankfully going in the complete wrong direction with his assumptions.

"My notes are just messy, Sherlock," Yasmin lied. "But I'd be happy to make new ones for you. I have plenty of extra notebooks."

Mason's eyes narrowed. He obviously didn't believe her, but he let the suspicion melt into his signature crooked smile, and Yasmin's heart skipped.

"New investigation, new notebook, right? Let's make a list of theories as to just what your new friend is." Mason's smile broadened, revealing his teeth and giving his face the powerful, predatory allure he so often hid. "If you have some good ones, I might even call you brilliant again."

45
YASMIN

"What's going on with you and Mason?" Gigi Davis turned in her seat.

Yasmin jumped at the unexpected sound, turning her eyes from the clock above Mr. Stern's head. She'd been counting the seconds until AP Literature ended. Mason would be at her apartment again after school. They planned to go downtown together.

The wisp buzzed beneath Yasmin's shirt. It had showed little interest in her classes, but now it peeped out the collar, trying to catch a glimpse of Gigi.

Yasmin pushed her braid over her shoulder to hide its glow. "I'm helping him with English." She kept her voice low.

Mr. Stern stood at the front, talking over a slideshow with notes on *As You Like It*. Pockets of chatter whispered beneath his voice. Not everyone was paying attention, but Yasmin didn't want to get called out.

Gigi twisted a short, blonde ringlet and pursed her cherry red lips. "But why'd he ask you? Isn't he friends with—?"

Yasmin followed Gigi's eyes to the front of class. Jeremiah sat in the corner. His lips pulled into a tight line, and he glared at Yasmin.

"He's been looking at you like that all day," Gigi whispered.

The wisp fluttered against the nape of Yasmin's neck, echoing her own nervousness. She'd noticed Jeremiah's looks. How could she not?

During lunch, Yasmin had met Mason in the library to go through the books he'd found on dragon fire spells. Halfway through, Jeremiah had appeared, a specter among the shelves, scowling his displeasure. Mason had said to ignore him, but it was easier said than done.

Does he know about the wisp?

Yasmin should talk to him.

The bell rang, and Mr. Stern cut off his slideshow. He reminded the class to check online for their next assignment as they began rising from their seats. Jeremiah packed his tablet near the front.

Yasmin grabbed her bag, but before she could move, she found her way blocked. Lydia Prince tossed her ponytail and leaned in. "You lied to Gigi. Something is definitely going on with you and Mason."

Gigi stopped to listen. So did several other girls. Jeremiah glanced up too, the disapproval evident on his face.

Brilliant. He was never going to trust Yasmin.

Jeremiah's head twitched. He glanced down and pulled his phone from his pocket. His eyes flashed with concern, and he began typing something.

"Kal and Zach think you're hooking up," Lydia continued.

A flutter of heat burst against Yasmin's chest. Kalvin and Zachary were Mason's friends. She doubted they'd make the mistake of thinking he had any romantic interest in her.

"No, they don't!" Yasmin argued. She glanced away from Jeremiah for a second. When she looked back, he'd vanished.

Why was he suddenly in such a hurry?

"You guys skipped school together. My sister saw you at the juice place," Lydia continued. She pulled out her phone and shoved it in Yasmin's face.

On the screen, was a picture of Yasmin and Mason at The Upside-Down Watermelon. His hand wrapped around her waist, and his head tilted toward her. They looked seconds away from kissing.

The wisp's heat could've turned Yasmin's entire body red.

The other girls leaned in, trying to see the picture on Lydia's phone. A chorus of gasps followed.

"When was this?"

"I love that dress!"

"Are you guys dating?"

Yasmin shook her head. "No, we're not—He was just— That picture's not—"

Ugh, she was perfectly articulate when she wrote. Why did her vocabulary have to vanish when she actually needed it.

The wisp buzzed in panic. It was right. They needed to get out of there.

"They're obviously not dating," Lydia said with a harsh laugh. She turned to Yasmin. "Mason's hooking up with you and hiding it, right? That is so sad."

The wisp sparked in fury against Yasmin. But it was a pinprick of anger in a massive wave of embarrassment. Her classmates were starting to whisper.

"Ugh. You're such a stalker, Lydia." Gigi pushed through the group of girls and grabbed Yasmin's arm. "Your sister saw Mason and felt the need to send you a picture. That's what's sad."

Gigi marched Yasmin from the room.

The wisp stopped shooting sparks. Instead, it crept toward Yasmin's neck, trying to peep out her collar again. She didn't block its view this time.

"Thanks," Yasmin offered, though the apology felt flat. "Did you save me because you were friends with Nima?"

"No. I did it because Lydia's being a bitch." Gigi kept Yasmin's arm linked with hers, simultaneously managing to pull out her lip gloss and reapply without breaking stride. "Everyone knows she's liked Mason for forever. She's just jealous he's not hooking up with her."

The wisp's hum softened. So did some of Yasmin's anger. She knew what it was like to lash out from jealousy.

"And we can all see how Mason's looking at you," Gigi continued.

"How's he looking at me?" The question slipped from Yasmin before she could stop it. Idiot. Did she have to make it so obvious that she cared?

They walked through Folkestone's main doors toward the front of the school. As they stopped by the benches near the foot of the steps, Gigi's eyes flicked down.

The wisp's glow came through the white fabric of Yasmin's shirt. She covered it with her free hand.

Gigi's brow furrowed in momentary confusion. She shook her head, recovered, and settled against the edge of an unoccupied table with a smile. "Like he's a little too happy to see you each time you appear."

"Oh." Yasmin didn't dare smile or move her hand. She could feel the wisp growing brighter.

Some kind of weapon. The only danger is it exposing my emotions.

A car honked. Yasmin turned and saw her brother waving to her from the front seat of their father's van.

Jerk.

Yasmin stepped toward them, paused, and turned back to Gigi.

"I like your lip gloss," she said.

Gigi beamed.

Amir pressed the horn again, and Yasmin hurried into the backseat. She'd almost forgotten about Jeremiah until the van rolled onto the main road beyond.

An indigo vehicle, with a sheen that reflected the night sky, had parked near the edge. Beside it, stood the first Castor policeman Yasmin had seen, the blond-haired werewolf who'd chased her and Mason to the old gym. Talking to him was Jeremiah.

Yasmin's eyes widened. The wisp trembled against her chest. Why was Jeremiah talking to the police?

She leaned forward and tapped her father's shoulder. "Slow down, Baba."

As always, he didn't listen.

46

YASMIN

"Why is Mason Wick standing by our door?" Hassan asked, grabbing Yasmin's arm and stopping her from stepping into the hall as the elevator opened.

Probably because he flew instead of catching a bus.

But her brother's tone suggested that it wasn't the timing of Mason's arrival that made him ask.

"We're working on—" Yasmin started with her usual explanation.

"Yeah, English, I know." Hassan rolled his eyes before shooting her his most innocent smile. "So what are you going to do if Baba comes home early and catches your dragon in your room?"

Mason, leaning against their wall, glanced at them, then away, pretending not to have noticed. If he could hear them, he'd have a lot of questions.

"We're not going in my bedroom," Yasmin said, certain her face had turned red. "He's just dropping off his bag. We're going downtown."

She hurried off the elevator before Hassan could pull her back again.

Mason watched with his usual crooked smile as she pulled the key from the plant pot and opened the door. Yasmin tried, and failed, not to keep glancing at him. Did he look *a bit too happy* to see her?

Hassan stomped forward and pushed his way in before either of them enter. He scowled at Mason.

"Did I do something to offend him?" Mason whispered, shifting his bag as he followed Yasmin toward her room.

She could think of only one thing though the wisp heated at the thought of mentioning it. "Maybe it has to do with Kalvin and Zach telling people that we're hooking up."

"Shit. Seriously?" Mason dropped his bag on the floor with a heavy thud. He'd been hefting around his usual school supplies and ten large texts from his fairy godfather's library. "I didn't tell them that, Yas. I swear."

A nickname?

The wisp fluttered against Yasmin's chest again.

Unlike the others, Mason definitely noticed. His eyes went straight to its glow, and his head tilted.

Can you please hide?

The wisp zipped up to the nape of her neck, settling beneath her braid.

"I know you didn't," Yasmin managed. She reached into her cupboard and traded her school bag for a smaller, over-over-the-shoulder purse. Kalvin and Zachary were the least of her concerns. There was a different topic she wanted to broach, but last time she'd accused Mason's family, it hadn't gone well.

Yasmin needed to tread carefully.

"That werewolf police officer who showed up on Friday

came back today. I saw Jeremiah talking to him when we left school."

"Okay." Mason bent over and tied the buckles of his bag with a large cord, sealing it shut. The additional protection probably wasn't necessary. Given his track record, Hassan would find books on magic and assume they were playing an elaborate game of Dungeons and Dragons.

"So, what do you think?" Yasmin pressed.

"That the policeman returned to do a follow-up interview, and Jeremiah went." Mason shrugged and stood. "Ready to go? Douglas gets crankier the later it gets."

———

Yasmin and Mason rode the subway downtown, then walked through the labyrinth of alleyways to arrive at the gift shop. Their conversation bobbed and weaved, dodging topics like they were thumbtacks on the floor. Mason was a master at changing focus.

"What did you tell Zach and Kalvin?" "That you're my English tutor. Actually, I do have some questions for you about Macbeth."

"Lydia's sister took a picture of us in the smoothie shop together." "Weird. Should we go there on our way? I still want to try that peanut butter flavor."

Yasmin made another attempt as they stepped into Dilly Dally's chaotic interior. "Does Jeremiah know about the wisp?"

As she mentioned it, the blue light flitted over her arm and zipped around her wrist—a glowing bracelet. The wisp had spent the journey hiding beneath her hair, only moving to her chest once when she'd caught herself admiring Mason.

"No, I didn't want to panic to him," Mason said, weaving through the dusty displays of out-of-place items. "Just told him I'm keeping my deal and teaching you about magic."

Yasmin fought the urge to tidy as she followed him. Fake store or not, couldn't Douglas sort the candy dispensers from the pens? "You don't think Jeremiah would want to help?"

Mason shrugged and plucked a bright yellow baseball cap from the display. He spun and fit it onto Yasmin's head with a grin. "Cute. You look good in yellow."

"That's not an answer." Yasmin pulled the baseball cap from her head. No way was she falling for such a cheap distraction. She followed Mason, who was now charging in the wrong direction. "Do you not trust me?"

Hurt she hadn't expected leaked into her voice.

Mason stopped. "It's not you, Yas. I just prefer to avoid unpleasant topics. Keep things positive, you know?"

"Jeremiah is a painful topic?"

"No, but—" Mason pushed aside a display of magnets, bottle openers, and lip glosses to reveal a smooth, dark door. The symbol on the top marked it as the bathroom. "Changes location. Neat, right? Now remember, going in here together is not an invitation to make out with me. No matter how pretty my wings are."

He had the audacity to wink.

Heat flooded Yasmin, along with a fluttered, high-pitched hum. The wisp echoed her embarrassment, but it wasn't just that.

The memory of smoke tingled on Yasmin's lips as they entered the bathroom. She watched him open the hidden staircase, but her mind conjured a different image: Mason pressing her against the wall, his fingers running through her hair like they had at the Drages' manor.

They descended the steps in silence, hands a breath shy of brushing. The wisp buzzed against Yasmin's chest. She didn't know if her next thought came from it or her.

Say something. Anything.

"You know we did kiss." The words left Yasmin before she'd thought them through.

Not about kissing, idiot!

Did the wisp have the power to take her back in time? Yasmin fought the urge to bury her face in the baseball cap still dangling in her hand.

"I do." Mason's lips tilted in his usual crooked smile. "But it's nice to know you're still thinking about it."

"That's not—" Yasmin's body transformed into a furnace as they rounded the last corner of the staircase. Maybe the wisp was capable of burning after all. "I'm not—"

Yasmin had no idea what defense she was about to offer, but she was spared the embarrassment of finding out.

"Again?" Xena groaned. The Amazon guarded the foot of the stairs. Frizz rose from her pulled-back curls, and the room's glowing lights flashed in her eyes. She tapped the pommel of her dagger but didn't draw the blade. "We'll get arrested with you at this rate."

"Think just working here is already illegal," Finnian's voice, deep and cheery, piped up from between the rows of luminescent magic. His mop of red curls appeared over the top of a dark shelf. Then, he joined them with such speed, the entire length of vine lit a multi-colored streak against the floor. He smiled at Yasmin. "My favorite customer. What happened with your witching ruse?"

Mason responded before she could. "*Our* ruse worked

perfectly, so well that we have something to show Douglas."

"Unless you're here to pay your debts, he won't be interested." Finnian leaned in, cupping his hand to his mouth in a conspiratorial whisper. "Between you and me, he isn't so thrilled about you bringing a *you-know-what* into his shop."

Yasmin's lips pursed. Seriously? Who would've heard if he said human?

"He'll want to see what we have," Mason insisted.

"Unless it's a million-dollar item, I doubt it." The two boys glared at each other. Despite Finnian's height, Yasmin's money was on Mason.

The wisp rose from her collar, trailing the length of her arm to glide across her fingertips. Yellow crackled like lightning in the center of the glowing blue. Its hum had turned hungry.

Xena peered around Finnian. Her eyes widened.

"Neat trick," Finnian said, looking at Mason instead of Yasmin as he reached forward. "You have impressive control. Can I—?"

The wisp whipped tendrils of blue flames against Finnian's fingers. He yelped.

"Drums! No need to burn me!" The elf shook his hand, then cradled it to his chest. Smoke coiled from blackened skin.

The wisp made a sound like someone licking their lips.

Yasmin gasped. "How? You don't burn."

"Like hell it doesn't." Finnian blew on his hand. "Xena, did you see—?" He broke off.

His companion had vanished.

A moment later, she reappeared from the back room where Yasmin had tried on the dresses. Douglas flew behind Xena, the old man's face drawn in a grizzled scowl. Fear flashed through his eyes.

"What've you got that's so important then?" he demanded.

Mason answered, "The item every media outlet is dying to hear about—the Drages' stolen flame."

47
YASMIN

Yasmin squashed between dragon and elves as they huddled over the desk.

The wisp flickered atop a glass plate. Douglas studied it through a silver magnifying glass, muttering to himself in a secret gibberish that was half curses and half beginnings of sentences that went nowhere.

"Did you know the Drages ran the Serpents?" Mason asked, his eyes on the fairy more than the wisp.

"Heard whispers," Douglas muttered. "But there's gossip about a lot of families."

"I don't think it's possible," Finnian insisted, voice the loudest of the group. "I know the Drages. I've seen them at dozens of balls. They're wealthy. Why would they lead a criminal organization?"

"How do you think they got wealthy?" Douglas asked. He rested down the magnifying glass and started opening drawers, rifling through the contents. Nothing within appeared expensive: scissors, calculator, loose pens. The fairy's fingers closed around a piece of gray fabric.

"Inheritance," Finnian suggested, laughing with the privilege of someone who had one. "Surely petty crime doesn't pay that much."

"I wouldn't call illegal weapons trafficking *petty*." Douglas found a bright red ribbon, pulsing with a magic glow. "Dust! This'll have to—"

"Dragons sell their fire," Finnian continued to argue. "It isn't illegal."

"It's not dragon fire," Xena whispered. "Or it would've burned her."

"I have a name," Yasmin reminded her, shuffling forward to avoid being squashed out of the circle.

Mason glanced at her. He was the only one.

Douglas tore a smaller strip from the cloth, then wrapped the ribbon around Xena's extended dagger to cut a smaller piece. He dropped both the gray fabric and the glowing red coil onto the glass plate. "Watch."

The ribbon blackened, crumbling to dust in the center of the wisp; the gray cloth remained unblemished.

"Why did it burn one and not the other?" Yasmin asked, taking the gray fabric from the wisp. Its hunger shifted to an appreciative purr as her fingers brushed it. She'd had to coax it onto the glass dish so Douglas could analyze it. "What's special about this piece of cloth?"

"Nothing," Douglas said, voice soft and eyes glued to the wisp. "That's exactly the problem. Only the ribbon had been enchanted."

Which means—?

The fairy moved away from the wisp. So did the elves.

Mason looked up. "My father said it's a weapon.".

"Yes," Douglas agreed, folding his wings without shifting his gaze. "A deadly weapon. The kind that even the

Serpents have gone too far in creating. This could cost us everything."

He pointed to the ashes in the middle of the wisp.

"This fire only burns magic."

48
MASON

The ribbon's ashes disintegrated until no sign of them remained. The wisp hummed in satisfaction.

"It's alive."

The whisper was so soft, Mason couldn't tell who'd spoken.

"That's not possible," Finnian said. He straightened from his slump, shaking his head at Douglas. "Why would any Castor make such a thing?"

"How the hell should I know?"

But Mason did. He'd spent his formative years with Lawrence, and how different were criminals at their core?

"To sell it," he said. "To whoever will pay."

"But no Castor would pay for this," Finnian argued.

"The Knights would."

"You think the Drages are in cahoots with the Knights?" Finnian laughed. But when no one else joined him, the prince's expression grew somber.

Behind his register, Douglas closed his eyes in what might've been a prayer. When they reopened, he glared at

Mason. "I should never have sold your father a doppelgänger spell. I don't deal with danger like this. Get it out!"

"No!" Finnian grabbed Mason's arm. "If all this is true, we have a moral duty to destroy this thing and protect the lives of our fellow Castors." The prince struck quite the figure—broad, tall, earnest, far too similar to a story-book hero.

But he wasn't wrong. The wisp existed to destroy magic. Only a villain would allow such a thing to flit into the wild.

"You can't hurt it!" Yasmin's voice trembled. She lifted her hand. The others leaped back as the wisp flew toward her palm. She turned to Mason. Her eyes were large and panicked, a silent plea: *help me.*

No, that wasn't the message. She was saying *help us.*

Yasmin thought she was connected to the wisp. Mason didn't blame her. He'd seen it follow her movements, respond to her emotions with its glow.

But what if that was only a pretense? A survival mechanism built-in to the weapon?

Yasmin ran. The elves would catch her easily. Mason had a split second to decide if to help her escape.

This is probably the dumbest thing I've ever done.

He summoned his wings and tail, lashing the latter toward Finnian. The prince, poised to speed after Yasmin, tripped forward. He had a long way to fall.

Before Finnian could find his feet, Mason encircled the prince with his wings. The cramped confines of The Portentous Purveyor allowed only a narrow prison, and his scales rubbed against the shelves.

And now his bodyguard attacks me.

Mason's tail lacked the spikes suited for war, but it

served as an adequate whip. Peering over his own wings, he watched for Xena to leap.

But she remained still, lips moving without sound, eyes caught on the glass where the wisp had been.

"Are you crazy?" Finnian dusted himself off. Mason's wings trapped him but did little to block the elf's view. "She's run off with a fire that could kill all of us. What if she's taking it to the Knights?"

Finnian's hand scrambled at his hip. But the prince bore no weapon, and even his ego wasn't big enough to attack a dragon with his bare hands. He was left with only his towering presence as he shouted at Mason.

"Do you not care because you can't burn? Do the rest of us Castors mean nothing to you? I've heard it said dragons are callous, but this is a new low."

"Of course, I care," Mason spat back. "But—"

Why was he blocking the prince? Mason didn't intend to take a pro-deadly weapon stance.

It's not about the wisp. It's Yasmin.

"She's not a knight," Mason said, as pathetic of an excuse as it was. "And that little fireball she's protecting is barely a drop of what exists."

Finnian's anger turned to fear. "There's more?"

"A lot more," Mason said. "If you're really worried about protecting the city, it's not Yasmin that's the problem. It's the Drages."

49
YASMIN

Yasmin's back pressed against the gift shop's crumbling brick façade. Her legs ached from racing up the stairs. Perhaps she shouldn't have avoided gym classes for so many years.

The wisp sheltered in the hat in Yasmin's hands. Its hum matched the pounding in her chest. Despite the hour, the sun remained stubborn. Daylight provided little opportunity to hide in the alleyway.

Should she wait for Mason or continue on her own? He could find her later.

A shadow swept across the ground, faster than should have been possible.

Yasmin squeaked. The wisp hid beneath her sleeve. But there was no time to run. Xena towered before Yasmin, blocking any chance at escape.

"Relax." The Amazon raised her palms, then leaned forward, reducing the foot of height between them. "I haven't come to hurt you. I doubt I could."

"Your prince wants to try," Yasmin said. Her knees

trembled, but she stuck her chin forward and folded her arms. "You obey him."

Xena snorted. "I protect Finn. But he's not our ruler. Not yet. Where is it?"

"Gone. It flew off when I came outside."

"The wisp would not have left you."

Yasmin's eyes widened.

She called it a wisp.

"Where's Mason?" Yasmin glanced toward the door.

"He and Finn are making plans, much to Douglas' frustration. The authorities can handle the Drages. I'm more curious about your wisp. I believe it's bonded to you, like a witch with a familiar."

"I'm human," Yasmin reminded her.

"Obviously." Xena's deep voice turned wry. "I'm not saying it has good taste."

Yasmin started to force a smile, then thought better of it and settled on a scowl. The gift shop's door swung open. Mason emerged, wings and tail glowing in the light. His eyes found Yasmin.

"But it's chosen you," Xena continued, speaking faster now that Mason had appeared. But she watched the door, not him, as though afraid someone else might follow. "The magic has made you one. And I think I know why. If you could just show me—"

Mason's wing spread between them, creating a shield of sunlit scales for Yasmin to hide behind.

But he didn't attack Xena. Instead, he watched her, eyes narrowed with curiosity. "How could that be possible? For it to bond with her, it would need to have—"

"A soul," Xena finished for him. She kept her eyes locked on Yasmin as she straightened to her full height, peering above the curved edge of Mason's wing. "Please, Finnian would be furious to know I'm discussing such things. It is forbidden knowledge, but—"

Mason watched Yasmin too. He wanted her to make this decision.

Should we trust her? Yasmin directed the question to the wisp beneath her sleeve. In answer, it slipped free, rising into the air just above her palm.

"A will-o-the-wisp." Xena's voice was reverent, barely a whisper. Her head dipped, eyes closed. "Living fire." She hummed a soft, mournful tune.

The wisp trembled to the beat.

Mason withdrew his wing, folded it against his back and approached, so that the three stood in a circle around the light. "You've seen something like this before?"

"No, but it's in one of our legends," Xena said. "The Harrow King, from before our rulers sacrificed such titles, could bend magic to his will like a witch. With it, he sought to capture the power of every creature in existence."

Yasmin had heard no such tale, but Mason must have. He nodded impatiently. "But when he sought the dragons, one of them burned him and laughed in his face because he wasn't fireproof. What's that to do with a wisp?"

"Your story ends with the Harrow King embarrassed. Elvish legend does not," Xena said, lowering her voice so that Yasmin had to lean in to hear. "The Harrow King returned to his people, determined to prove the dragons wrong. He sought to create a fire that would not burn him. But the price was steep. The flames demanded their fill of elvish blood."

Xena's eyes closed, and she muttered a prayer before continuing. "He sent his people on raids of other tribes, capturing elves to sacrifice to his flames. Thousands perished, and the fire was still not sated. The Harrow King turned on his own people until he was overthrown."

Mason's eyes glowed in the blue light. "You're saying, the Drages killed thousands to make a weapon."

"Not a weapon," Xena corrected him. "Will-o-the-wisps. The dead do not always pass on as they should. The Harrow King's dark magic trapped pieces of those he sacrificed. That's why his creation wouldn't burn elves. And why this one has bonded to you."

The wisp lowered, settling against Yasmin's chest. Its hum rose and fell with the rhythm of her heart.

Living fire.

The term clicked in Yasmin's mind. She understood.

The wisp on her chest wasn't a piece of dragon fire. It was the soul of another human.

50
MASON

When Mason suggested visiting The Portentous Purveyor, he hadn't imagined their evening would end at a restaurant with an elf prince and his bodyguard.

Scents of ginger, soy sauce, and hot oil wafted from trays of dumplings, carried through the circular tables by waiters in bright red. A dozen waving cats lined the counter near the entrance.

"Don't worry, it's my treat," Finnian insisted, waving them toward a table near the back.

Yasmin pressed the yellow baseball cap against her chest. The soft glow of the wisp radiated through a hole in the back. "That's so nice of you," she said.

Mason wanted to argue. Letting the prince buy her dinner annoyed him for some reason. But he couldn't borrow more money from Kira. He forced a smile as he took a seat. "You're too generous. Truly."

Finnian missed the sarcasm. He grinned back. "This is a good place to talk since Douglas kicked us out. Difficult to overhear." He waved over his shoulder, gesturing to the restaurant as a whole.

The owners had wasted no floor space. Tables and chairs packed close together. Customers' chatter mixed with the furniture scraping as they shuffled to let waiters pass. Voices rose from the kitchen where the staff shouted back and forth to one another without concern. Overlaying the noise was a constant loop of British pop music, entirely at odds with the restaurant's décor.

Before stepping in, both elves had inserted earrings, enchanted to both mask their appearance and soften their sensitive hearing.

"We'll go to the police together tomorrow and tell them what you saw at the Drages," Finnian said, adjusting the enchanted hoop before leaning in.

Mason tapped his fingers beside a pair of black chopsticks as a waiter rested the menus before them. "My word versus that of an elite family. No issue there."

"It doesn't matter if the Drages are rich. You're the one telling the truth," Finnian said, pointing a chopstick at Mason. "Plus, I'll vouch for you."

That would be the more important aspect.

An elf prince's word counted for more than some wayward dragon who'd turned his former foster parents into ash.

A flicker of resentment bubbled in Mason's chest, but it was quick to pop. How could he hold Finnian's privilege against him in this instance?

He's trusting me.

Finnian hadn't seen the chalice of trapped wisps in the Drages' manor. Most people would've ratted Mason out to the police for consorting with a human and hiding a weapon.

Not a weapon. A wisp.

Mason glanced to his right where Yasmin sat in the wooden chair next to his. Blue and yellow winked at him from where it had hidden beneath her braid—the soul of another human, or what remained of it at least. That sense of its identity had carried over into its new existence. It must've felt a kinship with Yasmin the moment she drew close.

"Being a prince won't be enough, Finn" Xena said, scanning her menu before dropping it onto her plate. "You need evidence."

A silence fell over the table until the waiter returned for their orders.

Mason pointed to every dumpling with shrimp. Elves could be finnicky about eating animals they didn't hunt themselves, but seafood was a different story.

Finnian watched the waiter travel back to the kitchen before turning to Xena. "I'll invent evidence. And before you argue, I'm not going to get caught or make it too ridiculous—"

"I wasn't going to argue," Xena objected, crossing her arms. "But it's important that whatever you say forces the police to investigate further."

"And you can't mention us," Yasmin added, glancing up from her lap. "You promised."

"Of course not. Mason will tell them about the Drages' chalice of fire. I'll give them a hint about what it does. You won't be mentioned." Finnian grinned, revealing a row of perfect, straight white teeth.

Why did he have to look like a prince from a fairytale?
And why do I care?

Mason flicked his tongue over his large canines. He

glanced at Yasmin, trying to gauge her opinion of the prince's smile.

Her lips pressed together, brow furrowed, too concerned about the wisp to worry about anything else.

Good.

"Mason was very insistent that we could trust you," Finnian said, leaning back, still smiling. "He said you're special."

Does he have to phrase it like that?

Granted, Mason had been effusive in his reassurance about Yasmin. But only because he needed to convince Finnian.

A waiter arrived with a tiered tray of dumplings. He rested it in the center of the table, poured water in the glasses, and vanished again.

Mason grabbed his chopsticks and shoveled dumplings onto his plate.

Xena poured soy sauce into her bowl. "What if you said you encountered a hooded person trying to sell it? That would save you from having to describe the features of the thief." Her eyes flicked to Mason. "You truly have no idea who stole it?"

His father's face, near identical to Mason's own, flashed in his mind. "No," he lied.

Mason couldn't betray his father.

Even if he abandoned me, hid a magic-burning wisp in my home, and didn't care—

Beneath the table, the wisp flew from Yasmin's sleeve. It settled on Mason's knee, spreading warmth through his leg. A soft, soothing hum reverberated with it.

Is it trying to comfort me?

Or was Yasmin? Had she sent the wisp to him somehow?

"Hooded man it is," Finnian said, lifting his water glass as though he intended to make a toast. "We'll say he did a demonstration of the fire, but kept his face hidden the whole time."

"Who said it's a man?" Xena asked. She still hadn't tried a dumpling. "The thief might be a woman."

"So she has a male partner who tried to sell it. I'd do that for you if you became a thief." Finnian laughed, but his face seemed strangely sincere.

Xena rolled her eyes. "Will you tell the police that the weapon is dragon fire?"

Mason glanced at the wisp, humming on his knee. He focused on the flickering blue instead of its yellow core and shoved another dumpling in his mouth. The elves' conversation was turning dangerous. He didn't want to risk being dragged in.

"Of course," Finnian said. The usual lightness vanished from his tone, and a commanding insistence tempered it with a regal edge. "That's what it is."

"All it is?"

"Obviously."

Xena lifted her chopsticks and finally took one of the vegetable dumplings from the top of the tray.

Finnian pouted, seeming more annoyed by her ignoring him than her arguing. "Ghost stories aren't real," he muttered, trying to grab the next dumpling before Xena could. "And the Drages can't create something they don't know about."

The wisp pulsed on Mason's knee, curiosity palpable. That was coming from Yasmin. Something sparked in her eyes—a theory.

Mason's chest tightened. He suspected he knew what it was.

The wisp proved that the Drages had learned the truth of the Harrow King's tale. Had they learned it from an elf?

51
YASMIN

Yasmin didn't speak during the meal, but her mind was far from quiet.

A human soul pulsed in the nape of her neck. Who had the wisp been before? What had happened to them? And what did it mean that it had bonded to Yasmin?

We are one.

Her thought? The wisp's? Both of theirs?

Yasmin needed to write all this down to process it. And she wanted to talk to Mason.

He plucked slices of ginger from the empty tray, eating them raw. They'd finished the dumplings minutes ago, but he'd continued to pick at the garnishes. Yasmin didn't think it was hunger compelling him. His eyes had darkened to the color of a stormy sea, and he moved on autopilot, forgetting to hide his less-human features. His tongue curled slowly around the ginger—precise, controlled.

Unprompted, the question slipped into Yasmin's mind: *What else can he do with—?*

Across the table, Finnian broke off mid-sentence with a laugh. He'd dominated the conversation most of the meal, inventing an elaborate story about the imaginary hooded man. But now, he'd caught Yasmin staring at Mason.

Heat flooded her neck. She snapped her head forward, focusing on the empty platter. Was Finnian going to make a comment about her looking at Mason instead of listening to his plan?

"I'm going to the bathroom," Finnian announced, pushing his chair backward with a heavy screech. He stood, and the top of his curls brushed the bottom of a hanging chandelier. He nudged Xena's shoulder. "Come with me?"

"Obviously. That's my job." She'd already been in the process of standing, fingers fluttering over the dagger on her hip. Either the waitstaff hadn't seen the weapon, or they'd assumed it to be fake.

Finnian winked at Yasmin as they walked off. He was giving her and Mason time alone.

Embarrassment flushed through Yasmin, so hot she worried she'd start sweating.

"Did Finnian wink at you?" Mason asked, eyes narrowed.

"No," Yasmin blurted the answer a bit too quickly. She fiddled with the edge of the hat, folding the fabric between her fingers. "Or maybe. I don't know. I didn't see. Maybe he was winking at you."

Mason tapped his chopsticks against the metal tray, making the fallen sesame seeds bounce. "What do you think of him?"

"Seems genuine, but I don't know." Yasmin shrugged. "Is that why you've been so anxious? You don't trust him."

"I haven't been anxious." Mason poked at the sesame seeds.

Yasmin raised her eyebrows. "Really?"

Mason sighed and rested down the chopsticks,

glancing in the direction the elves had vanished. "You're too observant, know that? Maybe I'm a bit on edge, but it's not Finnian. My mind just keeps wandering." He reached for his empty glass and pressed it to his lips, gulping air before he lifted his chopsticks once more. The charming, crooked smile flitted over his lips. "How many sesame seeds do you think we could pick up before the elves come back?"

Yasmin sighed as Mason fumbled to grab one of the tiny seeds with his chopsticks. He didn't want to tell her what was bothering him. Was it his family again?

"You know, you'd be a lot cuter if you stopped avoiding your feelings," Yasmin said.

Mason's eyebrow rose, and he glanced at her, clearly amused.

She'd been copying his own earlier advice about her forced smile, but it sounded dangerously close to flirting. Yasmin grabbed one of her chopsticks and rolled the top in what remained of her soy sauce, avoiding Mason's gaze.

The crooked smile dropped from his face. "It's not cute when I'm annoyed, Yasmin. I lose control. I don't want to hurt anyone again." Mason's eyes flicked to the wisp in her lap. His jaw tensed, his shoulders shuddered, and his blink lasted a second too long as he turned away.

The wisp's hum grew sad, a heaviness of guilt and sympathy woven into its music.

"Don't apologize. It's not your fault," Mason whispered. He was talking to the wisp. "I just have to stay in control of my emotions, keep a calm, positive outlook."

"What? Forever?" Yasmin couldn't keep the disbelief from her voice. That wasn't possible. Everyone got angry sometimes, even if only briefly. She'd wanted to snap at Lydia earlier today. And how many times had she threatened to strangle her brother. Or ranted about her sister in her notes?

Nima probably didn't deserve a lot of what I wrote.

"You were right about me being jealous of my sister," Yasmin admitted, lifting the chopstick she'd dipped in soy sauce and rolling it over the dumpling tray. Several sesame seeds stuck to the top.

"Clever," Mason said.

"Thanks."

"I meant me figuring out you were jealous."

Yasmin attempted to flick the sesame seeds at Mason. One landed on her white sleeve instead. Why did she bother?

Mason chuckled as he passed Yasmin a paper napkin from the center of the table. "Why're you thinking about your sister?"

"Because we've been messaging. And actually talking. It's been nice. She even showed me her secret hiding spot, which is a relief because Hassan—" Yasmin cut herself off. Mason didn't need to know all of that, just like he didn't need to know that Nima's last few messages had mentioned him.

"So you conquered your jealousy by confronting it," Mason guessed. "Congrats. I think avoiding might still be safer for me."

Yasmin shook her head. He wasn't getting it. "No, it's the opposite. I'm still jealous. Nima's easy-going, and pretty, and boys li—" She swallowed that last point. "The thing is that even knowing that it's not fair, those feelings don't just vanish. It's impossible to never have a negative response, even if it's unjustified. And I suspect yours are justified."

"Yasmin," Mason whispered her name, a plea for her to

change the topic. Pain flashed across his face. He didn't want to talk about this.

But Yasmin needed to finish.

"You can't never feel angry, Mason. Any more than I can never feel jealous. And that's okay. But you know, acknowledging it does help. It doesn't get rid of the feelings, but at least I'm not fuming at Nima in my head. Maybe if you faced things instead of always avoiding—"

Yasmin cut off as she spotted two tall, curly heads moving back toward their table.

The elves returned, filled the silence with their own conversation. The final details of their plan still needed ironing out. This time, Yasmin did her best to listen.

52
MASON

"Finally. You are so dead." Kira's voice greeted Mason before he'd stepped through the door.

His family had been busy that day. The parlor's walls had been stripped of their shredded hearts and covered in a palatable cream. Uncle Lee's ode to romance remained visible in the repaired pink cushions and bright red loveseat that must have arrived that afternoon.

But why did the room smell like raw chicken?

Mason's nose guided him to a bucket on the floor by the loveseat. Kira curled among the cushions beside it. Comet flew overhead. Judging from the great dragon's lashing tail, he was annoyed.

"I'm not cooking it on the stove. Lee will notice," Kira argued. She stuck her tongue out at Comet. "Not my fault you can't roast it yourself." She reached into the bucket, tore off a piece of raw chicken, and lifted it to her lips. A burst of green flame cooked the meat before she popped it into her mouth.

Mason's stomach fluttered. He dropped his bag beside

the door, giving himself an excuse to turn away. "You know you're not allowed to have that."

Their fairy godfather was particular about the food he allowed.

Mason walked toward his sister and feigned a swipe for her bucket.

Kira curled her limbs around it like a cobra. "You can't have the bucket, but you can have a piece. We won't get hurt if you use a little too much fire."

Mason's stomach tensed. Kira watched him, eyes wide with fascination almost as though she hoped he'd take her up on the offer. But it was only the middle-schooler's poor attempt at a joke.

"I already ate," Mason said, choosing to stand instead of joining her on the couch. "Why am I dead? Is Lee pissed I wasn't home to help this afternoon?"

"Probably. But Jeremiah's going to kill you before he does. He might hate you even more than me now."

"Jere doesn't hate you," Mason said. He'd hoped to shift to a lighter topic, but the mention of their brother did little to ease him. "Why's he mad?"

And why was he talking to the police?

Comet swooped in front of Mason. The great dragon swooned and batted his orb-like eyes.

"You left us with all the work while you enjoyed a candlelit table-for-two," Kira agreed, giggling as she charred another piece of chicken. "How is Yasmin?"

Mason rolled his shoulders, more embarrassed by their comments than he should have been. "It wasn't like that. We were working on an assignment."

Kira kept giggling. Comet hummed the tune of an old, Italian love song. The great dragon couldn't breathe fire, but he mimicked a piano with alarming accuracy.

Though maybe it was a bit. Yasmin had fallen asleep with her head against his shoulder. He'd pretended to drift off as well, but it was only an excuse to let his cheek rest against her hair. It was so soft, like silk against his skin. Her closeness made the surrounding air blossom with the scent of roses. In the crook of her neck, the wisp pulsed to the rhythm of her breathing like a lullaby.

But the elves had been with them at the restaurant. Mason considered explaining, but the fewer details his family knew, the safer. He couldn't risk them being implicated if something went wrong.

Not that it would. The police wouldn't question the word of an elf prince. Unless they had other evidence.

A horrible thought flashed across Mason's mind.

"It wasn't a date," he repeated, spinning toward the stairs. His siblings snickered below as he raced up, half-flying even with his wings hidden. Comet and Kira weren't the ones he needed to talk to.

Mason flung open Jeremiah's door.

The elf sat in his desk chair. The screen of his tablet showed a series of physics problems, but he wasn't looking at it. Jeremiah faced the door, his lips set in a sneer and his long arms folded. He'd heard Mason coming. Perhaps he'd overheard the entire conversation downstairs.

"Did you tell the police about Yasmin?" Mason skipped any pretense of small talk. "I know you talked to an officer after school."

"I didn't—" Surprise flashed in Jeremiah's eyes. He scoffed, swallowing his previous denial. "And your first concern is for Gul? Are you into her?"

Mason shrugged. So what if he was. His feelings for Yasmin weren't relevant.

"Rip off my ears and drown me in dust," Jeremiah

muttered a modified version of one of Uncle Lee's favorite curses. He slapped his palm onto the desk, stood, and crossed the few feet between them, his voice rising. "You've gone insane! I thought breaking secrecy and involving a human in whatever crap you're in was the worst of it. But now you're telling me it's because you *like* her. Dust, Mason. Which head are you thinking with?"

"She did me a favor. I'm not going to break my word and wipe her memory." Mason glared at his brother, refusing to step back despite Jeremiah's towering height.

"I think we're well past worrying about Yasmin's awareness of magic." A shrill, half-crazed laugh escaped the elf. "You gave her Eli's stolen fire."

It was as though a fork of lightning had struck Mason. His mouth moved. No words came. How did Jeremiah know about the wisp?

"Oh Stars! I'm right, aren't I?" Jeremiah slapped his palm to his forehead and stepped back. Another giggle escaped him. "You stole from the Drages. You broke secrecy. And now you've given dragon fire to a human."

Mason's tongue flicked over his lips. "I didn't—"

"Please! You think I'm blind? Yasmin had a blue light fluttering under her shirt. It kept beaming from her chest when you were in the library. I can put two and two together. What? Did you trap it in a glass gem for her to wear on her neck? A goddamn token of your sudden affection?"

Mason's fists curled. Heat rose in his stomach. His jaw twitched from the effort of keeping it closed. Jeremiah really thought he was the thief. And that he was reckless enough to give Yasmin dragon fire.

I'm not angry. I'm not.

Burn it. Mason was furious.

Acknowledging it did little to quell his fire. If anything, the heat in his stomach grew worse. He could feel it, licking against his insides, turning his torso into a furnace.

But it didn't creep into his throat. Maybe Yasmin's advice had some merit.

Mason clung to that small comfort, as he stormed from his brother's room.

53
MASON

"Phew! You're here." Finnian keeled forward on the sidewalk, breathing heavy. A few passing humans turned their heads, eyes narrowing in momentary confusion. To them, it must've looked like he materialized from thin air. "I was worried you'd go in without me."

Mason leaned against the wall of a parking garage soaking in the morning sunlight. The Castor's Police station loomed across the street. Its painted purple buildings with wolf paws stamped on the doors reminded him of a child's building blocks. If only its purpose were as whimsical.

"I should have," Mason said, pushing himself from the wall. "It's suspicious for us to arrive together."

Finnian waved away the objection just as he had last night. "We're friends. We discussed the fires we separately saw and realized the connection. Nothing suspicious about that."

Except the part where a half-orphaned dragon befriended an elf prince. But Mason didn't argue. Confronting the police had to be safer with a member of the nobility on your side.

"I was worried you weren't going to show," Mason admitted. He'd been waiting outside the garage for almost twenty minutes, counting the few cars that entered, and trying not to think about his fight with Jeremiah last night.

"I'm only five minutes late. I consider that on time," Finnian said. "Anyway, I messaged to tell you."

"I didn't bring my phone," Mason said, making it sound like an intentional decision and not a scatter-brained mistake. Honestly, he didn't know how he'd grabbed his wallet and keys but missed it. He always kept them together by his backpack.

"Probably smart. Wouldn't want the police to go through any romantic correspondence between you and your witch." Finnian winked, and Mason's stomach flipped. Was the prince alluding to Yasmin being human or trying to tease him about the nature of their relationship?

Mason rolled his shoulders, the back of his neck suddenly hot. "Don't mention her when we're in there."

"I know, I know." Finnian held up his hands. Even going into the police station couldn't dampen his grin. "I've never met her."

"Exactly." The less said about Yasmin, the safer for them all.

———

Mason's foot tapped against the floor of the interrogation room. He watched the minute hand tick on the wall clock. It had been an hour since the police separated him and Finnian. What a day to have forgotten his phone.

The door swung open, and Lieutenant Brager swaggered into the small, windowless room. Sweat dampened his uniform, staining his chest. He adjusted the collar, and his lips smiled. His eyes didn't.

"We meet again, Mr. Wick." Brager grabbed the chair on the opposite end of the iron table and spun it around. He spread his legs wide and set his arms over the back. His eyes flashed, reflecting the yellow of the single bulb overhead. "I must say, turning yourself in is quite a choice."

Doing what?

"I didn't steal anything," Mason said, narrowing his eyes at the lieutenant. Was this Brager's precinct?

The door opened again, and a young policeman with tanned skin and dark curls entered. Officer Lowe. He'd taken Mason and Finnian's initial statements.

Something dark and metallic glinted in the young officer's hands. He shifted, moving the object out of Mason's sight, before taking a position in the corner.

Is this some sort of test?

"I came to report what I saw at the Drages' Manor when I gave my alibi," Mason said, leaning back in his wooden chair. He crossed his arms, pulling them away from the manacles on the iron table, and pointed his chin toward Lowe. "He knows."

The young policeman shuffled nervously. With one hand, he pulled a notebook from his pocket. "He claimed to find a large fire that"—he flipped the page—"smelled human."

Brager waved his hand in dismissal. "Not a crime for Castors to be interested in strange scents. Though I can't say I'd appreciate it the way you would." He gave Mason another dead-eyed smile.

"To the contrary, sir, I think a werewolf such as yourself would notice it more than I did," Mason said. "And given the rumors I've heard—"

"About the Drages running the Serpents?" Brager scoffed. "A fact you claim to have heard from your father, Lawrence Wick. But if we ask your father..." He turned to his companion in the corner. "What did he say would happen?"

Lowe checked his notes again. "He said, *if you ask my father, he'll deny it.*"

"Sounds real believable." Brager exaggerated each word. "Your father, Mr. Lawrence Wick, also testified in court at his original hearing that he didn't know the identity of the Serpents' leaders. Are you saying he perjured himself or that he's suddenly had an epiphany about his current employers? Rather convenient. Did he have his wages docked recently?"

"No, my father didn't—" Mason's jaw clenched. He swallowed, trying to stifle the heat in his stomach. Werewolves could survive dragon fire but burning the policemen would do him no favors. He needed to keep his cool. "Forget about the Serpents. You have an eyewitness who saw a flame that destroyed magic. And the Drages are missing a flame. That's not a coincidence."

Brager shrugged. "I heard it was a painting that was stolen."

What is he talking about?

"You were searching my house for the fire a week ago."

Officer Lowe's eyebrows shot up. "L-Lieutenant?"

"That's nonsense." Brager scoffed, dismissing his inferior's concern with another wave even as his lips twisted into a sly smile. "I'm not looking for anything belonging to the Drages. None of us are. The family never filed a report. That theft was all hearsay."

Officer Lowe nodded, unable to see the smirk on the lieutenant face.

Cold flooded Mason.

News of the theft had only been in gossip rags like *Witch Whisper*, and even they'd claimed that the Drages never filed a report.

"You work for them." Shock tempered Mason's fire, keeping his lips numb and his stomach chilled. But it should've been obvious.

He and Finnian hadn't happened into Brager's precinct. The lieutenant must've had people alerting him whenever the Drages were mentioned in a report. That's why Mason had been left alone for over an hour. They'd been waiting for Brager to arrive.

"I need to speak to someone else." Mason stood.

Lowe shoved his notepad in his pocket and stumbled forward. Metal flashed behind his back. "S—sit down!"

"I'm only going to the door." Mason lifted his arms in a placating gesture. There was no reason for any of them to overreact. He'd entered the station of his own volition. He wasn't in custody. "I've given my statement. That's all I came to do, and my friend will be waiting."

Brager's smile stretched across his pale, thin face. He looked like a skeleton, at ease on his iron chair. "Oh, your little elf prince is long gone. And he gave me quite the tale."

Something about his tone made Mason pause. Did Brager seem amused?

"Muzzle him, officer," Brager ordered, and Lowe moved in, dark metal glinting.

Panic heated Mason's chest as he recognized it. But this had to be an empty threat. He needed to stay calm. "You can't muzzle me without cause. It's illegal."

"Good thing we have cause." Brager moved fast, a sick grin on his face. He grabbed Mason's arm and twisted, pinning him against the wall.

Fire bloomed in Mason's stomach, churning, threatening to overwhelm him. He needed to run.

But he couldn't.

Officer Lowe lifted the dark muzzle, drawing closer, voice shaky as he delivered the finishing blow. "You, Mason Wick, are under arrest for breaking secrecy and sharing magical knowledge with the human Yasmin Gul."

54
YASMIN

The wisp danced around Yasmin's arms as she packed her bag.

A human soul. Or a remnant of one at any rate.

"And now you're my familiar," Yasmin said, scooping the wisp into her palm. She expected the heavy sadness that the discovery had brought last night. Instead, excitement thrummed through the wisp. Bits of blue sparked from its yellow core, flying like miniature fireworks.

Yasmin smiled. "I'm glad you're not upset with the arrangement. Do you remember being human?"

The wisp settled against her chest, echoing her heartbeat and filling her with the same sense of kinship she'd felt when she'd found it hidden in the drain. Memories of its past life had been lost to the Drages' flames. All it knew was that it belonged with Yasmin. They'd bonded.

Yasmin pressed her hand to her heart. The wisp's warmth radiated beneath her fingers. It felt right.

How had she lived without the wisp before? How had she lived without magic?

Out of habit, Yasmin reached for her notebook to write

about the sensation. But she paused at the sight of the floral blue cover. Instead of embarrassing confessions, this one contained only facts about the wisp. Maybe it was better to keep it that way.

Yasmin's phone flashed on the shelf. The device had taken its time adjusting to the wisp's magic, but it had finally charged overnight. A message had come from Mason: *Meet me in the park before school. Bring the fire.*

55

MASON

The dark metal stung Mason's cheeks. The muzzle admitted enough oxygen for him to survive, but too little to fix the aching in his lungs. Every breath felt labored, a desperate gasp for air.

Forget acknowledging his emotions. He had to extinguish the fire.

Think positive. I'll get out of this. I just—

It was no use. Sparks flew from Mason's tongue. They grew into flames, swirling and raging in the confines of the muzzle. His lips cracked and dried as he curled on the cell's mattress. Mason would have sold his tail for a sip of water.

Or for the truth.

How had Brager known about Yasmin? Had Finnian really betrayed him? The prince acted friendly, but he'd initially rushed to defend the Drages. Maybe Finnian had planned to betray Mason this whole time.

Because who else knew Yasmin's secret? Mason, the three at the Portentous Purveyor, and—

Jeremiah never explained why he was talking to a cop.

Mason's stomach turned. He clamped his mouth shut.

The muzzle already too hot. He shouldn't think about his brother, or the prince, or anyone who might've—

Footsteps came from the dark passage, followed by a familiar voice, "And you just let him leave?"

Eli Drage.

Mason scrambled from the thin, foam mattress that managed to be less comfortable than a pile of clothes. He didn't dare touch the cell bars. They glowed like shadows, absorbing the light of the prisons, forged of the same stinging metal as the muzzle.

"Fuck's sake, Eli." Brager's voice was loud. "I can't arrest someone like that. People will notice. They'll go looking into what he said. Do you want that?" The policeman stepped in front Mason's cell. His lips quirked into a cold, cruel smile, and he pointed to a pair of shackles at the back of the cell. "Against the wall, Wick."

Mason was in no position to argue. He moved away from the bars, and Eli came into view.

The wealthy dragon's deep blue wings folded against the back of a crisp red shirt. His tail trailed along the floor, spikes digging into the ground. In his hand was a bottle of water.

———

"I am dreadfully sorry it's come to this, Mason." Eli sat on the edge of the thin palette. His arms spread in a sympathetic shrug as though the matter were beyond his control. "Under different circumstances, I imagine we'd have gotten along well. Unfortunately, theft and deception are poor foundations for friendship."

Shackled and muzzled, Mason was powerless to do more than glare.

"That must be torture." Eli pointed to the smoke sneaking through the edges of the muzzle. He shook the bottle of water. "Would you like a drink?"

"What's the catch?" Mason's voice strained to be heard through the metal, cracking and hissing from the heat.

"It's not poison." Eli rested the bottle at the foot of the bed, stood, and walked toward Mason. "I'm simply looking for answers. You tell me the truth, I give you a sip. More than reasonable, isn't it?"

Without waiting for a response, Eli reached up and unlocked Mason's muzzle.

Golden-yellow flames burst loose in a wild, desperate frenzy.

"You are impressive, Mason." Eli pulled a glass from his pocket. It must've been enchanted, for the fire swirled into its depths, allowing him to screw a lid over the top. "Raw strength and clever enough to fool me. I should have recruited you when you were younger. You'd have made a fine serpent."

Free of the muzzle, Mason gasped for air. His lungs filled too fast, and a fit of dry coughs racked his chest.

"I never gave much thought to what that old bastard sold. Perhaps I'll rescue some of his stock before he's smoked out of business." Eli spoke over the sounds of Mason's coughs, as relaxed as if they were old friends chatting over a meal. "Witch-scented perfume. A bit on the—" He tapped his nose, laughing at his own pun. "But burning her fingers so that it looked like the wisp had hurt her? That was inspired."

Mason only half understood. He licked his lips, but his tongue was too dry to be of use. The water glistened at the bottom of the bed. He strained against his manacles, trying to break just one hand free to reach it.

Eli slipped the captured fire into his pocket. Either dehydration was affecting Mason's vision, or the pants had been bewitched to hold more than the laws of physics decreed.

"Now"—Eli turned and lifted the bottle of water—"returning to my potions den when I invited you into my home was an absurd choice." He tossed the bottle between his hands. "I couldn't imagine the same criminal who broke past my security would be so reckless. When we found you, I didn't doubt—but I suppose your romantic attachment wasn't the lie."

He unscrewed the water bottle and lifted it to Mason's lips. "How did you and a human manage to rob me? Did you have help on the inside?"

Mason shook his head.

Eli didn't pour. "You must have. How else could you have known about the wisps?"

"We. Didn't. Steal it." Mason wheezed the words.

Eli tilted the bottle. A thin stream of water trickled into Mason's mouth. Less than a sip.

He savored it, sucking in his lips so he could feel the cool liquid against them. But when he swallowed, the trickle of water only accentuated his thirst.

"That was so you could talk. Not because I believe you. I'm already aware that your human has my wisp. Now, do you want another sip?" Eli shook the bottle, and the water sloshed within, promising relief.

"We found the wisp," Mason managed.

"Where?"

Mason's throat burned. He tried to think of a believable lie.

Eli tilted the bottle. Water trickled onto the floor.

Mason's resolve quivered at the sight, but he couldn't

crack. If he told Eli the truth, it would cast suspicion over his family— Uncle Lee, Kira, Comet, Jeremiah. He couldn't put them in danger.

And he couldn't rat his father out. Lawrence might've been an ass, but he was Mason's only blood relative.

And the Drages will kill him.

Eli sighed and shook his head, looking more like a disappointed parent than the leader of a criminal syndicate. He poured more water at Mason's feet. "Perhaps, you aren't as thirsty as I thought. How about a different offer." Eli smiled. "You know the story of the Harrow King, how those wisps were made."

A shiver went through Mason. That hadn't been a question, but he hoped answering might earn him another sip all the same. "You killed thousands of humans."

Eli's smile broadened. "Exactly. So you'll recognize it's no idle threat when I say that if you don't tell me the truth, your pet human will be an ingredient in my next set."

Mason's heart stopped. He'd imagined the worst they could do to Yasmin was wipe her memories. "You're planning to make more?"

Eli shrugged. "Wisps are more reusable than our flames, but they still have limits. Without a host, their little shriveled souls eventually vanish. No profit in selling a weapon our buyers won't pay us to replenish."

"The Knights."

"Perhaps. I anticipate we'll have offers from several groups after our demonstration."

"Your what?"

"To showcase the wisps. And remind people not to mess with the Serpents, of course. You know what they say. Three dead birds, one fire." He smiled. "Now, have you decided? Your human's life for the truth?"

Yasmin in exchange for Lawrence.

It should have been a difficult decision. Perhaps, a week ago, it would have been. Now, the quickness of Mason's response startled even him. "It was my dad. He stole the wisp and hid it down a drain. That's how we found it."

Anger flashed like lightning over Eli's face, from the furrow of his brow to the flare of his nostrils to the snarl of his lips. Then, a smile replaced it. "Selling out your father for a human? Perhaps you'd have made a poor Serpent after all."

He poured the last of the water on Mason's lips. The liquid still refused to offer the expected relief.

Mason had just condemned his father to death.

56
YASMIN

Gladwin Gardens was three blocks east of Folkestone High, beyond Yasmin's usual route. Pockets of fresh flowers splatter-painted the manicured lawn in bright patches of pinks and blues. Willow branches swept the grass, wind blowing the hanging tendrils so that Yasmin stood in a whirl of leaves.

At this hour on a Tuesday, few other people occupied the space—an elderly couple on a stroll, a jogger with earphones, and a man arguing on his phone at the end of a bench.

Why does Mason want to meet here instead of school?

Were the Castor's police at Folkestone again? But that shouldn't matter. They'd cleared his name. Now, he was the one filing a report against the Drages.

Is he worried they come looking for him?

Mason had hidden behind his optimistic grin but acting against the Drages made him nervous.

Yasmin's phone buzzed. The wisp trembled against her neck as she reached into her pocket. A message from Mason said that he was running late.

Something tapped her through the willow's vines.

Yasmin squeaked and spun around.

"Oh." She relaxed before growing annoyed. "Are you trying to scare me? Why are you—"

Before Yasmin could finish, a wave of white dust blew toward her. The wisp shot out to meet it. Neither of them noticed the glass jar until it was too late.

57
YASMIN

Something's missing.

Yasmin shivered, a chill like ice flowing through her veins. She'd never felt so cold.

Did I fall into a lake?

But it wasn't winter.

Blankets pressed against her. She felt their weight, but not their warmth. Her eyes fluttered open. She recognized the water stain near the corner of the white-tiled ceiling.

I'm in my bed.

That wasn't right. What was she doing in her room? She'd been at—Where? Folkestone?

Yes, she'd been at school.

Hadn't she?

She couldn't keep her eyes open.

"Allah!" That was her father, loud and panicked. He'd never done more than stick his head into their room. Now, his feet thumped against the floor like he was spinning in a circle. "Something's wrong. She left this morning but when I came back, she was here. She—she's roasting with fever. It's bad."

"Do you need me to come home?" Nima's voice came through a phone speaker.

"I—" His voice broke. "No, no. I can take care of my own daughter." He collapsed to his knees, and his hands grabbed Yasmin's own beneath the sheets.

———

Something's missing.

Yasmin's eyes fluttered open. Somehow, she was colder. She pulled a damp towel from her forehead and pushed the blankets aside. Sweat coated her body. Someone had dressed her in a blue nightgown.

Darkness betrayed that it was night. Yasmin stood and examined her body, expecting to discover she was missing a limb. But she had both legs, both hands, all her fingers and toes.

Am I going crazy?

Yasmin wrapped her arms around her shoulders and sat on the edge of the bed. Her eyes landed on a yellow baseball cap. She'd never seen that before. What was it doing on an empty shelf?

"My notebooks."

Yasmin leaped up, unsteady on her feet. She stumbled forward, hands running along the shelves. Her collection of biographies and mysteries twinkled near the top. All Nima's romances remained on the opposite side of the room.

But Yasmin's notebooks had vanished. The empty shelf instead had a bowl of melting ice, and a damp towel.

Is that what I'm missing?

It must have been. But how? Books didn't just vanish. Someone must've moved them.

"Baba!" Yasmin shouted, hurrying out the door and into

the hallway. Her feet stung as numbness gave way to pins and needles. "What did you do with my—?"

Hassan blocked her path before she could make it to the living room.

"You're up!" His arms wrapped around her. The hug lasted less than second before he stepped back, lifting his hand to her forehead. "You still have a fever."

"No, I'm freezing. Where's Baba?"

"He had an emergency job at an apartment building. I made him take it. He hasn't left the house since he found you on Tuesday."

What day was it now?

"He's going to be so relieved. Nima too. But you have to lay back down." Hassan took her hand to guide her back to her room.

"I can't." Yasmin pulled away, but her mind was spinning too much to run. "I have to find something. Hassan, did you move my notebooks?"

"No, I didn't. I swear." He traced an *x* across his heart. "I only read it the one time. I don't need to keep reading your Mason fanfic."

"My what?"

"Your story about Mason Wick." Hassan pressed his hand against her forehead again. "I think your fever has you delirious."

No, it didn't.

"I don't write made-up stories in my notebooks."

"Sure." Hassan didn't look like he believed her. "Let's get you back to bed. I'm sure you just hid your diary under your pillow or something."

Yasmin didn't fight when her brother took her arm this time. "Did you really read my notebook?" That seemed like something Yasmin should remember.

Hassan nodded. "But don't worry. I didn't tell anyone about your crush on Mason."

"I don't—" Yasmin started to object, but a strange flutter went through her chest at the thought of her class-mate with his perfect nose and crooked smile. Mason was cute, and clever, and sweet—No. Hadn't she always found him suspicious? Like his niceness was a mask that hid some dark secret?

No, it's just to hide his own pain.

Yasmin rubbed her head. Where had that impression come from? Maybe she was delirious. She let her brother help her back into bed. "What happened to me?"

"We were hoping you could tell us. Baba found you in bed, roasting with fever. You've been slipping in and out of consciousness."

A shiver went through Yasmin as she lay back against the pillow. "The last thing I remember, it was lunch. I didn't have anyone to eat with, so I went to the gym, and—I think I threw up."

Hassan's eyes grew wide. He felt her forehead for a third time. "Go to sleep, Yas. The fever has you confused."

———

Where is it?

Yasmin stared at the empty shelves. A swamp of scat-tered books, clothes, and stationery supplies spread across the narrow floor. She'd hunted through every nook.

Her sunflower notebook—the one she'd been so excited to use—had vanished, along with all the rest.

How? Years of writing couldn't just disappear.

Yasmin tied the string of her robe tighter. Sweat dampened her skin beneath the thick fabric, but the chill remained in her bones.

Where would I have put them?

Yasmin climbed over the bog of items to reach her door. She stalked through the apartment, a ghost haunting each room until she arrived at her father's own.

It remained as her mother had decorated: a king-sized bed with floral accents, purple curtains across the window, an incense burner on the dresser which no one ever lit. The apartment lacked storage space. Anything special was hidden beneath the bed.

Yasmin sat on a white and purple rug and pulled the boxes free: first aid supplies, tools, extra cushion covers her father likely didn't know existed.

"You're awake!"

The sound of her father's voice made Yasmin jump. She dropped the album. Amir didn't appreciate his children sneaking into his room. A lecture was imminent.

Amir rushed to his daughter. He knelt on the rug beside Yasmin and pressed both hands to her cheeks. Tears blossomed in the corners of his eyes. A smile spread across his face. "God is good," he whispered. "Your fever's broken."

Then why do I feel even colder than before?

"I was so worried. We were all were. I thought we might lose you like—" His voice cracked. A tear escaped from the corner of his eye, trickling across his cheek.

Yasmin had seen her father cry only once before. The night of her mother's funeral, he'd instructed his children to head up to the apartment alone. They'd gone to the elevator, but halfway, Yasmin realized she'd forgotten a book she'd been reading. She'd gone back to retrieve it and seen him—seatbelt still on, hands clutching the wheel, and head bowed as the tears dripped onto his lap.

She'd looked away. Watching felt invasive.

But Yasmin couldn't turn her head now. Her father's hands remained on her cheeks, forcing her to meet his gaze.

"Baba..." Yasmin's chest tightened. She didn't know what to say. For years, she'd worried her father didn't love her, that he wouldn't realize how much she did until she was gone. But here he was, crying because she'd had a fever.

Relief flooded her. It wasn't enough to get rid of the chill.

Something's still missing.

Yasmin rested one of her hands over her father's own, letting her fingers curl around his palm. "Did you move my books?"

"That's what you—" Amir's tears turned into a laugh. He patted his daughter's cheek before releasing her. "I am blessed to have a child like you. Unconscious most of the past forty-eight hours, and you wake up worrying about books. No, I haven't touched any of your things."

Did he say forty-eight hours?

Yasmin shivered. "What day is it?"

"Thursday." Amir reached out, rubbing his hands over his daughter's shoulders. "We should get you back to bed. I'll order food. Anything you want."

No, Yasmin couldn't lie back down. She had something to find. "It's okay. I'm doing much better. In fact, I think I'll go to school tomorrow."

And hopefully, her sunflower notebook would be there.

58

MASON

Three nights. Alone. In a jail cell.

At least when he'd been kept in isolation at the Reformatory, the therapists had checked in.

And the bed was comfortable.

Mason lay flat on the foam palette, staring at the dark ceiling. Did his family know where he was? There were no phone calls offered to Castors when they were arrested. The police department sent notice direct. Was Brager following protocol?

He must be, even if only for appearances.

After Eli's visit on Tuesday afternoon, a lawyer had arrived, likely in the Serpents' pocket himself. The rat-faced, graying man in a too-small suit claimed the case would be impossible to win. Absolute crap.

Yasmin wouldn't be the first human to learn the truth. Perhaps Mason had believed she was a woodswitch.

Whether a judge would buy that excuse, however, was irrelevant. Mason had information about the Serpents—their leaders and their weaponry. Any upstanding policeman would cut him a deal in seconds.

Except that Brager will discredit anything I say.

As though summoned by the thought, the lieutenant appeared, rattling the bars with his fist as he walked the short line of cells. "Wake up, Sunshine!"

Mason rose, gray jumpsuit flapping around his limbs. Unless someone had arrived overnight, he was the only prisoner in the station. He rubbed his jaw. The muzzle had stayed off since Eli's visit. Mason suspected there was something that quenched his fire hidden in the room-temperature soup they fed him for each meal. The Reformatory had used a similar trick. Mason didn't know why they bothered with deception. He'd drink liquefied spinach if it settled his fire.

"Breakfast?" Mason guessed, stepping toward the back of his cell.

But there was no tray in Brager's hand. Instead of food, he was accompanied by the lawyer. The rat-faced man wore a pin-striped suit that struggled to button over his stomach. What was his name again? Something like Sham.

"Good news, Mr. Wick," Rat-face said, scratching his chin. "You're free to leave."

Brager turned the metal key and shoved the door in.

Mason kept his back to the wall, waiting for the inevitable joke. When none came, he made it for them. "And return to the Reformatory?"

The two men exchanged a look.

Mason's chest tightened. Surely, a high school student breaching secrecy wasn't deserving of Ironvault Prison, especially while awaiting an official trial. Rat-face would have needed to do an exceptionally poor job to achieve that outcome.

Which is precisely what Eli would've ordered.

"You bastard." Mason's lips curled back as he glared at the man.

The lawyer's nose twitched. "I beg your pardon?"

"Odd way to say thank you," Brager said. "Mr. Shaw convinced the department to dismiss your case. He's here to escort you to freedom. Now get out my cell."

He pointed to the open door. Shaw, the rat-faced lawyer, continued studying his nails.

Mason hesitated. This had to be a trick. Unless he'd judged the lawyer unfairly. Maybe he wasn't working with the Serpents. But then why wasn't Brager more annoyed?

The lieutenant pushed Mason out of the cell, forcing him to accept his freedom.

Mason waited for an ambush at the end of the hall, then as he changed into his clothes, and again as he passed the jumpsuit to a policewoman behind a glass window. She passed his belongings in exchange. No attack came.

Somehow, that was worse.

Eli must have wanted Mason free. But why?

———

The breath caught in Mason's throat as he entered the Quintessential Living Complex. Lawrence's house appeared unoccupied as always—blinds drawn, no welcome signs, grass on the verge of needing to be cut.

Eli wouldn't have left him unpunished for the past three days. And yet, Mason couldn't relinquish his last desperate shred of hope.

Please be fine.

Lawrence was wily. Maybe he'd talked himself out of trouble. Maybe he'd fled the country.

Mason took a deep breath. His fire remained settled

from the previous night's jail-cell soup, but the heat was starting to return. He pounded his fist against the door. "Dad! Dad, let me in. Please!"

Mason's arm trembled. He tried the door. It opened. That didn't bode well given Lawrence's paranoia.

The kitchen waited in darkness, blinds blocking any trace of sunrise. The light entered only through the door, glinting on broken glass and outlining the toppled refrigerator. The scent of meats hit Mason, raw and bloody. Beneath was a faint trace of iron and smoke.

Dragon blood.

It dripped a red trail across the floor. Mason was too late. The Serpents had been here.

Or still were. The blood bubbled at Mason's touch, a sign that it was fresh. They'd gone after his dad the same morning that he'd been released. That wasn't a coincidence.

Mason stepped back from the townhome. Over the past few days, he'd replayed his last conversation with Eli over a hundred times. Dehydration made Mason's memory foggy, but certain pieces had burned into his mind.

He stole my fire. Then he said something about a demonstration.

There wasn't enough to blood to suggest Lawrence had died. Had Eli taken him somewhere? What good would a dragon be if he wanted to showcase the wisps? And why would he need Mason's flames?

Three birds, one fire.

That was the other statement that had stood out to Mason. Maybe the fire was metaphorical. But who were the three birds?

Lawrence. Mason. And...

Yasmin.

59
YASMIN

Yasmin flung her brother's books from his locker, anxiety mounting with every textbook she found.

"I told you, I didn't take it," Hassan said, voice soft. He offered nervous smiles to the few students that lingered in the hallway. Classes wouldn't begin for almost an hour, but many of the school clubs met early. In a parallel universe, Yasmin would be folding copies of the *Folkes News*.

"Then where is it?" Yasmin's fingers curled around the last stray piece of paper in Hassan's locker. Math homework he'd never finished. She crumpled it into a ball and flung it toward the garbage. It landed over a foot shy.

"Maybe you threw it out," Hassan suggested, scrambling to shove his textbooks back into his locker. "I haven't seen it in your room, and you wouldn't have brought it to school. Just, forget about it okay."

But Yasmin couldn't. A piece of her was missing. What could it be if not her sunflower notebook?

"I wouldn't have thrown it out," Yasmin insisted, perhaps too loudly.

Lydia Prince gave her a nasty look from the other end of the hallway. The tall brunette stood with a group of other volleyballers. She leaned in, whispered something, and they burst into laughter.

She doesn't like me.

Yasmin marched toward the end of the hall, ignoring Hassan's attempts to pull her back. "Did you take my notebook?"

Lydia's brow furrowed as she turned to Yasmin. "Why would I want your notebook?"

Jealousy?

That made no sense, and Yasmin knew better than to say it aloud. "Let me look in your locker."

"No way, weirdo." Lydia grabbed her bag and slammed her locker closed. She fell into a group with her friends and hurried toward the gymnasium door. Her whisper was loud enough to travel down the hall, "No wonder Mason's embarrassed to admit they were hooking up."

Yasmin ignored the comment. Clearly, their conversation had moved on to someone else, and she had bigger problems. The door to Lydia's locker wouldn't budge. The school locks were better than expected. Or Yasmin was incredibly weak.

"Can you open this?" Yasmin turned to her brother.

Hassan glanced at the door, shifting the bag with his cleats. "I have to go to practice."

"Fine." Yasmin waved him off and pressed her face to the slats, searching for a hint of yellow in Lydia's locker.

Hassan didn't move. "Yas, please. Stop. People are starting to—"

"There!" Yasmin slammed her fist against a locker at the bottom. One of the books had gold rings. She rattled the door, trying to pull it loose. Her arms ached from the strain. But she had to get it open.

Something was missing. Something she needed. Something she—

"Is your sister okay?" Gigi Davis ran forward as she entered the hall. Despite her volleyball shorts and sweatshirt, her lips featured their signature red. Before Hassan could answer, she crouched and rested her hand on Yasmin's shoulder. "Jesus, you're freezing."

Yasmin turned to Gigi. "Do you think Lydia would take my notebook?"

"I am so sorry," Hassan said, tugging on his collar. "She's just—She can't find her book, so—Uh. I don't—"

"She's delirious," Gigi said, biting her lip. She looked genuinely concerned. "I think I have some meds, but she shouldn't be here. This looks bad."

————

Yasmin pulled her limbs close, shivering beneath her blanket. She clung to a black polka-dot notebook full of half-finished notes. The cover labelled it as *Biology* with a heart atop the *i*, but it contained everything from math to English to a grocery list. Another time, Yasmin might've judged the disorganization, but she was finding it difficult to fault Gigi, who'd lent her the notebook and waited outside until Yasmin's father arrived.

She also asked me about Mason Wick.

Yasmin scribbled his name on the page. A flutter of heat broke through her chill at the sight. Odd. Especially since Gigi wasn't the only who'd mentioned him.

Lydia had made that strange comment in the hallway. Hassan claimed Yasmin's sunflower notebook contained a fictitious story about Mason. And there were the messages from Nima...

Yasmin leaned over pulled her phone from the pocket of her jeans, folded on her bedside table. She'd removed them and her bra not out of discomfort, but as a way to keep herself in bed. Her father had insisted, and logically, Yasmin knew he was right. She'd acted irrationally at school, and the cold felt like it might kill her.

But while she could force her body to stay put, her mind refused to comply.

Yasmin pulled up her sister's contact, writing her thoughts as she did. The most recent message from Nima had come after their family video chat last night: *Sounds like your memory got pretty scrambled. Didn't want to ask anything in front of Baba and Has, but did you remember about the birth control? xx*

It had to be her sister's idea of a horrible joke. There was zero reason for Yasmin to be on birth control unless she'd forgotten something *very* significant.

But what about the earlier messages?

Yasmin scrolled up further than intended: a few short texts over summer when Nima had the car—practical and to the point. Weeks of silence followed before a few requests to *chat*. Unusual, but Nima had probably wanted a favor. Her sister never communicated with her privately otherwise.

Until last Sunday.

Suddenly, there were dozens of messages sharing jokes about their relatives, memories of their mother, comments about Nima's new boyfriend, and then Mason.

Monday morning, Yasmin texted Nima asking to borrow a shirt. They messaged back and forth for the next ten minutes. Mason came up several times. Nima thought he was the reason for the request. Weirdly, Yasmin didn't deny it.

Had something happened between her and Mason?

Her sunflower notebook would have the answer. Yasmin needed to find it. She wasn't whole. Part of her was missing and—No! Yasmin grabbed a pillow and covered her face, trying to snuff out her spiraling thoughts. What she needed was rest. She closed her eyes, shifted beneath the blankets, and attempted to sleep.

———

Despite her best efforts, Yasmin was still awake when her bedroom door opened.

She slowed her breathing. Her father would feel better if he thought she was sleeping.

Soft footsteps padded toward the bed. A hand pressed against her forehead. Warmth radiated beneath the skin. It was like a fireplace on a cold winter day. Yasmin nuzzled against it on instinct, a soft sigh escaping her before the realization hit.

This was not her father's hand.

Yasmin's eyes sprang open.

Standing at her bedside, Mason Wick offered his usual crooked smile.

60

MASON

Relief flooded Mason.

Yasmin was alive, just concerningly cold. Why? Had Eli paid a witch to cast some sort of curse, or was she simply ill like everyone at Folkestone said?

Mason had visited the school looking for her first. Kalvin and Zach had broken away from soccer drills and rushed him. He'd barely needed to inquire about Yasmin before they filled him in.

She'd missed the past three days of school—just like Mason. A rumor had been going around that they'd run off together, though Kalvin assured him that no one with sense believed it. Zach agreed that the more popular theory was that they'd both contracted mono.

"You're in better shape than she is though," Zach had continued. "She came in this morning too, but totally out of it. Her dad had to take her home. She kept—"

Mason hadn't stayed to hear what. He'd thanked his friends, then run off toward the old gym. Kalvin had shouted something about Jeremiah, but most of the message was lost to the wind.

"Are you real? How did you get in here?" Yasmin glared at Mason as she pushed herself up. The sunflower-covered comforter fell from her.

She wasn't wearing a bra. And she was very cold. That was readily apparent.

"Uh..." Mason shifted his gaze before she accused him of staring, struggling to think of a response. He'd been so worried about Yasmin's safety, he hadn't considered how she'd react to his sudden appearance. "I used the key. Under the plant. I was really..."

A white bra with a red cherry print sat atop a pair of jeans by her bedside. Cute. He'd assumed Yasmin's underwear would all be black and practical.

Not that he'd thought about Yasmin's underwear. Or her current lack thereof. And was she not wearing pants?

Shit. Mason had gotten so good at avoiding difficult topics that he'd started doing it to himself. This wasn't why he'd come.

Eli's threat. My stolen fire.

"I think you might be in danger," Mason explained, pulling his eyes from the clothing. "When I went to the police, I walked straight into a trap. Brager's working for the Drages, and someone betrayed us and told the police..."

His voice trailed off. Confusion stamped itself across Yasmin's face. Her mouth hung open. Her brow furrowed. She kept blinking.

Reality slammed into Mason. Amnesiac powder.

He'd spent the past few days refusing to think about it. After all, Brager was corrupt. Mason's arrest was a farce. He'd given up his father to Eli. Maybe they wouldn't bother sending someone to wipe Yasmin's mind.

A stupid, childish wish.

"You don't remember," Mason whispered, and his heart

sank. This changed things. Nothing they'd shared these past two weeks mattered to Yasmin now. She'd forgotten magic, forgotten who he really was, even forgotten the wisp.

Guess that meant Xena's theory had been wrong. If Yasmin had bonded it, surely she—

Oh fuck.

Mason leaned in and pressed his palm against Yasmin's forehead. He'd never been good with judging human temperatures, but even he knew they weren't supposed to feel like they'd just stepped out an industrial freezer. This wasn't a hex, or even a sickness. This was much worse.

"There's no tiny blue fireball that's been flitting around you, is there?" Mason asked, crossing his fingers in a desperate last-ditch bit of optimism.

Yasmin shot him a glare as cold as her skin. "If this is a prank, it's not a very funny one. My dad's home. If I shout, he'll come. And he won't be impressed. Boys aren't allowed in my room."

"Didn't bother you before," Mason muttered, but he pulled his hand. He'd seen Yasmin's father when he snuck in. Amir was passed out on the couch with the television loud enough to drown a garbage truck. A shout might not wake him. Still, Mason preferred not to risk it.

If the situation was what he feared, he couldn't leave Yasmin on her own. She'd bonded with the wisp. Its heat had become part of her. Without it, she'd freeze.

"You've been in my room?" Yasmin squeaked the question.

Mason didn't answer. He paced the few steps between the opposing shelves and trying to think. His body gener-ated more heat than a human. It might be enough to stop

Yasmin from getting worse. But he couldn't be with her constantly. She needed the wisp.

Which meant Mason needed to find it. But how? He didn't know where to look. The Drages' manor, maybe. But Eli had something planned. What if he'd moved it? What if it was hidden? Would the wisp call to him like it had Yasmin? Should he bring her?

Fear churned in Mason's stomach, threatening to undo the effects of the soup. He had to fix this. But he couldn't choose wrong. What if he took Yasmin to the Drages and Eli fed her to his next set of flames? Or what if he left her and walked into a trap leaving her without even a temporary source of heat? Mason didn't know what to do. Not on his own. He needed—

"I need you," Mason realized, freezing in the center of the room.

Yasmin's eyes widened like a panicked doe. Her chest flushed despite her chill, and she wrapped her fists in the comforter, pulling it tighter around her waist.

A book dropped from the bed. Mason grabbed it, forgetting to slow his reflexes. The open page revealed Yasmin's current thoughts. Despite her refusal to admit it, she really did turn all her notebooks into diaries.

But this one's not hers.

Flipping it over revealed Gigi Davis' name on the cover.

Mason turned toward Yasmin's bookshelves. An entire row sat empty. How had he missed that?

"Don't read it." Yasmin's reflexes lagged several seconds behind his. Mason would have worried if that weren't her norm. She scrambled forward, reaching for the notebook. Her comforter shifted.

She was indeed not wearing pants.

The flash of cherries and exposed thigh would've made

Mason lose his train of thought at any other time. But he clung to it desperately now. This was too important.

Yasmin might not remember the last two weeks, but her memories weren't gone. She'd written them down.

The Castor police would've swept the room for anything related to magic. Instead of parsing her personal diaries, they'd likely just destroyed them. But the sunflower notebook hadn't been with the others. At least, not on Monday when Mason visited.

That meant, there was a chance.

"Yasmin," Mason's voice trembled, hope and fear battling. "We need to call your sister."

61

YASMIN

This had to be an elaborate prank.

Yasmin sat atop their clothes dryer, legs curled and sunflower notebook open in her lap. It had been in a crawl space in the ceiling, just like Nima said, folded inside of a pink dress. Finding her notes hadn't brought the sense of relief Yasmin had expected. Her missing memories read like a work of fiction. What were these elaborate descriptions of wings? Of Mason in general?

Yasmin's eyes flitted over a paragraph about kissing him: *Smokey lips... hands in my hair...shivers down my spine.* Had she drawn hearts around his name?

"Are you trying to read my notes?" Yasmin pulled the journal tight to her chest, glaring at Mason. He'd stopped pacing the narrow stretch of room, neck tilting toward her book.

"Of course not," he answered a bit too quickly.

If he saw any of that, I'm going to die right now.

But could Yasmin be embarrassed about something she didn't remember?

What if Mason wrote the journal himself to torture her?

He could've convinced Hassan and Nima to play along—maybe even the rest of the school. Except that Yasmin knew her own handwriting.

She hunched forward so the pages were less visible. Her head ached trying to read, but she couldn't stop. Page after page about Mason. About her family. About the wisp.

That's what I'm missing. That's what I have to find.

It felt like everything was finally starting to make sense. But what if that was Yasmin's fever? Logically, nothing in her notes could have been true. The commonsense assumption would be that she'd crafted a piece of fiction.

But Yasmin Gul didn't write fiction.

"Prove it." Yasmin slammed her book shut and straightened. "If everything in here is true like you claim, show me."

Mason rolled his shoulders and glanced around the narrow room. He stepped closer, lifted her hand, and pulled it beneath his shirt.

Yasmin's fingers brushed against his stomach, feeling the lines of his abs. Her heartbeat quickened. This wasn't what she'd meant.

"Can you feel how hot I am?"

"Um..." That had to be trick question. Yasmin pulled her eyes from where his shirt had risen, trying to feign nonchalance. It might've been more convincing if she'd moved her hand. "Some people have naturally high body temperatures."

"Do they also have teeth that could tear flesh?" Mason grinned, revealing a pair of large canines and a dimple.

Yasmin's heart stopped. He was right. Despite the boyish charm of his face, Mason's smile was inhuman. It was too powerful, too predatory. Her notes suggested that his tongue would betray his secret further, but her descriptions of it always trailed off like she'd gotten distracted. Or her thoughts had wandered in a direction she didn't feel comfortable committing to paper.

Either way, there was no way Yasmin was asking Mason to see his tongue. He knew what she'd meant when she asked for proof.

"Show me your wings."

"I don't know if that's a good idea, given your current —" Mason cut off, perhaps noticing Yasmin's insistent glare. He sighed and rolled his shoulder. "Fine. Just don't faint."

62

MASON

Mason unfolded his wings. The laundry room was too narrow to stretch, but he curled them forward, creating a scaled shield around his back and sides. He waited for a comment.

Silence.

"Did you faint when I specifically told you not to?" Mason twisted his head, trying to see over his wings.

If Yasmin heard, she didn't laugh.

Her fingers, feathery and cold, fluttered over his scales. Somehow, her touch managed to tickle the sensitive skin beneath, sending a shiver through him. Mason felt suddenly exposed.

"So, do they live up to the hype?' he asked, then realized his mistake.

Yasmin's notes described them as *sunflower petals gilded in specks of gold.* But Mason didn't know that because he hadn't been reading her private thoughts. Because reading someone's diary without her permission was a breach of trust. And he was a good person.

But come on! How was he not supposed to get curious when he saw his name with hearts around it?

She likes me.

A smile tugged on Mason's lips before he remembered the obvious. Yasmin *had* liked him. She'd lost her memories. Who knew how she felt now?

"Wow," Yasmin whispered the word, and her breath tickled the nape of Mason's neck. Sitting on the dryer gave her an extra few inches of height. "They're...wow. It's all real."

Mason folded his wings, rolled his shoulders, and hid them once more. He spun, afraid he'd find her sobbing or breaking down.

Yasmin's cheeks were dry. Despite the coldness that clung to her, determination burned in her eyes. "We need to find my wisp."

"Agreed," Mason said. "But we need a plan. I don't know if it's back on Eli's estate or already sold to the highest bidder. Without it though, I'm afraid you might..."

He couldn't say it, but Yasmin finished the thought for him with concerning certainty. "I'll die. I know. I keep getting colder." She pulled a pen from the notebook's gold spirals and opened to a fresh page. "Walk me through everything that happened after Monday night."

———

"He's definitely planning something," Yasmin muttered, tapping the page as she studied her notes. She'd written everything down as Mason explained, adding her own opinions on the situation. He hadn't pretended not to read over her shoulder this time.

"A demonstration of the wisps," Mason agreed. He'd already told her as much. "He'll use my fire to hide the damage and implicate me if something goes wrong."

Yasmin nodded, clicking her pen and studying he notes. "And it must be happening today, otherwise, the Serpents wouldn't have released you or taken your dad. They would've killed him at the house."

Mason's stomach turned at the mention of his father's death.

It'll be all my fault if—

He pushed the thought away and joined Yasmin on the washing machine. Her knee brushed against his thigh. Mason couldn't shake the feeling they were going in the wrong direction. "Dragons can't burn. My dad's useless in a demonstration of the wisps' power."

"Maybe the Serpents took him somewhere else then." Yasmin left the *to kill him* implied.

Mason squeezed his eyes shut. He couldn't worry about Lawrence. They needed to figure out where Eli's demonstration would be taking place. That would be key to finding Yasmin's wisp.

But they had to be related, didn't they.

"Three birds, one fire. That's what Eli said," Mason whispered. "My freedom, my dad's capture, the demonstration. It all has to be connected. Otherwise, what three birds could he have meant? We're the ones he wants to punish."

"But not the only ones!" Yasmin's eyes widened. She leaped off the drier, taking her notebook with her. She flipped through the pages. "Today is Friday, isn't it? That's the day Prince Finnian works at the Portentous Purveyor."

"You wrote down the days..." Mason trailed off as the weight of what Yasmin was saying hit him.

He hadn't gone to the police alone. And Yasmin's

disguise and the magic that had provided Lawrence's alibi had all come from the same place.

Three birds, one fire.

Eli had reason to want revenge on Douglas, Finnian, and Xena as well. And, unlike dragons, all three of them could burn.

63
YASMIN

Yasmin slipped the small jar of blue powder into the pocket of her hoodie as she tiptoed into the hall. She'd found zipped in a compartment of the pink dress. According to her notes, it was magic sleeping powder. The laundry detergents must've masked the smell from whoever had searched her house. Mason had been surprised when she pulled it out.

"Do you think I used too much on my dad?" Yasmin whispered as she led the way down the hall. The few windows in her apartment couldn't open wide enough for Mason to fly through, but she knew a building with a rooftop pool a few streets up where he could take off.

"He'll be fine," Mason assured her. But his soft gray clouded his eyes, accentuating the worry as he glanced from the rising elevator to her. "I don't know if you should come, Yas."

Yasmin's eyebrows rose. Was he joking? "I don't know if you should come."

"I'm serious." Mason's tongue flicked over his lower lip.

"We're racing into a situation we know nothing about. It might not be safe. If Eli's already there…"

"I have to find my wisp, Mason," Yasmin said. She meant it. The amnesiac powder might've wiped her mind, but her body remembered. She'd felt its absence when she'd woken up, known that a piece of her was missing. Whatever the danger, she had to find it. Mason wouldn't stop her.

He didn't try.

"You're right," Mason whispered. He held the elevator door open for Yasmin before following her in.

For the first time in days, Yasmin wasn't cold. Mason radiated warmth, spreading heat like a bonfire in the spring. She considered slipping her hands beneath his shirt again before quickly dismissing the idea. How would she even phrase that request?

Mason wrapped his arm around her waist. For a moment, Yasmin worried he'd read her mind somehow, but he'd pulled her in to hug her.

Yasmin's cheek dropped against Mason's chest. His heart pounded, and his head lowered so that his chin rested on her hair. She breathed in the wood-fire scent of his shirt.

"I'm sorry, Yasmin," he whispered. "If something happens to you, it'll be my fault. I could've wiped your memories in the first place, you wouldn't have bonded with the wisp, and you wouldn't—"

Mason's voice trembled. Like he was fighting back tears.

Because of me?

Yasmin reached up and pressed her hand to his cheek. The tension eased from his jaw. His eyes softened, blue managing to twinkle despite the dim light.

No wonder I fell for him.

"Mason, I chose to help you. I wanted to know about magic. I wanted to bond the wisp, and I'm choosing to go find it now. Whatever happens to me isn't on you."

"You know you're really beautiful, even without make-up, right?"

Yasmin's heart skipped, increasing its speed. Her body became hyperaware of Mason's muscles against her chest. Heat spread through her. Was he giving her a genuine compliment or just trying to change the topic?

Mason rested his fingers on her chin, tilted her face up toward his.

Was he going to—?

The elevator doors dinged open.

"Told you so!" A girl's voice shouted.

Mason dropped his hands. Yasmin followed his gaze toward the lobby.

A dark-skinned girl with silver bracelets and two loose curls pointed at Mason. Beside her stood a tall, scowling Jeremiah Quick and a concerned-looking corgi.

Mason's family had come to find him.

64

MASON

"Were you about to kiss a human?" Kira mimed gagging even as she grinned. "We've got to talk about your taste in girls.

Mason let go of Yasmin fast as he stepped out the elevator. He couldn't believe what he was seeing. "What are you all doing here?"

"Being right," Kira said, pulling a face at Jeremiah.

The elf scowled at a phone. "The location is off."

"I told you the numbers were on the buildings," Kira said.

"There were no drumming numbers on the building."

Clearly, there'd been a previous argument that Mason had missed. He didn't have time to catch up.

"Nice to see you all, but we're in a rush." He shot a half-smile toward Comet, who wagged his tail in greeting, then Mason grabbed Yasmin's hand and pulled her toward him. It would be faster if he carried her.

"Seriously?" Jeremiah blocked their exit. "You get lucky, and the police throw out your case, and the first thing you do is go back to her? Do you have any idea how worried we all were? We thought you'd come home. Even if just to get this."

He shoved the phone he'd been scowling at against Mason's chest.

Mason grabbed the device before it dropped.

This is mine.

Over a hundred missed messages showed on the bottom of the screen. Kalvin and Zach must not have been his only worried classmates. But Jeremiah hadn't looked at any of those messages. Instead, Mason's conversation with Yasmin was open. The last few messages had been deleted.

That was odd. Brager had claimed Finn had ratted them out to the police. But that had always seemed out of character for the elf prince.

"How did you find me?" Mason asked.

"Yasmin shared her apartment's location with you. It wasn't difficult to guess where you'd gone when you vanished from school."

"Right." Mason forced a smile and nodded at his brother. "Thanks for returning my phone, but Yasmin and I have somewhere to be."

"Have you gone insane?" Jeremiah started to argue, but what he had in speed, he lacked in strength.

Mason pushed past his brother with little resistance, pulling Yasmin behind him. Once they were outside, he wrapped one arm around her waist and another beneath her thighs.

Yasmin flung her arms around his neck as he scooped her up. "A little warning would be nice," she muttered, voice breathy.

Mason felt the same. This whole time, he'd been trying to keep his siblings out of this mess. Why had Jeremiah come looking for him?

And why were they all still following?

Kira jogged close enough that a sudden stop would have her barrel into Mason's shoulder. Jeremiah, who was impossible to escape on foot, matched their pace. Even Comet continued to waddle after in pursuit, panting loudly from the rear.

"Where are you going?" Kira asked. "Are you fleeing the city? I could help."

Mason grunted. Another time, the offer would've amused him. His siter had likely invented some star-crossed romance between him and Yasmin and thought they were running away to be together. At least Kira was offering assistance instead of lecturing him about dragon genetics.

"You're not really—?" Jeremiah sounded panicked. "Lee's waiting at home with a cake to celebrate. I mean, who gets released for breaking secrecy and then goes straight back to the human?"

Comet barked from over a block back.

"Yasmin probably doesn't even understand what's happening now. And we ought to wipe all this too. I've got more powder."

Comet barked again.

"He wants you to get him," Kira translated.

"Dusted great dragon," Jeremiah cursed, glancing around the streets without breaking stride. None of the other pedestrians paid them any attention. The elf sighed and blurred as he turned back.

"Mason, please, can we talk?" Kira pleaded as they jogged. "You don't understand—"

"No, you don't understand. None of you do!" Yasmin said, catching Mason off guard.

She'd been mostly silent since his family arrived, but

now she kicked her legs, forcing him to put her down. Once she was on her own feet, Yasmin continued, waving her arms, "The Drages are the Serpents. They've probably killed Mason's father, and he'll only be the first. They've got a weapon made of human souls that they're going to demonstrate. If we don't stop them and save my wisp, it's going to destroy everything magical. I'll be dead. Our friends will be dead. And Mason will be framed for all of it."

Damn. So much for keeping his family out of things.

Jeremiah froze a foot away, holding a slack-jawed Comet in his arms. Kira's brow furrowed deeper than a thirteen-year-old's should. All three shared the same wide-eyed bewilderment.

Kira found her voice first. "What do you mean *your* wisp?"

"I mean I'm bonded to it," Yasmin snapped. "So it's mine and I'm it's, and we need each other to survive. Otherwise, I'll freeze." As if to accentuate her point, Yasmin stepped forward, stretched her arm, and pressed her palm against the thirteen-year-old's cheek.

"Oh." Kira's eyes widened. Genuine fear flashed across her face. She licked her lips. "I didn't... I didn't know that you were... that humans could..."

"Hey, it's okay," Mason took Yasmin's hand, guiding her away from Kira. "We know where they are. Once the two of us act fast, we can—"

Comet interrupted him with a howl. The corgi-dragon wriggled free from Jeremiah's arms and leaped to the street. Then, he trotted to Mason and planted his butt on top of his foot. The message was clear—not *two* of us, *three*.

Mason lost what he'd been about to say. Warmth fluttered in his chest, but it wasn't fire. "I didn't mean...You don't have to come."

"Yes, we do," Kira said, voice soft. Her lower lip trembled, and her eyes flicked to Yasmin. "At least, I do. And you, Mason, but maybe it should be just us. Your human isn't fire-proof, and Comet is defenseless."

The corgi-disguised dragon nipped her heels in objection. Yasmin shot her a glare as well.

"Fine," Kira muttered, drawing closer. "We'll all go."

Not all of us.

Jeremiah hadn't approached. A crack across the sidewalk separated them like a metaphorical wall.

"I don't think I even understood half of what you just said." Jeremiah's voice was barely a whisper. "Wisps and the Drages and souls? I don't—Don't go rushing into danger, Mason, please. Let's call the police."

Jeremiah wanted to go to the authorities? Since when did he trust cops?

"Brager will intercept the call," Mason said, voice as quiet as Jeremiah's own. There was no fire in his stomach, not even the fluttering of a spark—just a cold, desperate wish. "It wasn't a coincidence that he showed up when we tried to turn in the Drages. Or that he knew about Yasmin. He's two steps ahead. If I call the police, he'll find a way to make sure it doesn't go through, and then it'll be too late. The demonstration will happen."

People would die. Yasmin. Her wisp. Finnian. Xena. Douglas.

And it would be Mason's fault. Whatever Yasmin said. He couldn't add another name to that list.

Dad.

"You could come with us too, Jeremiah," Yasmin suggested. "Mason could carry you and Kira could carry me." She held out her hand, reaching for the elf.

Mason's chest tightened. He loved Yasmin for asking,

but he could have guessed his brother's response. It was for the best. One less person for Mason to worry about.

Jeremiah shook his head. "I—"

"It's okay, Jere. Stay safe." Mason smiled, turned, and scooped Yasmin into his arms.

He jogged toward their launching building. Kira kept pace at his side. Comet panted behind them until their sister relented and lifted him.

As Mason predicted, Jeremiah didn't follow.

65
YASMIN

A human. A child. A corgi. And a dragon with a fear of fire.

If Yasmin wanted to assemble a team to take down a powerful organization, this wouldn't have been her first choice. She'd never shown much physical prowess. Neither of Comet's forms could unnerve an attacker. They'd barely been airborne for a few minutes before Kira had whipped out her phone to text Lee: *"Just in case we don't come back. He needs to know what to do with my things."*

Maybe Yasmin should've left a will too. Or she should've burned her sunflower notebook before leaving. If she died, Hassan might decide to torture her one last time and read an excerpt for her eulogy. What would he choose? The page she spent attempting to describe Mason's wings?

And she still hadn't done them justice.

Yasmin clung to him, arms locked around his neck, giving her the perfect view as he carried her above the clouds. Sunlight danced on his scales, catching on flecks of gold amidst the rich, glowing yellows. Unable to resist, she let her fingers trace the long, tapered shape. No wonder she'd compared his scales to sunflower petals

Mason shivered and pulled her tighter as if on reflex. Yasmin didn't mind. She liked feeling his warmth. And his muscles.

"You'll make me drop my phone," Mason said. He'd been messaging Finnian since they took off. So far, there'd been no response.

"His phone probably doesn't work with all the magic around," Yasmin reminded Mason.

"Look at you. No memories and you're teaching me," Mason quipped. The lightness in his tone felt forced. It was still morning. They had no idea when Finnian started his shift at The Portentous Purveyor. The prince's silence could be the result of something more sinister. Eli might have already gotten to him. They might be too late to save Finnian, or Xena. Or Yasmin.

At least if I die, I'll get to remember what it's like flying with Mason.

But Yasmin wasn't going to die. She was going to find the missing piece of her soul. The odds might be against her, but she didn't care. Yasmin was going to save her wisp.

66

MASON

I f Eli was at the Portentous Purveyor, he might see them approach by air. The group landed as close to the shop as was safe, then hurried through the streets. Mason led the way. Comet flew only inches behind, still in his true form. Kira and Yasmin remained several paces back. Mason had told his sister to keep an eye on her. Kira's heat could protect Yasmin as well as his.

Best case scenario? Finnian, Xena, and Douglas were safe within. Mason could warn them, let them flee, then lay his own trap for Eli to recover Yasmin's wisp. Worst case—?

A strange twang whipped through the air. Mason's head shot up in time to see threads of silver spinning toward him. A familiar figure with large limbs and a long face waved from an open window above: the guard from Eli's manor, Jarl.

Before Mason could fully process, Comet barreled into his side, knocking him to the road. An enchanted net tightened around the great-dragon's wings, binding him and dropping him to the street.

"Shit! Comet!" Mason scrambled to his feet. He caught Kira's eye at the end of the road and mouthed, "Run!"

At least Kira and Yasmin could escape. Comet too once Mason freed him. There had to be a weak point in the net. Could he snap the thread with his teeth? Why hadn't he considered that Eli might've posted a lookout around the building.

Jarl leaped from the window, spreading his wings with a sudden *whoosh*. Windows creaked open from the surrounding buildings. Men jumped to the street below. Not humans. One bore the orange skin and features of a goblin; the vines curling around the legs of another betrayed him as a nymph.

The final two were elves. They grabbed Mason's arms and dragged him from Comet, managing to hold him until reinforcements arrived.

Jarl landed on the sidewalk, a foot shy of where Comet wriggled against the net. The guard folded his green wings and focused his sneer on Mason without a glance at the captured great dragon.

"So good for you to finally arrive, Mr. Wick. We've been expecting you."

67
YASMIN

"We can't just leave him," Yasmin objected, trying to pull her hand free of the middle schooler. "Did you not see that net? It caught Comet. They could have another."

Kira's grip was like a vice. Dragons' strength was no joke. Yasmin should add more about that to her notes.

If she survived.

"They might kill him."

"They won't," Kira promised with a certainty Yasmin didn't share. "It's a sin to harm a great dragon, even one like Comet. And Mason is too powerful. You're the one whose life is at risk. So stop fighting me and follow. We need to get you that wisp, and I know another route to the old fairy's shop."

Yasmin turned toward the middle schooler. "You think you can get me to my wisp?"

"Yes," Kira whispered. She paused for a second, and her eyes flicked to Yasmin. Something flashed within.

Worry? Guilt? Maybe both.

"I don't want you to die," Kira said, pulling Yasmin

toward a new alley, too narrow for a car. "Humans aren't—I mean, you're a lesser species, but I wouldn't want *you* to die. Mason likes you."

Yasmin wasn't certain how to interpret that. She'd written a bit about Kira in her notes, but not enough evidently. What did she mean by *lesser species*?

Now didn't seem the time to question her, however. Kira's presence dulled the crippling chill in Yasmin's bones. Not as effectively as Mason's heat, perhaps, but it was better than descending into panicked icy delirium. And the middle schooler had promised to get Yasmin her wisp.

"And there's always exceptions to things," Kira continued, pushing aside a large trash can to reveal a hole in a low wall. She seemed to be talking more to herself than Yasmin now. Her speech came fast, reflecting the speed in her movements. "I don't like elves. But Jeremiah really cares about Mason. And Nigel's fine too, if kind of annoying."

If that was an elf Yasmin had met, she hadn't included him in her notes.

"But I wouldn't want people to die." Kira squeezed through the hole without releasing Yasmin's hand. The middle-schooler barely fit. "Not decent people anyway. That's not what we do."

Yasmin turned sideways to fit through the narrow opening and found herself on a thin strip of pavement that abutted the side of Dilly Dally. She wouldn't have recognized the location if the main street weren't visible around the corner of the building. How had Kira known this path existed?

There was no time to ask before the middle-schooler rushed Yasmin forward. The street outside Dilly Dally came into view.

Four men held Mason's limbs. A dragon with large

green wings stood over him. Comet still struggled against his net.

A lump rose in Yasmin's throat.

Once I get my wisp, I'll come back and save you. I'll be able to help then. Somehow.

The green-winged dragon turned. His eyes landed on her and Kira, inches shy of the gift shop's door. His teeth barred in a sneer. Then, he turned away as Kira pulled Yasmin in.

Dilly Dally's interior was as cluttered as Yasmin's notes had described. Pens and bottle openers shared buckets on the shelves. Hats, shoes, and inflated balls mixed together in a large plastic bin. A pair of dark boots stuck out beneath a rack of dresses, skirts, and kaftans.

"It's good that you want to save my brothers," Kira said, guiding her deeper into the store. "I appreciate it. Because they are my brothers. Even if we've only been together a year."

Yasmin froze. Were those legs attached to the boots? "Kira, I think..."

The middle schooler wasn't listening. She stopped but didn't release her grip. "Uncle Lee's home is the best one I've been in. I would never want any of them hurt. Mason just has to learn..."

"That he can't go running to the police when incidents occur." The boots stepped out from behind the curtain of clothes. Their owner was a man, handsome and somewhere in his twenties, with blond hair and eyes like ice. Yasmin didn't need her memories to identify him.

Eli Drage.

Kira turned to him, her expression somber. She kept her grip on Yasmin.

"The Serpents protect their own," Eli said, smiling as he

approached. His tone causal, almost friendly. "But Mason's initiation will be a tough one, I'm afraid. He has to learn that there are consequences to betrayal."

Eli reached into his pocket and produced a glass jar. A ball of brilliant golden-flecked fire raged within. He held it out to Kira.

"I trust you'll know what to do with this. After all, you have your own loyalty to prove."

———

Yasmin kicked her legs into the air, trying to break free of Eli's grip. He chuckled at her attempts, dragging her into the hidden staircase that led to the Portentous Purveyor.

"You are a fascinating human." Eli's relaxed tone held a sinister edge. "I think I'll enjoy keeping you as a pet. I'll get to explore some of your more *curious* qualities." His tongue flicked over the back of her ear.

Yasmin stopped kicking as her body tensed. Despite the dragon's warmth, the clamminess returned to her skin. "I think I'd rather die.

"That is the alternative," Eli said, chuckling as they descended. "Without a dragon's presence, you'll freeze. Kira's been telling me all about your special bond with my wisp. Sweet kid. You know, she really wants me to reunite the two of you."

"And will you?" Yasmin's voice was cold. She already knew the answer.

Eli's smile flickered at the corner of her vision. "I promised I'd do my best to keep you alive. Which I will. I think Mason will be a lot more compliant if he knows you're in my care, don't you?" His tongue flicked out again, this time tracing the edge of Yasmin's jaw.

She wanted to throw up.

The wreckage of the Portentous Purveyor waited at the base of the stairs. Shelves lay overturned, contents scattered on the floor. Spilled potions created oozing puddles of glowing liquids, bubbling and hissing like witches' brews. They'd sunk into the vine that decorated the aisles, turning the leaves brown and dry.

In the corner, colorful lights floated within a massive chalice, flickering and sparking like fires. Hunger emanated from them, a desire to spread, to consume.

The wisps.

But where was Yasmin's? Had Eli already disposed of it? Could she even recognize it without her memories? What if it wasn't here?

"Why did you bring me down here?" Yasmin asked. He couldn't think she posed any threat above. He carried her across the wreckage like a stuffed doll, leaping over the fallen shelves without concern for her weight. His shoes hit the ground. A still beating pig's heart squelched beneath his shoe.

"To save your life, of course. And perhaps I think it would be helpful for you to understand the consequences you'll face if you or Mason attempt to act against my family again." Eli smiled, revealing his teeth. One bite, and he could've ripped out her neck, killing her on the spot. Yasmin would be powerless to stop him. What consequences did he think she needed to see?

Eli stopped before a door in the corner where a pale dragon with moss-colored wings stood guard. Blood dripped from his eyebrow, and a bruise blossomed around a swollen eye.

"Bested by a human, then an elf. Might have to replace you, Jim."

The guard grunted. "She have more sleeping powder?"

"No." Eli waved the small jar he'd taken from Yasmin's pocket. Her only weapon—gone.

"Should use it to knock them all out," Jim suggested, stepping aside.

Eli's smile grew darker. "Don't be absurd. We'd miss hearing them scream."

68

MASON

Cold metal pressed against Mason's neck. One of the elves holding his arms had drawn a dagger.

"Eli prefers you alive," Jarl said, leaning close and pulling his lips back in a snarl that revealed his teeth. "But if you keep struggling, there might be an accident. My niece will forgive me."

Mason stopped struggling against his captors. But he must've misheard the guard. "Your what?"

"Don't see the resemblance?" Jarl's snarl turned into a grin. His cheekbones rose, and he traced an oval around his features. There was something familiar in the shape of the guard's face, but Mason couldn't place it.

Until Comet—mouth clamped by the strings—loosed a piercing whine.

The great dragon had managed to position himself such that his head faced the Dilly Dally gift shop. Mason twisted his neck in the same direction, forgetting the blade. A hot prick of blood boiled free. He felt it trickle toward the collar of his shirt.

Kira stood outside the gift shop's door. Her green wings

remained visible; curls framed her narrow face. Her long arms wrapped around a large glass jar. Golden-yellow flames leapt within.

She had Mason's fire.

"No." Mason couldn't believe it. He didn't want to. His foster sister was only thirteen. Stubborn and rude at times, but full of childish grins and big laughs. She collected bracelets, love ice-cream, had begged him to watch cartoon princess movies with her over the summer.

Comet whined again and his nostrils flared in accusation.

"I told you not to come," Kira snapped, but her eyes filled with tears as she looked at the great dragon wriggling on the sidewalk. "This had nothing to do with you. Just don't fight. No one has to get hurt."

Jarl sighed and rolled his eyes. "This isn't a movie, Kira. You don't have to give a speech."

"I want to explain," Kira said, glaring daggers at the guard. Their eyes were similar. How had Mason not noticed? "This is my fault. Mason, I'm so sorry. If I'd managed to recruit you properly..."

Something clicked in Mason's brain. "You sent me that text."

That initial message from the Serpents had started everything. Mason had assumed it to be a threat, then a trick, then an offer. In a way, it had been all three.

If Kira asked me to join them, I wouldn't have refused. I'd have been too worried about what they might do to her for failing. Eli knew that.

Mason's stomach turned. He wanted to throw up. "When did they recruit you?" he whispered, ignoring the threatening press of the blade at his throat. The Serpents wanted him to stay quiet. But he needed to know.

"They didn't." Kira's eyes flicked toward the shop as though watching for something. Then, she turned back to them, drawing closer. "My family are all Serpents. My parents died in a police raid. Then, Uncle Jarl took me in and trained me until three years ago when Eli wanted an orphan to steal a book from a pair of elves."

And dear, sweet Uncle Jarl had just agreed. Were all the Serpents equally shitty when it came to parenting?

No. For all his neglect, Lawrence never indoctrinated Mason, never had him commit crimes as a child.

Suddenly, Kira's comments about dragon supremacy made sense. Her accidental cruelty toward Comet, her constant stream of money, her constant skirting of Lee's rules, even her jokes to Jeremiah about the Harrow King.

She gave Eli the information about how to create the wisps.

Thousands of humans had died as a result. How much of that did the thirteen-year-old understand?

Mason's limbs stiffened. "Kira, where's Yasmin?"

"Safe. I promise." Kira drew an x across her heart. "I didn't know she'd bonded to the wisp. I-I wouldn't have taken it from her if I'd realized. I swear."

That didn't answer Mason's question. He tugged against his captors, and found their grip tighten on his limbs. Another drip of blood trickled from his throat. He shouted the question again. "Where is she?"

"Inside. Eli doesn't want her to die. Or you. He still wants you, Mason. Even after everything. He just thinks you need more training. To understand the consequences of betraying the Serpents. Loyalty is very important, you know?' Kira spoke fast, eyes wide with panic, flicking between him and the shop behind.

She was waiting for something. Mason was afraid to find out what.

69
YASMIN

Human shapes stirred among the boxes in the supply closet. As Yasmin's eyes adjusted to the darkness, she identified them as one might characters from a book.

A tall girl with frizzy curls and large ears twisted against restraints, which tied her to an iron pillar that stretched from floor to ceiling. Blood dripped from a slice on her cheek.

Xena.

A few feet away—Finnian and Douglas. The red-haired elf and gray-whiskered fairy had been bound back-to-back, ankles tied to ankles and wrists-to-wrists. The difference in height meant Finnian's back bent in a painful arch.

Their eyes turned to Eli as he carried Yasmin in.

"Please, Mr. Drage," Douglas begged. "We won't tell anyone what we've seen. We would never involve ourselves with Serpent business."

"You didn't," Eli assured him. "You three were just victims of a horrible tragedy. Wrong place, wrong time." He held Yasmin in one hand and took a rope from his pocket with the other. He bound her wrists, tightened the knot, and shoved her backward.

Yasmin stumbled into a group of boxes then fell to her ass on the cold floor.

Only then did she notice the final prisoner, spasming on his back. His limbs bent at odd angles, and his mouth opened in a half scream.

Even with his features twisted in torment, Yasmin didn't need the description from her journal to identify him. His hair was graying, his skin leathery and aged. But those were Mason's eyes, his nose, his chin.

"Lawrence Wick." Eli spat at the man writhing on the floor. "A former Serpent, who proved less reformed than society had hoped. He stole from his generous employers, and when his son found out, Mason ratted his father out to the police. Get up, old man."

Eli swung his leg at Lawrence's side. The old man gasped. After a few seconds, Eli grabbed Lawrence's shirt and hauled him upright, holding him steady so he didn't collapse again.

"Serpents know only one way to repay snitches, so an enraged Lawrence attacked his own son." Eli paused and pressed his free hand to his heart as though moved by his own make-believe tale. "Go on, Wick. Attack."

Lawrence, still trembling, opened his mouth. A puff of smoke escaped.

"Not like that." Eli tsked, acting like a theater director disappointed with his performer. "You can't hurt a dragon with fire. You need a blade." He wrapped his hand in a piece of cloth and pulled a dagger from his pocket.

How much could he fit in there? Did he always travel with props for his crimes?

Eli placed the handle in Lawrence's palm, curling the

old man's fingers. As though Mason's father were a puppet, Eli lifted the arm and took a slow, pathetic swing toward himself.

"That's better. Alas, in another tragic turn, Mason managed to get the weapon himself. Fueled by anger, he—"

Eli plunged the blade into Lawrence's chest.

Yasmin covered her mouth, stifling a squeak. Her eyes squeezed shut. Lawrence's body slapped to the floor with a heavy thud. His gasping stopped.

"Of course, killing his own father was too much for Mason's emotions." Eli's voice purred. "He lost control and burned the entire block. Killing not only humans, but an elfish prince."

"Rot in hell," Finnian spat.

Yasmin risked opening her eyes. Eli crouched before the elf prince. A cruel smirk danced across his lips as he reached out and plucked at Finnian's curls. "That will be all the tabloids can discuss. Why was the Star Elf prince in an illegal magic shop? I'm afraid your reputation will be ruined. Though at least they won't know that your girlfriend did more damage to my men than you."

Rage flashed in Finnian's eyes. His jaw tightened as he struggled against the ties tying him to Douglas. But the rope held strong.

Eli's teeth flashed. He turned his grin to Yasmin, still huddled among the boxes, and his eyes turned cold with amusement. He reached out and brushed his thumb across her cheek.

"You'll be the sole survivor, the one to see the flesh melt from their bones, smell the scent of their charred skin, hear their final screams. You'll relay all of it to Officer Brager, just how I tell you." Eli reached out and brushed his thumb across Yasmin's cheek. Blue sparks flew from his tongue. He leaned in, close enough that his breath heated her ear, and whispered, "Otherwise, Mason won't get the lawyer he'll need, and you'll burn too."

70
MASON

"You shouldn't have gone to the police. Or lied about having the wisp. Or pretended Yasmin was a witch," Kira continued. "I cleared both our names as soon as I realized Eli suspected we'd worked together to steal from him. But by then, you'd already lied about Yasmin being a woodswitch, and he wanted to meet her. He's always looking for magic users."

Of course he was. Eli hadn't made the wisps on his own. He'd wanted to vet Yasmin as a potential recruit.

It seemed obvious in hindsight. There was no need for them to visit the Drages' manor to prove Mason's innocence. Eli had been testing them. He wanted to observe them, decide if they were worth his time. Had they disqualified themselves by going exploring or had he been impressed by their tenacity? Maybe, he'd liked the idea of them being in a relationship because it gave him a weakness to exploit.

Or maybe, Eli's continued interest was simply because Kira kept vouching for Mason.

"After I heard you and Jeremiah arguing, I stole your

phone and realized what you'd done, I had to tell Eli. Otherwise, you were going to get in a ton of trouble. The Serpents kill people who betray them," Kira said. "But you didn't succeed, so it's not too late. Eli wants a Serpent at the Reformatory. You'll be arrested, but if you join us, he'll pull strings to get you in. It'll be a few years, and then you're out."

Kira sounded so earnest Mason could've cried. She didn't understand, was too naïve to see. Any petty crime could get Mason committed to the reformatory. Eli intended to frame him for murder.

"There are people inside, Kira," Mason said. He paused, waiting to see if his captor would slice his neck. But the elf's hand remained steady. "You heard us talking about them. Two elves, like Jere. And a fairy like Uncle Lee."

Kira shook her head. "No, the only person inside is your dad. Eli's going to—"

"Time!" One of the elves holding Mason's arms yelled. He moved his dagger to point at a coil of colorful smoke hissing through the crack of the gift shop's door.

"Release the fire, Kira," Jarl ordered.

Comet whined his objections, whipping his head, trying to free his jaw.

"Please, Kira, listen to me. I wouldn't lie to you," Mason shouted.

Kira rested her hand on the lid of the jar. She began to turn. Then, stopped and looked back at her uncle. "It is just Lawrence inside, isn't it?"

Another coil of smoke, pink this time, hissed onto the street.

"Burn me to hell!" Jarl shouted as he stomped toward his niece. "Of course it is. Stop worrying about elves and fairies and open the damned thing."

He reached for the jar. Kira twisted away, but her uncle batted it from her hands. The glass fell and shattered in the center of the road. Golden speckled flames exploded—too far from the gift store to reach. Jarl had made a mistake.

Mason enjoyed a moment of relief before the guard pulled something from his pocket and flung it into the flames.

An amplification spell.

Mason's stolen fire twisted into a massive tornado, spreading from the tarmac to the sidewalk to the gift shop's bricks. But it didn't stop there.

Sparks flew from the whirling mass, raining golden fire onto the street. The goblin whose weight pinned Mason's left leg screamed. The dagger clattered onto the ground. A second later, the four men holding his limbs fled as the street exploded into flames.

Everyone inside the buildings didn't have that option. They were trapped, doomed to burn in Mason's fire.

Once again, he was powerless to save them.

71
YASMIN

The air thickened with the scent of Lawrence's blood and the melting magic beyond. It was like a pan of blackened sugar—sticky and too sweet. Yasmin trembled, trying not to inhale.

They're all going to burn.

Colorful smoke twisted beneath the door. Yasmin refused to turn her head. She didn't want to look at the people around her. She didn't want to remember them. It would make everything harder.

An image of Mason pinned by a group of men flashed into Yasmin's mind. She'd watched it happen and fled with Kira. Idiot! Now Eli had them both.

No, he had them all.

A frenzy of hunger buzzed beyond the door. Douglas muttered prayers, Finnian curses as they twisted on the floor, avoiding the pool of blood spreading from Lawrence's body.

Was he still breathing? Yasmin didn't dare check.

Xena grunted, struggling against her binds. "Yasmin, get up" she said, voice sharp. "Your feet aren't tied."

Were they not?

Eli must have forgotten. Or, more likely, saw no need. Yasmin's legs were practically jelly. And his threats echoed in her mind.

Defy me, and you'll burn.

"Don't waste time," Xena hissed. "We need to move. Do you want to be that man's prisoner?"

No. Yasmin didn't want that fate for herself, or Mason, or her wisp. What if it was out there? She'd come here determined to save it. She couldn't give up.

Legs shaking, Yasmin struggled to her feet.

"There's a dagger on me that they missed," Xena said. "Strapped beneath my breasts, under the shirt. You need to get it and cut us all loose."

Yasmin nodded.

"What for?" Douglas broke his prayers with a humorless chuckle. "You can't fight heat with a dagger."

"I'd still prefer not to die hog-tied like a pig," Finnian grunted.

Yasmin found the dagger, its pommel the shooting star insignia. Her fingers trembled around it.

"Careful," Xena said. "It's sharp."

"Would never have guessed." Yasmin's voice was too small and squeaky for the intended sarcasm to translate.

"I'd rather not die at all," Douglas said, turning his head to look at the elf tied behind him. "But here's what your foolishness has gotten us. Tattling on the Drages to the police? Of course, they're out for blood."

"How was I supposed to know the police were on their payroll?"

"Yasmin, focus," Xena said. "You need to cut me loose."

"Your chains are metal. And there's a strange lock—"

"The dagger will cut through. Just hold your hands steady."

Yasmin inhaled, droning out Douglas and Finnian's bickering. Sweat pooled around her temples as she sliced.

Xena grabbed the dagger the instant her hands were free. She cut her own legs loose, then leaped from the pillar.

A desperate gasp came from the corner. Lawrence wasn't dead.

Mason will never forgive himself if his father dies.

Yasmin stumbled toward Lawrence. She'd never studied first aid.

"Flip him and plug the wound," Douglas said. The fairy —now free thanks to Xena—fluttered toward Yasmin. He passed her a large shirt, and she did her best to stop the dragon's wound, appreciating the heat of his blood on her fingers.

"Lot of good it will do," Douglas muttered. "If he survives this, Eli will kill him a different way. Same as us."

"At least we'll die with our dignity," Finnian argued, stretching his wrists, voice a fraction too high.

"Nobody is dying." Xena glanced at Lawrence. "Except maybe him. But Finnian, you and I are elves. We will run."

"And carry those who can't," Finnian agreed, grabbing Douglas before the fairy could object. He glanced at Lawrence, but the elf made no move to lift Mason's near dead father.

Yasmin imagined the elves could only carry so much.

"Lucky you're such a tiny human," Xena said, pulling Yasmin's up and holding her tight. The Amazon launched toward the door, flung it open, and screamed.

Green light danced on Xena's fingertips. Her skin blackened and crumbled to ash.

A wall of wisps blocked their path. The trapped souls whizzed through the now open door.

From the room beyond, Eli laughed.

72
MASON

A child's crying wailed through an open window. A woman shouted. The bricks were starting to melt. Mason's heart climbed into his throat, eyes full of dancing golden flames. He couldn't let his fire kill. Not again.

"It's like the sun fell," Jarl said, staring at the surrounding flames with a look of reverence. "Boss had better hurry. Some Castor will spot this soon, and the nearest station's only fifteen minutes away."

"I didn't think it would be so big," Kira whispered. "It's consuming everything."

Mason ignored them both, grabbed the fallen dagger, and ran through the spreading fire to Comet, slicing at the silver wires that trapped the great dragon's head. "We need to save everyone. I don't know how. Maybe I can get through the roofs. But Yasmin and the others are underground. If they come up, they'll burn and—"

"Hey! What are you doing?" Jarl barked, rushing toward them. "Your great dragon can't go free. He's seen too much."

"You can't hurt Comet!" Kira objected, trying to tug on her uncle's arm and pull him back. "Just let him go! He wasn't even supposed to come."

Jarl shoved his niece away, sending her spiraling into one of the burning buildings.

Mason hurried to cut Comet free faster. "On second thought, you fly off. I'll deal with this mess. It's my fire. I'm the one—"

Jarl leaped on Mason, grappling him to the ground. Mason tried to cling to the dagger, but the guard had training that he didn't. Jarl grabbed Mason's head and slammed it backward with force.

Pain exploded against the back of Mason's skull as it collided with the road. Spots blurred his vision. Jarl pried the dagger from his grip.

Something snapped. A wire.

In his blurred vision, Mason caught sight of Kira— golden sparks stuck in her curls—pulling the net from Comet. The great dragon shook his round head free, eyes locked on Jarl. He opened his mouth.

A roar boomed from Comet, spreading like a shock-wave. The force cleared the surrounding fire and flung Jarl from atop Mason.

What the hell?

Mason jumped to his feet, stumbling as his vision blurred. He touched the back of his head. Blood stuck to his fingers.

"Since when can you do that?" Kira demanded.

Comet barked and shook the remaining net from his body. He caught Mason's eye and tapped at the road.

He was offering to create a tunnel to free Yasmin and anyone else who was in the Portentous Purveyor below.

Cometsroar. The great dragon's full name had always

seemed like a cosmic joke. Now, it brought a smile to Mason's lips.

Maybe this wouldn't be like last time. Maybe no one had to die.

"They'll still die, Mason," Kira said, shaking her head. "They'll all burn when they get out. You guys should run. Eli won't let Yasmin die. He promised."

Across the street, Jarl clamored to his feet. They needed to be fast.

"Get them out, Comet," Mason repeated.

Comet nodded, unfurled his wings, and took off through the flames. Mason turned to his sister, seeing her through the growing yellow and gold blaze. She looked so small.

Mason rested his hand on Kira's shoulder. "Eli's lying to you. So is your uncle. People might die because—"

"Of what I did?" Kira whispered.

"No." Mason couldn't let this be on her head. Whatever part she'd played, it didn't matter. "It's my fire. This is my responsibility."

Somehow, Mason would get it under control.

73
YASMIN

Xena shook the green wisp from her hand, sending it spiraling toward a box near the door. It buzzed with hunger as it consumed the magic within.

"I knew it. We're dead!" Douglas pressed his back against the furthest wall from the door and grabbed Finnian's arm. "In my last moments, boy, I want you to know—I consider this entirely your fault. And my greatest regret is allowing you to work off your debt."

Finnian swatted the old man's hand away.

"We're not going to die," Xena insisted. But she retreated too, trembling as she stared at her blackened fingers, and her words came out frantic, like a plea to some otherworldly spirit. "We're not. I can't let anything happen to Finn."

Yasmin stood in the center of the room, heart pounding. The others shied from the wisps, but for her, their warmth felt like home.

"Maybe I could..." the offer died on Yasmin's lips. What could she do? These wisps were strangers. Even if she could reason with them, Eli waited beyond. The dragon had his own fire.

A piece of ceiling fell in the center of the room. Yasmin gasped and stumbled back. Forget Eli or wisps. They might be buried by falling rubble.

"What the hell?" Xena held her blade as though she intended to attack the stone.

A large orange eye peered through the hole in the ceiling.

Yasmin recognized it at once. "Comet?"

A roar blasted through the ceiling, sending more debris tumbling to the ground. Yasmin raised her arms to block the stray pebbles from hitting her eyes.

The great dragon shoved his body through the hole and chirped at her in seeming delight.

"You made a tunnel!" Yasmin could've kissed his orange scaled head. She turned to the others. "This is Mason's brother. He's here to save us."

"Some rescue party," Douglas muttered. "He might've buried us instead." But the fairy was already flying toward the hole. Finnian and Xena followed.

The Portentous Purveyor was deeper beneath the earth than a regular basement. Comet's escape route required wings or an incredible amount of physical fitness. Finnian, tall and spry, leaped up, hands and feet finding natural holds in the dragon-carved dirt.

More wisps latched onto the boxes. Hunger and hatred consumed them. Lawrence's body became lost in their glowing lights.

The door swung open. Shadows stretched across Eli's face. His lips twisted in fury, then a smile cracked his face. "From one fiery death to another. Do enjoy."

Yasmin hesitated beneath the escape tunnel. There was something ominous about his lack of concern.

"Come on, Yasmin." Xena reached through the hole, clinging to a rock and twisting her body so that her hand was low enough to grab. "Hurry!"

"No," Eli's voice snapped like a whip across the room. "You stay, Yasmin. You, I want alive."

That was all the motivation Yasmin needed. If Eli wanted her to stay, she needed to flee. She reached for Xena's hand.

A soft relieved hum rumbled beneath the fiery souls. It resonated within Yasmin's chest. She froze.

Even without her memories, she recognized that sound.

"My wisp."

Eli held it in his hand, encased a thick glass tube. He'd brought it with him after all. And he knew Yasmin wouldn't leave without it.

74
MASON

Only fire beats fire.

Lawrence's voice echoed in Mason's mind. For over eight years, his efforts had gone to swallowing his flames, calming them. Now, he needed to summon them.

Last night's soup continued to stifle Mason's flame. Only sparks flickered in his stomach. They wouldn't be enough. Tendrils of yellow-gold fire licked the air, threatening to spread beyond the block. The screaming within had stopped. Anyone within would have fainted from the smoke. Burning would come soon.

Jarl rushed forward, whipping his tail. The bones protruded like spikes on a morning star. There was no question who would win a fight.

Mason unfurled his wings and leaped into the air. Heavy flaps and gusts of wind echoed through the alley as Jarl rose in pursuit, cursing Mason as he followed him through the sky.

But the guard was the least of Mason's worries.

If he wanted to summon his fire, he'd have to get angry.

I hope you knew what you were talking about, Yasmin.

Mason zagged through gold tendrils of flame and rising yellow smoke. The colors twisted in his scales, camouflaging him as he set his gaze on the gift shop below.

Eli had killed thousands of humans, created a weapon that betrayed everything Castor's Grove represented, groomed Kira into serving him, threatened the lives of so many—Douglas, Finnian, Xena.

Yasmin.

Eli had stolen her memories, robbed her of the wisp, forced her toward a slow and icy death.

The sparks caught in Mason's stomach. His muscles clenched in fury. But with the soup dampening his power, it wasn't enough.

Mason stopped above the building, suspended in the flames. He closed his eyes, forced his mind into memories he preferred to ignore, felt the sting of his former foster parents' vines whipping his skin, the cold burn of the metal rod in his mouth, the rope biting into his wrists.

And how had he ended up in that situation?

My parents.

His mother might've wanted him, but when forced to make a choice, she saved herself and abandoned her son, leaving Mason alone with the man who claimed to have raised him.

My father.

Lawrence had kept Mason from his mouther out of spite. He'd never wanted to be a father. At the first chance, he'd turned Mason over to the foster system, told him to go be someone else's problem. Lawrence had ignored and belittled, robbed and cheated, cursed and blamed all his misfortune on his son.

And Mason still loved him.

He hated his father for that most of all.

The fire exploded in a roar within Mason just as Jarl grabbed him. The guard wrapped his arm around Mason's neck. From the pressure, he intended to cut off the airways.

But there was too much rage in Mason to be strangled into submission. He screamed and a whirl of golden flames rushed forth—a hurricane of sunlight attacking the inferno it had freed.

Mason felt the fire he'd just unleashed in the corner of his mind, attached to him still. It merged with the wild flames, battling and consuming them.

"Woah." Jarl released his grip as something barreled into him from the side.

Mason gasped and turned in time to see Kira pulling at her uncle's wings. Both dragons bared their teeth. Their tails whipped at one another in the sky. Mason's instinct was to help, but he couldn't be distracted.

The connection between him and the fire stretched like a string. How long before it snapped? Before he lost control like always?

I can't. Not this time.

Mason flew into his fire, hearing Yasmin's voice this time instead of his father's own: *acknowledging it helps.*

Sirens screeched from the ground. Purple lights flashed. Kira and Jarl danced in the sky.

Mason ignored it all and focused on his fire.

You're furious. I know, so am I.

The flames circled around his hands, wrapping him in a cocoon. Its rage pounded through him. He felt it. He understood. The connection glowed in Mason's mind. He was the fire, and it was him. Its pain, its anger, its power—it belonged to Mason. And for once, he felt it all, letting his body tremble with the strength of his emotions.

"I know. It hurts," he whispered the acknowledgement to the flames before shouting his final command. "But that doesn't mean we get to burn everything!"

75
YASMIN

"I'll make sure they die," Jim offered, cracking his knuckles and stomping toward the escape tunnel. His approach left Xena with no choice. She fled as the guard jumped after them in pursuit.

Yasmin alone remained with Eli in the bones of the Portentous Purveyor. The wisps had stripped it bare, burning its magic and its beauty. Potion bottles melted into puddles; the enchanted vine crumbled to ash. The wooden flooring and metal shelves remained, unblemished but obscured by roving souls and colorful smoke.

Eli stepped back, moving through the aisles, waving the captured wisp. He wanted to lure Yasmin deeper into the store.

It worked. She couldn't let the wisp out of her sight.

"Kira said it was easy to trap once she found you," Eli informed her with a smile as she followed him into the smoke. "It tried to protect you from the amnesiac ended up exposing itself. Sort of sweet, isn't it?"

The wisp hummed a soft, sad plea for Yasmin to run. Its new prison dulled its sound, making it barely audible above the frenzied fury of its siblings. But its hum resonated through Yasmin—precious and familiar.

Her body trembled. It wasn't fear. She was angry.

"Let it go," Yasmin said. Eli had led her to a dead end. His back was to the wall. She held out her hand and the back of her palm brushed a smoky purple wisp. Its hunger vibrated through her. "If you want me to live, you have to give it back to me."

"Oh?" Eli drew closer, cruel smile tugging on his lips. He stepped around her, his spiked tail carving a semi-circle on the wooden floor. "Catch then."

The blue-winged dragon tossed the glass prison. For once, Yasmin's reflexes didn't fail her.

She clutched her wisp, relief flooding her as she grabbed the cork at the top of the bottle. Eli might've trapped her in a corner, but she could free her wisp. Together, they'd find a way to escape.

Yasmin tugged the cork. It wouldn't budge. She clenched the glass in her hands and tried using her teeth.

Eli laughed. "I had that made special. The glass and the cork are both comprised of three layers, hiding the magic in the center where your little friend can't reach. It won't open."

No. There had to be a way.

Yasmin slammed the bottle against the metal shelf, trying to crack the glass.

Curiosity buzzed in the air around her. The purple wisp Yasmin had brushed earlier had stopped. It hovered close, watching her movements.

Eli didn't seem to notice. He laughed again. "Bullet-proof and reinforced," he said. "You'll miss hearing the others' screams as they burn, but you can watch your wisp shrink, life seeping from it until it fades."

Yasmin ignored him, slamming the bottle again. No regular glass was unbreakable. If she was just stronger—

Her hand brushed the purple wisp again.

You were human once. Please, you have to help me. Your friend is trapped.

Yasmin didn't dare speak the request aloud. But could it hear her? And could it help even if it could? The wisps only burned magic. Heating the chicken had been painfully slow.

But that was with only one wisp.

Trapped souls, shining like fiery, multi-colored candles, hovered above Yasmin, gathering like spectators around a soccer field. All filled the room with the same curious buzz.

Eli glanced up, noticing them for the first time. His brow furrowed. "They're attracted to you?"

Or they knew that Yasmin was trying to save one of their own. She held up the glass prison, staring at the floating souls. "Help us. Please."

The buzzing stopped. The room fell into silence. And then, the wisps flooded toward her, striking the glass like an arrow.

Shock flashed across Eli's face, but he laughed. "The outside isn't magic. They can't burn it."

But they could heat it.

Sweat pooled on Yasmin's temple. Her fingers burned before growing accustomed to the wisps' heat. A steady beat echoed inside her chest—determination.

Yasmin slammed the heated glass against the metal.

Crack.

The wisps slipped into the magical layer beneath, dissolving it in an instant. Yasmin continued slamming.

Eli lunged, slow to realize that his prison wasn't as

unbreakable as he'd claimed. He grabbed her arm, dulling the impact of her next hit.

"You're more of a problem that I expected," he said, teeth gritted as he forced a smile. Fury flashed in his eyes. "Maybe I should keep you in a permanent sleep instead."

Eli reached into his pocket and produced the same powder he'd taken from Yasmin. He unscrewed it with one hand, tossing it into the air.

Yasmin's eyes clenched shut. She wrinkled her nose. She couldn't breathe or—

Crack.

Her wisp broke free.

Warmth flooded Yasmin—sweet and soothing, like being whole once more. Memories flicked through her mind, like a movie sped up to show entire weeks in less than a second.

Finding the wisp in the bathroom drain. Visiting the Drages' manor. Kissing Mason.

Yasmin's eyes flew open in time to watch her wisp send a spray of blue sparks toward the sleeping powder. It wasn't alone.

The other wisps were helping. They swirled before Yasmin, creating a wall of colorful souls that reduced the magic powder to nothing. Eli released her, fury growing in his eyes until even his smile turned into a snarl. He shot fire, trying to break through the wisps.

But he'd forged the souls from flames.

They matched each of his attacks, their vibrations melding into a single continuous thrum of power, and life, and certainty.

We are human. We are you. We are one.

76

MASON

Mason's flames sank into the sidewalk until there was no sign of them but melted bricks and smoky air.

I did it.

Sweat coated Mason's body. His eyes fluttered closed. He dropped toward the ash-covered ground.

Hands grabbed the back of his shirt.

Kira had caught him. She flapped furiously to slow his descent. "You are not light," she muttered through her teeth.

Jarl flew toward them from several feet away. But his approach was slow and crooked. He kept veering off course, wing bent at an awkward angle. Kira had injured it somehow.

"I'm glad you decided to take our side," Mason said.

"I'm not. My uncle is going to kill me after this." The fear was obvious in the middle schooler's voice, but she kept her grip on Mason shirt as they descended.

A net whizzed through the air.

Shit! Had one of the Serpents who'd run earlier returned?

It missed both Mason and Kira, flying past them toward the lumbering Jarl. With his injured wing, he couldn't pivot, and the net wrapped around him, dragging him toward the ground.

Either the Serpents had terrible aim or—

A woman in a purple uniform lowered the gun that had fired the net. A pair of men in matching attire stood at her sides—the Castor's Police. There was no sign of Brager. Instead, Mason recognized the blond officer who'd showed up at their school. Beside him was Jeremiah.

"Damn. How bright was your fire?" Kira asked, sounding impressed. "I thought Eli had masked the area from view."

An orange streak burst through a hole blasted in the gift shop's wall. Comet stopped, flicking his tail like a traffic guard guiding cars.

Douglas flew after him, and Finnian stumbled out a moment later, almost as though he'd been shoved. Xena brought up the rear. She flung a dagger behind her as she ran.

Where is Yasmin?

Heavy green flames blasted after the group, forcing all but Comet to duck and freeze.

Jim ran into the street. But before he could unleash another attack, a massive golden wolf leaped at him, pinning him against the road. Jim struggled, but another policeman ran up and grabbed his head, snapping a muzzle across his face.

The wolf shook its fur, then transformed back into the familiar blond officer. He called Finnian, Xena, and Douglas to him, while his partner marched Jim away.

Still no sign of Yasmin. Someone else was missing too.

Mason landed on the sidewalk with a thud as Kira dropped him. Comet turned and caught his eye. The great dragon pointed toward the hole, baring his teeth and waving both front paws.

Mason understood. Yasmin was inside still.

And so was Eli Drage.

77
YASMIN

Eli stopped his attacks, winded from the exertion of his rapid-fire attacks.

The souls retreated to Yasmin, surrounding her in a rainbow of light. Then, they sank beneath her skin. Warmth filled her veins, with it came a thrum of power.

"What the—?" Eli wiped the back of his mouth, trying to catch his breath. He spat. A single spark flew.

Yasmin's wisp—the only one which had remained visible—pushed it back with ease before flying to settle on her palm. The others hummed within her.

A smile spread across Yasmin's face as she stared at the exhausted dragon. Mason had burned a house down as a child. Eli didn't even have enough fire left to hurt her.

"You're weak," Yasmin realized. No wonder he'd been so desperate to recruit Mason.

Eli snarled. "Burning would've been too quick a death for you. I'll keep you alive and rip limb from limb."

Yasmin stepped back. Her heel bumped against the wall. She'd never been fast, and now she was cornered. The wisps couldn't burn Eli. She needed another weapon.

The bottle of sleeping powder had fallen by Eli's foot. A few specks of blue remained within. The wisps hadn't destroyed it. If Yasmin could—

Eli lunged.

His hands were on Yasmin's throat before she could blink. Claws pressed against her skin, impervious to the light swirling where he cut.

Eli laughed at the wisps' attempts and bared his teeth to bite. "I'm going to enjoy this."

Suddenly, a force ripped Eli backwards.

Yasmin caught a glimpse of brilliant yellow. Mason had come to save her.

The wisps buzzed a cacophony of panicked disagreement. *Run. Hide. Fight.* Yasmin found herself frozen as Mason and Eli whirled before her, slashing with tails and teeth and using their wings as shields. The force of their attacks set the earth quaking.

"Go, Yasmin!" Mason shouted.

His voice snapped Yasmin to the present. She couldn't run. But she couldn't freeze either.

I have to help, Mason.

He was the faster of the two dragons, but the spikes on Eli's tail gave him an advantage. He whipped the spikes toward Mason, forcing him to block on two fronts.

Eli's tail bounced off Mason's wing, spinning upward through the air. It banged into the shelf beside Yasmin. The wooden frame tottered. Mason grabbed it with his tail, holding it steady so Yasmin could scramble to safety.

And Eli seized the opportunity. His tail cracked out again. The spikes jammed into Mason's leg.

Pain flashed across Mason's face. He let the shelf crash and spun to face Eli once more. His balance was off.

What had happened to the sleeping powder?

Yasmin crawled on her knees, keeping low as she searched. She tried not to glance at the dueling dragons, but their tails whipped like lightning. Each time scale collided with scale it clanged with a thunderous boom. Mason's breathing grew heavier. Eli filled the room with cold laughter. He was enjoying this.

There!

The unbreakable glass had protected the sleeping powder from the fallen shelf and dragon's attacks. It had rolled into the corner of the room. Yasmin reached for it.

The hum in her veins turned hungry.

Do not burn this. We need it.

Yasmin grabbed the glass. The wisps continued to buzz. She didn't know how long she had before they lost control and consumed the magic.

Eli had gained the upper hand. Mason was backed into the far corner of the room. He remained upright, but barely, swaying on his legs. Blood rushed from the wound on his thigh. There wasn't enough space for either dragon to take to the air.

Mason's eyes caught Yasmin's own

"Don't breathe," she mouthed.

And then, Yasmin blew the last of the powder into the air. It swirled upward on the current of her breath. Not close enough to reach Eli.

She'd failed.

Her wisp lost control. With a hum of resolve, it flew from Yasmin's side toward the powder, wrapping the dust in its light. She waited for the inevitable ash and smoke.

It didn't come.

Her wisp continued forward, flying toward Eli. The blue-winged dragon was too focused on attacking to

Mason to notice the yellow and blue light, or the sleeping powder it released.

Eli inhaled. Blinked. And crashed to the floor.

78
MASON

Eli's chest rose and fell in the steady rhythm of sleep. With the help of her wisp, Yasmin had knocked him out with sleeping powder from several feet away.

Holy shit.

Pain burned Mason's left thigh. He struggled to put weight on the leg.

Yasmin's wisp flew toward him, nuzzling against his neck. It offered a soothing hum before it whizzed back to her.

"I don't know how long he'll be asleep for," Yasmin said. Her wisp settled onto her wrist shining like a stone in bracelet. "Can you walk?"

Mason tried the leg again. Another burst of pain shot through it. He shook his head.

But there was no need to worry about Eli. Heavy footsteps pounded down the stairs of the Portentous Purveyor. Wolves with dark purple bandanas burst through the door. Two of them grabbed hold of Eli, wrapping their teeth around his arms and hauling him out.

One with brilliant golden fur remained behind, staring

at them both. It shook its massive body and shifted form, transforming into the golden-haired officer who'd shown up at Folkestone.

"Sergeant Henry Sable," the werewolf introduced himself, holding out his hand. He grinned as Mason shook it. "I've been trying to meet you for quite a while now, Mr. Wick. After I heard a rumor that you and Jeremiah had accepted a lift from Eli Drage, I thought you might have something useful for me. But I wouldn't have been this optimistic in my wildest dreams."

Mason couldn't believe it. "You were investigating Eli?"

"His entire family. Chief Amos has long suspected the Drages had a connection to the Serpents. I've been investigating discreetly for months and been intercepted almost every time. When Jeremiah called, I thought he might've been pulling my leg. I owe you and your friends a huge thank you. Including you, Ms. Gul."

Yasmin's eyes widened. "You know who I am?"

"Our records show that Mr. Wick was cleared of breaking secrecy regarding human Yasmin Gul. I can infer." The sergeant's eyes flicked to where Yasmin still had her fingers latched around Mason's hand.

Yasmin must've noticed. She let go at once.

Mason might've laughed if he weren't so focused on balancing. Sergeant Sable didn't care if they were holding hands. He was looking at the wisp.

"The magic-burning weapon," Sable noted. "May I see it?"

"Oh." Red crept up Yasmin's neck. She lifted her hand. The wisp hummed proudly on her palm, sharing its sound with the rest of the room.

"Extraordinary," Sable whispered. "Ms. Gul, I'm going to need you to come to the station with me."

"Then, I'm going with her," Mason said, answering before Yasmin could. Whatever her bond with the wisp meant, Yasmin was still a human. Who knew what the Sergeant intended?

Sable's eyes flicked to Mason's leg. His nose wrinkled. The scent of dragon blood could be strong. "I have questions for you too, Mr. Wick. But the only place you're going now is the hospital."

Yasmin gasped. A fearful hum emanated from within her.

Mason gritted his teeth, forced himself to stand on both legs. It hurt like hell, but he couldn't leave Yasmin to face the police alone. Mason managed five steps. Then, his leg buckled.

Sable caught him before he fell to the floor.

Dammit. This was not the impression he wanted to make, even if Yasmin was about to have her memory wiped.

Wait. Where was she?

Yasmin ran in the opposite direction, toward the back room. She opened the door, and the hot, smoky scent of dragon blood grew stronger. It wasn't coming from Mason's leg.

"Sergeant Sable," Yasmin shouted. "There's someone else who needs a doctor."

79
MASON

Sirens blasted as the first Castor's Care ambulance sped off. Mason climbed into the back of the second, wincing as his leg threatened to give out. He had to lean on the healer, a short nymph with green-tinged skin and a collar of leaves around his neck.

"Is he going to make it?" Mason asked, acknowledging the fear that sparked in his stomach at the question.

The healer shrugged. "Your dad was in bad shape, kid. They'll do their best. Can you get your pants off, or do I need to cut them? I need to examine that wound."

Brilliant. Mason balanced against the closest bed.

Magic transformed the Castor's Care ambulances into miniature hospital rooms. There were six beds in total, three on each side of the stretched interior. A rotating sanitization station in the center featured sinks, bandages, and an array of glowing poultices. Shelves with more emergency supplies had been bolted to the far end of the ambulance's interior.

Mason gritted his teeth as he tugged the pants down. It was only pride that stopped him form letting the healer cut them. Given the holes from Eli's spikes, the pants would have to be tossed.

The door to the ambulance opened.

Yasmin?

Mason's stomach flipped. She'd insisted she'd be fine going to the Castor's Police Station on her own. She probably would be. When Mason arrived in the Portentous Purveyor, he'd seen Yasmin fending off Eli. Light rose from her, then sank beneath her skin—the wisps. She'd absorbed them. More than that, she'd gotten hers to carry magic without burning it.

Yasmin Gul might have just become the most powerful human in existence.

In contrast, Mason boasted a mangled thigh and a pair of hotdog-covered boxers. Just how he wanted her to find him. He turned, searching for a joke that would cover his embarrassment.

"Kira?"

The middle schooler didn't smile, not even to make fun of Mason's underwear. Instead, she stared at his leg. "Eli hurt you."

It wasn't a question. Kira's voice was unaffected, but her eyes gave her away. They widened as she crossed to the bed opposite Mason, never moving from his wound.

"It's my fault," she whispered. "If I'd recruited you properly, then—"

The ambulance door opened wide again. Comet flew in. Jeremiah leaped after him.

"You two aren't hurt," the healer said, giving both a brief glance. He shook his head and pointed to the door. "Only family ride with the injured."

"We're his brothers," Jeremiah said, slamming and

bolting the door behind him. Comet landed on Mason's bed and clicked his tongue in agreement.

Neither had mentioned Kira.

The healer's eyes narrowed. He looked like he wanted to object. Few elves claimed to be related to dragons. But a few seconds after the door closed, the ambulance started to move. Jeremiah stumbled forward a foot before finding a handhold dangling from the ceiling.

The healer sighed, shooed Comet off the bed, and pointed to Mason. "Lie down and turn on your side."

Mason complied, wincing as the healer rolled up the left side of his boxers.

"Twigs, your spikes are nasty!" The healer peered into the cut as though he were speaking with it. Maybe he was. Healers tended to have unusual gifts. "This could've ripped the entire tendon. Worse if it higher. You're lucky your species is adapted to fighting, or you could be dead."

Being a dragon had nothing to do with it. Mason owed his survival to Yasmin. And his siblings. All of them.

"What is wrong with you?" Jeremiah asked, clinging to the handhold as the ambulance picked up speed. "Your leg's all mangled. You should be screaming in agony. Not smiling like a lunatic."

Mason kept grinning. "How'd you know where to find us?"

"Your phone's been sharing location with me since you first took off with Gul." Jeremiah tapped his own pocket until a sudden corner sent him scrambling for another handhold. He chose the end of the sanitization station. "I found Kira with it the morning you got arrested. I should've figured it out sooner."

Jeremiah glared at Kira for the first time since climbing

onto the ambulance, but he continued to speak as though she weren't present.

"A few minutes after you left, I realized you were walking into a trap. Kira knew exactly which building Yasmin's was, and when you started talking about a wisp..."

He trailed off. But Mason understood. Kira hadn't questioned what that was. And there'd been other signs. Kira's constant supply of money. The *friends* that she disappeared to visit. Her strange comments about dragon superiority.

Mason had missed them all. He'd failed Kira. If he'd paid more attention, he could've—what? Saved her from her family's grooming?

Maybe.

Family wasn't an easy thing to abandon, even when they deserved it. Mason knew that firsthand. But, when it mattered most, Kira had switched sides.

Mason opened his mouth to reassure her. "Ki—Yow!" He clenched his jaw as the healer poured a cold, white poultice over his thigh. It stung like hell.

Jeremiah winced on Mason's behalf. "I should've told you about Sable when you asked. I knew he was investigating Eli. And he seemed trustworthy. I just—I really thought we'd all be better off not getting involved. And there was the Yasmin of it all. I don't suppose this is the last we'll see of her?"

Despite his arms trembling from the effort of holding himself steady, Jeremiah looked almost optimistic.

Comet flew back up to the end of Mason's bed. He pointed with his tail and unfurled his wings, almost knocking the healer over.

"I don't speak great dragon," the healer said, barely glancing at Comet. "But I'm pretty sure he's saying your *brother* here likes that girl."

No shit. Comet had folded his wings into a heart. Mason rolled his eyes. He would've feigned a kick at the great dragon too if he had use of both legs. But the poultice had numbed his left.

Jeremiah groaned. "That's exactly what I was afraid of."

"I like Yasmin," Kira whispered. "She didn't run when things got scary. She wanted to save Mason."

Three pairs of eyes turned to her. The healer had crossed to the far wall and opened one of the drawers among the shelves. Given the size of the vehicle's interior, he'd be out of earshot if they kept their voices low.

Jeremiah did, but his whisper stabbed like ice. "You almost killed her."

"Not on purpose. I didn't realize...I didn't want anyone to..." Kira's voice broke. Tears spilled from her eyes.

In the time she'd lived with them, Mason had never seen Kira cry. Now, it seemed she couldn't stop.

Comet flew from the edge of Mason's bed. He rested his head on the middle schooler's knee, staring up at her with large, unblinking eyes.

"Ki—" Mason lost his train of thought as the healer returned, holding a massive pair of metal tweezers in both hands. "What the hell are those for?"

"Dragon spikes splinter and leave nasty little strips of bone. Can cause an infection if they're not removed. She'll be next." The healer pointed to Kira over his shoulder. A brief hint of sympathy flashed in his eyes. Then, the sadist rammed the tweezers into Mason's thigh.

It didn't hurt. The poultice had seen to that. But the sight made Mason's flames churn.

"I'm sorry," Kira choked out words between sobs, apparently unfazed by the healer's return. "I'm so sorry. I shouldn't have—I should have realized when I went for the wisp. Eli warned me that I'd need to catch it, so when it burned the first set of amnesiac powder, I didn't question it. I just grabbed it and knocked her out and then I lied to you all because—I didn't think—But then, all those people screamed. And it was so real."

Comet curled his tail around her, wrapping her into a hug.

"Those people are alive thanks to you, Ki," Mason said, shifting despite the healer's protests. He sat up, making sure he could see all his siblings. "I was only able to get control of my fire because you kept Jarl away. And Comet," —Mason smiled at the dwarfed great dragon, who opened an eye to peer at him beneath Kira's cheek—"Cometsroar, I should say. Without you creating a tunnel, Eli would've had three Castors to use as hostages when the police arrived. And they'd never have found us without you, Jere."

"You're making us sound like heroes." Jeremiah snorted.

"No, not heroes." Mason shook his head. They were in his opinion, but that wasn't what he was getting at. "Family. We've got each other's backs. All four of us."

Mason held out his hand. Comet stretched his wing. They couldn't reach, but that wasn't the point.

Kira wiped her eyes, trembled as she rested her hand on Comet's wing. She glanced at Jeremiah. "All of us?"

The elf sighed, offered her a thin smile, and stretched his arm toward Mason's too. "All of us," he agreed. "Family."

80

YASMIN

Yasmin sat in the waiting area of the Castor's Police Station. The metal seat felt extra cold against her thighs, at odds with her internal warmth. She'd insisted Mason go to the hospital. But Yasmin and the wisps weren't alone.

Douglas sat on one side of her, Xena and Finnian on the other. They'd given their statements to Sergeant Sable too and were now attempting to reassure Yasmin.

Their strategies varied.

Douglas assured her that he was the one who was in for it. He'd operated without a permit and indulged questionable clientele. He kept muttering under his breath about Iron Vault Prison and what he wouldn't give to be a human in this situation instead.

Finnian chattered on about the officers who puttered around them, pointed each out to Yasmin and identifying them by species. Most were werewolves. But there was an occasional witch or nymph among the bunch.

Xena spoke only once. "We have your back. We won't let them punish Mason or wipe your memory."

"They can't," Yasmin assured her. One of the officers had tried. Her wisp destroyed the amnesiac powder before it could get close. But Yasmin did worry about Mason. They'd locked him up for breaking secrecy before.

A pulse of uncertainty came from the end of Yasmin's braid. Her wisp had settled there, disguising itself as a band. No one had even glanced at it since. Not even when Yasmin twisted her hair, and the light fluttered around her fingers.

The wisp's hum shifted at her touch. A sense of wholeness thrummed through her veins—thousands of souls, at peace within Yasmin.

Sable stepped out from behind a large staircase. He'd gone up to confer with his Captain given the *special circumstances*. The Sergeant was quite striking. His blonde hair was a rich golden color, and his light eyes twinkled. A gold ring shone on his left hand. Yasmin suspected there'd been a lot of girls vying to put that on him.

Not unlike Mason.

Sable's serious expression spread into a grin as he approached. "Great news. You're free to leave."

Douglas leaped off his seat. His wings popped loose like he intended to fly off at once. "All of us?"

"Yes, Mr. Fairweather. Whatever our suspicions about unsanctioned enchantments in your establishment, the fire burned them all away. And you have Prince Finnian vouching for your good character." Sable's eyes narrowed at Finnian, and Yasmin got the impression that the sergeant didn't approve of the prince's word carrying such weight. "However, there is one thing we need from you all first."

Sable glanced at the nymph receptionist, who was the only other person in the room. She manned an old landline behind a thick wall of glass. Vines uncurled from her arm to press the receiver to her ear while her green tipped fingers sorted through papers.

The sergeant continued in a whisper, "Knowing that a weapon that destroys magic exists would shake the community into a panic. And we have several enemies that would dedicate themselves to its creation."

"You're going to wipe our minds," Xena guessed, standing with the fluid ease of an Amazon warrior. She positioned herself before Finnian. And before Yasmin. The elf's hand reached behind her back.

She didn't still have the blade hidden on her, did she?

Worried Xena might attack in the middle of the station, Yasmin jumped up.

Sable seemed more amused than annoyed. "I'm asking you three to sign non-disclosure papers." He gestured to the receptionist. "We need your memories for the trial. Your testimonies will condemn Eli to life in Iron Vault. You have no idea how good that'll feel. I begged Amos for this assignment. He was skeptical if... Well, it doesn't matter. The Drages will get what they deserve."

Following Sable's instructions, they filed toward the receptionist. Yasmin found herself between Xena and Finnian. But the sergeant pulled her aside. "Somehow, I doubt having you sign enchanted papers will go well. You're coming upstairs with me. Captain Amos wants to meet you."

"Then we're coming too," Xena said, spinning at once. She grabbed Yasmin's arm.

Yasmin pressed her lips together, trying not to grin. "You care about me."

Xena huffed.

Finnian laughed. "More like Mason will kill us if we let something happen to you."

Heat rose to Yasmin's neck. She fought harder to contain her smile. Was that true? Her veins hummed with excitement as she recalled just a few hours earlier. Mason had raced down to the Portentous Purveyor to save her earlier. And he had. If he hadn't pulled Eli off and fought him, Yasmin might've been dead.

It was the bravest thing she'd ever seen, like something from one of her sister's romance novels. Mason was a knight quite literally armored in shining golden scales. Not that Yasmin needed another reason to like him.

"Actually, the reason Captain Amos wants to meet you pertains to Mr. Wick," Sergeant Sable said, voice a bit too sly. "We'd like to confirm the nature of your bond with the small piece that remains of the weapon." He pointed to the visible wisp on Yasmin's braid.

Amusement skittered inside her veins. The Sergeant had no idea. No one did besides Mason.

Xena kept her hand on Yasmin. "What does Yasmin's relationship with the wi—weapon have to do with Mason?"

"It's a crime to tell a human about magic," Sable explained. "Especially one you've already been accused of breaking secrecy for. But it's not a crime to tell another Castor."

Yasmin's eyebrows rose. Excitement made her heart pound and set the hidden wisps into a flurry within her. Was he saying what she thought?

Sergeant Sable smiled. "I want Captain Amos to start paperwork to change your classification. You might be a human, Ms. Gul, but that bond you've developed with a piece of magic should officially make you one of us."

81

YASMIN

Tap. Tap.

Yasmin's eyes fluttered open. Had she fallen asleep? Sunlight snuck through the small windows above her bed. Her sheets tangled near her feet as though she'd grown hot and pushed them off during the night. Something cool pressed against her cheek—her phone.

Had Mason messaged her back yet?

Yasmin pushed herself up and grabbed the phone. Her wisp shuffled against the nape of her neck before whizzing toward her fingers to peer at the screen.

After leaving the police station, Yasmin had sent Mason several messages updating him. She'd had a dozen different questions as well. Where was he? How was he? Had the healers fixed his leg? Was his dad okay?

Maybe Yasmin shouldn't have sent that last one. Or the sixty-five prior. Sixty-seven messages in a row were too many. But she'd been excited. Then worried. Then nervous. Having hundreds of souls echoing her emotions back to her hadn't exactly helped.

But exhaustion must've won eventually. Yasmin could've written a hundred different articles on the events of yesterday alone. In less that twenty-four hours, she'd rediscovered magic, flown in Mason's arms, faced a dragon, rescued her wisp, and become a Castor.

Yasmin's wisp buzzed and shot blue sparks toward her phone. There was a notification on the screen.

"He responded!"

Within her, the other wisps reacted to Yasmin's excitement. They zipped about her veins, making her hands tremble as she unlocked the phone.

One single message had come in response to her sixty-seven: *Do you not understand what a magical hospital does to phone signals? Mason will get out tomorrow. He'll come see you then – Jeremiah.*

Did that mean Jeremiah read the sixty-seven messages she'd sent? It didn't matter. Nothing was embarrassing about them.

Except the quantity.

Yasmin groaned and buried her face beneath her pillow.

Tap. Tap.

Someone was knocking at her door.

"Mason?" Yasmin flew out of bed, searched for something to throw over her pajamas. The only thing she found was her sister's green bathrobe. She pulled it on and opened the door.

Hassan stood outside dressed in soccer shorts and holding a ball in his hands. At the sight of his sister, he burst into laughter. "You thought Mason Wick was outside your door and that's what you answered in? Maybe you do still have a fever."

Yasmin's face heated. Her body followed suit, wisps

increasing their burning. If her brother touched her, he'd likely grow concerned again.

Yesterday, he'd arrived from school to find his father passed out and his sick sister missing. He'd been so panicked he'd gone racing around the building and then the neighborhood looking for her. Yasmin had found him at the bus stop when she returned. He'd been red-faced, short of breath, and showing a picture of her to everyone who walked by.

Yasmin had been messaging Mason at the time. She hadn't even thought of her brother. She'd have deserved every insult Hassan wanted to scream at her. Instead, he'd wrapped his arms around her, sobbed, and told her how scared he'd been. When they got home, he'd begged her to stay in the living room with him, even offering to let her choose what they watched on television.

Evidently, sleep had erased that momentary sweetness. Hassan kept laughing as he kicked the soccer ball from knee to knee.

"You can't—" Yasmin cut herself off. The past few days, she'd been too sick to parent her brother. It had been nice. She sighed, pulled the robe off, and chucked it back into the room. "Practicing today?"

"Yup. Coach is definitely going to play me next game. Especially if Mason remains... distracted. What's really going on with you two anyway?" He smirked at her, taking his eyes off the ball and sending it too high.

It bounced against the narrow wall and hit the ceiling, almost crashing into the overhead light.

"Hassan!" Amir's voice barked as he rounded the corner into the corridor. "Don't mess around with the ball inside. You might break something. You're supposed to be telling your sister that her friend is here."

"What?" Yasmin's eyes shot toward the corridor.

"Yeah, your *friend* is in our kitchen." Hassan grabbed the ball before it rolled too far and turned to grin at her. "But that shouldn't shock you since it sounds like you were expecting him."

Hassan lifted a finger and began tracing a shape in the air.

Yasmin considered taking off the robe and hitting him with it. Was he drawing a heart? In front of their father?

No. It was even worse. The jerk was trying to draw wings—a horrifying reminder that he'd read her notebook. That was one memory Yasmin might've preferred not to get back. Now he knew—Wait.

"Mason is here? Now? Really?" Yasmin needed to get out of this bathrobe. Fast.

"In the kitchen," her father said, pointing with his thumb.

"Yup," Hassan confirmed. "He said he came by to ask you on a date."

———

Her brother was messing with her. Yasmin knew he was. It hadn't stop her from agonizing over her outfit. And it didn't stop the wisps from fluttering every time she glanced at Mason now.

Sunlight highlighted his hair with gold as they traveled along the sidewalk. The color of his shirt made the blue in his eyes extra bright, and the fabric emphasized his muscles.

Mason filled her in on everything that had happened as they walked. The ambulance had taken him and his siblings to Castor's Care Hospital. Uncle Lee, their fairy godfather, had met them there. He'd ordered pizza, and they'd celebrated Mason's release from prison, and listened to a lecture on when to involve him as their godfather.

Neither Comet nor Jeremiah had been injured. Kira's scrapes from her uncle had been easy to heal. Mason apologized on her behalf for the role she'd played in everything.

"She's a kid, you know? She didn't mean for you to get hurt. Broke down about the whole thing. Lee thinks they'll be able to get the charges dropped against her seeing as no one died."

Yasmin's ears perked up. Did that mean—?

"They gave me something to heal my leg, but it put me to sleep. My phone was still dead, and I made the mistake of putting it by my bed. I had no idea Jere had responded to you until this morning when I reached the end of your messages," Mason explained, pausing beside a pedestrian crossing. He leaned against the sign, looped one thumb in his pocket, and shot her a crooked smile as an apology. The sun made his eyes sparkle.

Yasmin's heart stopped. Her wisp, disguised as a clip on the side of her head, fell silent with it. Had she really spent three years pretending not find Mason handsome?

"A quiet Yasmin Gul." He raised his eyebrow, turning to walk backward across the road so that he was facing her. "Must say not what I expected. Guess you got all your words out in your seventy messages."

"Sixty-seven," Yasmin corrected him, as though that somehow made it better.

Mason grinned like he'd made the mistake on purpose. "Did you really absorb the wisps?"

"More like they sank into me." Yasmin stopped when they reached the sidewalk. A small supermarket created a hotspot of cars and pedestrians in the parking lot beside them. No one seemed interested in them.

Yasmin lowered her hand from view, focused, and spread her fingers.

The wisps came as she envisioned, unfurling on her palm like flower petals of different hues: smoky purple, bright pink, leafy green, lime, indigo, cobalt with peach flecks.

"Wow," Mason whispered the word with reverence. "You really are a vessel for fractured souls."

A smile tugged at Yasmin's lips. She'd relayed that theory around message thirty-five. Which meant Mason wasn't lying about reading them all. It also meant he was avoiding on purpose. "What happened to your dad, Mason?"

He stopped in the center of the sidewalk, forcing a pair of women to pass on either side of them. His eyes focused on a strand of Yasmin's hair. For a moment, she worried he'd ask why she hadn't braided it in an attempt to change the topic.

"Lawrence is still in the hospital," Mason admitted. "He lost a lot of blood. But they think he could pull through."

"That's good."

"Yeah. Though I bet the first thing he does is blame me for what happened." Mason sighed and flashed her a crooked smile.

There went the wisps again. Yasmin froze, mouth dry, and insides trembling.

"Come on. Or this breakfast date's going to turn into lunch." Mason grabbed her hand, intertwining their fingers.

He just called it a date. And took her hand. Did he mean it like a *date* date?

Her wisp hummed in delight by her ear. The other souls created a frenzy of excitement that echoed through her chest. Mason couldn't feel that, could he?

"You're quiet again." Mason chuckled nervously as they rounded a corner and entered a commercial section of the city. Brightly painted shops and restaurants, stacked in multi-story buildings, crowded each block. "What are you thinking?"

Yasmin's cheeks heated. Should she come out and ask him? Somehow, the question stuck in her throat.

"I'll have to assume you're daydreaming about my wings and how they look like sunflower petals dipped in gold."

Yasmin almost tripped over her feet. She stumbled to a stop, grabbing a pink wall for stability. Mason hadn't just come up with that description on his own. Had Hassan told him, or—No, even Yasmin's brother wasn't that cruel.

"You were reading my notes." Yasmin pulled her hand from Mason and twisted it around her hair. She wanted to glare with righteous anger. Instead, her voice was high and squeaky. The wisps set her limbs fluttering in panic. They wanted to burn a hole in the wall behind her, so she could disappear inside.

"I wanted to make sure you'd written down all the important things. I wasn't expecting you to write so much about our kiss."

Heat flooded Yasmin. Her lips tingled as she remembered Mason's mouth on hers. Whatever embarrassing description she'd written, he'd never let her live it down.

"Or for you to write that you liked me." Mason's grin grew too large to hide his teeth.

Burning a hole in the wall and disappearing was starting to sound like an increasingly good idea. Yasmin struggled to find a response that wouldn't end up with him teasing her for the rest of the year. "I didn't mean that in a romantic sense. Obviously. Just as like a friend. A buddy. A pal."

What the hell was she saying?

"That's too bad." Mason's smile faltered only a little. He stepped closer, until Yasmin's back pressed against the wall. He rested a hand beside her head and leaned closer, eyes shining as they met her own. "Because I definitely like you in the romantic sense."

82

MASON

Why isn't she saying anything?

Mason had expected his admission to be met with one of her own.

Yasmin's seventeenth message had said the amnesiac power's effects had vanished when her wisp returned to her. Her forty-second message alluded to her first meeting with Xena; her fifty-third referenced their trip to the Drages' manor. Admittedly, she'd said nothing about remembering that she liked him, but it stood to reason, didn't it?

"You like me," Yasmin repeated the words slowly, almost like a question. She rose onto the tips of her toes, and her arm moved toward him, hesitant until it wrapped around his neck. Her fingers tickled his skin.

Mason's breath caught, wings threatening to spring free from the sensation.

Yasmin stepped closer. Her body brushed against his. He swore he hear her skin buzzing. "You like me."

"Very much," Mason whispered, unable to tear his gaze

from her eyes, large and brown with lashes like an old Hollywood starlet.

A smile fluttered over Yasmin's lips, shy and sweet and genuine. Mason's breath caught. How had he ever found her annoying?

Yasmin pulled his lips to hers. Their kiss started like her smile, sweet but shy. Her lips brushed like a whisper against his own. Her hand rested on his chest.

The scent of roses intoxicated Mason. Yasmin tasted just as sweet. He needed more.

His arm wrapped around her waist, and he pressed her against the wall, trapping his fingers against the small of her back. He didn't care.

Heat radiated through Yasmin. It met Mason's own as his tongue traced her lips. Her body trembled against his, humming with desire. The sound echoed in his ears. Unexpected, but not unappreciated. The excited buzzing made Mason bolder, and he pressed her further against the wall, tracing the curve of her cheek with his thumb.

Yasmin's fingers curled into fists around Mason's shirt. Her other hand traced the muscles on his shoulder.

Mason pulled on her lower lip. She moaned, and her mouth parted for him. Their tongues twisted into one before a need for breath finally broke them apart.

A boy a few feet away whistled. An older woman shot them a disapproving glare.

Mason fought back a grin. He didn't want to reveal his teeth if he could help it.

"Why is there always someone watching we kiss?" Yasmin hid her face in her hands

"Next time, we can find somewhere more private."

Yasmin lowered her hands enough that he could see her face flush at the statement. She shook her head in disapproval, but when she spoke, her voice was still breathy and nervous again. "Does that mean this is a real date?"

"Obviously." What else could it have been? Mason had asked her to breakfast with him, and she'd said yes. Her brother had even shouted *enjoy your date* and started drawing hearts in the air.

Yasmin's lips, pink and swollen from their kiss, fluttered into another smile. "Where are we going?"

"Took you long enough to ask. Right here." Mason tapped the wall and grinned, letting his teeth show for a moment. "You're leaning against a magical café. Castors only. Which includes you now. So, what do you say, Yasmin Gul, ready to officially begin your life as a magical being?"

PLOTWORKS PUBLISHING

Thank you so much for visiting the magical city of Castor's Grove!

If you enjoyed *Dragon's Wisp*, please tell your friends, or leave a review in the place where you purchased it. It would mean so much to me!

Then visit Plotworks Publishing to keep exploring the Castor's Grove universe! Sign up for the newsletter and get a discount!

You can also follow me on Instagram: @aj.renwick

The Castor's Grove Universe consists of several stand-alone novels about the many creatures living in the city. In fact, I suspect that Yasmin and Mason have a sequel in their future—you can't topple a criminal syndicate without some sort of reaction! I also plan to explore Finnian and Xena's relationship in a novel about the elves. If either of those interest you, keep an eye out for future releases!

In the meantime, you can learn about other supernatural species in *Angel's Feather*, the city's witches in *Banshee's Breath*, and the news story that originally ruined Yasmin's reputation in *Changeling's Dagger*.

Now check out the book that launched the series—turn the page to find the first chapter of *Orphan's Egg!*

CASTOR'S GROVE

ORPHAN'S EGG

a young adult paranormal romance

A.J. RENWICK

ORPHAN'S EGG

Frances West froze on the sidewalk as she stared at the familiar gray door.

It was the first thing she'd recognized since returning to Castor's Grove three weeks ago. Though she'd been born in the city, Fran's return had felt less like a homecoming than she'd secretly hoped. The streets were easy to navigate with buildings organized in square grids, her temporary apartment on the edge of downtown was clean and conveniently located, and there was nothing lacking in the environment. With the ocean on its south and east borders, forest to the north and west, and dense urban high-rises in its center, Castor's Grove was a city that boasted something for everyone.

But there was nothing special about a city that everyone could enjoy. Fran liked it, but it was in the same way any visitor might. While waiting to hear back from the adoption agency, she'd wandered the streets, avoiding the usual tourist activities, waiting to see something that sparked some long-buried memory or wander into someone who would recognize her.

Now, it was happening.

But instead of the sense of belonging she'd imagined, Fran's chest tightened and her breath caught. Her anxiety buzzed in her brain.

There was an image of a sword burned into the door. It stretched almost the entire length, its hilt hovering only a few inches above a sunflower welcome mat that looked far too normal in the context. Who lived in this house?

Your foster parents. Fran grappled with her anxiety to take control of her own thoughts. *They're probably into Dungeons and Dragons, or one of the kids they cared for did it.*

Either way, it was nothing to worry about.

Fran took a deep breath and pushed her hands into the pocket of her large black jacket. It wasn't cold, but she wrapped it around her as she walked up the steps. There was no doorbell. She tapped her elbow against the wood.

No response came from within. Fran could've tried again. It had been a light knock.

This is too weird. They might not even live here anymore. What was I thinking just knocking on their door?

She should just leave a message. There was paper in her pocket; she could buy a pen somewhere nearby, write a letter, and slip it into the mailbox.

"Upon my honor."

Fran spun around to see a thin middle-aged woman with olive skin. Short gray hairs frizzed around her temples, narrowly escaping the band that pulled the rest into a black ponytail. She wore an oversized green dress with a canary yellow jacket that matched the shopping bag in her hand.

The woman took a few steps closer, keeping her eyes on Fran. There was a wariness to her expression.

"Um, I was just—"

There was nothing suspicious about knocking on someone's door in broad daylight, but Fran felt suddenly guilty. "Do you know if the Franklins still live here?"

"We do." She narrowed her eyes, glancing between Fran and the door as though she thought the teenager was blocking her path. "Is this a university project? Are you doing a census?"

Fran was tempted to lie, tell Mrs. Franklin yes, and bolt, but she'd made it this far, so she shook her head. "No, I'm not with the university. I'm actually, well I was, one of the kids you fostered. It was like fifteen years ago. You probably don't remember—"

"Frances Buckler."

The sound of her original name rang like a bell in Fran's ears. Her lips mouthed the word *Buckler*, trying to wrap themselves around the harsh first syllable and the slur of the second. She'd whispered it to herself every night since she'd learned it, but it still felt like it belonged to someone else.

"It's Frances West now, actually."

"You've dyed your hair." Mrs. Franklin reached toward her. Fran flinched, but she was too slow to stop the woman from grabbing a clump of black hair. Mrs. Franklin ran her finger over the ends as though testing if the dye would rub off. Then she dropped the hair, pulled a set of keys out from her bag, and turned to the door. "Come inside. You shouldn't be out here."

"Oh." Fran pulled her jacket tight again. Her first instinct was to refuse. Stranger danger and all that. But how did she expect to get information about her parents if she didn't talk to Mrs. Franklin? "Maybe for a minute, but I can't stay long."

The strange yet familiar door led to a normal and therefore relatively forgettable living area. There was a fireplace in the corner with olive green couches and a squat brown coffee table. Paintings of flowers hung on the walls.

Fran's stomach tightened as she stepped in. *Why doesn't it match the door?*

"Sit." Mrs. Franklin instructed, pointing at the couch.

Fran hesitated, but the woman kept smiling and staring. Eventually, she gave in and sat on the edge of one of the chairs. Mrs. Franklin didn't join her.

"You must tell me about your life, dear. What's brought you back to the city?"

"Nothing in particular," Fran said, fingers crumpling stray pieces of paper in her pockets as she tried to guess what Mrs. Franklin's angle was.

There's no angle. She's just a nice older lady who took care of me for six months when I was a toddler. Don't listen to your anxiety.

"Although, I was wondering if you knew anything about my parents," Fran forced the truth out. "I wouldn't bother you about it, but there's no record of them anywhere, no birth certificate on file for me, but you're the one who recorded my last name as Buckler, and my dads said you sent that gift with me, so I just thought, maybe you'd known them?"

Fran held her breath as she waited for Mrs. Franklin's response. This was it. Her former foster parents were her last chance of learning the truth about her birth parents. Who had they been? What had they done? Had they loved her?

The woman before her might have those answers.

Mrs. Franklin's smile faltered. "What gift?"

"You know," Fran said. If the woman had been able to

recognize Frances after fifteen years, she must have remembered it. "The Faberge egg. It's purple with gold details."

Mrs. Franklin's smile stretched so tight that it looked like her skin would snap. "You still have that?"

"Obviously." Sarcasm leaked into Fran's voice before she could stop it. Did the woman really think she'd have thrown away the only gift she'd ever received from her parents?

"It's here with you? In the city?"

Fran stiffened, feeling her heart thump in her chest. That was a strange question. It wasn't just her paranoia.

"No. I left it back in Lansing."

"Excuse me a moment. I need to make a call." Mrs. Franklin spoke with the smile frozen on her face.

Fran nodded. Her eyes flicked to the front door. It was close, but not so close that the older woman couldn't grab her before she got to it.

Mrs. Franklin didn't leave the room. Eyes trained on Frances, she pulled a phone from her pocket, pressed a button, and raised it to her ear.

Fran struggled to keep her breathing steady as she stared at the woman.

"Dammit." Mrs. Franklin's smile finally dropped as she lowered the phone. She knelt on the carpeted floor before Fran, and rested her hands on the teenager's knees.

Fran was small, but the woman before her was frail. She could push her off. But her body was frozen. All she could think about was the fact that she should've hidden her knife in her pocket instead of her boot.

"Listen, Frances, I have the answers you want, okay? But we need to be honest with one another. What's the address of your home in Lansing?"

There was no way Fran was telling her that.

"Never mind. Two dads, West? I'll look it up. Just wait here until I'm back, okay? I'll tell you about your parents then."

Before Fran could fully process what the woman had said, Mrs. Franklin had raced out of her own house. The tension in Fran's body slackened as she realized that she was alone, but her heart continued to quiver. This was all far too weird, and try as she might, Fran couldn't pierce through her anxiety to come up with a logical reason for Mrs. Franklin's actions.

I need to leave.

But Mrs. Franklin knew her parents. Fran could finally learn who they were, who she was.

The longing burned within her, begged her to stay, just as her anxiety screamed at her to run. The result was that Fran sat on the olive chair for a lot longer than most sane people would have. And she might have remained there until Mrs. Franklin returned were it not for the noise.

A loud twang shook the floor beneath Fran's chair.

That settled it. She leaped up and grabbed the door handle without hesitation. But it wouldn't budge. Mrs. Franklin had locked her in.

Crap.

Trustworthy people didn't lock teenagers in their houses. Whatever claims Mrs. Franklin made about her parents could easily be false. She couldn't stick around.

But how could she escape?

The Franklins' house had only one entry, and there were bars on all their windows. Except for the ones in the basement.

It was the design of all the houses in this area. Fran had noticed it while walking through the neighborhood. But the strange noise had come from the basement.

Fran reached into her boot and pulled out her knife. Fingers trembling, she managed to get the blade free. She held it before her, afraid to breathe as she searched for the basement door.

It didn't take her long to find it in the kitchen.

Cold sweat trickled down Fran's back as she stared down a long flight of steps. There was no sound now save Fran's own pounding heart.

Maybe the noise she'd heard was a cat. People owned those. They knocked things over. At least, they did in television shows.

And I think I'm too smart to die in a horror movie? This is the dumbest thing I've ever done.

But waiting for Mrs. Franklin would've been just as foolish. So Fran tiptoed down the stairs, knuckles white around her knife.

A stream of light from a high window illuminated the bottom of the staircase. The tension eased from Fran's body. It was too high for her to climb through, but there might be a ladder or something she could stand on down below. Maybe she wasn't about to die.

"Dust!" a boy's voice exclaimed.

Or maybe she was.

"Couldn't you at least give me a few minutes to try to escape? Maybe we could make a trade?"

Fran's legs turned into metal rods, anchored to the ground, unable to move. Her heart did its best to escape them. It took all her effort to turn her head toward the voice.

Her mouth dropped open. The only thing that stopped her from gasping was that her chest was too tight to let the breath escape.

Trapped underneath a silver net was a boy about her

own age with a mass of red curls. But it wasn't the net or the color of his hair that made Fran feel as though she were about to faint.

He had wings.

PLOTWORKS PUBLISHING

And now turn the page for a peek at another A.J. Renwick series, *The Warlock's Homeowners Association*, a comedic suburban fantasy!

the
WARLOCK'S HOMEOWNERS ASSOCIATION

presents...

BOOK ONE

SUB DIVISION BATTLES OF THE DEAD AND UNDEAD

A.J. RENWICK

SUBDIVISION BATTLES OF
THE DEAD AND UNDEAD

On a cold night in the middle of June, at exactly 10:57 pm (though when the story was retold, the time would be changed to midnight for dramatic purposes), a dead man strode into The Clover Motel.

A brown messenger bag hung from his shoulder, and beneath his arm, he clutched a black chrysalis. It shimmered with iridescent light and radiated with the heavy heat of the underworld.

Bartholomew Whitlock wasn't dead in the traditional sense, or even the untraditional sense. His heart still beat. His breath was steady. He had no desire to moan, hold his arms stiff before him, or eat brains. His death was a metaphorical one.

Gone was Bartholomew Whitlock, exalted among the Acquisitions Department of The Bearded Syndicate, in his place was—

"Bartholomew Bartlow?"

Rebecca Willis, the woman stuck working the night shift at the motel's front desk, peered at the identification card through a pair of pink-rimmed spectacles. Had she looked closely, she might have noticed a curious sheen on the plastic, like it was turning brown in a pattern of lines and dots. But the news was reporting on a plane crash, and Rebecca took a morbid delight in listening to tragic stories, even if only so she could inform her husband the next day and chide him for his lack of empathy when he remained indifferent. She was eager to get this new guest checked in so that she could get back to the television.

Still, she attempted to make what she considered polite conversation as she typed Bartholomew's information into the old computer. "I'll bet school was tough for you."

Rebecca cracked a sympathetic smile and looked at the man before her desk.

He stared back, dark eyes serious beneath a pair of thick black brows that matched the curls on his head. His lips were drawn in a tight thin line. "No," he said, "I was an excellent student."

Rebecca stared at him. There was something unsettling about his voice. In the moment, she couldn't place what it was, but when she recounted the meeting later, she'd realize. Though Bartholomew's face was smooth, not a day over thirty, he spoke like a radio-announcer who was pushing seventy.

"No, I meant— Right, well..." Rebecca waved her hand in dismissal and continued entering the information. "And do you know how long you'll be staying with us, Mr. Bartlow?"

"Who? Oh that's me." He nodded. "No, not yet. But I'll need a pet-friendly room. I'm about to get a cat." For some reason, he shifted the black chrysalis in his arm as he spoke. An arc of light shimmered around it, as though it were wrapped in a rainbow.

Rebecca blinked. She'd never seen anything like it,

which wasn't surprising. Most people, even magical and undead ones, hadn't.

"Very good, Mr. Bartlow. Pets are only allowed in rooms on the first floor. We have one still available." The Clover Motel in fact was mostly empty, but Rebecca had been instructed to say otherwise by her boss, who was under the mistaken assumption that the lie gave the establishment an air of desirability. "We'll keep your credit card information on file until then. Wi-Fi password and information are in a binder on the side table when you go in. Room is right down the hall, second on the left. Here's the key."

She dropped it into Bartholomew's waiting hand. Like the rest of his body, his fingers were long and thin. Unlike the rest of him, they had a tendency to twitch like the limbs of a dying spider. They curled around the key with a snap.

He turned, took two steps toward the hall, and stopped. His fingers flitted into his pocket and retrieved a green bill.

As a habit, Rebecca's interest in guests ended the moment the room key was exchanged. She'd already begun switching the computer tab back to the news. However, the glint of green caught her eye.

It wasn't often that guests bothered to tip her.

And it wasn't a one-, or five-, or even a ten-dollar bill that Bartholomew was crinkling in his fingers. Rebecca recognized Benjamin Franklin's shiny forehead, and even if she hadn't, the two zeros beside it could have only meant one thing.

Bartholomew had her interest once more.

He rested the hundred-dollar bill on the desk. "If someone with a beard shows up, tell me."

"Absolutely!" Rebecca grabbed the money before Bartholomew could change his mind. She would have responded just as eagerly to a ten.

Of course, she would have been just as inefficient if he'd given her a thousand.

Two bearded men would visit the motel in the next week, and Rebecca would inform Bartholomew about neither. Not due to malice, but because the entire encounter slipped from her mind, replaced instead with facts about the night's disaster.

The private plane had exploded mid-air, killing three individuals: the pilot, co-pilot, and a single unnamed passenger. His face flashed across the screen: a man in his thirties with a black beard, long, slicked back hair, and dark eyes that seemed strangely familiar.

I bet he'd be handsome if he shaved, Rebecca thought, and then immediately imagined a new, and incorrect, face for the deceased passenger, which drew more than a little inspiration from the hero on the cover of a romance novel that currently waited beside her bed.

It would be years before she realized that she'd rented a room to a dead man, or even remembered Bartholomew's request. And even then, it would be only for a second before a bearded man plucked the memory from her mind.

PLOTWORKS PUBLISHING

Visit Plotworks Publishing to continue exploring the Castor's Grove universe—and to find many other titles as well!

ABOUT THE AUTHOR

A.J. Renwick is a lover of all things fantasy, from mermaids and unicorns to vampires and dragons. She writes young adult paranormal romance with strong plots, dual points of view, and happily ever afters.

When she's not writing, A.J. Renwick enjoys reading (duh!), baking (some things more successfully than others), and spending time with her three dogs (the Dragon Squad).

www.ingramcontent.com/pod-product-compliance
Lightning Source LLC
Chambersburg PA
CBHW030757020726
47495CB00012B/389

* 9 7 8 1 9 6 0 9 3 6 7 0 7 *